Books by John Patrick

I0655746

Non-Fiction
A Charmed Life: Vince Cobretti
Lowe Down: Tim Lowe
The Best of the Superstars 1990
The Best of the Superstars 1991
The Best of the Superstars 1992
The Best of the Superstars 1993
The Best of the Superstars 1994
The Best of the Superstars 1995
The Best of the Superstars 1996
The Best of the Superstars 1997
The Best of the Superstars 1998
The Best of the Superstars 1999
The Best of the Superstars 2000
The Best of the Superstars 2001
The Best of the Superstars 2002
What Went Wrong?
When Boys Are Bad
& Sex Goes Wrong
Legends: The World's Sexiest
Men, Vols. 1 & 2
Legends (Third Edition)
Tarnished Angels (Ed.)

Fiction
Billy & David: A Deadly Minuet
The Bigger They Are...
The Younger They Are...
The Harder They Are...
Angel: The Complete Trilogy
Angel II: Stacy's Story
Angel: The Complete Quintet
A Natural Beauty (Editor)
The Kid (with Joe Leslie)
HUGE (Editor)
Strip: He Danced Alone
The Boys of Spring
Big Boys/Little Lies (Editor)
Boy Toy
Seduced (Editor)
Insatiable/Unforgettable (Editor)
Heartthrobs

Worldwide Praise for the Erotica of John Patrick and STARbooks!

"John Patrick is a modern master of the genre! ...This writing is what being brave is all about. It brings up the kinds of things that are usually kept so private that you think you're the only one who experiences them."
– Gay Times, London

"Barely Legal' is a great potpourri ... and the cover boy is gorgeous!"
– Ian Young, Torso magazine

"Collections of stories have become increasingly popular in the past couple of years: leading the way is the prolific and consistently entertaining John Patrick who, under the STARbooks imprint, has edited fifteen or more collections of erotica written another dozen books himself and published several handfuls more by other authors. ... Burly (500-plus pages) anthologies of erotic writing, the perfect bedside companions..."
– Richard Labonte, Q Magazine

"A huge collection of highly erotic, short and steamy one-handed tales. Perfect bedtime reading, though you probably won't get much sleep! Prepare to be shocked! Highly recommended!"
– Vulcan magazine

"Tantalizing tales of porn stars, hustlers, and other lost boys...John Patrick set the pace with 'Angel!"
– The Weekly News, Miami

"...Some readers may find some of the scenes too explicit; others will enjoy the sudden, graphic sensations each page brings. Each of these romans clef is written with sustained intensity. 'Angel' offers a strange, often poetic vision of sexual obsession. I recommend it to you."
– Nouveau Midwest

"Angel' is mouthwatering and enticing..."
– Rouge Magazine, London

"Superstars' is a fast read...if you'd like a nice round of fireworks before the Fourth, read this aloud at your next church picnic..."
– Welcomat, Philadelphia

"Yes, it's another of those bumper collections of steamy tales from STARbooks. The rate at which John Patrick turns out these compilations you'd be forgiven for thinking it's not exactly quality prose. Wrong. These stories are well-crafted, but not over-written, and have a profound effect in the pants department."
– Vulcan magazine, London

"For those who share Mr. Patrick's appreciation for cute young men, 'Legends' is a delightfully readable book...I am a fan of John Patrick's...His writing is clear and straight-forward and should be better known in the gay community."
– Ian Young, Torso Magazine

"...'Billy & David' is frank, intelligent, disarming. Few books approach the government's failure to respond to crisis in such a realistic, powerful manner."
– RG Magazine, Montreal, Canada

"...Touching and gallant in its concern for the sexually addicted, 'Angel' becomes a wonderfully seductive investigation of the mysterious disparity between lust and passion, obsession and desire."
– Lambda Book Report

"John Patrick has one of the best jobs a gay male writer could have. In his fiction, he tells tales of rampant sexuality. His non-fiction involves first person explorations of adult male video stars. Talk about choice assignments!"
– Southern Exposure

"The title for 'Boys of Spring' is taken from a poem by Dylan Thomas, so you can count on high caliber imagery throughout."
– Walter Vatter, Editor, A Different Light Review

Entire Contents Copyrighted © 2010 STARbooks Press, Herndon, VA.

All rights reserved. Every effort has been made to credit copyrighted material. The author and the publisher regret any omissions and will correct them in future editions. Note: While the words 'boy,' 'girl,' 'young man,' 'youngster,' 'gal,' 'kid,' 'student,' 'guy,' 'son,' 'youth,' 'fella,' and other such terms are occasionally used in text, this work is generally about persons who are at least 18 years of age, unless otherwise noted.

First Edition Published in the U.S. in December 2000
Library of Congress Card Catalogue No. 99-094938
ISBN 10: 1-934187-75-5
ISBN 13: 978-1-934187-75-3

Herndon, VA

HUGE 3

A Collection of Erotica
Edited by
John Patrick

STARbooks Press, Herndon, VA

Contents

Editor's Note

Most of the stories appearing in this book take place prior to the years of The Plague; the editor and each of the authors represented herein advocate the practice of safe sex at all times. And, because these stories trespass the boundaries of fiction and non-fiction, to respect the privacy of those involved, we've changed all of the names and other identifying details.

MEASURING UP

Question: I would like to know how to suck a 12-inch dick?

Answer: So would I!

Instinct magazine's "Sex Advice for the Clueless"

# # #

"For me, size does matter, especially in a fantasy like porno videos,"

A gay porn fan named Joe T.

# # #

"I blew Jake Andrews in the bathroom at the Robin Byrd Show and he's got a huge cock it's definitely a mouthful."

Porn star Will Clark

# # #

"In my extensive field research on the subject, black and South American men are generally bigger than other ethnic groups, if you catch my drift."

Filmmaker Bruce LaBruce ("Skin Gang")

# # #

"A small dick is boring, I can't feel it. ...Yes, it's psychological, but a small penis doesn't excite, doesn't stimulate fantasies and emotions. But from big penises, a sea of fantasies can arise!"

Andrei, quoted in "Military Trade"

# # #

"I was at the Palladium to judge some silly contest. I had had a bit too much to drink and I found myself in a bathroom stall telling someone (I don't know who) that my biggest fantasy was to try a nine-inch line of Special K off a 10-inch dick. What a surprise to find he had both! I happily indulged myself with shameless gusto."

Party boy James St. James in "Disco Bloodbath"

INTRODUCTION: SIZE DOES MATTER

John Patrick

The esteemed writer Edmund White says that, contrary to a wide-spread belief, not all writers are bottoms: "I have a French friend who is a poet and a top and he said he's very campy, even though he's a top he says, 'Well, Darling, I'm the only writer top in the world.' But he's one of these guys who has a huge dick, so I don't think people would let him be a bottom. I used to know a chick-with-a-dick, who told me that even dressing up and everything, she still couldn't get fucked. She always had to do the fucking, because the minute they saw that huge dick...."

In his book Buddy Babylon, Buddy Cole recalls one of his more memorable brushes with bigness: "There came a knock at the door. There stood a vision covered in sweat and copper dust, holding a bundle of dirty clothes. It was Romeo Gouter, the sexiest boy in the mine. Romeo was actually a man, nineteen years old and considered a bit of a rogue because he ironed his curly hair flat. I thought he was super-fine.

"'Where's your maman?' he asked.

"'She's taken everyone to see Madame Levesque's goiter,' I answered.

"'Oh, yes,' he said. 'I saw it three days ago. I was the first in line.'

"I was very impressed. Not only gorgeous, but morbid, too.

"'So are you alone?' he asked.

"'Yes,' I said. 'But I am still authorized to take your laundry.' I flushed hot.

3

"'Okay,' he said. 'Here.'

My hand trembled as he handed me his precious garments. It was mid-July and the heat was intense. Sweat glistened on his brow and fell in rivulets into his sexy brown eyes.

"'Sure is hot, eh?' he said, the consonants in his speech heavy with straight intent, the vowels dancing with gay possibility. I said nothing. I just stared at his belt buckle, which announced him as a regional curling champion. 'I forgot one thing. I hope you don't mind.' He undid his curling buckle and his pants fell to the floor. Quickly stepping out of them, he casually slid his boxer shorts down to his ankles. His thick, uncut penis swung out. I looked at it. It was like looking right into the sun. 'Ever seen one that big before?' he asked.

"Actually I had. Many times. My brothers were all bigger than him, but I already knew a lot about the male ego, so I lied and said I hadn't. He smiled with pride and scooped the warm boxers up with his foot. He stuck the foot with the underwear hanging off it in my face. It smelled like fresh bread. I reverently took it and placed it gently on the pile on the floor. Then, mustering up all my self-control, I turned to him. 'It should be ready by tomorrow. I'll take care of it personally myself. Come by around noon.'

"'Okay,' he replied, his voice husky. We just stared at each other. This was as far as I was willing to take it. I had what I wanted. Then he slipped his pants back on, very slowly did his belt up, and went to the door. The window of opportunity had passed. He paused. 'See you tomorrow.' I closed the door and watched through the window as he walked down the path to the road. He looked even more beautiful from behind, which was something I didn't understand then, but would become clearer to me later in life. Then I got his underwear and began to dance...."

John Fergus Ryan in the book Watching describes the time he was permitted to watch his neighbor, a well-endowed hustler, at work: "Bud, who has the attic apartment in my building, is Clam Manager at an Italian seafood restaurant and makes a lot of money on the side giving whippings to masochistic men. Bud makes two hundred dollars a day, sometimes more when he is willing to extend himself. Two sessions a day is best, Bud says, because after two, it is impossible to keep a hard-on, which is his big selling point, since Bud has ten inches, uncut.

4

"He is thirty, keeps his weight down and exercises daily, running along the Hudson eight or ten miles a day. He is a big man with blond hair and a handsome face, who advertises his services in some of the bondage magazines and in the little newspapers they keep under the counter at newsstands. Bud thinks of it as just a job. He considers himself some sort of actor, like in a pageant. He tells me he meets the client or customer in black leather pants, black boots, a black leather jacket with no shirt, a black leather motorcycle cap and dark sunglasses.

"One day Bud told me he was expecting a client at two o'clock and asked me to let him in if I heard the bell.

"On the off chance, I asked Bud if I could watch. He thought about it a moment then said, 'Yeah.'

"The client arrived at the front door on the appointed hour and I let him in and showed him up to the attic apartment, where Bud was waiting in the doorway. He was wearing black boots, black leather pants, a black leather jacket, black sunglasses and a black leather motorcycle cap. He was holding a short black leather whip in his hand and was leaning against the door frame with one of his legs crossed over the other.

"The client was about thirty, not very tall and a little overweight. He wore a yellow sweater, khaki pants and a pair of shoes that looked a little like dancing slippers. He saw Bud in the doorway and stared at him, saying nothing. Bud pinned him down with his eyes, like a hawk would eye a mouse helpless before it.

"Bud spoke. 'Strip!' he ordered.

"The man started to undress in a terrified frenzy. When he was naked, Bud ordered him to crawl into the bedroom on his hands and knees. The man started to comply and Bud walked along beside him, flicking the man's bare ass with the whip.

"I followed them into what looked more like a gymnasium than a bedroom. There was a sort of vaulting horse and a large thick mat covered in plastic, inside a sheet metal tray with sides that came up about three inches.

"Bud ordered the man to stand and put his hands behind his back. Bud handcuffed him then put tit clamps on his nipples and the man writhed in pain. Bud turned him around, pushed him down across

5

the vaulting horse and started beating his buttocks with the whip. The man seemed to like it and kept calling Bud 'Master.'

"The rest was what must be a standard workout. Bud took off his leather clothes, one piece at a time, with short intervals between each item, and forced the man to perform oral sex on him then give him a rim job and suck his toes.

"I noticed the man did not have an erection and Bud commented on it, demanding to know why he was not excited.

"'I'm too excited, Master!' he said.

"Bud spent another thirty minutes with the man, then took off the tit clamps and while the man was sighing with relief, put them back on again.

"I noticed that Bud did not have much of an erection either by now, but I presumed it was the consequence of a busy week at his trade.

"Bud took off the tit clamps and the handcuffs and ordered the man to lie down on the plastic-covered mat on his back. Bud sat on the man's chest and masturbated, shooting his load in the man's face.

"'Open your mouth!' Bud ordered. The man obeyed. Bud stood up and started pissing, aiming for the open mouth and hitting it. The man swallowed the urine and I noticed he started to have an erection. Bud kept on pissing in his mouth and the man's hand became a blur and he reached a climax, gasping and bucking as he continued to swallow Bud's piss stream.

"Bud noticed the man's excitement and sneered at him. 'So, you're nothing but a little piss queen!'

"'Yes, master!' said the man.

"Bud ordered the man to get up. He handed him a towel and ordered him to sop up the urine in the metal tray. He did so.

"The man must have been there before for he picked up his pants, pulled a one hundred dollar bill out of a pocket and handed it to Bud.

"The man was covered with urine and semen.

"'Get dressed and get out!' barked Bud.

"'Yes, Master!'

"After he left, Bud turned to me and held up the hundred dollar bill and smiled."

A man named Martin admits he has spent his life collecting data on famous stars who supposedly have big dicks: "I am fixated with them: Ed Marinaro (in the '70s he could frequently be seen walking around sans underwear) was huge! Zach Galligan ('Gremlins') has a huge basket! Peter Horton, Fred Dryer (big dick, and what an ass)!"

Another fan says that John Schneider of "Dukes Of Hazzard" fame is supposedly "gifted" in that department, but he also seems to have found religion of late: "Got some gay-guilt feelings there Johnny boy?"

"I've been a serious Michael Dorn fan since I first saw him out of makeup. He was the token black cop during the later seasons of 'Chips.' In some of the reruns, Michael Dorn seems to pack a good bulge in his tight patrolman's uniform. Another guy who's too handsome to be straight. Howard Stern got Jim Carey to admit on the air he had "two good handfuls."

Another movie fan said, "I hear Matt Damon is packin' a third leg! Who could protest that rocker Tommy Lee isn't hung after seeing the infamous Pamela Anderson Lee sex tape! I could hardly believe Tommy Lee's big, beautiful slab of meat ... I think I want to become a groupie!

"Actress Dana Delaney, who starred on China Beach a few years ago did a movie with James Woods and William DaFoe, and she said when all three of them were in a scene together and their dicks were so huge the lens wasn't wide enough. Of course she exaggerated but to make the point.

"David Cassidy: just watch some of those old 'Partridge Family' reruns and watch him running down the stairs in those white jeans and you can see it's true."

Ice T, in an article in Details magazine, when asked about his alleged big dick, verified that it was no exaggeration, and supplied proof that the writer did not show the readers.

Slash of Guns 'n' Roses is also said to be more talented than most in that area. "There is a scene in 'The Spanish Prisoner' where major babe Campbell Scott is walking towards the camera and sporting quite a large bulge."

And speaking of big bulges, Ray Stricklyn, in his sad autobiography, "Angels & Demons," shares an amusing anecdote about the legendarily mega-hung Forrest Tucker. "Now, as far as I know, Forrest Tucker was as straight as they come. But he was also well aware of his assets. When he was touring with 'The Music Man,' a legendary theatre story goes that when the show first started, he called all the male dancing gypsies into his dressing room. He reportedly said to them, 'I know all the whispering behind my back, so let's get it out in the open right now, so you can concentrate on your work.' He proceeded to show them his penis, and then quietly put it back in his trousers and resumed putting on his makeup. The boys left satisfied and the whispering stopped."

Bruce LaBruce, in his fascinating autobiography The Reluctant Pornographer, likewise admits to being an unrepentant size queen: "Although lip service has been paid to miscegenation in the form of an occasional blowjob, 'queer' remains primarily a snow movement. I must say I do sometimes prefer black men in bed. I know I may be crucified by the left for making such a statement, but in my extensive field research on the subject, black and South American men are generally bigger than other ethnic groups, if you catch my drift. Sorry. Anyway, I always seem to have a hot affair with a black man while in Los Angeles or New York City, and this trip was no exception. His name was Leroy, a strapping six-foot-two peroxide blond lawyer and frustrated fashion designer (only in New York, kids). He picked me up at the Bijou, an old movie theatre-cum-sex-club on the Lower East Side.

"After sweeping me home and depositing me in his bed, Leroy informed me that he had a confession to make: he knew who I was on account of my Jodie Foster tattoo, and had chosen me because he'd 'always wanted to fuck a porn star.'

"'Me too,' I thought to myself, although I did once accompany Vaginal Davis to a sex club in L.A. where Joey Stefano happened to be hanging out (literally), and she insisted that he was cruising me, which I find hard to believe, seeing as we're both hopeless bottoms. But I digress.

"Anyway, I don't mean to brag, and I'm only telling you because you asked, but Leroy did say that I was the best fuck he'd ever had."

Bruce also recalls, "I picked up a Colombian named Ishmael at a Gino Colbert Film Festival at the Tomkat porn theater on Santa Monica Boulevard and took him home ... He seemed kind of dumb and could hardly speak English, but he had a big dick even when soft and a good thing too, since crystal meth is an erectile inhibitor which, roughly translated, means I sucked on a limp dick for seven hours straight."

Many porn stars are themselves unabashed size queens. Consider cutie Jeff ("Tailspin") White, who says the most sexually adventuresome thing he's ever done was at Mardi Gras, before he got into porn, and all it took was a look at a stud's big dick: "I was out on the balcony on Bourbon Street down in New Orleans, telling all these straight boys walking by to show me their dicks. And their girlfriends would pull down their pants so we'd throw pity beads at them. Then out of nowhere, this guy shows up. Very gorgeous, looking like an International Male model blond hair, nice tan, wearing tight blue jeans, white shirt, ohhh.... So I yell at him to show me his dick, and he yells back, 'Show me yours!' So I do and he shows me his, and it is so beautiful and so big! And he starts shaking it at me and says, 'I want to fuck you with this!' So I tell him if he wants to fuck me, he has to be up on the balcony in two minutes.... And the bar was so crowded, I figured he'd never be able to make it up that fast, but the next thing I know he is tapping me on the shoulder. I turn around, he has his big dick hanging out, shirt lifted up showing those abs of steel, and I am getting harder than hell. So he says, 'Are you ready for it?' and pushes me up next to the bathroom, where he throws me this great fuck right there in front of about 20 people! I still jack off to this day on the memory of it."

I know from personal experience just how much porn star Tony Cummings enjoys having sex with a guy with a big dick. In fact, in San Francisco during one of his semi-annual appearances at the Nob Hill, he became reacquainted with a mega-hung black dancer he had met years before in Charlotte. This incident has been combined with another to form the story that appears in this volume. Also while staying in San Francisco, Tony found out that a new Falcon star Tony LaFont from Amsterdam was staying at his hotel, seeing clients when he wasn't filming scenes. Tony managed to get an introduction and LaFont invited him in for some more afternoon delight. As we know from the Falcon videos, LaFont has a beautiful, very large, uncut cock and Tony loved sucking on it. After a few minutes of cock-worship, LaFont took Tony doggie, then flipped him over and slammed it into him missionary for a good half an hour. Neither of them came since Tony had a show to do and the stud had six clients that day, but Tony said it was one the hottest, most memorable fucks he had ever received.

Porn fans love big dicks, too, of course, but often complain that the dicks they see on film don't match up to the hype. Porn star David Rinaldo, for instance, didn't appear to be as big on video as he did in stills, and Mike Donner at All World Video responded, "David Rinaldo has a very big pinga and sometimes when these guys are that big, the blood isn't 100% flowing down there, so it takes some time for them to get the blood pumping. As for his blowing some stud on film, we can only wait ... and hope. I'm glad you're a big fan of 'big pingas'. But the great thing about this biz is that there is something for everyone. Not everyone gets as excited as we do over endowments, and it's not because I'm a bottom! Most of my personal experience with well-endowed men is that they are feisty bottoms!"

I recall that Rick Donovan told me his problem was "blood flow," that it took a long time to fully engorge a schlong that huge. Rick was seldom really hard in his videos. One fan remembered exceptions: "With Matt Ramsey in 'The Bigger The Better' (well who possibly could blame Rick for being hard there?) and his scene in 'The Big Ones' with Josh Taylor (who was the first porn star I ever saw in real life ... I nearly fell off my balcony in WeHo). Likewise Rod Garetto, who never is hard. Compare him with Mac Reynolds, Dick Masters (who occasionally flagged), Karl Thomas who, on a good day, is enormous, Tom Steele, Michael Brawn, Mike Nichols, Jeff Stryker (who has a great dick even if the rest is a problem) and of course the wonderful schlong of Vince Rockland, which is attached to a fairly amazing specimen of man flesh. One should mention also Ken Ryker: a disappointing dick often hand-held except with his scenes with Jake Andrews and Trent Reed, where he showed some arousal."

"The biggest one I've ever seen," a fan named Matt recalls, "was that of Ken Foxx, a not-very-well-known guy, who is in 'Jack Off Giants.' He had a cock that measured at least 13 inches when he's about to come and in this video he has one of the biggest and intense orgasms I've ever seen. I've been trying to find him!"

"I am never turned on by a guy with a small dick, not in front of my VCR, not in bed," a fan named Phrennzy says. "The best thing about porn, for me, is seeing a huge, shaven, hard cock. Period. My favorite performers are Mike Nichols, Cole Youngblood and Todd Stevens. I find that far too many guys in porn have too small a cock."

"Size matters, visually, in a porn flick," a fan named Pinga Boy agrees. "I find those horny hung Hispanic guys to be the most exciting. Sucking an uncut ten-inch schlong has to be life's greatest pleasure."

"Size is indeed interesting," according to a fan named Charles, "but to me the major criterion is the hardness of the erection. That is why I have no interest in those guys with large cocks that cannot keep them fully erect at an angle of at most 90 degrees when measured from their belly and who are forced to use a tight hand around the base of the cock. This may explain why one of my favorite performers was/is Eric Stryker...."

In Eclipse magazine, columnist Woody Miller answered a young man's letter in which the youth wondered how gay porn studios manage to get all the guys with big dicks. Why couldn't he find these hung men?, wondered the writer. Well, Woody says, that's because it's all faked. Well, pretty much. "To begin with, the camera makes things look bigger than they really are. One industry cameraman estimates that the video camera makes the cock look up to 30 percent larger than it really is. Trimming pubic hair and using a vacuum penis pump before a scene to engorge the cock with blood also help. (The pump's effects are only temporary.) And then there's that little thing called proportion: Slap a six-inch cock on a boy who is only five-six, then stand that guy in a room where you can't tell how tall he is. ...It's all blue smoke and mirrors, folks."

Tim Evanson of RAD Video suggested those interested in dick size check out "The Male Genitalia Kit" from InfoMedica: "They are an online health site (www.afraidtoask.com.). The kit comes with a ruler and some information on the size of American men's trouser trout. You can find out what percentage of the population has a bigger or smaller, thinner or thicker, curvier or pointier, penis than yours."

A fan in London says, "My ex was the kindest and most caring guy I have ever known and the only person I have ever loved in my life. He also has the most fantastic cock I think I shall ever see. better possibly than a porn star cock because it was real and always mine. My ex was almost eight, genuine, uncut inches and real thick. He was only five-six, which made him look incredibly huge both soft and hard. My only hope now is that his new boyfriend worships that beauty with the love and attention that it requires. I know I shall always love him and have strength in my memories of our fabulous lovemaking."

Samuel R. Delaney, in his book, Times Square Red, Times Square Blue, recalls some of the mega-hung boys he met at the various theaters in the area over the years. One of his favorites was a one-legged fellow named Arly, who was "good-looking, with a hard body, and a solid ten inches, uncut; and while a few people were put off by the missing leg, he seldom lacked for takers. He demanded endurance. But he was attractive enough and big enough that he could afford to be choosy. As I slid in beside him, he grinned up at me and grabbed my arm to pull me down: 'Aw, this is good, now I got the man here who really knows how to do it!' You'd have to be a habitue to understand just how fine a greeting like that can make you feel."

He recalled another lad, the hugely hung Joey, who had incredible sexual self-confidence. Delaney remembers, "I was the one, though, who, after a month or so, missed our assigned Thursday meeting. Hustlers are just not my particular thing. ...When I ran into Joey on the street, he was all professional concern: 'I was worried about you, man. I mean, I was hoping that nothing had happened to you or anything. The money I could always get from somebody.' ...Oh, we had a couple more encounters. The last, most pleasant, messiest (on my part) and loudest (on his) was in a doorway on Forty-eighth Street, one night when I'd had a couple too many. Afterwards Joey put me on an uptown bus, then tramped off over the icy street into the December dark. It was only five bucks that night."

Then, a bit later, at (the Eighth Avenue) Cats, a black drag queen with exquisite crimson nails and a red-blond wig frowned at Delaney over her drink, then asked, "Did you know a kid out here named Joey?" Delaney said he did. The queen said that Joey had dropped dead of a heart attack, then confessed: "Oh, that boy was just the sweetest! I used to let him stay with me all the time. On my couch. He was always so nice. ...I have never known anyone who could get into sex more than he could. I mean, that boy loved to come! ...I have a few little kinks, myself, and he was always the world's most obliging lay. ...That boy was so talented. I don't think he'd his twenty-ninth birthday yet."

"Paul Morrisey's 'Trash' (1970) is remarkable for a lot of things, not least of which is an ongoing display of Joe Dallesandro's consecrated cock in a happy variety of situations," Greg Morris in The

Bay Area Reporter said. "Ironically, this icon-stud plays an impotent junkie, but Warhol superstar Jane Forth, seeing the objet d'sacre for the first time, says it all in a mantra that devoted dicksters will repeat like a Buddhist chant: "Oh, my ... you're rather large.""

But, you see, size is, after all, relative. When one is young and immature, one sees things differently. Stephen Fry recalls his schooldays in Moab Is My Washpot: "Yes, I might have been tall, yes, I might have been growing almost visibly, yes, my voice might have broken, but what was happening down there? Fuck all, that was what was happening.

"If I heard the word 'immature' used, even in the most innocent context, I would blush sCarlet. Immature meant me having no hair down there. Immature meant me having a salted snail for a cock. Immature meant shame, inadequacy, defeat and misery. They could peacock around without towels, they could jump up and down and giggle as bell-end slapped against belly-button, and heavy ball-sack bounced and swung, they could shampoo the shaggy pubes and sing their brainless rugby songs in the hiss of the shower-room, it was all right for them, the muddy, bloody, merciless, ape men cunts.

"...I remember being at the bedside of a boy at prep school, playing with his (as it seemed to me at the time) colossal and strainingly hard penis. I stared at this phenomenon and I can recall this scene so exactly in my mind in its every detail I thought to myself, What now? I know this is fun, this has meaning, this is part of something big, but what now? Do I eat it? Do I kiss it? Do I try and merge with it, become one with it? Do I cut it off and take it back to my own bed? Do I try and stuff it into my ear? What is this supposed to lead to? I don't find this cock attractive or pretty, in fact it's frankly rather ugly, but I do know this: it is part of something that matters.

"I had been there then, at the bedside, worshiping at the throne of the cockhead as it were, knowing that this was something that was always going to have meaning for me. But it was disconnected, it was just a great gristly fat thing all the poor lad wanted was for me to finish him off so that he could get to sleep of course, he had no interest at all in my psychic or romantic destiny but for me this thing in my hands was at once a potent symbol of something that mattered and just a dick belonging to another boy, nothing more; the very disconnectedness of this dick, coupled with its swollen urgency and such a perplexed presentiment in me of the momentous weight and meaning such scenes as this were to have in my life, made the whole experience, and the dick itself, highly absurd, highly comic and very slightly frightening. "So I giggled."

Then there are those who are famous simply because of their spectacular cocks. Michael Musto noted that New York character Jonah Falcon is a "self-described actor/screenwriter (who) parades around in seemingly painted-on spandex shorts which highlight his gargantuan schlong, thereby giving one the willy ('It's 13 and-a-half erect, nine-and-a-half soft' he informs). He leaves me messages like 'I want to tell you about how I showed my penis to Leonardo and his friends' and 'I'm the guy with the large penis. I'm sure you noticed me dancing in the audience at the Donna Summer concert last night. I made quite a scene.' Lately, he's been faxing and enthusing about his appearance on HBO, in which he talks about his penis."

And if the real thing isn't handy, there's always a dildo. In Queer PAPI Porn, S'Naughty Spice recalls she might not have the stuff to fuck a queer boy but she found a big dildo to do the job: "I push his face and shoulders to the mattress while I spread his legs, presenting him quite attractively. Smearing on some lube, I contemplate his ass, deciding how to begin. I slide my finger, slick and wet, down the base of his spine to his asshole.

"I let my finger rest there, touching that sweet pucker of skin. He is silent, barely breathing, and tense with anticipation. I slowly increase the pressure on my finger and ease it in. He tries to push back against me to force my finger deeper, but I can easily hold him down from this angle, and keep my movements gentle. I tease him with my slender fingers and he shivers with impatience, wanting more, but not daring to admit it.

"When I feel he has waited long enough, I enter him. As I slide my fat, fourteen-inch dildo into his ass, Mino sucks in his breath with a wet noise. I pause for a moment to let him adjust because today, I am very, very big. Slowly, I begin to move, grabbing his hips. As I begin to thrust a little faster, I hear his breath quicken and I can feel heat rising from deep within his body to the surface of his skin.

"He tries to shift as I am grinding his knees into the bed, but I have the advantage and keep him in position. He is grunting as I begin to pound him really hard, with a fast, even rhythm. When I reach around to grab his balls tightly in my fist, he gives a deep-guttural moan, one that surprises me. Even with the paper-thin walls of our two-bedroom flat, I have never heard him make this particular sound. It excites me, so I work a little harder, leaning into him with my full weight, slamming him...."

Fred Eggan, in the same collection, recalls, "...The one that fucked me the best was a Chinese man who lived by the Cow Palace tall, wiry, smooth, with a dick that was way big for me back in the days when I was first getting fucked. Centuries of tradition left him no need to be butch, just a man who knew how to fuck. And then he gave me beautiful porcelains."

In the book Lila's House by Jacobo Schifter, about male prostitution in Latin America, in the male brothel, the prostitutes, in their efforts to attract clients, are eager to display their attributes: One boy, Cerebron, for example, wears tight jeans that subtly show off "his package," as he refers to his penis. Jose sits with his legs open to achieve the same effect.

The prostitutes consider passive receptive anal sex as something that "isn't done" and which differentiates them from their clients. The prostitute known as Vernol says that he has "a huge dick and clients can't wait to be penetrated or to give me oral sex. Very few can take it, and sometimes I spend half an hour trying to get it in. But when I am, they shed tears of joy.... They're very tough to take something of that size. I couldn't do it."

The hustlers at the house contend that it is precisely the clients' enjoyment of fellatio that enables them to have erections. Lila himself acknowledges that the quality of the oral sex performed by clients is what hooks heterosexual youths on male prostitution. Some of the boys in the brothel have been receiving oral sex from clients since the age of ten, before moving on to other practices. "Women don't know how to perform oral sex, and the guys go crazy from the blow jobs they get from their clients," says the brothel owner.

Cerebron says, "I'll be honest. Not everyone can charge the same because not everyone has this (he grabs his crotch). Clients choose me because I'm good-looking and because I can give them a good twelve inches of pleasure. They're willing to pay more for a good hunk of meat. Just like anything else, right? If you go out to eat, you're not going to pay the same for a hot dog as you would for a filet mignon. So, for clients who like a good banging, here's where they can get it."

Another prostitute, Hugo, says: "What most clients are looking for is a big dick." Hugo says that clients are interested in a big penis, "like a horse." When asked if some of the guys have been rejected for being less well-endowed, he said, "No, not very often. However, clients discuss all our characteristics among themselves. Maybe the first time they'll go with someone small, but the next time they'll look for the biggest one."

Bisexual clients also differ from homosexual clients. Bisexuals are more attracted by the prostitutes' youth, while homosexuals are attracted by their masculinity. Mono explains why: "The homosexuals who come here are looking for a man. What attracts them is not youth, but masculinity. In gay bars, there are masculine homosexuals but they are a minority. The younger "fairies" who want to feel like women come to be penetrated. When you're with them, they act and talk so much like women that you feel like you're in a hen house. Some guys like them because it's like being with a woman. Others hate them for being effeminate. The masculine clients, on the other hand, are respectable family men, some are even grandfathers."

In terms of sexual practice, there is also great variety. Cerebron prefers older customers because "they treat you more like a son" and "They help you more, they don't beat around the bush, and if you need something they give it to you because they know they're old. They're not so interested in sodomy." Hugo agrees that clients who are married and have relations with women "are different from homosexuals. They're not so demanding."

Married men, demanding or not, seem to love glory holes, and gay guys love servicing them. A man in Connecticut once wrote to Winston Leyland about his experiences with such men during a typical day at the dirty bookstore: "There are four booths with glory holes. Upon arrival, I saw how one of the glory hole booths had one person in there so I promptly went in the other side. The guy had grey hair but it was probably premature as he looked to be about 35, medium built, and had a thick, dark bush around his cock. I signaled for him to stick his dick through and he did.

"While I was sucking him, I maneuvered his balls through the hole, too, and was able to suck them also. After he came and left, another guy came into the booth. He was about 40, medium built also, and wasted no time taking his cock out and sticking it, soft, through the hole. After I got him hard I sucked it until he came. The first guy was about six inches and cut; the second about eight inches and cut. Both were medium thick.

"Anyhow, I had to leave but I came back later that night. There was this blond guy there I had met through a mutual friend; he ignored me, and I ignored him. I went into a booth with a glory hole ... I looked through it and there was the blond guy, jacking off. I could not believe the size of it! When he stuck it through, I had eleven inches of pleasure to work on. After sucking this thick monster up and down, I sucked on the head, playing with the foreskin with my lips and tongue and rubbing my lips up and down the shaft. After he came, I moved to another booth. A guy came in, was playing with his dick through his pants. Finally, he took it out and stuck it through the hole hard, eight inches cut, and not too thick. I started sucking that cock, giving it my all, when the guy withdrew, knelt down, and whispered to me, 'Let's go out to the car.'

"So we went and ended up at a park around the corner where we both lay out and I sucked his dick for about two hours, making him come four times. It was great feeling his hairy, taut body while I sucked him. We went back to the bookstore. He went home and I went back inside.

"The first booth I went into had a cute blond guy in it and as soon as I peeked through, he stood up and stuck his cock through the glory hole. It was about eight inches long, uncut, and thin. I wished I could have gotten at his large, hairless balls, but before I knew it, he was ready to come so I withdrew. "Then came the attitude. He signaled for me to stick my cock through, which I didn't do, but he never looked to see, as he opened the door to the booth and slammed it so if my cock was there, the door would hit it. Nasty.

"The next guy that came along had a nice seven-incher, cut and thick, and nice balls, like two golf balls in his sac. I got him off ... then went home to sleep, dreaming about my half-dozen big cocks for the day."

Sometimes you can have too much of a good thing, as "BD" of Manhattan, who is 38 and a topman but occasionally likes to bottom for a big cock, found out. First, he hired Chad, a popular escort who is listed on the escorts4u website and was featured in the February 2000 issue of Inches magazine (pgs. 44-51). BD gushed, "I found he's got a slim but very sexy body, nice skin, good attitude, and an absolutely sensational cock. While almost all guys exaggerate their measurements,

Chad is completely accurate and unassuming about his, which is refreshing. According to Chad, some guys say he's ten or eleven inches. He himself says he's 9 2 inches, and if you see it for yourself, you'll realize just how much most other escorts exaggerate their endowment. His pictures do not show his cock off to best advantage since he's not fully hard in them, but he gets hard with me. He's got a bunch of tattoos, which are hot, and a pierced tongue. I sucked his cock while he loosened up my butt with his fingers to get ready to fuck me. I wish he were a bit more passionate, but he's still a lot of fun." Then he had Chad with "Mike4hire@aol.com," and "that was amazing, but with two enormous cocks to take care of I could hardly walk the next day!" What a way to go!

Another john said that he also hired Chad and, after some idle chit chat, they proceeded to the bedroom. "He kissed me with his pierced tongue (which I found to be really hot), and began to disrobe. When his huge dick popped out, already hard, I exclaimed 'Whoa, what a show dog!' He was everything he claimed to be and more. He was active and passive, orally. He was an active top. I had to ask him to stop after about 20 on bottom. His huge member was too much for me. At my request, he straddled my chest and jacked off on my face. Then he made me shoot."

MAM also hired Chad and asked him if he got into scenes or dominance and he said he could do that. MAM said he was really into a rape type scene and he gave Chad his address and told him he'd be on bed in the dark apartment with the door unlocked. "Chad came over and as soon as he walked in the door came over to the bed grabbed my arms and cuffed them together. He then blindfolded me and proceeded to use fowl language, spit, and smack me around (all of which I wanted). He wouldn't listen to my whimpering to him stop. He then spit on my hole and began to probe with fingers then his massive cock. I have been around and have never felt anything so big as his. After a while he pulled out of my hole and began to urinate on me. He then jacked off onto my blindfolded face. When he finished that he uncuffed me took of the blindfold and kissed me!"

Another john, a 22-year-old student at NYU, said he saw Chad's ad in Next magazine and arranged a date. When Chad arrived, they chatted for over half an hour before Chad began to undress. "Chad has an enormous penis and I couldn't wait until his pants were off to suck it. I'm not into anal and was just happy pleasing him orally. Chad doesn't cum easily so it took me the remainder of the hour to finish him off, which was fine because I could suck on his dick all day."

Another john said he reached Chad on his cell phone and Chad admitted that he had just had a client and thought it best to wait a while so he could perform better. "I thought this was cool of him. I called him the next day and set up to meet at a hotel he recommended. ...I had him sit on the bed and proceeded to undo his pants so I could suck his huge cock. Chad kept grasping my head and forcing it down his huge pole chocking me often. After a while of this he stood up and we completed undressing. Chad asked if I liked to get fucked and I said I wasn't sure if I could take him. He assured me that 'a little lube goes a long way.' We got on the bed and I was on all 4's blowing him while he put on a glove and starting prepping my hole. Soon he had three fingers in my hole and told me he thought I was ready. Chad turned me around and gently kept pressing the head of his cock in my hole. Finally it popped through and I got a quick shot of pain which soon subsided and I felt only hot pleasure. I've never had anyone his size in my ass before and it felt great. I asked Chad to pull out and shoot on my face, which he did. It was great."

When it comes to truly awesome cocks, you'd have to go some to beat the dudes in Black Inches magazine. In one story therein the author expressed the fascination very well: "...Kissing his neck, I ripped open his shirt, and this caramel gang of hard, roping muscles heaved and panted. His nipples were gigantic, dark thimbles standing erect. I grabbed at his overdeveloped chest and devoured each tangy man tit, one by one. Slowly moving down his hard, pounding belly, I licked his rough dick hair as he shivered. He pushed my head farther to that long, wicked disturbance pulsing through beige gabardine. My teeth probed the cloth. Nasty boy no drawers! His leaking dick produced a warm wet spot. I reached inside, glided my hand down his scratchy pubic thatch and clutched his hardened cock. ...Oh, this Brother had crazy inches going on! The dancer in him swerved. He oscillated his hips just once, and then with a thrust it flopped down, torqued up and a gush white gold petered out! It rose in jerks before my eyes, a long, tan, tubular titan throbbing at my lips. Mmmm! Enormous dick! Encased in a tight, velvety skin, it tumbled forth from a leather-studded cockring and the motherfucker looked stately! Crazy long. Succulent meat. The dark shaft curved at the middle. Oh yes, this was a bone made for sucking! Sucking slow and wet...."

Meanwhile, indulge yourself with some hearty tales of the humongous not done with smoke and mirrors, we promise you.

FIRE ISLAND FLING
Daniel Miller

A lot of gay guys today look back on the '70s like they were one nonstop, cum-dripping, cock-busting fuckfest. When I tell them I came out in New York City during that mythical decade, they look at me with awed fascination. Generally, I just smile and play it cool. I don't bother to tell them that, until the summer of 1976, I was probably the last gay virgin in the Big Apple.

It wasn't that I didn't want to feel some hot, humpy stud's big tool crashing into my too-tight hole or hosing down my pulsating tonsils. In fact, in the six months since I'd finally admitted my desire for men, I'd thought of almost nothing else. The problem was that, as a sheltered teenager who'd just fled a small Midwestern town, I honestly didn't know where to start. Whenever I spotted a man who looked promising, I'd get totally freaked out at having to admit my inexperience.

Eventually, I confided my dilemma to a few of my new friends. Though they laughed at first, they were sympathetic enough that they decided to solve my problem. So a bunch of them got together and arranged for me to spend a long holiday weekend at Fire Island. If I couldn't get laid there, they said, I might as well hang up my cockring for good!

Stepping off the ferry onto the docks of the appropriately named Cherry Grove was both a revelation and a shock. All around me, the summer air was alive with buff, suntanned bodies and handsome heads of flowing, sun-bleached hair. As I approached the steps of my guesthouse, clutching my duffel bag in sweaty hands, I passed a group of gorgeous body-builder types sunbathing completely naked on a ground-level deck. My mouth went instantly dry, and I felt my balls constrict in my cut-offs. This scheme was doomed to failure, I knew. If I couldn't even approach a guy in a bar, how in hell was I going to walk up and proposition someone whose uncut 10-incher was dangling right in front of my face?

My heart pounding, I dashed up the stairs to my room, which ironically turned out to be a narrow, closet-sized space. Throwing myself onto the bed, I hauled out my cock with trembling fingers. Shivering with lust and frustration, and banishing all thoughts of my own miserable predicament, I began desperately stroking its rigid, throbbing length.

Before long I felt that familiar clench in my guts, and my pisshole dilated wildly as the first spurts of hot cream shot up into the air. I guess seeing all those naked hunks on the terrace had inflamed my libido even more than usual, because I soon came so hard and so long that a shower of gold and white sparks danced in front of my eyes. My sauce just kept bubbling out of the head of my cock, sliding down my wrist in thick, frothy waves, and gushing down over my heaving, hairless torso. I was about to groan and flop onto my back on the bed when I heard someone walk by in the hall. That was when a truly bizarre thing happened.

Looking back on it later, I figured that in my haste to beat off, I'd neglected to shut the door all the way. The vibrations from the hall floor must have jarred it open just as my fellow resort guest sauntered by. But when it actually happened, I didn't have time to mull things over. All I knew then was that I was crouching on my bed with my shorts around my ankles and my naked, cream-coated cock in my hand. On the other side of the now-open door, wearing only a pair of skimpy black swim trunks, stood the most magnificent man I'd ever seen. He looked about my age, and like the guys on the deck, he sported pumped-up pecs and a broad-shouldered frame that had tanned to a sleek, mellow bronze. The skin around his nipples and at the base of his throat shimmered with sweat, as if he'd just come in out of the hot sun.

As his wide brown eyes darkened with lust, I sat there with my legs wide open and my dribbling hose clenched in my fist. My gaze drifted between his sinewy legs, too, and I swallowed hard when I saw the huge sausage stuffing that tight thong. His fleshy tube was growing by the moment, swelling up like someone was pumping air into his suit. Knowing that the sight of my cock had done that to him got me turned on all over again. While he watched, fascinated, my own prong stiffened up and pushed against the confines of my cum-stained fingers.

He shifted his weight from one foot to the other, and I saw the ponderous weight of his full balls settle in the pouch of his suit. Then, before I could say or do anything, he cupped his bulge with his right hand and stepped quickly inside the room. This time he reached back and pushed the door shut all the way.

"I get the sense you're looking for some company," he said quietly, moving to sink onto the bed beside me. "I'm Desmond."

"Jesse," I whispered, shifting so that his muscular body could fit comfortably beside mine. I could never have predicted it, but the overpowering horniness that suddenly welled up in my body gave me a burst of confidence I'd never felt before.

I heard Desmond's breathing quicken as his fingers crept up my sides, peeling away the cum-spattered cotton tank top I still wore. I moaned as he traced the outline of my own naked torso, his fingers playfully returning every so often to tweak my stiff nipple. I humped my naked body toward him, letting my rigid cock poke forward until it brushed against his rippling abs. The contact sent a fresh current of lust through me, and I imagined that I could actually hear my pre-cum sizzle against his bare skin.

Guided by a horny instinct I didn't question, I reached out and slipped the elastic band of his swimsuit down away from that pulsating swell between his tanned thighs.

Finally, I looked down and got a close-up view his meat. His elongated, mushroom-shaped cockhead glistened with a silvery drop of pre-cum, while his thick shaft seemed to pulse softly with a web of plump blue veins. Light brown fuzz that smelled like coconut oil and male arousal covered his wrinkly, low-hanging balls.

Though I was still nervous, my throat was burning with the need to sample the goods. Slowly, keeping both hands on his splayed thighs, I stretched out on the bed, keeping my hips turned sideways so he could still access my own throbbing hard-on. I sucked back a deep, calming breath, then dipped my head and got my first taste of another man's cock.

The crisp flavor of spiced meat, seawater, and salty pre-cum filled my head, and my senses reeled as I flicked my tongue along his bloated base and swelling nutsac. Swiftly I tongued his juicy nuts into my mouth and rolled them hungrily around in my mouth.

23

With a growl, Desmond tensed up and rammed all his weight into me, sinking his fiery bulb down past my tonsils on the very first stroke. The sensation was so startling that I coughed and gagged a little, jerking my head so that he slid halfway out again.

Not noticing my difficulty, Desmond started a fuck-rhythm of his own, mashing his groin harder against my upturned lips and cramming his fat cock all the way into my gullet. It took some effort, but before long I figured out how to relax my throat and breathe through my nose. Soon I was hauling down his meat like I'd done it a hundred times before.

As though he'd been hit by a bolt of lightning, his pulse quickened and his body grew feverish with need. When I gave his balls a squeeze, I felt them start to pull up in my tightening grip. Then, to my delight, Desmond reached between my legs and began to massage my bulging boner with a surprisingly steady hand.

The exhilaration I felt was too much for my own poor cock to bear. "Yes!" I hissed. "Here I ... come!" All at once, I felt the floodgates open, and a torrent of my virgin spunk gushed all over Desmond's pumping hand. Wet, sticky heat soaked my thighs and ran down his wrist and my legs. Far from minding this impromptu shower, Desmond began twisting his body like he was losing control.

"Me, too," was all he could rasp. "Don't stop!"

Though I'd enjoyed every moment of our blow-job so far, I'd never even tasted my own cum and had no idea what to expect. All I knew was that the idea of letting him unload in my guts was setting me on fire from the inside out!

He went rigid all over as he fired his wad deep into my thirsty, clenching throat. Dizzy with my success, I swallowed load after load of his warm jizz as it cascaded down my throat in a scalding, continuous stream. Raw heat coursed through his cock, filled my mouth, and radiated into every corner of my naked, trembling frame. The harder I sucked, the more cream he unloaded. Though I hardly stopped to taste it in all the excitement, I knew it was something I would never get enough of.

When he had emptied himself out, I spent a long, lingering moment tonguing off his dome and flange. Then I popped his softening rod from my lips and moved lower to nuzzle his balls, lapping up the leftover cream that had pooled there. His eyes squeezed shut, Desmond kept fucking the air like he imagined that my wet throat was still wrapped around him.

We rested awhile, and I had to fight to keep a big, goofy grin off my face. I'd done it, I kept telling myself, my heart and cock throbbing with equal excitement. Now I could actually go home and tell my friends I'd blown another guy-and shot my own wad all over him to boot.

In fact, I got so carried away with congratulating myself that I never noticed Desmond's cock springing up beside me, ready for more action. Before I had time to register that fact, he had rolled me over on the mattress and was peeling my ass-cheeks apart with both hands. I sucked in a deep breath, willing myself to relax while he wrenched my butt-hole open with both thumbs. Slowly he positioned himself on top of me, his pointed cockhead brushing my fiery rim while he took careful aim at my cavern. Then, while I lay there holding my breath, he humped his hips and shoved his cock halfway into my ass.

"Ohhhhh," I moaned, spreading my legs as wide as I could while he bucked his hips and skewered himself a few inches deeper. It hurt a little at first, though I was so excited that I didn't notice much beyond the sweet, stinging pleasure that ripped its way into my hot, willing bowels. Melding my body to his, I managed to wriggle and shimmy until my sphincter was gripping his tool as tightly as my mouth had done moments ago. He seemed amazed at my tightness-amazed, but pleased.

"I've never felt anything like your ass on my cock," he grunted, and I had to admit that the reverse was true as well. I couldn't imagine anything could ever feel as satisfying as his thick plug did in my drainpipe, especially when he thrashed his hips and rubbed himself up and down my chasm.

My own boner sprang up between my crotch and the bed sheets, squirming against the cum-stained mattress like a horny anaconda. As I ground my hips against the bed in slow, agonized circles, I could feel sparks of pleasure fire all the way into my balls.

When Desmond hit my prostate with a hard, well-aimed shove, I felt my nuts let go for the third time that afternoon.

"Oh, yes," I shouted. "Fuck me! Fuck me, Desmond!"

"You got it, Jesse," Desmond grunted, riding me like a bucking steer, while I pumped my hips against the firm mattress. Before long, we both started spurting. My ass sucked up Desmond's spunk like a dry sponge, though he unloaded so much ball-fuel that some of it leaked out over the rim of my ass and drenched the bed all over again. When he finally exhausted himself and pulled out with a gasp, I bent over and licked a big, tasty wad off the sheets.

I smacked my lips with satisfaction as he rolled me over and licked my now-flaccid cock. It ached like someone had squeezed it in a vise, and my balls felt like they'd been turned inside-out and emptied. My asshole felt like it had been ripped open and stitched back together with carpet thread. But it was the sweetest discomfort I knew I'd ever feel.

Desmond left about a half an hour later, and I didn't run into him again until I was heading for the ferry two days later. We made arrangements to meet in the city, but by then I'd spent most of my vacation sucking and fucking myself sore with a variety of other hot guys I met on the beach, in the clubs, and right there in my own guesthouse. I still go back to Fire Island every year, and I make it a point to stay on that same floor in that same guesthouse.

Every now and then, I walk by my old door just to see if it will still swing open the way it did for Desmond all those years ago. And, once or twice, it has.

CONTACT SPORTS
Daniel Miller

The Colorado scenery outside was nothing less than breathtaking, and a blanket of fresh, crisp snow surrounded the lodge. Most of my fellow competitors were out on the slopes with their snowboards, practicing for the Championship match the next day. Ordinarily, I would have been out there with them, fine-tuning my jumps or scoping out my rivals. But for now, I was a lot happier inside my room, bathed in the glow of the big-screen TV in the corner. My legs were on the coffee table, and I'd pulled my sweats down just far enough to expose my balls and rigid boner. As my fingers flirted up and down its rocky length, my eyes were glued to a hot video I'd sneaked out of the chalet to rent.

In keeping with the spirit of the place, I'd chosen a flick with a sports theme. On the screen, two gorgeous hunks were by themselves in a locker room, their hard bodies draped in nothing but a few steamy trickles of sweat. A blond guy was sitting on a bench, his nine-inch dick curving like a crowbar from his doubled fists. The other man, darker and every bit as muscular, stood in front of him. His torso was tilting wildly back and forth as he pumped his swollen boner in and out of the blond's throat. On every upstroke, I could see the thick, purplish veins on his shaft ripple against the sides of a translucent condom. The blond guy's lips were stretched out so far they'd lost their color.

Pretty soon, the dark guy shot his rubber full of cream just as the blond dude detonated all over both their naked chests. I've always taken pride in my self-control keeping my body and mind in perfect sync was what had gotten me to the Snowboarding Finals in the first place but when I saw those shiny gobs of white slithering down those quivering muscles, I totally lost it. My right hand snapped into a fist and began to milk my bloated shank with every ounce of horny strength

I could muster. I could feel an intense pressure building in my nuts, and my puckered cockhole flared with an onrush of heat.

Clenching my jaw, I tightened my fingers and focused on siphoning my jumbo-sized load. The first pearly tendrils had just burst from my dome when I heard a scraping sound behind me, and a jaunty voice shattered my concentration. In my haste to start watching my tape, I'd apparently forgotten to lock my door.

"Hey, Dane, what's up? I was wondering if you felt like whoa, sorry!"

My spewing dick still in my hand, I whirled around and found myself staring at the tall, blond-haired Californian from the room next to mine. In his mid-twenties, he was a bit older than most of the other contestants, though so was I at 22. I'd gotten to know him a little over the past week, and we'd done a few practice runs together. Oddly enough, I'd already pegged Colin as my biggest obstacle to taking the trophy home at the end of the week. His quiet determination and serious grey eyes, not to mention his skill on the slopes, marked him as the type of competitor who could take an unwary opponent by surprise. And he had certainly done that just now!

Considering the rather awkward situation, and the fact that both my hands were now covered with frothy jizz, I expected Colin to sputter some kind of apology and bolt from my room. Instead, he stood rooted to the spot, apparently mesmerized by the sight of my softening sausage. At least he had enough sense to close the door while he stared at me.

"That looks pretty hot," he murmured, though I wasn't sure whether he meant my prong or the video. His husky voice was almost drowned out by a series of muffled moans and grunts from the TV set.

The look on his face, not to mention the lump that had spontaneously formed in the front of his ski pants, suddenly got my cock ramrod stiff all over again. Instead of attempting to cover myself, I spread my thighs wide open. My shaft snapped bolt upright between us and my big balls popped out over the cum-stained waistband of my sweats.

"You can come in and watch the end of this with me, if you want," I said, leaving it up to him to decide if I meant the fuck flick or the hand-job. With exaggerated nonchalance, I dropped my hand back into my cinnamon-colored nest. Colin's jaw went slack with lust as I gave my stiff cock's rigid base a squeeze, then began to stroke slowly up and down my entire eight inches. My pointed crown soon filled with hot blood, and my shaft flared both horizontally and vertically as a burning pressure gripped my nuts.

The action on the TV screen suddenly heated up again, the two guys now sixty-nining on the floor of the locker-room shower. All the while, Colin just stood there, speechless, which got me confused for a moment. If he was as much into guys as I was, why wasn't he down on his knees with my hose up his gullet by now?

Pausing, I confronted him. "So what's the scoop, Colin? You into guys or what?"

"Well, I am, sorta when I'm not practicing my verticals."

I couldn't help laughing. No wonder he was such a terror on the slopes. He poured all his sexual energy into his relationship with his board! "Well, I can't say that I've mastered those yet myself but I'd be happy to give you some tips on getting horizontal, if you're interested."

"I...uh...I'm not sure," he stammered, forgetting all about the video. "We're competing tomorrow and....." His words trailed off and he blushed furiously, his cheeks going almost as red as my cock did when I gave it a playful pinch and aimed it in his direction. At that point, whatever objections he'd been turning around in his mind must have vanished, because he slid to his knees and stuck his face right up next to my cock. He extended a long, pink tongue to lap my balls. My right hand went right on choking the chicken while the left shot to the coffee table beside us. My wallet lay there, and I hastily extracted two wrapped condoms. One I tossed on the sofa, and one I plopped over my again-gushing cockhead.

"Go for it, man," I hissed, wrapping both hands around the back of his head and crushing him suddenly against me. I felt my shrink-wrapped cockhead slide up into the very back of his throat just as the first steamy tendrils of pre-cum squirted into the condom's soft rubber membrane. Colin dug down harder, a flood of acrid sweat rushing from my bush to coat his face, gluing us together with sticky heat.

A deep flush crept across my thighs as he opened his mouth as wide as he could and inhaled me up to my chubby hilt. When I was safely lodged against his tonsils, he half-swallowed and tightened the muscles in his throat. With a moan, I started pushing my hips forward and then pulling them backward in tandem with the movements of his head. The two of us were soon humping and pumping in a sensual fuck-rhythm, Colin rolling his head from side to side to put added pressure on my shank.

While he sucked me, the two of us grappled with my sweatpants until they formed a dark blue puddle around my ankles. While Colin went on slurping me, using his chin to compress my aching balls, his fingers crept around my ass-cheek and tickled my asshole. I writhed in pleasure, fucking my cock deeper into his windpipe, then shuddered with surprise when he suddenly stiffened his fingers and plunged right on in.

His entry was clumsy and hurt a little at first, which supported his story that he wasn't all that experienced. Still, what he lacked in technical skill he made up for in enthusiasm, so I shifted my hips and wriggled my ass until his invasion began to feel more comfortable. When he added a second and then a third finger to the mix, a smoldering flame of arousal spread through me. It almost felt like a cock reaming me back there, and I wanted to suck it deeper and deeper into my bowels. At one point, I fantasized that his energetic lips might be able to slurp his own fingers right up into my crotch. Then he'd be able to fondle my balls from the inside out!

It didn't take long before my reawakened cock lashed out against the confines of his throat in a sudden fit of lust. I wheezed and pulled his hair while I drained my guts out through my throbbing main vein, my condom expanding so much that his cheeks puffed out like a chipmunk's and his eyes grew wide and glassy. I could tell that he was fighting off a gag, so I reached down and gave my balls a final, emptying squeeze.

"Finished," I grunted, as I jerked my hips back and slid my wilting meat from his mouth. His tongue seemed to have melted into the sweltering rubber, because it burst right out along with my shaft. He remained crouching beside me, his juicy licker dangling from his open lips like a Saint Bernard's. I could even hear him panting as he gulped air to replenish his lungs. Slowly he withdrew his fingers from my ass.

"OK, now it's your turn," I growled as soon as I'd recovered my composure. Reaching down, I executed a perfect Double-Handed Grab on his asscheeks and hauled him onto the couch next to me. In 15 seconds flat, I had him naked and sprawled out in front of me.

I reached between his open legs and wrapped my hand around his hard-on. It was no lightweight, as I'd suspected from the mound in his ski pants, but needless to say it looked even better exposed. An intricate web of dark veins surged up the entire nine inches or so of his bloated shaft, while a deep, sexy groove split the underside of his distended mushroom-shaped head. His pisshole winked at me like a naughty black pupil.

Delighting in the thick, hot feel of it, I went to work rubbing its length and scratching at the tender underbelly with my nails. In no time at all, his whole groin was quivering visibly with need, his tight abs streaked with sweat. By tilting my rear end forward, I even managed to rub our cockheads together for a while. Colin really liked that.

I started to slide the second condom onto his rod, but his hands on my wrist stopped me.

"No," he whispered, "wear it yourself. I want your cock up my ass."

I was a little surprised at that, since he seemed to be on the point of explosion and my pole was still on the wane from my most recent detonation. Colin had apparently taken this into account, however, because he quickly dropped my wrist and moved both hands to his stick shift. A few strategic yanks and twists, and my fuck-engine started back up with a vengeance. He slicked the waiting condom on me himself and spread his legs eagerly.

Hunkering down on my knees beside the couch, I maneuvered his ass to the edge of the cushions and nudged myself just barely inside him. He felt tight, so I explored the insides of his ass-tunnel slowly, moaning as his fuzzy balls tickled the insides of my thighs. The hot skin of my blunt cockhead rubbed my deeper recesses until his whole ass spasmed with pleasure. Colin raked his nails against my steely thighs while I took a deep breath and slicked all the way inside him.

"Oh, yeah, perfect," he grunted, while I eased his buttocks as far apart as they would go and pressed forward. Soon my rubber-clad cockbase was wedged tight against the stretched-out girth of his asshole. His sphincter muscle spasmed, contracting and then flexing open with obvious pleasure.

I started an explosive in-and-out fucking motion, nearly losing control of myself when he started contacting his butt muscles. At one point, he got so into it that he wrapped his legs around my waist and forced my cock deeper into his ass, his sphincter squeezing my shaft like a clenched fist. His glute muscles were rippling like gleaming snowdrifts in a high wind as I thrust into him, my condom filling with yet another load of steamy pre-cum. Before long I had squeezed my eyes shut as a searing heat rocked my hips and ignited my whole groin.

All the while, Colin's own shank seesawed back and forth between his splayed legs, untouched but close to bursting. His mouth was still open, but his eyes were half-closed and unfocused. It was like he was lost in a daze of total, mind-numbing ecstasy. I was astonished at his patience and self-control. It made fucking him a mind-blowing experience, but it would sure put me at a disadvantage on the slopes the next day!

To hell with that, I thought. There'd be other snowboarding finals, but I'd probably never find another competitor like Colin! Firming my jaw, I put everything I had into making him come. Soon my bulging head hammered his innards with such urgency that I might eventually have mashed his prostate into pulp. Only then did he let out a single, powerful wail like the Abominable Snowman monster claiming a mountainside. His doubled fists flew to his stalk, and a single, powerful squeeze sent his white cum raining over my bare shoulders. I blasted the condom with a third load of my own unfortunately much smaller than either Colin's or my first two had been and held onto the rim of the condom as I sagged, exhausted, between his legs.

"Shit, Colin," I wheezed when I could speak again. My whole body was drenched with so many white, trickling pellets of cum that I looked like I'd just come in from a snow flurry. The TV screen had long been showing nothing but scratchy static. "If you're as good at snowboarding as you are at fucking, I don't have a chance out there tomorrow!"

He opened his sea-grey eyes sleepily. "Actually, I'm not sure I do, either. I usually try to save up all my energy for a big match like this. But you just looked too damn good to resist."

That made me feel better and, as it happened, neither one of us made the top three of the competition. Since we'd both been heavily favored to win, no one could figure out why we didn't seem at all disappointed. The truth was that we were looking forward to doing the whole thing over again the following year!

TOO MUCH
John Patrick

Mark had been directed to the old two-story house behind the Boylesk theater. It was used to house the dancers and to provide a place for them to meet clients. Officially, it was a massage parlor, or so the sign on the door said.

Mark entered a reception area, where an overweight, bearded gent dressed only in a towel took his money and checked him off in his spiral-bound appointment book. He stared at Mark blankly for a moment. What kind of expression was Mark expecting anyway? Maybe the man had already gotten so used to escorting men in and out that he simply could not respond at all. But even so, even if he was completely used to it by now, there should still be a special look on his face, Mark thought.

Finally came a half smile, and the attendant pointed across the room to a long hallway. "Room seven," he said, and, with a quick slap on Mark's ass, Mark was sent stumbling down the hall. "Have fun," the attendant said.

The door to room one was half open, and Mark could hear moans of pleasure mixed with slurping and sucking noises. Mark couldn't resist peering into the doorway. A young blond was naked on a massage table and was receiving a blowjob from another young blond. When the sucker saw Mark he gently eased the door shut. Mark continued on. All of the other doors were closed.

Mark got to room seven and knocked.

"Come on in," a deep voice called out.

Mark opened the door and there he was, Chad Carpenter, star of over 100 videos. Chad had done everything, and he had fascinated Mark as no other porn star had for nearly three years. When Mark heard Chad was dancing for a week's engagement over the

Thanksgiving holiday, he tried to book a flight but everything was filled. Mark decided to drive, see some relatives along the way.

Chad's show was disappointing to Mark because there are state laws that prohibit totally nude dancing, but the boy was charming and a terrible tease. Chad wore his blond hair considerably longer than in the videos and he appeared to be much smaller and more delicate. But Chad's ass was even more splendid that Mark had remembered it, and Chad delighted in bending over and opening it up a bit for his adoring fans. Mark sat way in the back for the first show, and then moved up front for the second. It was after that show Mark saw Chad in the lounge and Mark agreed to meet Chad "next door" the next afternoon.

Chad apparently had the star's quarters. There was a huge bed, covered only with a messy sheet, a small refrigerator, tables, chairs, and an adjoining bathroom.

They sat across from each other for a few minutes, chatting pleasantly, and then Chad jumped up and served champagne in cheap glasses.

Mark don't know what he expected, but it wasn't this. Champagne in the middle of the afternoon with Chad Carpenter! A fully-clothed Chad besides! He guzzled his wine, while Mark sipped it. Chad re-filled his glass several times. He appeared to be a nervous sort, and Mark confronted him: "Is there something wrong?"

"What?"

"I just wondered if I'd done something wrong."

"Oh, no, nothing's wrong," Chad said, getting up to fill his glass again. "You're just a very attractive boy, you know. People who visit here, well, you know, it's like my job, that's all."

Mark was terribly flattered. Maybe, he chuckled to himself, he could have some of his hard-earned money back? "Actually, this is a first," Mark said. "I mean, the first time I've ever been with anyone, well, famous."

Chad blushed, and suddenly lost his balance, plopping down on the bed. He quickly regained his composure, sat up, and the contents of his champagne glass spilled as he drew it to his lips.

He finished the wine, and told Mark to come over to him. Chad blinked as Mark sat down next to him and began stroking his stomach, his armpits, then his crotch. Mark simply couldn't hold back; he at least had to fondle the merchandise. This was suddenly too much for Chad, apparently. He dropped his glass on the floor and grabbed Mark's wrists and pushed him backwards across the wide bed. He fell forward against Mark, pinning his body beneath him, using his weight to full advantage to quiet the now wriggling mass beneath him.

Suddenly Chad rolled heavily sideways, landing on his back with Mark above him. Mark held his arms crucified away from his body.

Chad smiled an oddly wistful smile. "Fuck me," he begged.

With that Mark tilted his head down and kissed him. And like so many before him, Mark lost himself in the joy of kissing those well-kissed lips. If there was one thing Chad had learned in all those hours before the cameras with cold women and men under hot lights it was kissing.

In all Mark's life, he had never experienced such passion hitting him full force. The room was burning with Chad's kisses. And Mark was writhing against him, and finally Chad let his hands go, uncertain what else to do. Mark seized the opportunity, and quickly reached own to his waist, and pulled off his T-shirt. The sight of him nearly naked was too much, somehow. Mark was speechless. Having this universally beloved, and beautiful, porn star in bed with him took Mark's breath away. Chad reached out suddenly and turned off the bedside lamp, as if he sensed asking Mark to fuck him in bright light was just too much.

Before Mark could start thinking whether it was too much even in darkness, Chad was pulling off Mark's shirt as well. Soon he had their jeans removed. Chad wore no underwear and, Mark thought, his cock was every bit as gorgeous as it appeared in video after video, sliding in and out of innumerable mouths, cunts, and asses.

Chad gently directed Mark now because Mark seemed lost, and Mark took his direction flawlessly. As Mark removed his briefs, Chad slapped a palm against his ass, then fingered his tits. He seemed to be surveying Mark, as if he were casting him for one of his videos. "Tight little ass," he noted, "Smooth chest, juicy cock." He ran a finger through the tuft of dark hair at Mark's crotch. He sighed then, and leaned back on his elbows, offering himself to Mark. Mark took Chad's raging hard-on in his mouth and sucked on it, lost in long-suppressed desire. He had wanted this for a long, long time.

Mark straddled Chad's torso, and ran his hands over his chest, lightly flicking his nipples. Chad's body stirred slightly under Mark. Mark bent down and they kissed again.

In a matter of seconds Mark was stretched out full length on top of Chad, clasping his head with his hands and kissing him as if his life depended on it. Mark began pumping his hips, grinding his stiff prick against Chad's sweat-slicked belly. Chad's hands slid down his back and cupped his ass, squeezing the cheeks with every thrust of Mark's body. Chad's fingertips dug into Mark's crack. Mark's mouth worked its way on down, kissing Chad's throat, his shoulders. Mark's head swung lower and he gently took Chad's left nipple between his teeth, flicking it with his tongue. Chad groaned, and his body squirmed gratefully, blissfully beneath Mark. Mark's tongue made a wet trail across the incredibly hard ridges of Chad's belly to the first fringe of his dark blond pubes. His fat cock had stiffened to full hardness now. Mark took it in his hand and gazed at it, the cock he had seen being sucked and adored and glorified by so many gals and guys. He traced the veins along the meaty, ivory, cut shaft. It must have been at least eight inches long, this magnificent cock. "Oh, it's beautiful," Mark sighed.

Chad smiled. He never tired of hearing men admire it.

Mark rolled his tongue around the cockhead, gently, teasingly, and then suddenly descended, taking the entire shaft down his eager throat. Chad cried out, "Oh, god," and seized Mark's head with both hands. Chad began pumping his hips, cramming his luscious cock deep into Mark's mouth. After a couple of seconds, Mark found his stride, matching each upward thrust of his with a downward plunge of Mark's own. Mark reached up, gripping each of Chad's hard nipples between thumb and forefinger, and squeezed. Chad's groans of delight at Mark's technique took on an added intensity. Chad wrapped his legs around Mark tightly and rolled them over. In this position Chad could easily ram his dick down Mark's throat.

After a few minutes of the most marvelous face-fucking Mark had ever enjoyed, Chad pulled out, and Mark was able to bathe his nearly hairless balls with his tongue. Mark looked up to see Chad was staring back down at him, his eyes bright and feverish. Chad took his cock in his hand and slapped Mark's face with it, rubbing it over Mark's nose, eyes, cheeks. Pre-cum coated Mark's skin.

Mark's hands wandered up and down the length of Chad's hard, muscled torso, kneading the sweaty flesh, then again pinching his nipples. Chad took his balls out of Mark's mouth and went back to fucking his face. He reached behind him and grasped Mark's dick, pulling on it with short, quick strokes. Finally, he got some lube and coated Mark's cock.

"I want you to fuck me as hard as you can," he said.

"Sure," Mark smiled.

Chad took a big dollop of the lube and worked it into his asshole, then sat on Mark's erection. The cock slid right in. Soon Chad was gasping, arching his back. Mark plowed into him as energetically as he could. Sometimes he pushed all the way in and stayed there, as Chad began to grind his hips into Mark. Gradually, Chad picked up the tempo, and Mark's cock was plunging in and out with a hard, fast rhythm. Chad jacked off while he fucked Mark's cock. Cum soon was spewing out of Chad's dick, in one ropey loop after another, splattering across Mark's chest, and Mark's cum was soon filling Chad. Mark reached up to pull him down, and kiss him as he finished.

A few minutes later, Mark held Chad close. Chad seemed in no hurry for Mark to leave. Chad lay there humming, his head on Mark's shoulder. Mark said to him, "Well, you sound happy."

He twisted his head to look up at Mark's face. "You fucked me good, mister."

"No, you fucked me."

"Whatever. It was good." Then Chad paused suddenly, his eyes locked on Mark's smiling face. He put up a hand to caress Mark's face. With that, Mark leaned down to kiss him goodbye.

#

Mark arrived just in time for the midnight show. He was lucky and got a seat in the front row.

Chad danced last and was joined on stage at the end of his act by the five other dancers. Here he just held his own, blending indistinguishably into the crowd as he pressed his way forward among the men standing there, sexy, well-built men just like him, to step over to him and bend down and kiss him.

The crowd roared. A star was what he was and now, and in one of the defining, unforgettable moments in Mark's young life Chad whispered in Mark's ear, "Why don't you come next door and fuck me?"

This time, the fat man at the door smiled the moment he saw Mark and told him to go right back, that Chad was expecting him. Mark felt as if he was being given a second chance when none was needed really, and it wasn't costing him a cent.

Chad was naked, fresh from a shower. No words were spoken; he just took Mark in his arms and kissed him. Then he said, "That was great. Just how I like it. You're a great kisser."

Mark beamed, and dropped to his knees before him. It was party time. Chad's cock was only partially hard. Mark leaned forward and kissed the knobby, circumcised head. The sleek crown twitched and spasmed a moment. Mark gave it a couple of licks and kissed it again. Then the warm knob was in his mouth, pulsing and throbbing between his lips, stretching and hardening as he sucked.

Mark laved the bulbous head and pre-cum oozed from it. Chad's right hand dropped down to the back of Mark's head. The cock was now rigid in his hand. He pumped him steadily, his lips working the crown, sucking and licking the knob. Suddenly, Chad shuddered. His cock twitched and spasmed. His cum filled Mark's mouth.

"Shit!" Chad cried, pulling Mark's head into his groin, his hips jerking and quivering. Chad's cock jabbed at Mark's mouth, then the rhythm slowed. Soon, the famous cock lay peacefully on Mark's tongue, the pubic hair tickling his nose.

"I'm sorry," Chad said. "I haven't come all day. I usually come two or three times and...." He paused, stroked the back of Mark's head. "Damn, you're good, Mark."

Mark released his cock and got to his feet. The penis he had fantasized about so often glistened lewdly between Chad's legs. Mark stroked it as Chad started removing Mark's clothes. Again Mark saw the delicacy, the fragility of him despite the taut muscles. Mark wanted to make love to him, slowly and sweetly. But there was another part of him that knew that Chad wanted to be fucked until it hurt.

Soon Chad was on his knees on the bed, his ass high in the air. Mark covered Chad's magnificent ass with little kisses. His tongue probed Chad's shaved asshole and Chad flinched. Mark steadied him with a gentle hand as he licked his crack up and down, over and over, until he cried out, desperate for cock. Mark smeared the lube all over his erection. He entered him slowly, and it was simply too good. Mark became dizzy, thought he was going to pass out, it was that good. Chad collapsed to the bed, letting Mark fuck his ass harder and harder until everything went black around Mark, and Mark came harder than he had ever come before.

Yes, it was all too much. Much too much.

PUNISHMENT
Ken Smith

My neck ached and my head felt like shit. I guessed I'd been hit with something and my brain had ceased to function.

Shit! I thought. Where the fuck am I?

Two steel rings hanging from his pierced nipples were the first thing I noticed, then the smooth mountain of a chest sporting them. Oh, Jesus, this guy was bloody enormous and his shaved head looked threatening. I couldn't see his thighs, they being hidden behind a towel, but the muscles, just above his knees, gave me a good idea of their formidable fortitude.

Had I dropped a clanger, or what?

I made an instant promise that I would never burgle another flat, but knew I couldn't keep it. God damn it, I was out of work and needed to eat. Anyway, the stupid bastard shouldn't have left his flat open. Problem was, I reckoned I was just about to be flayed alive.

His fearsome eyes hadn't blinked once and were screwing me into the bed's headboard. My brain issued an adrenalin-induced command for me to run. My minuscule muscles flexed for the daring dash but when you are in a state of fear and you are being bombarded with alternatives, it's funny how things go unnoticed like your hands having been handcuffed behind your back! I hadn't even noticed they weren't in their normal position or even defending my body.

What an asshole! What did he think I was going to do? Me, a sixteen year old David. Him Goliath. I didn't even have a sling!

Goliath dropped his towel. "Right, you little shit!" he roared. "You've got two choices. I call the cops or you suck this!"

"So that's what you hit me with, you bully," I muttered. Then thought, "What a bitch of a world. How come I didn't have a dick that size?"

Hey, I'd met faggots before. They were all fruity fairies who'd run at the sound of a fart, weren't they? Not anymore. It would seem they were now all beef and biceps.

Then it struck me what he'd just said. He was planning on being Tarzan with me his Jane.

Now, I could see a problem developing here. My choices? Well, it made no difference. Either way I was going to get banged up. It was lock or cock!

This was turning into a real crap day.

Well, I can be butch as well and I told him straight, any attempt to use my mouth as an asshole simulator and I'd bite his bell end off.

Sadly, that was not a good move, and what I thought was a big dick was now a really big dick. What's more, it was pressing against my lips, almost prizing them apart. The problem with keeping your mouth shut I wished I had! you have to breathe. Not really difficult until some bastard with a cock the size of a cucumber has it pressed to your mouth and grips your bloody nose.

Opening my mouth, I gasped for air, got some but mostly got cock and couldn't breathe again until my nose was released. Fighting back, I sank my teeth into the solid savaloy. But, shit, he loved it and his cock gained in girth and length.

I began sucking in lifesaving air through my nose, but the bastard shoved a bottle of poppers up one nostril. My brain exploded!

His dick hit the back of my throat and I gagged as three inches went past the critical point. My eyes watered.

I breathed deep and fast through my nose but the poppers were still jammed up there. My eyes spun.

Now then, this was not such a particularly friendly event, so why then did my dick straighten in my pants and an overwhelming urge for the bastard to grab hold of it and pump it wildly surge throughout my body?

He got right above me now, his meaty thighs either side of my boyish face. He tipped my head right back. I guessed this was it. I was about to get the whole length.

I wanted to suck in some ordinary air but the Poppers were still jammed up my nose. The blood-pumping gas was doing its job all right. My cock was bigger and stiffer than it had ever been!

In one thrust he gave me the whole length of his cock. Not roughly. Deliberately slow. Feeding my throat until his pubics met my nostrils and his balls dangled over my chin. I was more than surprised that I could still breathe. I was even more surprised that pre-cum was dribbling down my dick.

No, I wasn't enjoying this oral attack. Shit, that's a lie. Hell, I was loving that thick, firm prick pressing my palate, the bulbous head opening my esophagus. But I shouldn't have been, should I?

I guessed it was because I, too, was a guy and knew the sexual bliss my seducer was swimming in. I knew he couldn't stop even if he wanted to. I guess, because of this, I sucked and sucked on that delicious dick, eager for that hot spunk to siphon into my mouth. Eager for him to shoot his stuff. Gorging on that glorious gristle as if I were gorging on my own.

Then, just as I was getting into it, the bitch changed tactics. Not deep anymore. Just tickling the back of my throat. I arched up, trying to get more, trying to get it past the puking part but the bastard wouldn't give it to me.

I moaned, groaned, begged and cried for his cock. I don't know why. You tell me!

At last he gave me the whole length, moving the final inches back and forth so I could feel the swelling head deep in my throat as it prepared to deliver his load. I whimpered.

Hey, fuck off. I'm not queer! Tip to base, his cock sank. Tip to base. Oh God, tip to base!

Suddenly the monster was staring me in the face, pumping spunk all over my cropped hair. I came in my pants at the same time, almost as much as him.

My punishment administered, he cunningly grinned, then released me from the handcuffs.

"I suppose you want to shove that big cock up my arse now, you bastard!" I shouted.

Goliath shook his head.

"Well, you fuckin' well better had," I screamed, "or I'll tell the fuckin' cops!"

BIG & BEAUTIFUL
John Patrick

"...Not only was it big, perhaps the biggest I'd ever laid eyes on, it was breathtakingly beautiful."

"I was fifteen then," he told me as he made himself comfortable on the couch. "I was workin' at Bill's Butcher Shop for the summer. It was a very hot day near the end of summer. I made a delivery to a woman, who invited me to come in. She gave me a drink of iced tea. We talked a little. I was up against the sink, drinking the tea, and she came over and stood in front of me and took hold of my dick. I just stood there. I was scared. Nervous. She said, 'My god...!' Then she asked, 'Does this feel good?' 'Yeah,' I said. She asked me if I'd ever been with a woman, never taking her hand off my dick. I told her I'd only been with little girls. She laughed and she took me into the bedroom and started to undress me, kissing my chest. I kept asking if she was sure her husband wasn't coming home. She said he wouldn't be home for hours. Then she went right down and started to suck me. She was the first person ever to tell me how big I was. Once I was fully hard, she got up and took her clothes off and I thought how big she was. God, she had a big, fat ass! She took my hand and put it on her cunt. 'Do you like it?' she asked me."

"And did you ... I mean, did you like it?"

"Yeah. I mean, she was nice, but it was weird, you know, doing it in the bed she shared every night with her husband. And it wasn't like banging a little girl. The girls I'd been with were not too experienced either, they kept their clothes on, they were so embarrassed. But with her ... well, I knew she wanted more. There were things I knew I didn't do right. Like, I came right away. She didn't say anything but I know she was disappointed. She just lay there, running her hands up and down my thighs, playing with my cock. I think she was trying to get it up again."

"And did you?"

"No. After I come, I come so much, I just need to rest awhile. A couple of hours at least."

"Yes, of course."

"But it was good for me, you know. It was the first time I realized it wasn't about me getting off. It was about pleasing somebody else."

"You felt you had pleased her?"

"No, I knew I hadn't. But what I mean is, it taught me what my job was. I got dressed and she lay there, nude. She made me come over to her and she kissed me. She stroked the bulge in my jeans and she told me I could come back any time."

"And did you?"

"No. I had to go back to school. I never told anybody about it."

"Maybe you thought whoever you told would go over and fuck her?"

"No." He looked out the window. "Well, maybe...."

Now, after telling this tale, he was incredibly wanting. He didn't hold my hand but grabbed my wrist. He took my open palm and drew it down to his crotch.

Through his jeans I could feel what I knew would be there. His tool was pressed hard against his jeans. I looked down to watch as I slowly rubbed my palm the length of his dick. It didn't stop till I'd gotten a few inches down his thigh. I squeezed the head through his pants, then slid my hand back up and between his legs. I could feel so much heat coming off his crotch, I thought he might come. I looked back up at his face. He looked drugged. His eyelids were heavy. His bottom lip was trembling. I rubbed the side of my hand hard against the full length of the massive member and he caught his breath and lightly moaned.

His hands squeezed my shoulders as I undid his belt and unbuttoned his jeans. His eyes were nearly closed, so I didn't bother looking at them. I was too captivated by what I was unleashing. With his fly open, I slid my hand into his pants to feel his dick through the cotton of his CK briefs. My other hand was left to manipulate his hard ass. Through his briefs I could feel all the contours of his cock; the incredibly solid shaft, the spongy head and a small, wet drop where his slit hit his underpants. As hot as he was, he was even more turned on than I thought possible. All his nervous energy wanted to be released now.

In one motion I had his briefs and jeans around his knees. His cock pointed straight out and a little bit upward. Not only was it big, perhaps the biggest I'd ever laid eyes on, it was breathtakingly beautiful. I could tell that even the breezes caused by our movements were more than his dick could take. He was flexing it involuntarily and it appeared to be waving at me. I got on my knees and used a couple of fingers to grab the base. I slid my other hand up his shirt to caress his flat, warm stomach. There wasn't much hair, just a trail down from his navel. With his cock in my control, I aimed it toward my mouth. Slowly, I ran my tongue underneath from the base to the head. It was a long, long trip. At the head, I ran my tongue around in a slow circle, stopping at his slit. I could taste the tangy cum oozing up from his balls all the way to his opening.

I took a deep breath before resting the entire length of the beast in my mouth and throat. I could feel the veins as they rode past my lips and tongue, disappearing inside me. I let it sit there for a minute, my mouth sucking against the sides and my tongue moving slowly underneath. I thought I might choke, but I didn't want to move. It felt amazingly nice to have something that big in my mouth. I tried to swallow, but the head of his dick got in my way. I pulled my mouth back and he moaned again.

I pulled my own dick out and started massaging it. I'd been wanting this since I'd seen the boy almost as much as my dick did. I threw my head on him again, sliding my mouth over his cock relentlessly. He was moaning and more pre-cum started spilling slowly from his shaft.

After jacking myself for a few minutes I had to stop for fear of coming too soon. I took a bit of a breather while one hand groped his balls, the other had a free finger to play with his asshole. My shoulders were resting against his thighs and I could feel them tremble. His leg muscles got stiff and I knew he was going to shoot. I put my mouth on it again as he began. Mercilessly, I sucked on his cock, trying to suck everything out of him, sliding my mouth over it again and again. His hands grabbed my hair and I thought he was going to pull it out. He wasn't forcing my head onto him, he just needed to hold onto something tightly.

The hand I'd been using on his balls went back to my own swollen cock, but the other was still busy, having managed to squeeze a finger past his tight sphincter. I'd gotten past the tightness and he was squirming under the pressure.

His cum shot deep into the back of my throat. It was still a bit tangy and heavy globs of it filled my mouth. He made sounds like he was in pain, but I knew he was happy.

My finger was still lodged inside his ass and he kept riding it, begging me to continue. Begging for more, perhaps.

Catching his breath, he asked, "You gonna fuck me now?"

I could hardly believe my ears.

"If you'd let me...."

He nodded and parted his thighs wide so I had full access to him. His placement on the sofa was perfect for me and I added another finger and plugged as deep up his ass as I could. I leaned down to give his popped-out nipples a rough sucking. My mouth moved from first one tit to the other, while my hand rotated his buttocks with big, circular movements, my fingers expanding his hole to prepare him for my cock.

When I pulled my fingers out of his hole, they made a wet, slurping noise. I released his tit from my mouth, and his fluttering ass lips kissed the underside of my dick when I slithered it up and down in his ass crack. He whimpered softly when he felt my knob enter him. There was just a little resistance, even after all the finger fucking I had given him. I pushed.

He squealed loudly, and wiggled his ass around to assist me.

"That feels good," he whimpered.

Once past the barrier of his resisting ass ring, inch after inch of my long cock easily surged deeper into him. He was definitely helping all he could now.

His hole tightened around my throbbing cock. Each time my dick plunged in, his body tensed and I continued to play with his tingling nipples furiously. Droplets of milky pre-cum drooled out of his bobbing cock and glistened in the dimly lighted room. He grunted softly with each deep thrust of my cock. I slid my dick in and out smoothly when his hand cupped the back of my head to pull my mouth down against his muscular chest. His arching pec trembled as my tongue flicked his taut nipple back and forth. I nipped at it with my teeth. I flicked it, nibbled on it, and then sucked it until he was writhing in ecstasy, overwhelmed again by the sensations that seemed to be radiating outward from his sensitive nipples. His tits were both hard and pointy, looking just like little pricks on the curving crest of each muscular pec.

Keeping my mouth sealed over one of Scott's nipples, his cock rose up unassisted, tall and straight, pointing toward the ceiling, throbbing violently as cum started to flow gently out and trickled down his thick shaft.

Finally I demanded my own release and I slipped my hands under his body, cupping his magnificent buttocks tightly. I lifted his thighs in the air, pressing his knees back against his nipples until his buttocks were spread wide open. When I shoved my cock into his slick asshole, his hips began to gyrate as he thrilled again to the pressure of my cock expanding his slick ass walls. He shoved his bottom up against me, making certain my throbbing cock plunged balls-deep inside him. His hips were a blur as he humped against my probing dick while he urged me to "Fuck it ... fuck it good!"

I leaned forward into the vee formed by his uplifted thighs and continued the fuck. His hips seemed to have a mind of their own as he propelled his plump buttocks furiously against my hard cock, and he was wide-eyed with pleasure as I came deep inside him.

I had his fee waiting when he emerged from the bedroom, freshly showered, ready for his next client.

He smiled and shook his head. "No, man, keep your money. Just call me again."

And he knew I would.

PRINCES
Lewis Frederick

Kurt Braun was the first true asshole I ever loved. That's speaking metaphorically of course. At sixteen, I didn't know much about the mechanics of man-to-man sex, but Kurt taught me a thing or two before we were done.

The way he pronounced his name should have tipped me from the start. He said it: "Cooort!" Just like that, exclamation mark, and all. When teachers called for him during roll, he made a big point of ignoring them, pretending he didn't know who they wanted because they didn't say his name right.

After the third or fourth try, most instructors got exasperated. "I see you back there, Braun! Why don't you answer?"

"Oh, you were looking for me?" he would ask, full of deference. "I didn't realize. You see, the name's 'Cooort'. Perhaps you've never encountered it, the Aryan pronunciation that is. My father escaped Austria before the great war to avoid joining the Nazis; he was a brilliant professor who died in political exile writing tracts against Hitler."

By now other students would be squirming in their seats and the teacher would be fuming. "Sit down, Braun. That's enough out of you."

I had never seen anyone stand up to adults like that. It's embarrassing now to admit how I fell for it.

Kurt had all kinds of other affectations I fell for as well. He liked to don a cultured British accent when he met someone new. The Beatles were big at the time and all the guys at school sported carefully coiffed bangs on our foreheads, snapping them out of our eyes with a toss of the head as often as possible. But Kurt's bangs were just a little bit longer, a little bit greasier, and tossed a little bit more often than anyone else's. Over institutional school lunches, he used his eating utensils in the European way, fork and knife turned upside down.

Every detail was just what you'd expect from a genuine foreigner. It was weeks into fall term before I realized he was just another American, though certainly one with his own idiosyncrasies.

He couldn't drive because his mom wouldn't sign for his permit. I had just gotten my license, so I was prime meat for him to bum rides from when nobody with a sportier car was available. Usually he had me drop him off a few blocks from his place.

"I'll enjoy this fall air the rest of the way home," he'd say with a faint Eton drawl. Soon I began to get curious.

"I'm in no rush," I insisted one day. "Let me take you to your door."

He seemed a bit flustered but directed me the rest of the way. Once there, I was ashamed for him. It was a simple apartment, a little shabby in fact for the prosperous East End neighborhood where it was located. From the airs he put on, I had expected nothing less than a mansion.

"Thanks for the ride," he said jumping out. "I'd ask you in, but today me Mum's ill." He almost ran to the door.

I didn't see Kurt for a while after that. He had all kinds of allergies and was out sick for several days. When he finally did reappear at school, he sidled up to me by my locker as if nothing was amiss.

"Hey, Marcus," he said, speaking pure American for a change. "How's about we double this weekend? I've got a couple of girls dying to go out with me and I can't handle them both. Plus I got no wheels."

Not much into dating, I hedged. "My parents need the car, I think."

"Aw come on, man, I'm desperate," he moaned. "I'm so horny, I don't know what I'll do without a girl."

He held a certain mysterious charm over me and I found myself waffling. Besides, I had begun to formulate indescribable fantasies about what a guy like Kurt might do without a girl to siphon off his sexual energies. He was the tallest boy in our class and the only one shaving already. In a lot of ways, he seemed more man than boy. But then he would open that big mouth and spoil it all.

"I'll see," I said and rushed off to my next class.

#

"God! Don't you just think Paul is the cutest thing you ever saw. I mean totally cool! So much cuter than George or John or Ringo. He's just the greatest!"

Some girl named Vicki or Nikki or something rhyming with "ickie" bounced up and down on the front seat beside me, hugging her knobby knees and chattering about the movie we had just seen until I thought I would steer the car into a tree. Even so, I preferred her voice to the grunting, slurping sounds coming from the back seat where Kurt and his date wrestled full length across the cushions, coming up now and then only for air and to check for cops passing. Their acrobatic contortions made it hard for me to drive.

Eventually I heard him shout an ominous warning. "Now! Now! Now!" he cried. Then all was still from the back but for the sounds of heavy breathing.

"So!" Nikki-Vicki chirped into the sudden quiet. "Which Beatle do you like best, Marcus?"

I just stared into the moonlit park road ahead, trying hard to avoid looking in the rearview mirror.

#

Once our dates were delivered to their doorsteps, Kurt thanked me so many times on the way home I got embarrassed and told him to shut up.

"No, man, really," he insisted. "You don't know how long it's been since I got any."

I didn't have to wonder what he would say if I told him I'd never gotten any. I knew. He would blow me off as some inexperienced kid.

"So how'd you make out with what's-her-face?" he leered, lighting up a cigarette.

I had asthma but didn't want to confess that shortcoming too, so just opened the power windows throughout the car and tried to act cool. "Okay," I said. "She's pretty, nice, I guess, just ... kinda ... talkative."

"You know how to stop that, right?" he punched my arm painfully.

"Yeah, sure," I said. "Only, I was sorta tired tonight. I wasn't much into ... well, getting any."

Kurt almost choked on his cigarette. "Not into it! What's the matter with you, man? I don't go a minute of the day that I'm not into getting some."

Hot blood rushed into my face and I was glad for the pale light of the dashboard just then. Truth was, I'd known for some time what was wrong with me. Girls sought me out, clearly interested, sending notes and inviting messages through friends. I never responded, never had any desire to. So far, most everyone had written me off as shy. But every now and then, someone raised another issue. Maybe Marcus just wasn't interested in girls?

We had reached Kurt's apartment so I was spared further questions.

"Damn!" he said, searching his pockets. "I've forgotten my key. Will you stick around until I know Leah's up?"

Calling his mother by her first name was another of Kurt's peculiarities. I had never known anyone who called their mom by name.

"Sure," I sighed, wishing I'd never let him talk me into this endless evening. He jogged up to their front porch and began pounding on the door.

I pushed buttons on the car radio, looking for something listenable, finding weather reports and ads instead. The sound of glass shattering cut into my search, and I looked up to see Kurt reaching through the door pane he had just broken to let himself inside. I thought he would signal back to me to go on, that he was in now. But silence issued from the dimly lit flat.

I began to get nervous and called for him several times. No answer came back and I knew then something serious must be wrong. Someone was sick or something. I hopped out of the car and raced into Kurt's apartment, calling his name, hating the panic in my own voice.

I still wish neither one of us had ever seen what greeted us there.

Inside, it was a pretty nice apartment after all. Kurt's mom had some good antiques and a few expensive prints hanging on the walls. I knew because I'd begun to get interested in interior decorating and had started studying the contents of local galleries.

The furnishings in Kurt's apartment weren't the problem. The problem was the inhabitants.

I had never seen a more filthy place. Dickensian images of gin houses came to mind. A pall of dust and cigarette smoke hung thick over everything, obscuring the patina of the few good antiques, dulling the clarity of the few good prints. Oriental rugs that had once been valuable lay wasted, plush altars to good taste defiled beneath fat piles of cat feces and overturned ashtrays. Empty beer cans and liquor bottles littered every table top.

In the midst of the squalor, an unlikely courtesan lay propped like some leprous thing between the snoring forms of two hairy men. It was Leah, Kurt's mother, stark naked in a drunken sleep. Her sagging breasts rested on the faces of her bearded courtiers, her bloated belly lifted up and down with her labored breathing, above a thatch of graying pubic hair.

I turned to Kurt, unable to find words. He was staring at his mother's white body, shaking his head, mumbling something I couldn't understand.

"You could come to my place," I offered, feeling this consolation prize was a little lame under the circumstances.

"Whore!" he intoned with Old Testament indignation and strode with great drama out the broken front door.

#

Without ever intending to, I adopted Kurt that night. My folks were asleep by the time we got home so it was no big deal to sneak him into my room. First we raided the refrigerator and Kurt helped himself to some of my dad's imported beer. Right from the start, he stamped through the house as if it were his own, smoking a cigarette and dropping ashes all over the place.

"Nice place," he said between whistles of appreciation. "Your parents pretty loaded?"

Uncomfortable, I shrugged and changed the subject. "We better turn out the lights and lock up. You want anything else before we turn in?"

"Sure," he said and helped himself to the refrigerator again.

It was as if the trauma at his place had never happened as far as he was concerned. Meanwhile, I felt a residual nausea, thinking of his mom sandwiched between those hirsute men in that fetid room. Marveling over Kurt's nonchalance now, it eventually hit me he must have walked in on even worse scenes in the past.

I managed to shuttle him up to my room, shushing him all the way, and get him behind closed doors where we could talk in normal tones.

Once there, he crowed "Wow!" and dived onto my bed, spilling Heineken and cigarette ash all over the spread. "I could get used to this," he said, looking around with a smug smile.

I had to laugh in spite of myself. It was like watching a kid's first Christmas. So many playthings filled the spacious room a stereo, color television, chemistry set and telescope most of which I seldom used anymore. Trying to see the room through Kurt's eyes, I decided I didn't have it so bad after all.

"So, you've been holding out on me," he grinned, coming and grabbing me in an unprecedented bear hug. "Why didn't you tell me you were a fucking prince!"

He smelled of cigarettes and English Leather mixed with his date's Ambush and other body smells. His beard stubble against my neck triggered the beginnings of an erection, and I hoped he wouldn't brush close enough to feel me swelling there.

"Come on, let's wrestle," he said, taking me to the floor. We rolled around on the carpet for a bit, giggling and cursing, till my asthma and his cigarette smoking brought us both down with a shared coughing fit. We just sat for a while then, panting and wheezing, sizing each other up with silly grins on our faces. That's when I first knew I was falling for him.

It didn't make sense. Oh, he was a handsome guy, all right, but he didn't have a thing to offer except that incredible self-confidence and a genuine love of the good things in life. Maybe that was the appeal. I had a lot of good things no one else had ever seemed interested in. Maybe Kurt made me feel needed.

Whatever the inexplicable reasons, Kurt Braun wormed his way into my heart that night in a way that left me different ever afterward.

The next morning, I had some explaining to do, but it was hours before my parents even knew there was a visitor in the house. My family was so disengaged at the time, we often went days without encountering each other much at all. Having stayed awake most of the night talking in the dark, Kurt and I slept till noon. Finally up, we sauntered down to the breakfast room, where my mom and dad were still lingering over the Sunday paper.

That was a rare domestic scene. My natural father had just returned home for yet another attempt to reconcile with my mom. They had divorced years before, but he still reappeared now and then between her other liaisons, just to see if they might make a go of it again. I couldn't imagine why he tried so many times. Mom could be pretty cold when she wanted to be.

"This is a classmate, Kurt Braun," I told them. "He stayed over last night."

I watched them encounter the predictable confusion with his name. "What was it again?" Dad asked.

That was all Kurt needed. He was off in a flash, explaining the pronunciation, giving his family history, putting some extra drama and detail into his usual speech just to impress my parents.

It didn't work. I could see the immediate antipathy in their eyes. It was hate at first sight. That was okay, though. Their hating Kurt just elevated his stature with me all the more. This was going to be interesting, I thought.

Kurt continued his monologue, helping himself to coffee and toast, then lighting a cigarette and blowing smoke rings between sips of coffee and chatter, till my parents both asked simultaneously to see me alone.

"Who is this person?" Mother demanded once we were out of the room.

"Just a friend," I shrugged. "He got locked out last night by mistake. We didn't want to wake his mom so I invited him here."

"Well, don't do it again," Mother said in a steely voice.

Dad saw me set my jaw and jumped in to mediate. "Son, we might be held responsible in some way if there were any misunderstanding about your friend's whereabouts. You can understand that, certainly?"

I had to concede the point and agreed to get permission first before inviting Kurt for an overnight again. "How about next weekend?" I asked.

"We'll think about it," Mother ruled, ending the discussion there.

Kurt had heard every word, of course. "Sorry to cause a row," he said as we sauntered out to the yard to examine the fall garden.

"Don't worry about it," I said in a voice just as steely as Mother's. "You'll come here anytime I want you to. That is, anytime you want?"

He beamed. "Sure! Hell, we're brothers, right?" Throwing an arm around my shoulders, he started quizzing me about the bulbs and perennials, the chrysanthemums and tulips, wanting to know every name, how the plants grew, how we took care of them, appropriately appreciative of each specimen's beauty and cost.

I have to give him this much, even now. He really knew how to work me.

So began the autumn of Kurt Braun. We became inseparable companions, spending every possible minute together. When we weren't with each other personally, we were on the phone or writing notes to shove into each other's locker about the plans for our next venture.

I had never had such a close friend and found the whole thing a little intoxicating. My hypothesis about Kurt needing me soon proved true. Not only did he need a home away from home, much to my parents' chagrin, he needed just about everything help studying, help budgeting his scant spending money, help figuring out what to wear or eat and how to get himself wherever he needed to be. Despite a bright and inquisitive mind, he couldn't focus his energies to accomplish anything productive. Little by little, I moved into the role of manager in his life.

It was kind of like having a really big, really special puppy that never grew up. For my part, I felt amply compensated by the genuine appreciation he expressed, at first anyway. Having lived so hard, fabricating his own family mythology and happiness, he seemed truly grateful to have someone actually care for him. Later he would grow complacent and begin to take me for granted.

On my end, it all felt almost spousal. Sometimes I found myself straightening his clothes or wiping crumbs from his mouth, wherever we might be. He basked in this attention and never seemed to mind the occasional glances my ministrations brought from onlookers. My parents' reactions were another thing.

Kurt spent every weekend at our house and sometimes school nights as well. His mother never seemed to notice or care how little he came home to their tacky apartment. After a while, he quit calling to let her know where he was staying. She never took any initiative to track him down.

All of which irritated my own mother no end. The longer my infatuation with Kurt endured and the more he was around our house, the angrier she got. She never showed it openly though. That wasn't her style. She worked through sidelong comments and manipulations employing my dad, sending me messages through him about when Kurt could and couldn't stay overnight, what I was expected to do for her in order to earn the privilege of Kurt's company, sometimes rescinding a plan she'd agreed to on short notice without explanation, other than the maddening words: "Because I said so."

I hated her at these times. As for my dad, my lack of respect for him crystallized as he let her dictate to him and me both. He was so spineless he didn't deserve any pity.

Then something happened one night that put a different spin on things.

Kurt and I had been on another double date, but he hadn't been so lucky this time. Not only did he not get any, he got a firm fist in his mouth for pawing his date once too often.

"Bitch!" he fumed, working his jaw on the way to my house afterward. "She's probably a lesbian."

I masked the secret pleasure I felt seeing Kurt strike out with a girl. These staged outings had begun to get on my nerves. Something about them didn't feel right, didn't feel clean. I always drove, listening to some perky ingénue talk my ear off in the front seat while Kurt conducted an orgy in the back. Later he'd recount every detail to me; what he did, where he touched her, how she responded, how long and how hard they both climaxed at the end, as if I couldn't hear for myself. I was beginning to suspect the real agenda for these evenings was the reconstructing of his sexual exploits for me afterward. That sounded crazy, though. Why would anyone want to do that? Again, I didn't think right off what he might have experienced in his own home before now.

That night, he went on and on about how horny he was, what a prick tease his date had been, how badly she'd led him on. "You just can't trust women," he said time and again.

Back in my room, which I had begun to think of as "our room," he finally pushed too far. We were lying in separate twin beds, him smoking and ruminating aloud about where his date went wrong, me flipping through a magazine, conveying colossal disinterest, when he decided to vent his frustration on me.

"So what's up with you tonight? You've been acting like you have a corn cob up your ass all evening."

"What are you talking about?" I said.

"You know what I'm talking about. You've hardly said two words all night."

"I didn't know I needed to. You do enough talking for the both of us.

He stubbed out his cigarette and sat up in bed. "You really are pissed, aren't you?"

"Look, Kurt, it's late ..."

"It's always late with us. We stay up all night, remember?"

"I don't feel much like talking now."

"You'd rather pout."

"Aw come off it, Kurt. You know what this is about. You just like to show off your sexual prowess and rub my nose in my own lack of experience. You tried it again tonight only your date didn't play along so well this time."

The artful attack surprised even me, for it was so spontaneous yet so on the mark. He was taken aback.

"You're talking crazy talk. I just like the women. It's the way I am. There's nothing more to it than that."

"Oh yeah?" I said. "Then why is it you only like them in front of me? You never have a date on your own, never ask anyone out without me as an audience."

"What are you saying?"

I didn't know myself. Words for thoughts and feelings I had never conceptualized were bubbling to my mouth uninvited, spilling out, taking their toll. At the same time, I knew somehow they were right. Emboldened by my own honesty, I pressed on, relentless now.

"Admit it, Kurt. This isn't about women. It's about you and me ... and a whole lot more you haven't got the guts to face."

The startling, scary, sacred words were out. You and me. Things to face. All of a sudden, I felt like a giant.

We sat on our separate beds, eyeing each other with a newfound mixture of caution and respect, both knowing almost anything could happen now, neither one of us wanting to make the next move. His blue eyes were unfathomable. One moment I thought I saw cockiness, the next moment fear. What the hell, I finally decided. Time for the kill.

"This is about you being sexual with me, isn't it Kurt?"

Just then a loud rap on the door broke the spell. I went to the door and opened it a crack.

It was Dad, pulling his robe on in haste, looking agitated and unhappy. Across the hall, I saw Mother's shadow retreating into her room. Her door whispered closed behind her.

"We need to talk, son," Dad said, between demanding and beseeching. "Meet me downstairs, okay?"

I muttered assent and grabbed my own robe. Kurt looked like a deer caught in headlights.

"What the hell is happening here?"

"I don't know. Just go to bed," I said and hurried down the darkened stairs after Dad.

We never made it to the first floor. Somewhere between the first and second landing, his hand reached out and dragged me down to sit with him on the steps.

"You have to get that boy out of this house right now."

I felt the hairs rise up on my neck as my Dad pinned me against the wall. Kurt's last words echoed in my mind. What the hell was happening here?

I wrenched free of the frantic grip, backing up against the stair treads behind me, breathing hard, wordless.

"I'm sorry," Dad said. "I didn't mean to do that. It's just that we're so worried. Your mother and I."

My jolted senses rallied and I laughed outright. "You and Mother worried about me?"

Crouched on the carpeted stairs there together, inches from each other's face, I could barely see him in the faint light from the street lamps outside. But I could register this much: he winced and bit his lip.

"Maybe we deserve that, son. We haven't been very ... present, I guess. But we're here now, and very concerned about your welfare. This Kurt, this ... relationship troubles us both very much."

The wheels were racing inside my head. No matter how much adrenaline pumped through my body and no matter how hard I tried to find some frame of reference for this discussion, I couldn't find anything anywhere in my experience to guide me. Silence seemed the only safe alternative.

He pulled back and took a deep breath. Maybe he had the same thoughts I had. My eyes adjusting to the dark, I could see him clearly now, leaning against the balustrades, trying to get his act together, trying to figure out how to deal with me, his sometimes-son.

He was a gentle man, forced to cope with a complex life he never envisioned. He came from a time when work, home and food were blessings. He'd survived the Depression, seen combat overseas, and come home to a world turned upside down women doing men's jobs, children thriving in day-care. Mother and I presented him with murky emotional material he could barely comprehend, much less manage. I felt a sudden sadness for him, watching him retreat into himself against the stair rails.

Then he surprised me with a gift I never expected.

"I think it's time we talked," he sighed. "Not just talked but really shared some things." He shivered in the cold draft on the landing and raised the terry collar of his robe against his neck, looking away from me, at the geometric streetlight patterns on the shadowed foyer below us.

"Love's a funny thing," he said, staring off into the darkness. "You can't know when it will come to you. You can't know who will bring it. But when it's there, it's there. No doubt about it. You just know this is it. And that's all there is to it."

Something in his tone scared me. I wanted him to stop, wanted to clap my hands over his mouth and tell him it was okay, he didn't need to say anything more. But he kept going.

"Sometimes love comes in a nice neat package, one that everyone blesses ... a new baby ... a pet."

"Dad, please," I pleaded. But it was too late.

"Other times ... most times ... love comes in strange ways, ways we may find hard to accept. A woman we're drawn to across a ballroom floor, all the while knowing she's not good for us; a child we never wanted, never planned, couldn't support, who somehow seized our heart nonetheless."

I was starting to feel sick. A tremor began somewhere deep in my gut and spread through my body until I felt like I'd been plugged into an electric outlet. Still he kept on, clearing the slate, exorcizing ghosts.

"Other times it's someone we clearly shouldn't love ... someone toxic to us ... someone sick, damaged, married, unavailable ... someone out of our reach, whatever the reason."

The clock in the hall chimed just then and set me to thinking how late it was. When it was done he looked up at me with total candor. " Men just can't love one another at all. We try and try, but we just can't seem to get the thing right."

I put my hands over my face and waited for the rest.

"I spent a lifetime once in a foxhole with a guy. He was an ordinary fella, came from somewhere in Ohio. Couldn't tell you where. We didn't have a thing in common except that hell-hole we shared.

"Here's the strange part, though. Everything about this guy was pleasant. Every minute with him was easy, in between dodging bullets anyway. We were a mess all the time, couldn't shave, didn't bathe for weeks on end. But when his butt bumped up against mine in the night, I felt nothing but good just glad to be there with him, glad to feel his heat.

"Even when the shell hit, even when I was trying to figure out how to get his face back together, holding it in my hands, putting the pieces in place like some crazy puzzle, I never minded the mess. There was just something about this fella. Nothing else mattered but being with him."

He seemed to come back to himself then and remember where he was at last.

"When he died, the others thought I was crazy I couldn't let go of him. Medics had to sedate me and pry my fingers off him."

Dad sat for the longest time, staring down at the pool of light at the bottom of the stairs. Finally he looked up at me.

"I know something about loving men," he said. "Do you know what I mean, son? Do you know what I'm telling you here?"

I wanted to cry, throw up, run. But something in his soft voice and earnest eyes reached out to me in a way he never had before. I stood my ground.

"I think so," I said. "Only, Dad? That's enough. All right?"

He sighed and nodded. "I agree."

I stood, feeling a hundred years old, and started up the plush stairs, one slow step at a time. He coughed behind me.

"There is one more thing," he said in a business-like voice. "Your mother will want to know Kurt's plans."

That was it, I thought, and turned like a snake. "Tell her this then, Dad. Kurt stays or I go."

He leaned back to escape my force. Something between fear and admiration filled his face. I didn't care which. I knew what I wanted at last.

"The whole community can read in the paper how some silly socialite let her son run off with his best male friend to do God knows what," I said. "Or we can all come to terms. It's her decision."

I thought I saw a little smile flicker across his lips. "I'll tell her," he said and looked away again.

Head reeling, I trudged up the stairs, wondering how life got so crazy all of a sudden. Turning the knob to my bedroom door, I looked over my shoulder and saw that the crack of light beneath Mother's door was still there.

"'Night, Mom," I called loudly and went into my room.

Kurt was propped up in his bed in the low lamplight, lighting one cigarette off another, pushing an empty beer bottle under his pillow.

"What gives with you people?" he said. "Are you all plain crazy or just too rich for my blood?"

Unable to process one more word with one more person for the rest of the night, I bit my tongue as I pulled off my clothes and threw them to the floor.

Kurt didn't handle silence well. "Do they want me to leave now or what? Do they hate me that much?"

I walked over to his bed and took a hard look at him. He needed a good haircut and his fingers and teeth were tobacco stained. But he was still a fine-looking youth, thin as a whip and muscled everywhere, all without a moment of exercise as far as I could tell. Genetics were capricious gods. I reached out and took the newly lit cigarette from his hand, stubbing it out in the ashtray on the bedside table.

"What are you doing? I just lit that fag."

I turned out the last light in the room and threw back his coverlet. He was completely exposed under a merciless moon, taut muscles, lithe limbs and a glowing erection, all rising up to meet me in the now silent night.

I crawled into bed beside him and put my fingers on his lips, pressing my naked body into his for the first time. There was so much ahead for us, countless arguments, questions, doubts. But tonight was about something we couldn't do in our heads.

"Just shut up" I said, working an arm around his waist. "For once in your life, just shut up, will you?"

To my surprise, he nodded a small nod and let out a short breath, easing a bit into my embrace. And for once in his life, Kurt did keep his mouth shut. Or rather, he didn't open it to speak for a while. Lying beside him there, I could feel the heat rising from his groin and the warmth drew my face to his crotch like a magnet. I leaned down to explore the newfound plaything there, just eyeing at it with frank appreciation for a while.

The proud pink swell of his erection bobbed gently with each beat of his pulse. Eventually I couldn't wait any longer and bent to kiss it softly. Taking it reverently in hand, I traced a path with it against my jaw, where it left behind a thin, warm coating of pre-cum. I worked my way down to his balls, taking them in hand as well to lift the low hanging sack to my nostrils and inhale deeply of their ripe scent..

I began to kiss and tongue his balls, taking them into my mouth one at a time, then eventually together in a mouthful that stretched my lips until they hurt. Like everything else about Kurt, his penis and scrotum were a little larger than life a little too florid, a little too wet, a little too fragrant. For a change, however, the excess here proved infinitely attractive. I leaned back on an elbow and drank in the sight and smell of him, tasting the salt sweat from his cock and balls on my lips as I did. He lay there with his eyes closed and an arm raised over his head. The damp hair curled under his armpit gave off a musky, animal odor and I found myself drawn there next, kissing and tonguing the dark cleft hungrily.

Kurt began a low, guttural moaning and began working the loose foreskin around his cock up and down so rapidly that the combined sight of his hand, cock and balls soon became a blur, like a centrifuge spinning. I reached down to do the same to my own neglected shaft, rock hard now and oozing precum. As I jacked myself, I rubbed my cock, balls and pounding fist against his smooth, hairless chest, bringing on louder moans from him.

Seeing his big ball sack begin to tighten and hearing his breath come in short, feral grunts, I knew he was about to come. Suddenly I couldn't decide what I wanted more -- to watch him come, feel him spray across my chest, come myself, come inside of him, or what. Falling back on pure instinct, I turned my body so that I straddled his head with my thighs and positioned my face above his moist crotch. My dripping cock dangled right above his mouth and I glanced down to see his reaction.

He had an almost frightened look on his face just then and I thought he was about to terminate the whole proceedings. Then with a sudden, hungry growl, he opened wide and took the entire length of my shaft in his mouth, all the way up to the base, burrowing his nose into my balls. With that, I unwrapped his hand from his long dick and took the drooling purple tip between my lips. I had hardly begun to suck in earnest when he let out a muffled cry and shot his load, spasm after spasm wrenching his lithe body as he lifted his hips off the bed and pumped a torrent of thick cum down my throat, filling my mouth till it dripped out around my lips. I savored the tart, bittersweet taste as it rolled around in my mouth before gratefully swallowing it. That was all it took for me to climax as well, and I drove my pelvis down into his face as I shot a hefty load of my own down his throat.

After we came, we lay frozen in place for a time, not knowing what to do next: disengage, dry off, order a pizza, or go at it again. Soon I felt the bed shaking under me and realized Kurt was the cause. At first I thought he was crying but then I recognized his snide chuckle.

"Christ, Marcus, you've fuckin' drowned me," he laughed.

"Look who's talking," I said, turning to position myself alongside him again. "Besides, I don't see anything left to drown in. Looks like you've swallowed cum pretty well for a guy who 'really likes the women!'" And with that he got pissed and began tickling me hard.

We fell onto the floor giggling and wrestling. There, when we ran out of breath, we exchanged the first of a million kisses that would follow in the time ahead for us. For the rest of our days together, moonbeams and magic would make me masterful with Kurt.

Yes, Kurt and I would teach each other a lot.

TAUNTING TONY
John Patrick

"I am a sex addict!"

– Tony Cummings, star of "Beverly Hills Hustlers" and dozens of other porn videos

Allen glances one way, then the other, but only for a second, to see if anyone is noticing him enter the Boylesk theater. Fumbling with his wallet, Allen pulls out three tens and hands them to the cashier. Admitted now, he grumbles to himself about paying the higher admission price, but he has to admit the place has been beautifully renovated since his last visit several months ago, when porn star Tony Cummings was making one of his occasional, highly advertised appearances. Allen first tours the downstairs, with its 120 different porno flicks and its buddy booths, with windows open to the adjoining booths. There's little action so early in the afternoon, so he goes to the main room. He enters the darkened theater just in time to catch Tony's first show. Allen has come back to see Tony, who so aroused him the first time he saw him. Now, Tony's first time through the audience, wearing only socks, he stays facing Allen and jerks his hard, six-inch, nicely cut dick constantly. Allen can tell that Tony's enjoying himself immensely, and he tips him.

Tony's second time through the crowd, Tony shoves his ass into Allen's astonished face. Allen can't control himself, he has to touch the pretty butthole. Tony jumps, smiles, gives Allen a "you know you can't do that" look, smiles again, then lets Allen continue rubbing his butt cheeks. After a few moments, Tony leans over and lets Allen spread them apart, and Allen chuckles when he sees the moistened butthole winking at him.

After the show, Allen goes to the so-called "shower-showcase," gets into a booth and waits for Tony. Tony now puts on another show, lying on the floor of the shower room, legs spread as far as they can open, finger fucking his ass one finger, two fingers, one finger, two fingers! Tony goes from window to window until he comes up to Allen's window. Allen begins rubbing his crotch against it and Tony licks where the bulge touches the Lucite. Tony makes sucking motions with his mouth, and looks up into Allen's bewildered face. Smiling, Tony gets back on the floor and begins finger-fucking himself some more.

Suddenly, Allen feels unworthy to watch any longer. His cock pulsing along with his heart, he turns away, leaves the booth, relinquishing it to a Latino man, a good-looking stud, who makes eye contact with him, but quickly turns his attention to Tony.

Moments later, in the lounge, Tony, in his jockstrap, talking with another customer, looks up, smiles at Allen. Allen can hardly bear having Tony acknowledge him. He wants to ask him what he is staring at. "Can I help you?" he would have said if they were anywhere else. To Allen's eyes, Tony is perfection and Allen wants him desperately. It's a feeling so pure that he wants to cry. How terribly unfair that his whole self aches because of the shape of an ass, a winking asshole. Yet, for Allen, there is the glow of real personality behind the staged. To Allen, Tony seems to enjoy what he is doing.

Tony leaves the other man and approaches Allen. "Hi," Tony says. And Allen wants to touch him to see if he is real, this boy of his dreams. They exchange small talk for a few moments and Allen is shaking again, as he did when he was a boy and in the company of those boys who he wanted so desperately but couldn't have. And why shouldn't he be nervous now? He is a loyal husband, who, reaching out, touching this porn star, has always honored his vows. He does not move his hands or his fingers, just holds them against Tony's wonderfully smooth skin, so warm, almost hot. Tony takes Allen's hands in his own, presses them to his ass, and then Tony begins to massage Allen's crotch. This arouses Allen, as before. Tony is an expert, Allen finds, someone trained in an art. Over and over, Tony whispers, "I want you to fuck me with this big dick...." Allen hasn't been so aroused in years. Allen is breathing deeply, leaning up against the wall now in a near-panic. Allen tells himself that having Tony fondling his cock is an aberration, just like his coming up those stairs, into this theater.

He had only wanted to see Tony, to watch the show. He'd gone up the stairs a faithful husband, a working man taking an afternoon off.

And now, minutes later, a different man emerges: a violator of his matrimonial bonds. Allen considers leaving the theater now, though his legs feel hollow and unsteady. And there is also his erection, diabolically hard, bringing to mind all the lewd thoughts he'd had about Tony for weeks after the theater started advertising his appearance.

Allen is so close to climax that he is afraid to move. He wants to get away without having to face the enormity of his pleasure. He remains still, his hand clutched tightly on Tony's perfect buns, and thinks of his wife waiting at the bus stop, his wife soon at home, wondering where Allen is.

And yet here, grinning at him, is Tony. So wonderful, his ass, his skin. And the skill with which Tony is touching him. The mere idea of Tony is so enticing it pushes him past control. Allen lets go of Tony's ass and lets the shame rush in and fill the emptiness, so that even his hollow legs feel solid and full once again.

But Tony will not so easily be denied. He says, "Come back to my room with me."

"Your room?" Allen asks, not understanding. He does not know the headliner gets a room at a nearby fleabag hotel.

"Yeah, across the street," Tony smiles, continuing to stroke Allen's penis.

Immediately there is plotting. Now the deceit grows. Allen told his wife he was going to the gym before dinner, that was the plan. But now Allen's erection builds strength and, he fears, he might actually come if Tony keeps rubbing it.

"C'mon," Tony coaxes. "It'll be worth it."

Allen starts to ask how much Tony charges, but thinks the better of it. Whatever it is....

"I'm all right with that," Allen says finally.

"Okay," Tony says, a big smile on his face.

Allen inhales, exhales. Tony tells Allen to wait right where he is, that he will be back in "a flash."

Allen stands there obediently, afraid to touch his erection. He could leave now, run into the street, go to the gym, be faithful his wife. In life, Allen has always felt there is a path to be followed. Either you stay on it or you stray into darkness: this is the choice that is offered. Allen checks his watch. There is time enough to go to the gym and reach the bus. Steeling himself, he has to decide now to run, to leave Tony. But then Tony re-appears, dressed in jeans and a T-shirt, and Allen is overjoyed as simple as that. It's over. Tony smiles and moves his hand, placing it on top of Allen's. Tony squeezes it and says, "Let's go."

Allen stands openmouthed; Tony is simply too beautiful for words. But there is no time to contemplate him. No, Tony is in a hurry; he has to squeeze in these little private dances between shows.

They cross the busy street and enter the hotel. In the elevator, Tony strokes Allen's cock all the way up to the ninth floor.

In the room, Tony goes to the bathroom. Allen is already taking off his jacket and undoing his shoes. He uses one shoe to kick off the other.

When Allen is naked except for his watch, Tony comes out of the bathroom. Tony is now wearing only the jockstrap he wears for his show.

Tony drops to his knees before Allen and starts sucking his erection. Tony understands Allen's wishes, and Allen realizes no one has ever sucked his cock like this before. He wants it to go on, but yet he doesn't. He fears he will come if Tony keeps this up at this pace. Tony senses this too, and he leaves him, rushing to the double bed, which has recently been made up.

Allen walks toward the bed. He moves slowly and with an air of detachment. Just the right amount, he feels, befitting an object of desire, for he understands that it is Tony who desires him, that is the game being played here.

Tony lies on his back, spreads his legs, giving Allen a better view. Allen smiles at the sight, and Tony moves his hand, placing it on Allen's erection. He squeezes it and repeats his mantra, "I want you to fuck me with this big dick...."

Allen nods, climbing on the bed, getting between Tony's outstretched thighs. Tony reaches over to the nightstand and gets a condom and the lube.

He slides the condom over Allen's cock, then applies lube to it. Slowly, Tony draws the cock to his hole, intently watching Allen's openmouthed expression of great anticipation as he does. Tony does not grease his butthole because it has been well-prepared. Allen has no idea that, three hours earlier, Tony had been, on this very bed, squatting over Michael, the studly black dancer at the theater, slowly letting the dark, ten-inch, uncut cock enter his asshole. When Tony had all of Michael's cock in him, he began to bounce up and down on it while Michael moaned and groaned with delight. Tony ran his hands over Michael's sculpted body as he rode the cock that he hadn't enjoyed for almost three years. It was exciting seeing Michael again after all this time, and Tony could hardly wait to get the stud back to his room and renew his acquaintance with what was undoubtedly one of the biggest cocks Tony had ever had inside him.

At one point, Michael flipped Tony over on his back and slammed his cock back into him. Tony gasped and began wriggling his ass, corkscrewing against Michael's drilling cock. Sweat poured from Michael's shiny black body, and to Tony he looked like a glowing, lithe panther. Having Tony again was more than Michael could stand; he could not stop himself, he had to come after half an hour of fucking Tony in the missionary position, even though he had an entire day of shows to do and was instructed to have at least one orgasm per day before the public. As Michael came, Tony kissed him hard on the mouth. Tony did not come, however; it was satisfaction enough for him to have made Michael happy.

Now Allen is entering the passage that had earlier been so stuffed by Michael that Tony thought he would pass out from the ecstasy of it. Allen's cock, about two inches shorter and not nearly as thick as the black's, is really more of Tony's ideal: big but not too big, and incredibly hard. Tony hates a big cock that cannot become fully erect no matter how much he sucks on it.

As always, Tony controls the entry, squirming his ass as the cock slides into him. The pain subsides soon enough, and Allen falls over Tony's body and takes the boy in his strong, tanned arms. Allen kisses Tony on the forehead as his cock disappears completely into Tony. Allen barely begins before Tony senses he is approaching orgasm. Allen fights against it, trying to relax himself, trying to think of other things. Allen's breath comes in gasps. He clenches the muscles in his legs, and his tight buttocks harden into stone footballs. Automatically. Against his will. On the edge of a glorious ejaculation, he throws his head back and clenches his eyes shut. Tony moves now, holding Allen off, pushing his cock out of his ass. Allen blinks and looks down at Tony. He smiles at the boy and his breathing slowly returns to normal. Tony lightly strokes Allen's big cock; it is like an iron rod, a bludgeon, that taunts Tony, demands his attention. Tony allows Allen to shove it into him again.

From the jockstrap, Tony pulls out his own cock and he jacks it as Allen starts again. Allen puts only the head in and lightly strokes Tony's inner thighs. Tony's breathing quickens slightly, as Allen enters him fully, moving his sinewy body over Tony's. Allen embraces Tony and Tony mouths the words he has said a thousand times before with clients and on porn sets: "Fuck me with that big dick. Oh, yeah, fuck me."

Tony squirms visibly, moving his hips in a rhythmic motion. "God," Allen whispers. "You are so hot." Allen thinks nothing has ever felt quite so nice and naughty and amazingly natural at the same time. Allen has always dreamed of fucking a boy, and now he has the one of his dreams beneath him, loving every moment of it. For Allen, this is almost too much to bear. As Tony strokes his cock heatedly. Trembling now, he places a timid hand on Tony's balls. Tony's breathing comes harder now. Allen plays with Tony's balls, as if trying to push the cum from them. It is too much for Tony; he knows he should not come now, should hold off until later, for the last show, but he simply cannot. He is groaning now and it seems as if someone had cranked up the room temperature a thousand degrees.

Suddenly, Tony feels an intense explosion inside his groin and he moans audibly. Allen also is breathing rapidly, and his mouth finds Tony's, kissing him passionately until Tony's quickened breathing begins to subside. Tony sighs a long contented sigh, and watches with fascination as Allen dips his fingers in Tony's cum, then sticks his dripping fingers into his mouth, licking Tony's juice from them.

"Oh!" Tony wrinkles his nose. "O-o-oh, how can you do that?"

Allen smiles. "Mmm," he teases, then he goes down and sucks on Tony a bit.

It pains Tony to have a cock in him after he has come, and he pushes Allen's cock from his ass. Allen leans back and pulls off the rubber. Tony's hands lazily stroke Allen's sweaty torso as Allen jerks his cock.

Tony sees Allen is very close and he spreads his legs, trembling in anticipation. He glances up long enough to see Allen's closed eyes and his slightly open mouth. Unable to resist the ultimate act of his fantasies, Allen jerks his cock with one hand as he shoves a finger into Tony's ass.

Losing track of time and space, Allen comes and comes, while Tony strokes his skin. So filled with ecstatic delight, Allen is only faintly aware of cum dripping down onto Tony's thighs. Sighing, Tony rolls over on his stomach and hugs the pillows. The sight of Tony's freshly fucked ass is too much for Allen, because he does something he has only dreamed of in his own secret fantasy world. Tony's hips move in a definite rhythm as they push his mounds into Allen's face, and Allen begins to explore Tony's ass with his tongue, caressing his hips and legs, feeling an unexplained oneness with the youthful dancer as he rims him. Again the intensity increases, accelerating rapidly beyond all control, and Allen goes back to jerking his dick.

Keenly aware Allen's arousal has not yet fully subsided, he feels a fierce renewed desire to be fucked again. Allen works the now moisture-laden opening sucking, licking, and exploring more expertly than he had ever dreamed possible.

Allen could feel Tony's ardor build again, his breathing quicken, his rhythm accelerate. "OK," Tony whispers, "stick it in me again."

"Are you sure?" Allen hesitates.

"I've never been more sure of anything in my life!"

Allen has no time to sheath the cock in latex. He simply shoves it in, once again burying his big prick into Tony's warm, sweet ass. Tony becomes totally immersed in Allen's sweaty embrace, as if they are one body. They lose track of how long they were in locked together and how many times they come, until they both sink from exhaustion into the damp bed.

When Tony comes out of the bathroom after his shower, Allen is dressed and ready to leave. He says he will shower after his workout at the gym.

"Wasn't that enough of a work-out?" Tony teases.

"Yes, but...."

Tony interrupts him with a tender kiss.

Allen fumbles with his wallet. Tony stands back, watching, waiting. Allen has a hundred, two fifties. He hands the money to Tony. Tony likes nothing more than the feel of crisp bills between his fingers.

Sometimes, after he's been given twelve hundreds for an overnight stay, he falls asleep gripping the cash in his fingers.

Tony looks up into Allen's sad eyes. "I charge three hundred for an hour...."

"Oh, I'm sorry," Allen says, opening his wallet again.

Tony clasps his hand over Allen's. "But that's okay." Tony kisses Allen on the cheek. "Will you come back to see me?"

"Oh, yes," Allen says, backing up towards the door. "But I have to go, really."

Tony smiles at Allen as the older man opens the door, hesitates, then finally is gone.

Editor's note: The above was based on the true experiences of porn star/dancer/escort Tony Cummings; to respect the privacy of others involved, the names and identifying details have been changed.

HUNG FUCKBUDDIES (AND OTHER LOVERS)
David MacMillan

I glanced over at Ian and grinned as we both stepped onto the sidewalk in front of the restaurant. He plopped his butt on the hood of the car and looked back at me.

"Jose is the sweetest guy," I told him and felt warm and toasty all over as I thought of the manager of the restaurant we were about to enter. I sat down beside him and took his hand in mine.

"Knowing you, I'll bet he's got a big dick too."

"Fuck you, asshole," I growled good-naturedly. "He's only the third guy to plug my butt you and Manny were the only ones to hold that honor until a week ago."

He looked away. "Sorry, Geoff. I didn't mean anything by it. It's just that I'm going to miss our getting together."

I realized Ian was hanging back. It was almost like he didn't want to meet the man I'd decided to give myself to. Even after he'd pestered me the past two days to introduce them. Ever since he found I wasn't willing to drop my pants and bend over for him anymore.

"We'll still get together, buddy."

"Yeah, but we won't be fucking like we were doing."

Ian was a strange duck. His next door neighbor porked him every night. He considered his butt belonging exclusively to Manny; only, he liked to fuck me every chance he got. Ian was in love with his neighbor but he wasn't completely ready to give up his image of what makes a man a man.

I hadn't been around much the last week to give him the relief his dick thought it needed, though. I'd been with the Mexican inside the restaurant every chance we had to be together. And I didn't have any delusions about wanting to be a top not with Jose and his dick to love me like I knew I wanted to be loved.

Ian was right, though. Jose did have a big dick. A huge dick, as a matter of fact, but it fit my ass perfectly! It filled me up so much I couldn't think of anything except blowing loads while it was inside me. And I couldn't imagine anyone else plowing my butt now that my own personal young Mexican had claimed it.

"Well, yes, he is hung, but he's a lot more than just a big dick, Ian. I think I'm in love with him."

"Jesus!"

"You've got Manny."

"Yeah...." He looked down at his hands. "And you deserve more than being just being my fuck buddy, Geoff. You deserve somebody really special."

"Hey!" I threw my arm around his shoulder. "You just got lucky first. And I'm not complaining about what we had, it's just that ... well, I now have a chance for the whole enchilada. Like you've got. I want to take that chance."

"Just make sure you're protected, Geoff."

I pushed off the hood as I growled: "Nobody gets through my backdoor without a cover. Not you, not Jose, not anybody." Jose stood at the register as we stepped into the restaurant. Shiny black hair cut short, wide chest, tight abs, slim hips. Liquid brown eyes and pearly white teeth. A permanent bulge in the front of his jeans I had come to know well. Twenty-one and I knew that only because he'd showed me his papers. He looked up and when he saw us, he smiled from ear to ear. "Geoff!"

"I brought a friend over to meet you," I told him. "Jose, this is Ian Norton. Ian, this is Jose Corrida."

"A social meeting?" The smile disappeared as he looked from one to the other of us.

"Ian's been my best buddy forever."

Jose's lips twitched. "And he maybe wants to make sure I'm good enough for you?" Ian blanched, then turned crimson. Corrida studied me for a couple of moments and nodded. "It's a good idea. I'll show him what I'm made of, Geoff."

Jose led us into the supply room/office of the restaurant and pushed the door closed behind us. "It is only three o'clock, mis amigos." He looked from me to Ian and back. "We've got half an hour now even an hour when it's dead and mis muchachos don't need me." He raised a brow questioningly.

I understood immediately. Jose had loved on me enough the past week that his body language came across loud and clear. I didn't know how I felt about this guy I already saw as my lover showing his stuff to anybody, Ian included. But I also understood it was a matter of pride for him. Jose had something to prove. My claim to him had to take second place to that.

I frowned and glanced over at Ian. "If you think he's nice in his clothes, you ought to see him with them off."

"Geoff!" Ian's pale English complexion again turned crimson before our eyes.

"You would both like to do something, yes?" Jose's hand touched my thigh and I nodded, accepting that was what he saw as being necessary.

"I think Ian would like to check your equipment out."

"You would want me to show him it is in working order?"

His pride thing was vital. I could understand that. But I had some pride myself. "This one time only," I told him.

He nodded and grinned broadly. "Then, we must get down and dirty, mis amigos."

Ian stared at me for a long moment and I couldn't read what he was thinking. He turned slowly toward Jose. His eyes didn't get above Corrida's chest but quickly found their way to his crotch. The restaurant manager pushed off his sneakers and opened his jeans, exposing a triangle of flat, tight, brown skin beneath his shirt.

Ian sighed and reached out to pull the lapels of the jeans apart.

Jose wasn't wearing underwear today any more than he had any other day the past week, and his cock quickly sprang out for my best buddy's inspection.

"Jesus," Ian groaned and licked his lips.

"You'll help me out with this, Ian?" the restaurant manager asked as his fingers wrapped around his meat and pointed at it my buddy. His cock became pinga grande and I grinned at how my buddy's eyes bulged as he stared at it.

Ian nodded and leaned forward to lick the nearly exposed cockhead before him. His lips pulled the skin down over Jose's helmet. His teeth nibbled at the hem of that skin. Corrida shuddered, then moaned his approval.

"Come, Geoff," Jose whispered. "I want a taste of yours."

Ian sat on a box that elevated him just enough so his face was even with Jose's groin. He wasn't paying any attention to our conversation he was nursing a cock that was as big as Manny's and twice as nice and making every attempt to take it all.

"You want to?" I asked in surprise. Me getting blown hadn't been on the menu since the first time we got together. Ian was the only guy who regularly tooted my horn. I slurped on Jose's just enough to lube it for the main event of our sex together.

"Sit on the box above Ian so I can reach you."

I happily shucked shorts and briefs and climbed onto the box, grinning back at Jose as he put a hand on each of my knees and leaned into me. My cock rode my stomach. My balls fell across my asspucker. My legs splayed as I gingerly moved my butt to the edge of the box to give him better access. His tongue touched my ball sac, his lips outlining my nuts. They nibbled up to my root and out along my shaft. I lay back against the boxes stacked behind me and gave my dick to the very best of young Mexico to possess as he had already come to possess my ass.

His lips reached the head of my skinned dick and spread over it until they were anchored behind the flange. His tongue pushed into the slit before he brought his teeth gently down around my shaft just behind the flange. As his knowledgeable lips slid toward my pubes, he directed one set of fingers to pull on my ballsack.

I leaned back and gave myself up to what he obviously knew how to do well.

His other set of fingers moved to begin exploring my abdomen, pushing my t-shirt up on my chest.

I lay back and listened to the slurping noises coming from beneath me, my ass planted on the edge of the box, and let myself slide toward orbit the slow and easy way.

The fingers that had tugged at my balls traced ever tighter little circles around my asshole and the ones from his other hand tweaked one nipple and then the other. I was close and getting ready to jump over the edge.

I didn't even realize Jose's lips had left me until he spoke.

"Reach above you, Geoff," his voice caressed me. "Hand me one of the packets you find there."

I reached above me automatically. My fingers found condom packets on top of the box above me. His fingers left my nipples and I felt a sense of loss. I smiled as I remembered his other fingers now plugged my butt. I tightened every muscle I had in my gut and ground against them.

As I handed the packet to Jose, I leaned forward and looked down between my spread legs to see Ian still slurping on Corrida's tool. It took a moment for Ian's fist moving on his hard, jutting cock to register. It took another moment for me to realize he'd pulled his shorts and underwear down and they were bunched at his ankles.

I grinned. My best buddy was naked and about to find out just how nice Jose really was.

Ian gave up the cock in his mouth unhappily. He looked up as Jose put both his hands on his shoulders and pulled away from him. That blank look that covered his face told me he wasn't even thinking about me. He wasn't even thinking about Manny. He wasn't thinking about anything but Jose's dick and what it could do for him. Just like me when I was alone with Corrida.

Jose smiled and raised the condom packet between them. "I'm going to show you all of me so you'll know I am good enough for your friend."

Ian sighed and a shudder ran through him. But he turned around to kneel over his box beneath me, hiking his butt up for the taking. I lay back, my legs spread. I stroked my meat slowly. And moaned in appreciation when Jose's fingers returned to my ass.

Ian's grunt as Jose entered him brought my favorite Mexican back to my horn. His lips caressed my cock helmet. My feet found his shoulders again. His tongue tortured my meat with ecstasy, his fingers came out of my butt and pulled gently on my balls, and his other fingers again tweaked one nipple then the other forever.

Ian's soft moans in the room were a constant as were the soft splats of Jose's thighs against his cheeks, a rhythm carrying me deeper into orbit. "Oh, shit!" my best buddy groaned below me. "I'm going to yeah!"

My balls rode my shaft and Jose pulled on just the skin of my sac. He deep-throated me in synchronization with his continued movement in Ian's ass. My hands moved to Corrida's head to push him away. "I'm almost there," I mumbled and Jose's lips moved to my shaft and started to jack me. Ian's voice was a continuous moan beneath us.

I was coming and grabbed Jose's hair, pulling his lips into my thatch. Rope after rope splattered against his neck and onto his back.

He groaned, pulling me back into reality, and I let go his hair. He smiled up at me as he let my shriveling cock go. "You like what Jose does for you, Geoff?"

I pulled myself out of the euphoria sweeping over me. I nodded and smiled at him and ruffled his gleaming black mop of hair.

"You'll come to my place tonight after work?"

Our eyes locked on each other's, he kept his dick's tempo in Ian at a steady pace.

I nodded again, immediately looking forward to having what he was giving Ian and getting hard all over again.

"I want to give you all of my love." Both his hands roamed over my backside to claim me gently.

I nodded again and leaned forward to kiss him.

Below me, long, steady strokes possessed my buddy's ass. Ian ground against the invader that had taken his hole. His moaning got louder and I broke contact with Jose's eyes to watch his cock thrusting into my friend's hungry hole. After watching this hot action for a few minutes, I suddenly thought of my best buddy's nice mouthful of meat for the first time since I realized Jose Corrida was quite enough for me.

"Can I suck him off while you're fucking him?" I asked.

"You want to do that?"

"This one last time only, Jose," I said carefully as I tried to understand what I was really saying. "I want to say good-bye to what we used to have in a really nice way."

He nodded. "You must do it then, Geoff. He's your good friend."

As I hopped off the box, Jose's hands went to Ian's chest and pulled him back against him. My buddy's face was a picture of a saint's hitting rapture.

I knelt beside them as Jose tweaked Ian's nipples. My buddy moaned as my fingers touched his nearest hip and caressed their way toward his bush and the hard, drooling dick jutting out from it. Corrida continued to move slowly in his ass, plowing his guts gently.

I sat on the box before Ian and smiled up at my buddy as he reached behind him, behind both of them, to grab Jose's backside. I reached out and cupped his balls as I knelt beside him. He stared blankly down at me as I spread a rubber over the wide helmet of his cock. He moaned as I pulled all of him into my mouth.

"Suck him well, Geoff. This afternoon needs to be a special memory for long years to come."

I nodded around the cock sliding in and out of my mouth. Jose understood me completely.

Corrida's forward movement pushed Ian's dickshaft past my lips, his helmet hard against my tonsils. His dick's retreat from my best buddy's ass pulled Ian from me, leaving just his covered cockhead. I laved it with my tongue each time before re-forming a chute on which Ian's meat slid back into my throat.

I pulled on his ball sac, my finger slipped between his thighs to feel Jose's cock slide across its tip into my buddy and pull almost out. I kept my lips tight on Ian's shaft as it moved through them.

"I'm close, amigos," Jose groaned. His thrusts into my buddy's ass quickly became short and hard, pushing Ian onto his toes each time Corrida banged into him. Ian was singing a soft moan continuously and, no matter how much I tugged at his balls, they bunched around his dick, strangling it.

Ian's hands grabbed the back of my head and pulled me on to his dick. My face buried in his abs and his bush tickled my nose. His cockhead grew in the back of my throat, pushing at my tonsils as Jose banged his ass hard. He held me there. And unloaded.

I could feel his jizz blasting the rubber wedged in the back of my throat as he jerked and shuddered to his orgasm.

Jose heaved against my buddy one last time, shoving Ian up onto his toes. And held there. Blasting his spunk into the rubber deep in Ian's guts.

I was the first to break the sexual magic of the moment. I had to breathe. I pulled off of Ian only to return to kiss the head of his dick. I rose from the box and took his face in my hands. And kissed his lips.

Jose pulled out of him and Ian collapsed against me. Both of them were gasping as their bodies cooled down from the twin work-outs that had got them off. I watched Corrida's cock deflate and smiled as he remembered to pull the rubber off before it could slip off by itself.

Ian pushed off me stiffly. He looked from me to Jose as if he were trying to figure something. He turned and faced Corrida. And stepped up to him without a word. He kissed him, his arms going around his back and pulling him to himself. Jose's fingers caressed his butt cheeks in appreciation.

Ian pulled away and smiled at the man who'd fucked him. "I think we need to go." His smile widened and he nodded. "Just take care of Geoff here, Jose. He's a very special buddy."

Corrida nodded back, his face serious. "I'll keep him well as long as he wants."

My buddy picked up his clothes and started pulling them on. He glanced up at me and shook his head, wrinkling his nose. "Damn, Geoff, I've got to get home before that big-ass Manny does. You're driving, remember?" I nodded. "Well, get the lead out. This really nice guy is going to be here tonight waiting for you just like he will be every night."

I picked up my clothes. Jose patted my butt and I looked up to see him smiling at me. I smiled back and started pulling on clothes. "I'll meet you here at ten?" I asked. He nodded.

As I pulled up in front of Ian's house, my buddy turned to me and nodded. "You're a lucky man, Geoff. You've got just about the best guy in the world in love with you."

"Manny isn't so bad, either."

Ian chuckled. "You're right and all of me is his now - after this afternoon. Just like you'd better be Jose's, if you know what's good for you." He moved closer and reached out to pull my face against his. "For old times' sake," he mumbled as our lips touched.

He kissed me, and what we once had together, good-bye.

BIG WHERE IT COUNTS
Thomas C. Humphrey

"It's huge!" I gasped. "How do you keep it in your shorts on the tennis court?"

"Well, I'm big where it counts, man," he had snapped back at his hunky older brother's teasing about his slight build. He had even bunched his baggy shorts for emphasis as he left the dinner table, much to his mother's embarrassment. Now, if Jimmy Moran had his way, I was about to find out whether that had been an idle boast or a statement of fact.

On the elevator up to my room after he drove me to my hotel, Jimmy backed me into a corner and held on to my swollen crotch as if he was afraid I would somehow jump through the tiny service door in the ceiling and escape from his fervid clutches. The truth was that I had to brace my weak, trembling body against the side rails to keep from collapsing submissively at this beautiful boy's feet. I tried to be rational about what I was allowing to happen, but my mind had become as dysfunctional as my body. My only thought was centered in the aroused flesh beneath the demanding fingers of a kid whose mother fretted that he was too passive and unassertive!

Minutes earlier, he had stopped me from getting out of his Mustang by dropping his hand on my thigh and squeezing firmly.

"I want to have sex with you," he said in a throaty whisper, easing his hand higher for emphasis.

He caught me totally off guard. I had dreamed about getting him to bed since he first appeared in the hotel lobby to drive me to his house after the car rental company screwed up my reservation. But even as I dreamed, I never remotely expected it to become reality. For one thing, he was a high school jock, which I figured pretty well ruled him out as a sex partner. But more important, he was the son of a colleague on the lecture and workshop circuit and a friend of long standing, which would stagger me with a burden of guilt if I attempted to make a move on him.

Maybe he knew that. Maybe his knowing it explained his frequent physical contact and his clever innuendoes, a teasing intimacy that had kept me tingling with desire all evening. But, despite what should have been some telltale signs, I had assumed that he was completely straight, that he would dump me in the hotel parking lot and hurry off to spend what was left of this school night with his teenage friends. I never expected his blunt proposition.

I opened and closed my mouth several times, but words of protest stuck in my throat, especially since his hand now rested in my crotch and his probing fingers were setting my throbbing cock on fire.

"Jimmy...." I finally managed.

"You've got to be gay," he said, almost prayerfully. "But even if you're not, I want to have sex with you."

"We need to talk, Jimmy," I gulped out.

"Let's go to your room and ... well, discuss things," he said, giving my stiff dick another firm squeeze. A suggestive leer belied the innocence of his years. And so, we boarded the elevator, headed toward God only knew what.

I barely managed to close the door to my room behind us before he had me in a rib-crushing bear hug more like a wrestler than the All State tennis player he was.

"We were going to talk," I said.

"Let's talk later." He slid his hand inside my shirt and reamed my navel with a finger.

"You're sure you know what you're doing?"

"I know what I want to do."

He eased both hands up my sides until my shirt bunched under my armpits. He leaned in and gently sucked at a nipple and then shifted to the tuft of hair in the cleft between my pecs. He grabbed a mouthful and tugged on it until I thought he would pull it out by the roots.

Pinpricks of sensation radiated through my body, and a new surge of blood had my cock as stiff as if I was sixteen again. As it throbbed and pulsed and fought against my briefs, I forgot my friendship with his mother, forgot that he was barely eighteen, ignored the possibility that he was virgin or near-virgin and might feel completely different once this experiment ended. I gave myself over to an intense desire that matched his. I tilted his head up and kissed him. I explored the sweet wetness of his open mouth with my tongue as his own tongue battled mine for dominance. He grabbed both my ass cheeks, pulled me tight against him, and ground his erection into my groin.

I pushed back for a moment and just looked at him to confirm his astounding beauty. A mass of calculatedly disheveled deep blond hair swept down and framed his evenly tanned face, the tip of each strand bleached almost platinum by the fierce Florida sun. His watery green eyes, set beneath nearly invisible lashes, gazed up at me, glimmering like depthless twin sea pools. He still had a teenager's thin neck, but it supported a firm chin and strong jaw line, his face accented by a sharp, slightly upturned nose and full, sensuously molded lips. All in all, his appearance was delicate, but not in the least feminine.

That was all I knew of him. The rest of him had remained a tantalizing mystery, obscured by an oversized Tommy Hilfiger shirt and baggy white shorts. Now, I was driven to see all of this strikingly beautiful youngster.

I grabbed his shirt and yanked it up. He raised his arms helpfully, and I slid the shirt over his head and let it trail off one arm onto the floor, offering my first view of his torso. He was hard, lean, and muscular everywhere, not a hair on his upper body. I slowly teased both hands down his surprisingly broad chest and lingered to pinch the large chocolate-drop nipples which adorned each sublimely muscled pectoral. I moved on down across his ridged abdomen and circled the dark cavern of his navel with a finger before following a faint trail of blond fuzz until it disappeared on its provocative plunge toward the as-yet undiscovered treasure buried in his baggy shorts.

Impatient, he fumbled with trembling hands to unbuckle my belt. I pushed his hands away.

"Not yet," I said. "Here, sit down."

I led him to the edge of the bed and he obediently sat. I knelt between his legs and removed his boat-sized Filas and socks. Starting at his ankles, I tickled and kissed my way up both legs, past knotted calves and onto strong thighs. Every time I touched him, his muscles flexed, shattering the light into dancing splinters among a tangle of nearly transparent hair. When I reached the hem of his shorts, I inched both hands up his sensitive inner thighs until I almost reached the prize.

He sucked in a quick breath of air and rose slightly off the bed. "Oh, God!" he sighed, "Oh, God, it feels so good, Mr. Gilman!"

"Under the circumstances, I think you'd better call me Graham. Or Gray ... that's what my friends call me," I suggested.

Ignoring the prominent mound which had rapidly formed in his baggy crotch, I pushed him back onto the bed and stretched him full-length on the mattress. I hurriedly stripped down to my briefs. As I tugged my socks off, Jimmy lay fingering his erection and licking his lips in anticipation. He reached up and pulled me down beside him. His lips locked onto mine in the hungriest kiss I'd ever experienced. In the midst of it, he grabbed my stiff dick and squeezed tight.

I ran my hand across his tight abdomen and beneath the waistband of his briefs, through a small prickly thatch of pubic hair. My fingertips stalled at the wide base of his cock, which had pushed out through the left leg of his briefs and lay across his thigh, thick and long. I followed its path beneath his briefs and then into the open, where the fleshy, veined shaft of his dick projected out beyond his leg, the huge bulbous head pulsing with each rapid heartbeat.

"It's huge!" I gasped. "How do you keep it in your shorts on the tennis court?"

"It's hard," he said.

"I know it's hard," I answered, giving it a quick squeeze.

"No, I mean it's hard to keep it in my jockstrap," he explained with a laugh.

"Stand up," I ordered. "I want to see just how big it is." I practically shoved him off the bed.

He stood before me, and I slowly eased his briefs to his ankles. As he kicked them off, I sat inches away from a heart-pounding hunk of stud-cock jutting straight out toward me. It was almost nine inches long, but on his slight frame, it looked almost twice that. And it was thick, nearly as thick as his wrist, with prominent veins running its length. He was neatly clipped, and his foreskin just covered the flange of his wide magenta cockhead. It was mouthwateringly beautiful.

Wrapping my hands around his taut full buttocks, I pulled him toward me and took his dick in my mouth. His buttocks tensed and then trembled like the flanks of a nervous filly. He inhaled deeply, held his breath for seconds, and then exhaled with a long, "Aaaah!" He grabbed my hair with both hands, spread his legs wider, and not exactly gently mouth-fucked me, driving past my tonsils time after time. I tickled and tugged at his tight, almost hairless nutsac with one hand and eased the other between his ass cheeks, a finger searching for the opening, which I reamed without trying to penetrate it. I could see the tremors running through his loins and knew he would explode soon ... much too soon.

He knew it, too. He popped his thick rod out of my mouth and knelt between my legs. I raised my hips as he tugged my briefs off. He pulled my dick away from my body with a thumb at the base and studied it intently for a second. He bent down and began to suck me. Though not expert, he was pretty good, good enough to show some prior experience, good enough to have me ready to cream in nothing flat. I pried him off my cock and half-lifted him onto the bed. I spread his legs and knelt between them.

"Have you done this a lot?" I asked, flicking my tongue into his navel and making him squirm.

"Not really," he managed. "Just with Aaron, and he's too uptight to go all the way with it. So we wind up just jacking off. But I want more than that." He stroked my head tenderly.

I knew from dinner conversation that Aaron was his tennis doubles partner and, according to his mother, about the only person Jimmy spent any time with. Now I understood why. But I forgot Aaron and concentrated on giving Jimmy more of what he wasn't getting from the other kid. Using every move I knew, I carried him to the brink of explosion time after time, only to sit back and toy with his balls or lean in to suck and bite at his nipples until he cooled off a little. I had him hunching and thrusting and grabbing and sighing in ecstasy, not wanting to bring him to his peak and thus end it.

Once when I almost let him go too far, he pushed me off his dick and sat up, his thighs pressed tight against me. He cupped my face in both hands and gazed at me with those irresistible deep green eyes.

"Gray?" he asked in a thin, tentative voice. "Gray, can I, you know, put it in you?" He smiled an oddly bashful smile.

I needed a little time to think. I am not naturally a bottom, and I've never really enjoyed the role. Faced with this mammoth cock, I was not at all sure I wanted to be fucked, no matter how beautiful Jimmy was.

"I don't know," I hedged. "That thing should be registered as a dangerous weapon. Have you ever done it before?"

"No," he said with a twinge of sadness, "Aaron won't even talk about letting me, won't even think about it. But I want to ... with you. I want to know what it's like. Please."

The "please" got to me. I reached into the bedside table for condoms and lubricant which I had stashed when I unpacked, always the optimist. With him kneeling between my thighs, I tore open a rubber and struggled to stretch it over the broad head of his cock and roll it down the shaft. I reminded myself to buy some large size ones next time. I squeezed a generous supply of lube on my fingers, lay back, raised my legs, and dabbed the goo around my opening, shoving a big glob up inside with two fingers. God, I felt too tight for this!

"Okay, let's give it a try," I said, raising my spread legs higher. "But go easy with that monster!"

"Like this?" he questioned. "I thought - on your stomach or hands and knees, maybe."

"We might get around to that, but let's start like this," I said. "Come on, I'll help guide you in."

He grabbed my thighs and pushed my legs almost back against my chest. I wrapped my hand around the base of his dick and led it to the opening. When he pushed inside, I had to bite down on my forearm to keep from yelling out. I had never been stretched so wide before. But I forced myself to relax and enjoy the sensation of his thick cock burrowing into me. When he had most of that long rod buried in my yielding passage, I pulled him down on top of me and wrapped my legs about his waist. He set up a steady, unhurried pattern of alternating deep and shallow thrusts, gyrating his pelvis each time. He nuzzled into my neck and nipped at my earlobe as his hands strayed through my hair. I reached back and felt his firm round buttocks straining and flexing with every thrust of his pistoning tube.

After too short a time, his thrusts became harder, deeper, and faster until he was ramming that huge thing full length in me. I rotated my ass and raised up to meet every thrust. I was loving every cruel lunge. His movements became spastic, his breathing ragged. His cock ballooned inside me. A flash of intense pleasure shuddered through his body, and he collapsed on my chest.

"Wow! That was cool! I didn't know anything could feel so good!" he gasped out, struggling to catch his breath.

When his breathing slowed down, he raised up onto his knees, keeping his dick inside me. He reached down and slowly jerked my rigid cock until I shot a bountiful load all over my chest and onto my chin. After he had squeezed the last droplet out of my sensitive cockhead, he sat back and popped his softening dick out of me.

"Thank you, Gray," he said in a little-boy voice.

As we showered together, Jimmy went to his knees and took my swelling cock in his mouth. Trying out some movements he had picked up earlier from me, he had me trembling and hanging onto the grab bar with approaching climax before I knew it. I tried to pull his mouth off me, but he clung tight until I exploded a second copious load deep in his mouth. He took it all before spitting into the drain.

After we toweled off and returned to the bed, he fingered my limp cock.

"This thing's not exactly small, either, you know," he said. "It's sort of scary, but next time, I want you to fuck me with it." "Oh, you mean there's going to be a next time?" I teased.

"Yeah, every night for the week you're in town ... if I don't fuckin' wear you out. And you have to come see me play tennis," he said. "But right now, c'mon and suck it."

I grinned and eagerly dropped to my knees between his legs to reconfirm that he really was big where it counts.

HORNY AS HELL
Anonymous

I ride the subway each workday from Queens to Manhattan. Every day I ride back and forth with the same people. I know where they live, what kinds of coats they wear, what they eat for breakfast, but I have no idea who they are. We go in and out together and are entirely anonymous. Do they recognize me? Do they notice that some days I look better than others? Do they suck dick? Will they fuck a gay boy?

Some mornings it gets very crowded, with too many people jamming into the cars, and it isn't unusual for someone to brush up against my crotch or ass. Most of the time, I have to believe it's intentional. Sometimes they linger, sometimes they squeeze, sometimes they rub. There is no point getting angry. To be honest, I find it rather exciting, having a complete stranger touching me in public. Since my boyfriend broke up with me a couple of months ago, I've had fantasies of some guy feeling me up, taking him home, and fucking my brains out. I knew I'd never have the nerve to do it. Still....

At the token booth one morning a couple of weeks ago, the man behind the counter said that due to some emergency work, there would likely be delays today in the tunnel. It was possible that the train might be stopped for a half an hour, maybe more. Sorry for the inconvenience, blah, blah, blah....

I almost turned around and went home. Who the hell needs the aggravation? Then I remembered I had to open the art gallery where I work that morning; my boss had left for Europe the night before. I had to go in.

Grudgingly, I paid my fare and went down to the platform to wait for the train. It was chilly that morning so I wore my leather jacket and my best jeans. On the platform, I waited for the train. The platform was only a little more crowded than usual, and I hoped maybe the problem had been exaggerated. The train arrived fairly quickly. It was crowded, but I had seen worse. I stay on the train for fifteen stops; it usually takes me about 45 minutes. The doors closed and I hoped for the best. I grabbed onto a pole, took out my New York Times and began to read.

For the first three or four stops, the train moved at normal speed. Unfortunately, it got jam-packed. The people around me had their backs to me, I was in a little shelter formed by their bodies. The train slowed down and crawled along between stations, stopping intermittently. It was during one of these short stops that I felt a hand resting lightly on my ass. Fingers were gently pressing against the denim covering my ass. I knew I should do something to stop him, but I figured it was harmless, and after not having had sex for over two weeks, I was horny as hell.

The palm of his hand pressed slightly harder against my ass. I pushed my ass back a little into his hand, signaling my awareness of and consent to his actions. At that point, the train again started to move slowly and my molester squeezed my ass cheek firmly. He began to move his hand over my denim-covered ass knowingly. My cock began to harden.

His hand drifted lower and I allowed him to reach under me and squeeze my crotch. The train was so packed that nobody new got on. As the train left the station, I felt the zipper of my jeans being toyed with. I blinked, wondering just how far he thought he could go on a crowded subway train with people all around us. I felt the pre-cum dripping from my cock onto the denim as his hand struggled with the zipper. His actions became more urgent. I brought my newspaper down on his hand and he removed it from my zipper. Enough was enough.

While his one hand roamed freely over my denim-covered ass, rubbing, squeezing and probing, his other hand reached for my free hand near him and took it to his crotch. He pressed my hand into his cock. It was hard under his pants. He moved my hand up and down over his prick. I gasped; this was one huge piece of meat. Oh if only we weren't on a fast- moving train!

When he let go of my hand, I continued rubbing his prick on my own. As he squeezed my ass, the train slowed. I ran my fingers and nails teasingly along his bulge. I surveyed its length with my hand. I figured it to be at least eight inches.

Just outside the station, the conductor announced over the loudspeaker, "Ladies and gentlemen, the area of the emergency track work is just ahead...."

Other passengers groaned and cursed. My molester turned me to face him. Until this time I had not seen the person who was feeling me up. He was a Puerto Rican, maybe 15 years old, and a bit shorter than me. He smiled and wished me a good morning in Spanish.

A minute later, the lights in the train went out and we remained there, as if frozen in time, and I continued stroking his bulge while he squeezed my ass.

Finally the train began moving again and we chilled until we got to my stop. Using what little Spanish I knew, I asked him if he wanted to come to work with me. He grinned. "My boss is in Europe," I explained. He nodded, seeming to understand.

I was taking a terrible chance with this boy but I was overcome by my sexual need; I had taken such risks before, but never at the gallery. I took him in through the back door, keeping him in the storeroom. It was nearly nine, and we had only a half hour before the other assistant, Charles, would arrive. I explained all of this to him while unleashing his cock from his jeans and dropping to my knees before him. My mind was in a daze as he began slapping my cheeks with his semi-hard cock. I moved my mouth to it and took it between my lips. I ran my tongue over his cockhead as I sucked more and more of his prick into my mouth. His prick stiffened and I was able to take the entire shaft down my throat. I moved my head back and forth along his hard cock. I reached up and touched his hairy balls. He took my head in his hands and guided my cocksucking movements. I continued to suck his cock from head to root. I flicked my tongue all along his long shaft, then I moved my mouth to the underside of his prick and licked down to the root. When I got there, I sucked one of his balls into my mouth. I worked on his balls for a short time. While I did, I encircled his cock with my hand and jerked him off. Soon my lips returned to his cock. This time, he held my head steady and fucked my mouth. I used my tongue on his shaft as best I could. He suddenly buried my face in his pubic hair, his cock down my throat and shot his load of warm, sticky cum into my mouth. I licked up every drop I could.

Breathing heavily, he held my head and kept his cock in my mouth. I felt his prick go limp between my lips. He wouldn't let me get up. I was afraid Charles would come flying through the back door and see me on my knees, and a Rican cock in my mouth. Still the boy held me there. Finally, with his hands, he motioned me to stand up, and his still-impressive cock slid from my mouth.

"Tomorrow?" I asked him as he put his jewels away and zipped up.

He smiled, nodded, and vanished out the door.

My new Rican lover was not on the train the next morning. There were no delays and I arrived at the gallery much earlier than usual. I knew nothing of him, so I was free to imagine everything. I conjured entire lives for the youth while I jacked off, not once but twice. I was no longer horny. Still, although I didn't get my hopes up, I did prepare my asshole just in case. Then, shortly before nine, there was a soft knock on the back door. My heart began pounding as I opened it and saw him standing in the shadows, his hand stroking the bulge in his jeans. He smiled.

Again, I kept him in the store room and, after getting him hard, I let him turn me around and slide my pants off my hips to expose my ass.

I leaned over the work table as his finger probed me; he realized I was ready.

As he spread my asscheeks, I reached for his now fully erect prick and guided it to my asshole. Slowly he worked his cock up into me.

I gasped. The entry was painful, but I was prepared for that. What I was not prepared for was how urgent his thrusts were; I knew he would come soon. I flexed my ass muscles around his prick desperately trying to milk him dry. He didn't disappoint me. He grabbed my asscheeks hard and pushed into me as far as his prick could go. Seconds later, I felt his cock pulsate as he filled me with his cum. He stayed in me and began rocking slowly back and forth and played with my cock with both of his hands. Seconds later, with his expert fondling of me, I came, my jism splashing on the floor in front of the work table.

As he pulled out of my ass, I sighed. Catching my breath, I stayed bent over the work table. His hand squeezed my ass one last time and, when I turned to look at him, again he had vanished.

I KNOW YOU WANT IT
Frank Brooks

"I'll suck that big, hard cock. Fish it out of your pants and I'll suck it off right now...."

"Suck my big one," the older kid growled in a low voice. He was tall and blond, a beefy, football-player type. "C'mon, I know you want it."

"Fuck you!" said the younger, shorter kid. He was slender, boyish and dark-haired.

They were both cheeky checkout boys, standing behind the counter of the video-rental annex of the 24-hour warehouse supermarket, and they hadn't seen me as I came in, turned away from the entrance as they were, and engrossed in their banter. It was just after seven on a blizzardy morning and they were in the middle of a shift change and not expecting to see any customers, and I walk quietly by long habit.

I slipped behind some shelves, my eight inches of uncut meat hard and throbbing in my jeans as I spied on them and eavesdropped. The bigger kid persisted, kept saying, "Suck my big one," and the younger one kept telling him to fuck off, although he didn't sound especially convincing. The younger one had spent the night working and was ready to go home, while the older one had just come on duty.

"I'm fucking horny, man," the blond half whispered. "I always wake up with the biggest, hardest, fuckingest cock you ever saw, and when one of my girlfriends isn't around to take care of it, it fucking drives me nuts. Come on, I know you're drooling for it."

"I'm not one of your girlfriends, man."

"But you're a cocksucker. I can tell. You're just dying to suck my big one."

"Fuck you, I'm going home."

"Wanna see it? You won't believe how big it is."

"No thanks. I'm leaving."

Well, then leave, I thought. What are you waiting for? Then I mentally urged the blond to pull it out and show it to him: Come on, he won't be able to resist it. But he was all words and no action, repeating "Suck my big one" like a broken record.

I was horny and impatient. I'd just spent the night behind the wheel of a snow plow. In fact, I'd still be out there plowing the streets if the blizzard hadn't let up. I don't usually work nights, and I don't usually have to spend eight hours at a stretch behind the wheel of a truck, except in a fucking snow emergency. My usual shift is days, and my usual job is to make the rounds of the city parks and other public areas to make sure the maintenance workers have done their jobs. My foreman position gives me frequent and ample opportunities to relieve my pent-up lust as I make my rounds during the day, but last night it was all work and no play.

"Suck my big one!"

"Fuck off!"

I'd had enough. I stepped behind a black curtain into the Adults Only room, grabbed a video called College Cock off the shelves, and marched straight up to the counter.

Both boys gaped at me in red-faced shock, wondering, I'm sure, where in the hell I'd come from. As the older one checked me out, mumbling nervous small-talk about the snow, the younger one acted like he was actually and finally going to leave.

It was time to act. "I'll suck it," I growled in a low voice. "I'll suck it off for you."

The younger kid froze in his tracks and the older one stared at me open-mouthed.

"I'll suck that big one," I repeated. "I'll suck that big hard cock. Fish it out of your pants and I'll suck it off right now."

Neither boy made a move. Both just stared. I glanced down the hallway that led to the video annex and saw that it was deserted. Not wasting a second, I slipped behind the counter.

"You can't come back here," stammered the blond.

"Well, I just did." I started to unzip him.

"Christ, somebody will see you!"

"Who's going to show up this early in a snow storm? Besides, your buddy here can keep watch." I forced down his jeans. His sweaty stud-cock stood out straight and throbbing. It had to be eight inches plus, and thick as my wrist. He was true to his word, "big" was the word for it. I licked my lips. "Beautiful!" I dropped down to taste it.

"Fuck!" he panted. "Oh fuck!"

I licked his plum-sized balls, savoring their musky flavor. I licked his shaft, nibbled and lapped at his swollen, sizzling, purplish glans. Juice oozed out and I drank it. He pushed down on my head, forcing his flesh into my mouth.

"Suck it! Eat it! Suck my big one! Yeah!" Gripping my head, he fucked my face.

Experienced cocksucker that I am, I took it without choking. Experienced is the wrong word. "World-class" says it better. World-class cocksucker. I've been sucking off five or ten cocks a day for more than 30 years, and more on good days. You do the math. That's a lot of cock sucking.

As the blond grunted and screwed, his cock pulsing and sliding in my mouth and throat, its bulging veins rippling against my lips and thrilling them, I heard a rhythmic slapping sound near my head. The younger kid had fished out his dick and was pounding it. I reached up to feel it seven inches of bone-hard, uncut young rod, hot as a branding iron. I thumbed the tip and felt slick juice oozing out, which I smeared over the glans.

"Wow!" the boy whispered.

The blond started rise up and down on his toes. His dick flexed hard and nearly lifted my head off as his spunk shot into my mouth. He was gasping. The bursts of young cum were profuse and hot, and they came fast. the big cock swelling and contracting squirting, squirting, squirting. I gulped it all and sucked for more.

The younger boy's cock turned to steel in my hand. Cum splashed against my cheek. I turned my head, letting the blond's cock slip out of my mouth, and I caught the younger boy's cock between my lips as it was delivering its second spurt. He gasped, squirming and humping, squirting boy-cum against my tonsils: "Drink it!" I didn't need to be told. I could have guzzled his sweet load all day.

The blond started shaking me by the shoulder. "Shit, somebody's coming!"

I didn't panic. Public-sex addict that I am, I'd heard those words daily for three decades. In fact, I expected to hear them. They were part of the experience and added to the thrill. Wiping cum off my cheek and licking my lips, I backed out from behind the counter on my hands and knees and straightened up, as if I'd just dropped a coin and had bent over to pick it up. The intruder, entering the store, was none the wiser.

"Call me anytime," I said to the boys, pointing to my phone number on the video rental form. "Any time."

Out in the parking lot, sitting behind the wheel of the truck, I took out my pulsing hard-on and stroked it, working the foreskin up and down. The knob was swollen huge and purple, its piss slit open and oozing clear juice. I could still feel those boys' cocks sliding in my mouth and throat, could still taste their salty young meat, not to mention their sweet, tangy young spunk. The snow had stopped and the sun was trying to poke through the clouds, and I debated whether to blow my load then and there or to head for the nearest glory hole. Even early on a snowy winter morning there might be a hungry cocksucker at one of the nearby parks who would appreciate a hot load of pent-up man-cum to warm him up.

I was the expert on the public glory hole scene in this town. My job required me, among other things, to check out all the public restrooms in the city at least once a day to see that they'd been cleaned and maintained, so I, more than anybody, knew what action went on regularly where and when. It was my doing that the glory holes were never covered over. Why bother, I told the maintenance crews why waste your time when the holes will just be re-bored and the workers were happy to have one less burdensome task to perform and left the holes alone.

I dipped my finger into the slick sap oozing from my pisshole and tasted it. My dick was ready to jump out of its skin, ready to shoot off any time. I enjoyed postponing my orgasms sometimes, enjoyed the sweet torture of it, but if I held off too long, I'd end up with blue balls. Damn, those checkout boys were hot, I thought, and hoped that one or both of them would call me sometime soon, although I knew from experience that the odds of that happening were 50-50 at best.

But, I thought, why beat off when I could get sucked off? I would head to the nearest park for a blowjob and then head home for some sleep.

As I was driving toward the exit of the parking lot, my hot dick sticking up out of my open fly, juice oozing out of it with each throb, I spotted somebody walking. Drawing up alongside the figure, I recognized the younger checkout boy. I rolled down the window.

"Want a ride?"

He looked up and recognized me. His face turned red. "I don't take rides from strangers."

"I'm no stranger. You've got my phone number I hope and besides, I'm a public servant. This is a city vehicle I'm driving. If you can't trust a public-works engineer, who can you trust?"

"I never rode in a snowplow before," he said, as if that might justify his accepting a ride from me.

"Then hop in. You're in for a thrill."

As soon as he'd climbed in beside me, he spotted my pulsing erection. "I think I'd better leave."

"Relax, I don't bite. And there's no need for you to do a thing. You can just sit back and watch me jack off. Have you ever watched a man jack off before? Or I'll suck you off again. Whatever you like."

He didn't say anything, but he didn't leave, either.

I stroked my cock and he watched me and I watched him watching me. His hand went to his crotch, squeezing, rubbing. He was excited.

"Ever suck a cock?" I asked.

"Hell no!"

"Try it sometime, you might like it."

"I don't think so," he said.

I squeezed lubricant out of my swelling erection and licked it off my fingers. "Mmm, good stuff! You ever taste a man's juice?"

"No way."

I stared down at my cock and licked my lips. "Big, sexy piece of meat. I'd suck it off myself, but I can't bend down that far. I guess I'll just have to jack off."

After working my meat a few strokes, I let go of it and let it stick up in the air and throb as I slumped back with my eyes closed, as if I'd fallen asleep. In the close confines of the truck cab, I could hear the boy's breathing getting heavier. I heard him unzip and start to work his stiff cock. I resisted the urge to open my eyes and watch. I wanted to see what he'd do. I felt hot juice ooze from my pulsing cock and trickle down the shaft and over my hairy, swollen nuts.

"Shit!" the boy whispered, and then he was leaning over me, breathing on my cock.

I held my breath, flexed my cock a few times.

"Fuck!" the kid whispered, and his tongue flicked at my naked glans. He started to nibble it. With a moan, he took my cock into his mouth, swallowing half of it.

"Yeah baby, suck it!"

"Mmnn!" he growled, sucking.

I opened my eyes and saw his head bobbing in my lap. He sucked noisily, with juicy smacks of his lips, which rode up and down around my spit-lubed shaft. With each down-stroke, my cock sank a little deeper into his throat. His spit trickled over my balls. The sight of my gristly, rock-hard man-cock sliding in and out of his cute, boyish face sent such thrills through my loins that I couldn't hold it. I wanted to it last, but I couldn't hold it.

"Oh, I'm coming!" With a groan, I exploded into his mouth.

He choked, but he didn't let up. He wanted it.

"Suck it...!" I writhed on the seat, seeing stars.

His mouth overflowed and cum ran down my balls. I held his head, fucking his throat and shooting juice straight down his gullet. He was squirming, but not because he was trying to break free. Cum shot from his cock, splashing on my pants and boots. The truck cab filled with the spicy scent of it. I wiped it off my pants and licked it off my fingers. When we were both spent, I pulled his face up to mine and kissed him smack on the mouth. He didn't resist.

That evening I did something I rarely do: sat home and waited for the phone to ring. Would one of my checkout boys call? It wasn't likely, but the thought of missing a call from either of them had me sitting home, restless and horny. I'd shot off only once today down the throat of young Jaimie, the checkout boy who'd climbed into my truck cab this morning. After that after dropping off Jaimie a few blocks from where he claimed to live I'd been a good boy for the rest of the day, sleeping most of it, then avoiding the glory holes later on. I wasn't used to only one orgasm a day three to five a day had been my average for the past three decades and now, as I fantasized about both checkout boys, my hard-on was ready to split out of its skin.

I'd learned from Jaimie that his co-worker at the video store the tall, blond, beefy stud with the huge cock was named Brent. Jaimie claimed to know little about him except that he worked the day shift and bragged about having a dozen girlfriends that he fucked regularly. Sure! I thought. Judging by the load Brent had shot down my throat this morning, I reckoned that he hadn't fucked anything in days.

I opened a beer and put on the videotape I'd rented: College Cock. It hadn't been rewound, and when I pressed the Play button, a pair of blond college boys appeared immediately on the screen locked naked in a 69 embrace, each with the other's cock down his throat. I imagined one of those big cocks down my own throat and salivated. I didn't dare stroke myself, knowing I'd blow my load in less than a minute if I did. It was an exquisite torture, one that I enjoyed in a strange way, but finally I'd had enough. Glory holes, here I come! I thought, and, as if on cue, the phone rang. It was Brent and he sounded drunk. He wanted to know if I remembered him. When I said I did, he laughed, then slurred, "Suck my big one!" I said I'd love to and offered to pick him up. He said he could find his way over and I gave him directions.

A half hour later he staggered in, unzipping his fly and freeing his gorgeous, monster cock before I could lock the door. With a growl, I dropped to my knees and went down on him. His cock tasted of beer, piss, and sweat. He stood over me, swaying drunkenly and mumbling, "Suck it, suck it, eat it!" I pushed him backward onto the couch, where he slumped, his legs spread, my head bobbing between them. In half a minute he was ready to blow, so spit out his cock and sat back.

"Aw man, I wanna get off!" he whined.

"Relax," I said. "I'm going to make you super good." I slid down and untied his shoes.

"Aw man, just get me off!"

I ignored him. I got his shoes off and rubbed his naked feet. He sighed and spread his legs. I hauled off his jeans, then his t-shirt. He had a smooth torso with bulging pecs. I licked his nipples, then slid back down and sucked his toes.

"Man, what're you doing?" His cock was pointed straight at the ceiling, throbbing wildly. His toes flexed in my mouth.

I took my time, enjoying the taste of him, moving up his legs, jack-knifing his thighs so I could lick under his balls and taste his ass. I slipped my tongue inside him and he gasped: "Oh fuck!" He wiggled his ass as I tongue-fucked it and his heavy cock flip-flopped against his belly. I slid up and licked out his navel, lapped up and down his flanks, sucked on his nipples again and nuzzled and tasted his armpits.

"Suck me!" he groaned, grabbing my head, forcing me down on his cock. "Suck my big one!" He fucked his cock all the way down my throat. "Eat it, cocksucker!"

I was salivating so profusely that my spit ran down his shaft and balls. As I began to suck, he let go off my head and slumped back. I slid my mouth and throat up and down his incredibly thick, long, hard cock, swallowing every inch of it, smacking my lips, sucking for his load.

"Deep-throat it," he moaned, "Hot damn!"

I jack-knifed his legs again and he assisted by grabbing them under the thighs and holding them up for me. As my head bobbed, my mouth devouring his meaty cock, I tickled his asshole with my spit-wet middle finger and gradually worked it into him.

"Fuck!" he gasped, "Fuck!"

I pumped my finger in and out of him and he squirmed, his asshole contracting. I felt his prostate swell against my finger and I prodded it, tickled it, tortured it. His cock swelled even more. He started to whimper, his toes clutching.

"Oh Christ!" he gasped, and hot spunk hit the roof of my mouth. Cum filled my throat. A stream of hot cum flowed down my gullet. I churned my tongue, smacked my lips, and sucked, sucked, sucked until he could shoot no more. He lowered his legs and seemed to pass out. With his cock still in my mouth, I shot off against the side of the couch.

When he finally opened his eyes, he said, "I gotta go."

"What's your hurry? I'll suck you off again. And again and again, all night long."

He stood up unsteadily. "Gotta go. Got a date."

Jaimie called the next evening. I couldn't believe my luck. If this kept up, I'd give up the glory holes. The kid didn't have wheels, so I picked him up where I'd let him off yesterday. On the drive back to my apartment, he wouldn't let me touch him, afraid, I guess, of somebody spotting us making out in the front seat of my car. But once inside my apartment, things changed. Immediately, he unzipped me, fished out my hard-on, dropped to his knees and went down on me. He sucked with such hunger that after a minute or two I had to make him stop.

"You keep that up and I won't last another ten seconds. Come on, let's do this right."

He was hesitant to take off his clothes, but as soon as he saw me naked and standing there with a pulsing hard-on, he gave in. He had wonderfully smooth skin, and his rock-hard seven inches stood out and up at an acute angle, its foreskin retracted. I went down on him, swallowing his young pecker to his velvet-skinned balls. He rose up and down on his toes and rocked his loins, moaning as I sucked his cock and stroked his belly and pecs and tweaked his nipples. I left off sucking his cock so I could taste his armpits. When I kissed him, he didn't pull back, but slipped his tongue between my lips. Continuing to kiss him, I pushed him down onto the couch and stretched out on top of him. He drooled into my mouth and I swallowed it. We rocked against each other, our bellies getting slick with the pre-cum oozing from our excited cocks.

"How old are you?" he asked, breaking our kiss.

"Forty-five," I said, lying. I was actually ten years older.

He looked shocked. "You're older than my dad."

"Can you do with your dad what we're doing?"

"Pervert," he said, and pushed me off him.

I grabbed his hand and pulled him off the couch. "Come on, little boy, let's go in my bedroom."

"I don't think so," he said.

I picked him up, carried him into my bedroom, and dropped him on the bed. He was light as a feather.

"What are you going to do with me?"

"What would you like me to do with you? Turn over."

"Why?

"So I can look at your cute boy-ass."

Reluctantly he flipped over and looked back at me over his shoulder. I stood there lusting for him, my gristly man-dick throbbing a mile a minute. The sight of it seemed to excite him and he squirmed. I crawled forward onto the bed, spread his asscheeks, and started licking up and down the crack.

"What're you doing to me?"

Instead of answering, I shoved my tongue inside him.

"Fuck!" he gasped.

Fuck was the word. Fuck was exactly what I was going to do to him. I was going to drive eight, thick inches of throbbing man-dick up his boy-pussy. I sat back on my heels, my dick standing up like a billyclub between my hairy thighs. There was lube in the drawer of the bedside table, but before I could get it, the kid flipped over and went for my cock like a hungry shark. Dazed, I felt on my side beside him. We were in the 69 position and he pushed seven inches of sweet, satin-smooth young dick into my mouth. He started growling and I started growling as we gripped each other's head between our thighs and sucked, sucked, sucked. I wanted him and he wanted me, and before I knew what was happening, I was pumping cum into his mouth. He choked a few times, but sucked for more, and then he was pumping his own cum down my throat. We drained each other and lay there catching our breaths. He rolled off the bed and stood up.

"Where are you going?" I asked. "Need to use the bathroom?"

"I need to get going or I'll be late for work. And I could use a ride."

Over the next few weeks, both boys came over several times, but not often enough to suit me. On evenings when neither one showed up, I cursed myself for wasting precious glory hole time waiting for them. Brent always showed up half drunk and in need of an instant blowjob. Jaimie always wanted to kiss and sixty-nine, and somehow I never got around to fucking him. I wondered if I'd ever get to fuck him. Then, one evening Brent showed up drunker than usual and the unexpected happened.

I got Brent undressed and into my bedroom, where he lay sprawled across my bed, his muscular legs spread, his over-sized hard-on throbbing against his flat stomach. His eyes were closed and I couldn't tell if he was still awake or had passed out. I sucked his cock for a good ten minutes, savoring it, but he failed to come. Usually, he had his first orgasm within a few minutes of arriving, then would let me take my time teasing a second load out of him. I wondered if he was too drunk to have an orgasm. When I slid up to suck his nipples and to lick his armpits, he all at once rolled over onto his belly, mumbling as if he were talking in his sleep.

What an ass! I kissed it, then spread his asscheeks and buried my face between them, licking and sucking his succulent asshole and finally slipping my tongue inside him. He sighed, grinding against the mattress. As I continued to rim and tongue-fuck him, I found myself getting hotter and hotter, and almost mechanically, almost without thinking, I reached over and opened the drawer of the night table and fished out the container of lube. Kneeling between Brent's legs, I greased his asshole and worked one, two, then three fingers into him. He moaned, but offered no resistance. Continuing to finger-fuck him, I greased up my cock, then slipped my fingers out of him and pushed my cock between his asscheeks. He soon opened up and I sank into him, screwing all eight inches of my cock up his tight asshole. He groaned as I settled down on him. I licked the back of his neck and began to screw. He sighed, rotating his ass. I could hardly believe it.

He had to be awake, I thought, but I wasn't about to break the spell by asking him. Clinging to him, biting his shoulders and neck from behind, I screwed away, grunting and groaning as his slick asshole gripped my sliding cock like a muscular fist. I hadn't fucked such a gorgeous, tight ass in years. I wanted to leave my cock inside him forever. Then just my luck the doorbell started buzzing away. I tried to ignore it, but whoever was out there was stubborn and kept at it. Finally, I pulled my cock out of Brent.

"Stay right here. Don't move."

In the living room, I punched the intercom, ready to tell the pest probably some sex-crazed old trick stopping by to be serviced to come back tomorrow, but when I heard Jaimie's voice at the other end, I buzzed him right in. When I opened the door and Jaimie saw me standing there naked, with a greased-up hard-on, he acted as if he didn't know whether to come in or flee.

"What's up?" I asked. "I thought you had to work tonight."

"I've got the night off. I was in the neighborhood thought I'd stop in. What's going on?"

I pulled him inside and locked the door. "Take off your clothes."

"What's going on?"

"Come on, I'm not in the mood for game-playing." I undressed him on the spot and hauled him into the bedroom. He paused at my bedroom door when he spotted the naked body lying face-down on my bed.

"Don't worry, he's alive," I whispered. "But I'm not sure if he's asleep or awake. Recognize him? He's a friend of yours. Your big-dicked buddy from work."

Jaimie turned pale. "Maybe I'd better leave."

"Don't be silly. Guess what I've been fucking him. Screwing his ass. You don't believe me? Just, watch. Stay put and watch me. He loves a big dick up the ass."

I left Jaimie standing in the doorway and climbed back on the bed to mount Brent. He moaned as I sank into him. I looked back at Jaimie. He was jerking off. I humped Brent. Jaimie moved closer into the room, so close that I could hear him pounding his hot meat. I turned my head to the side, tongue out, begging for his cock. He wouldn't give it to me.

"Let me fuck him," he whispered.

I was slightly shocked. I pointed to the lube and Jaimie grabbed it and greased up. I rolled off Brent and Jaimie climbed aboard, sliding his hard-on up Brent's half-open asshole. Without a pause, he started to ram. I caressed his smooth, bouncing butt and slid a greasy finger up and down his hot crack. I found his pucker and slipped my finger up his asshole. He kept fucking in earnest, panting like a dog. I pulled my finger out of him, got up behind him, and shoved my lusting hard-on between his asscheeks. Then I was inside him to the hilt. I was surprised by easily he took it all and by his moan of appreciation. Gripping his skinny, rocking hips, I began to screw.

"Fuck!" Jaimie gasped. "Oh fuck!"

I screwed hard and fast, matching the rhythm of my thrusts to the rhythm of his own. "Fuck him good, baby," I growled in Jaimie's ear. "Ram that hot ass."

I settled down on him, squashing him between Brent and myself. My cock was buried in him. I couldn't enter him any deeper. With each grinding thrust I gave him, he delivered one equally deep and hard to Brent. The three of us, joined together, became a mass of writhing, sweating male flesh. I gnawed into the back of Jaimie's neck. He whimpered,

Whether Brent knew who was fucking him, I couldn't be certain. He seemed too dazed to care. But he had to be conscious of what was happening that he was getting fucked by somebody of that I was certain. Squirming under the two of us, he moaned so loud that I feared the neighbors would start banging on the walls.

I sucked on Jaimie's ear, growling into it. His skin felt like hot, oiled velvet against me. His asshole felt like an electric socket into which I'd plugged my cock, and jolts of pleasure shot to all the way to my nipples and toes. I'd never fucked a hotter, tighter ass, and I let go completely, fucking full blast, fucking to climax. "Baby, I'm coming!"

As I exploded into Jaimie, he shuddered with pleasure and his asshole went into spasms. "Oh fuck, oh fuck!" he kept gasping. As I fucked my love-juice into him, he fucked his own into Brent. Our orgasms seemed to go on for minutes. When we uncoupled, all three of us drenched in sweat, I saw that Brent had shot off all over the sheets.

Even now, Brent kept up his act. "Hey, where am I? What happened? Man, am I drunk!"

I didn't buy a word of it, and by the look of disbelief on Jaimie's face, I knew that he didn't either.

Brent, flustered, grabbed Jaimie's head and forced it down over his cock. "Suck my big one, cocksucker!"

Jaimie didn't resist. Finally, he was sucking Brent's big one.

PLAYING HARD TO GET
P.K. Warren

"Sex is life, and life is unlimited."

– The late Scott O'Hara, who, it was said, possessed "the Biggest Dick in San Francisco"

It was the Tuesday before Thanksgiving, 1978. I was sitting at the kitchen table when my dad came in and tossed the day's paper down in front of me, right on top of the peanut butter and jelly sandwich I was going to eat next after I finished my chicken soup. Any other time, such a stunt would have been the spark for another heavy row between us, but I'd promised I'd bite bullets in keeping the house peaceful for the holidays.

When I pushed the paper aside to unveil my sandwich, he shoved the plate beyond my reach and brought the paper back before me. "Do you mind? I'm tryin' to eat right now," I said, trying to control my anger.

"Never mind that. Whatcha think of that?" He pointed to an ad he had circled with red ink: "CUT and CARRY". I didn't get the point; we hadn't had a real tree in the house for five years, and Dad did have his reason for never having one again. The last tree he had bought ended up decorated on our front porch because, two day before he was to bring it inside, a friend of his had lost his home in a tree-related fire. So, to save the spirits of my younger siblings, Scrooge dashed out and brought home the cheapest artificial tree he could find to sit on top of the TV.

I looked up at him. "I don't understand."

"Simple. Look, with just a hundred of 'em, you'd make a killer profit at fifteen to twenty a pop in the city."

"Me?"

He shook his head in dismay. "Yeah, you! We're going into the woods!"

"No way!" I screamed, as Mom's wish for peace over the holidays quickly flew out the window.

We argued, off and on, for three days straight, but I finally relented anything to get Dad to shut up about it. Little did I know that Dad had sucked his buddies Buck and Sonny into his latest scheme.

Finally the day came and we were up and dressed and fed at five in the morning. By the time the yellow sign for Sonny's Garage came into view up the road, where we were to meet both Sonny and Buck, my nerves were in a total frazzle. Dad honked the horn and Buck and Sonny scrambled into Sonny's pickup and off we went. Sonny drew up behind us, honked his horn. I turned around and he gave me a wave. I blinked; there was just something about Sonny, something I couldn't explain, couldn't understand.... I snapped around to keep my eyes on the road ahead.

I simply couldn't believe I was heading off to the mountains with this trio. Buck was much like my dad in a lot of ways, but while they'd both get pissed over the smallest things, my dad could shake it off in a few hours, Buck would hold a grudge for years. He was on his second marriage and was totally pussy-whipped. I couldn't stand Buck.

Sonny, however, was another matter altogether. He was the youngest of my dad's drinking buddies. He was a mechanic and extraordinarily handsome. He stood six-two, with straight black hair, mustache and wicked blue-green eyes. I had been desperately in lust for Sonny from the first day Dad took me over to his garage. Sonny looked at me with those devilish eyes as he shook my hand, and I just about passed out with a whimper. I had many nights of dreaming of Sonny after that. Over the years, it became obvious to me that Sonny, in addition to liking his booze, had a penchant for getting hooked up with, as he put it, "bitches." Little did I realize why.

When we reached our destination, Dad and I took the tractor and tow-sled into the woods, because Buck and Sonny assured me they could handle the tree binding and loading. After a half hour of knocking trees, he let me be and started towing them out to the road. Contrary to his opinion, I was no stranger to man's work nor being in the woods, so I kept him out of my hair by keeping a pile of trees waiting for him on return trips. It began to snow and, by dinner time, it was obvious that we were going to have to spend the night at the lodge. This, of course, led to Dad and his buddies promptly getting drunk.

After dinner, I went to take a piss and Sonny followed me. I stood at the toilet and Sonny stumbled in. He was feeling his booze more than usual, if that was possible. He wrapped an arm around me from behind, shoved his crotch into my ass.

"Too bad your dad's here," he breathed into my ear. "It would've been nice being snowed in with just the two of us."

I pushed him away. "You're drunk."

"C'mon kid. We both know the story...."

I zipped up and tried to leave, but Sonny wasn't to be discouraged. "I remember how close we came that time...."

"That was two years ago, Sonny. You were drunk. That shouldn't have happened. And you're drunk now."

"Hey, I wasn't drunk. I knew what I was doing. And I'm not drunk now. You've never seen me drunk, kid."

The incident he was talking about had been my first brush with fire, with the potential of sex with Sonny. We had all been together for a "fish fry" at the Dew Drop Inn. It was on these occasions that everybody had too much to eat and too much to drink, and I was feeling miserable, looking for a way out and Sonny provided it. His "bitch" at the time drank even more than he did. She passed out and Sonny asked me to help him "get her home."

After a wild ride to her trailer, and after we put her to bed in the bedroom, Sonny decided he needed a "real" drink. This led to my sipping on a Coke while Sonny belted a few down as we sat at the little table in the kitchen. Then Sonny decided he was too drunk to drive so he asked me to drive myself home. I agreed, but by the time I got to the door, Sonny was asking me to spend the night. He cupped my ass and pushed what was obviously an erection into my crack. Terrified, I pushed him away and fled. Now here he was asking for the same thing once more and again I was so terrified I was speechless. I raced out of the bathroom. Maybe there would be a better time. There was always hope; I knew that now. Again, little did I know.

Feeling no pain by now, Dad led us upstairs to pick our beds for the night. The largest bunkroom offered one full-sized bed and Sonny climbed into that. I took the lower bunk and Dad scrambled into the upper. I turned away from Sonny, for fear I'd get so excited I'd have to jack off. Amazingly, I slept soundly through the night, but I was rudely awakened in the morning.

"C'mon on, you sleepy head, time to wake up," came Sonny's voice, his foul breath hitting my face.

I tried to roll away from him but he had his hand on my thigh. My eyes snapped open just as his hand fell on my piss hard-on. I jerked away. "C'mon yourself...."

Just then, Buck came into the room. Sonny froze, turned around and said, "Kid's never gonna get up," and stormed out.

I rolled over and tried to ignore Buck as he went about getting his gear together. After he left, I raced to the bathroom, locking the door behind me. After I peed, my hard-on still wouldn't go down. In the shower I re-played Sonny's two failed attempts at seduction, imagining that he had forced me to suck him the first time and that he blew me while I lay in bed. I came instantly.

Late one afternoon three weeks later, Sonny, driving his pick-up, stopped me as I was walking home from school. He said he'd closed the shop early due to lack of business so close to the holidays. He offered me a ride home. I didn't realize the home he was talking about was his.

When he missed the turn to my house and kept on going, my cock began to twitch in my jeans. "Where are we going?" I asked.

"Home," was his tart reply.

I remained silent, giving my consent at last to whatever it was Sonny had in mind.

As we neared his girlfriend's trailer, I noticed her Mustang wasn't parked in the carport. "You're alone for the holidays?" I asked.

"Yeah. The bitch has gone to her folks. I can't stand her folks."

"That's a shame."

"What's a shame is that you've been playing hard to get all these years," he said, reaching over and rubbing my crotch. Finding I was hard already, he chuckled. "Yeah, it's a shame all right. I can feel it."

As I followed Sonny into the trailer, fear gripped me. I had so many wet dreams about this, there was no way the reality could measure up. So it didn't surprise me that as soon as I was inside the trailer, Sonny was all over me. I could smell the liquor on his breath and knew he'd stopped off at the Dew Drop Inn before picking me up. Still it was Sonny, and what he was doing with his hands excited me.

But when I wanted to touch him the way he was touching me, he pushed my hand away. A few flips and turns of his wrists and my jacket was off, my shirt was off, and my slacks cascaded down around my feet.

He knelt before me. I held on to his shoulders as he slipped my shoes, socks, and slacks off me so I was just standing in my briefs. He reached up and took hold of the waistband. I closed my eyes, waiting for the final unveiling and sweep of cool air between my legs and around my erect cock when it would spring free from its cotton wrap but it didn't come.

I glanced down to find Sonny staring up at me.

"What's the matter?" I asked.

He swallowed hard. "I can't believe this is finally happening...."

"Me neither." I couldn't stop shaking. He took my hands in his and held them.

"I've always loved you...." he stammered, hugging me to him.

"Hey, Sonny," I groaned, "it's all right."

"Hmmmm," he moaned as he nuzzled my crotch. He slobbered all over my cock through the fabric.

Finally my briefs were slowly slid down off my ass and my cock snapped free. Sonny caught it with his mouth and an electric shock surged through me as he took more and more of me into his mouth and throat. One hand slipped through my legs to hold my ass as the other came to cup and massage my balls. In one steady rhythm he took my eight, thick inches of cock to its root without so much as a flinch, his nose buried in my tiny patch of pubic hair. He twisted the head a bit before slowly drawing back off and my toes dug into the carpet. He took me fully down his throat several more times in rapid succession and I was fast climbing to the point of no return. It was the blowjob of my dreams and I could hardly believe he was the one administering it. I had always thought I would have been the cocksucker, servicing this renowned ladies' man.

He knew precisely what he was doing, stopping before I could come, drawing off, letting the head pop out of his mouth, leaving me sucking air through my teeth as he palmed my balls to his mouth, only to proceed to stroke me with his hand. I bent down over his back to hike his T-shirt up. He pulled off to permit me to take the shirt off him, but he went right back down on me. I jerked my hips a bit and again when I was close, he pulled off.

"I've waited so long...."

"Me too."

"But God, it was worth the wait," he said, stroking my slick cock. "This is one big dick, kid."

"Thanks," I said, still trembling with fear. "Almost as big as yours, I'll bet."

He didn't respond, just went back to sucking me. My body was still shaking as my orgasm raged through me, and I could only stand there as wave after wave crashed through my bones. When the intensity began to subside, Sonny drew me down to the floor with him. He wiped his mouth with the back of his hand.

"What a load!" he cried.

"Oh, Sonny," I said, hugging him. "Please, let me do you."

I moved to one side so he could stretch his legs out and I started by pulling off his boots and socks. As the zipper of his jeans descended he warned me that he didn't wear underwear. I chuckled at that because, somehow, I had figured as much, from the way his jeans bulged. A glorious column of ivory skin sprang up at attention in the "V" of his open jean fly. I couldn't wait and stretched out on my stomach on his legs and got as much of that cock in my mouth and throat as I could. The male-musk that wafted up from his crotch and the taste of his prick was a heady mixture. I wasn't in the proper position to handle more than half of him before I gagged. Propped up against the couch, he watched me intently as I explored his cock and balls. Kissing, nibbling, sucking. I wasn't sure how long it was but it was at least as long as mine, and thicker.

"Like it?" he asked.

"Hmmmm," was all I could answer since I refused to take my mouth off of it.

"I'll teach you everything. Don't worry about a thing."

I wasn't worried about anything at that point. I was finally where I wanted to be: between Sonny's thighs, with his cock in my mouth.

"But not tonight. Your dad'll be missin' you."

I couldn't stop now, but Sonny insisted. "No, please?"

"No. Not tonight. Christmas Day. After dinner. I'll get boomed and you'll have to take me home, okay?"

"I didn't know you were coming for dinner."

"Yeah, when your dad found out the bitch was gone, he invited me."

"I don't know...." I didn't want to give up the cock. I kept kissing it.

"C'mon, be a good boy. Wait till Christmas. I'll give you a present you'll never forget."

I took him deep, came back up for air. "Promise?"

"Promise."

Sonny let me play with his cock all the way home. I even sucked on it a couple of times. He let me out a block from my house. It had started to snow and I told him to drive carefully.

He said he would, that he was going back to the trailer and jack off thinking of me.

"Or," he said, "I may not. Maybe I'll just hold it till Christmas."

Everything went as planned. Sonny drank a lot, but not as much as usual. By the time dinner was over, he asked Dad if I'd mind driving him home. By that time, Dad was so smashed he would have agreed to anything. Mom was the one who was worried, me driving Sonny's pick-up on icy roads, but we were determined. On the way to Sonny's, he hatched a plan: I would call Mom and tell her the roads were really treacherous after all and I had decided to stay overnight. This would be accepted, he said, because of his reputation as a ladies' man. He was, truly, above suspicion. I agreed and the first thing I did when we arrived was to call Mom.

While I called, Sonny busied himself in the bedroom. I felt strange going in there, seeing him in bed, nude, stroking his cock. "C'mon," he said, waving it at me, "finish what you started."

And so I did, at least so far as sucking it a bit, getting accustomed to the size of it in my mouth. But it was my cock Sonny wanted and my cock Sonny would have. I was treated to the first part of my Christmas present, a long, leisurely suck job, before he started poking around my asshole with his fingers. This was something that I hadn't really considered. I knew this sort of thing was done, but I was so naive I had no idea what was involved. I would have been perfectly happy just sucking him while he sucked me, but when he began sticking his tongue in my butthole, I realized what I had been missing. He rolled me over on my stomach and moved his cockhead into position to tickle my asshole. I was so worked up that I didn't even care that he hadn't lubed it. The head slid in between my waiting lips, parting them easily. He started to press against it. I tensed, waiting to feel the big prick tear me open. I groaned as the huge head penetrated me. I was amazed at how I stretched around the cock. Sonny's hands were on my shoulders, digging into my skin.

He fucked me with slow strokes at first, with only the first few inches of it in my ass, teasing me mercilessly as he massaged the most tender part of me in quick thrusts. He would pull all the way out, and I would whimper for him to fill me back up, but he took his time, working me up to where he wanted me, to where I could take it all. I was aching with the need to come when he finally slid the entire length of it back into me, causing me to lose my breath, I felt my ass begin to spasm as my walls gripped his shaft, trying to keep it locked inside me.

"Yeah," Sonny sighed, "I knew you could do it." He hugged me tight against him and kissed my neck. "Just relax."

That was easier said than done. He drew out so just his fat cockhead teased and threatened to pop free, then he slowly pushed back in all the way. He swiveled his hips and ground his coarse pubic hairs into my ass. Slow and easy, hard and fast, he plumbed my ass wide and deep. Little by little he speeded up. I clawed the pillows on the bed as Sonny snorted and grunted above me. He pulled me up so that he could play with me while he fucked me. He could tell I was close. "Now, come with me!" he insisted and, after more ass-stretching dick plunges and cock strokes, he howled, "Now!" and my cum soaked the bed sheets while Sonny's cock was thrusting in and out of me. Soon he was jumping and shooting his cum deep into me.

He collapsed on top of me, shoving me into the mattress. Time passed and his breathing leveled off into a smooth, easy rhythm and I assumed he had fallen asleep with his cock still in me.

And then, "Are you all right, kid?" he whispered.

"Uhmm, well, I think so."

"There aren't many who can handle me, you know. Guy or girl."

"Doesn't it ever go soft?"

He lifted himself up. "It doesn't stay like that with just anyone, you know?"

"No, I wouldn't know...."

He started again.

"Oh, god," I moaned.

"Can you take some more?"

"Yeah, go ahead," I said.

Again he pinned me to the mattress with his full weight, and, with me squealing into the pillow, he shot a second load up my ass. Finally he pulled out of me, rolled over and set the alarm clock. "Maybe it'll snow all night," he said, taking me in his strong arms.

I woke up with Sonny sucking my cock.

"Now this is the way I enjoy waking up," Sonny said, moving my legs around his hips.

While he sucked me, he slickered two fingers and worked them up and into my sore ass. He sucked and gnawed my nipples until they stood in little nubs, air-sensitive and tingling, before I reached down to guide him in. And it hurt like hell as Sonny pushed all the way in slow and easy.

Then he rolled us over so that he was on his back.

"Ride me, Phil. You know, somehow you were made for me," he said, sliding his rough hands up and down my torso.

I worked my happy ass up and down his long, fat cock, wiggling my butt over his nuts upon taking him to the root over and over. Up and down, up and down, my ass hummed along his shaft, hovering at the bottom and strangling the head at its end. Sharing lascivious looks only encouraged me to fuck myself on his nine inches of incredibly stiff man-meat.

When Sonny reached and took hold of my cock I was so close to shooting that I took hold of his hands and moved them to his shoulders. "Not yet," I told him.

"But I'm 'bout ready," he said, with the hazy look of want in his eyes.

After a couple of up and down strokes of my ass on his cock, Sonny's back arched and he thrust up and into me with his hips. I pushed down with my ass to bury his spasming dick all the way in me. "Oh, god," I gasped. His cock flexed and warmth arrested my ass in a rapturous outward flow. I raised my asslips to the crown of his cockhead and thrust down his mighty length once, twice before he grabbed hold of my shoulders to pull me into a kiss and thrust his cock into my ass until his climax ebbed. His butt fell to the mattress and he pulled out of me with an air-sucking pop. I reached back and guided him back in me all the way, until my ass rested on his hips.

"Oh, Jesus, Phil!" he gasped. "That was fuckin' unbelievable!"

Sonny sat up and bent down far enough to get the head of my cock in his mouth, then wanked my shaft with one hand and fondled my balls with the other. All it took was a few hand strokes and I was coming. He swallowed and sucked and pumped me for more, swirled his tongue around my sensitive head and probed my dick's eye for all he could get. He didn't miss a drop and sat back licking his lips.

#

That winter, I met Sonny occasionally, always at the garage, always in a rush. He'd give me a blowjob, send me on my way. The fucking never happened again. One day in early spring, I went to the garage late in the afternoon. Our signal was that the "CLOSED" sign was hung on the door if Sonny was receiving visitors. I'd go to the side door, which he would leave open for me. I entered, made my way to the back where his office was. I heard voices and I stopped. I crept along the wall until I was where I could look into the office. There was Sonny, his pants down to his ankles, and spread out on his desk was little blond-haired Billy, the son of another of Dad's drinking buddies from the Dew Drop Inn. Sonny was fucking the hell out of Billy's ass, and the kid was loving every thrust. I couldn't believe it: Billy was only 13!

I tried to move, to run, but a crazy inertia held me there. Finally, after watching them for a few minutes, I turned and suddenly I was outside, and the spring air filled my lungs.

I walked home following the river, nearing flood stage now, but everything was quiet on the water. My body weighed nothing; it wanted sleep. Memories came up in my head. Now and again I heard Sonny's voice the way it was that night and that morning he fucked me. "I'll teach you everything," he'd said. My hands trembled, my legs were weak. When I got home, I sat down on the lawn in the damp grass. There weren't any lights on in the house. I had no idea what time it was.

SLAVE TRADE
Blaise Bulot

"...It was magnificent, his cock."

Grandpa was a successful cotton factor, so successful he bought a big house on Royal Street. But my pa wasn't so successful because he couldn't stay away from the racetrack. So all we had left was one hand we didn't ever call them slaves Zoe. Poor old Zoe; she was our cook, and she was deaf and getting on in years. She tried to be everything besides cooking, she was the maid, the butler, the laundress. The quarters behind the house were mostly empty.

In those days, it seemed as if I was always horny as hell; it was so bad, I thought there must be something wrong with me. I don't know whether it was the phase of the moon or what, but I'd get so horny I just didn't know what to do. I'd beat my meat. I'd wiggle my fingers up my asshole. I'd squeeze my nipples 'til they hurt. It didn't do any good. It just made me hornier.

One day I thought it might take my mind away from between my legs if I went out for a walk. So I put my clothes back on and went out the door.

I was passing the St. Louis Hotel when I saw a big poster declaring: AUCTION.

I scurried back home, got the money I'd been saving from underneath my carpet, went back, and went in. The big domed room was full of people, voices, and cigar smoke. Nearly all of them were men, but a couple of them were ladies who I bet were not so lady-like. The merchandise was assembled up front behind the selling block. A motley crew men and boys, women and girls. Some were all spruced up in fresh clothes in the hope of bringing a higher price. But some were in rags. And there was one big brute who was naked. All he had on was a collar, shackles and a chain. He had sores on his wrists and ankles and his back was criss-crossed with scars. One ear and two fingers had been cut off. He must have been mean or a repeat run away.

There was a lot of interest in the mustee. He was fine-looking, but I knew mustees are bad news. They can be mean; and it's easy for them to runaway because they can pass for white. There was also a lot of interest in a beautiful octoroon girl. She had both looks and carriage. Many present must have wondered how she came to such a sad predicament.

Louisiana law, the Code Noir, strictly prohibited sex between master and slave, but of course it was very common and everybody looked the other way. Some hands, male and female, had special features that made them particularly desirable as sexual objects. They were called "fancies." There was once, I remember, a fancy with a fourteen-inch cock! Everybody went to that inspection and auction, and for what he brought you could have bought a small farm.

But this time there was a rare fancy, or more accurately, a pair. Handsome, bright twin boys. I left before they were sold, but I'm told a bent, old guy with white whiskers bought them for a bundle. I wondered what he planned to do with them.

There was little interest in the youth who caught my eye. He was, I would guess, barely eighteen then. He wore no shirt, no shoes, and wore only a pair of dingy trousers. There were, I was careful to note, no tell-tale marks on his wrists, ankles, or back. He stood upright, proud, staring straight ahead, avoiding eye contact with anybody.

Nobody wants to buy a pig in a poke, so the inspection can be very thorough. Just as with horses, you always want to look at their teeth. But, if the potential buyer wants them for breeding, he'll shuck the pants down and heft the weight of their balls in his hand. If he wants them for field hands, he'll feel their muscles, all of them, and have them bend over and spread their cheeks so he can inspect them for hemorrhoids.

Acting as casually as I could, I made my way up to his side.

Looking down at his feet, he murmured, "Please, suh, don' shuck me down."

But I did; I did it myself. I unbuttoned his pants and pushed them down 'til they fell down around his ankles.

I blinked. Fine, very fine indeed! His cock even stiffened when I touched it. And his ass was perfect. My cock stiffened. I pressed it against him, slipped my fingers between those perfect buns, and whispered, "If I buy ya, will you play with me?"

"Oh yes, suh," he answered softly as a single tear stole down his cheek.

I wasn't sure whether it was a tear of sadness or happiness that such as me would desire him. Whatever, I was in lust with him now.

The bidding began. At about the end of the first half hour he was put up for sale. Prices were weak. The owner of one of the biggest plantations up the River Road, like Pa, couldn't stay away from the racetrack. (I won't mention the gentleman's name nor that of his plantation.) The house and the lands were auctioned off, and the hands, more than a thousand of them, were auctioned off separately. This sudden infusion into the market had weakened prices. So I could afford the slave. I was the high bidder. And he was a bargain.

Pa was at the track, Ma was taking her afternoon nap, and Zoe was snoozing in her kitchen. The coast was clear. I hurriedly smuggled my new acquisition into the bathroom.

I shucked him down again, then stripped myself. Now I could examine the cock more closely. To me, he had a perfect cock. Oh, it was huge, all right, but not too big. The cock was in perfect proportion with the rest of him.

My cock was almost as long as his, but not as thick, and it stood out straight at him, stiff as a stick. He looked surprised. He'd probably heard a lot of snickering in the quarters that white boys had itsy-bitsy pink worms. His cock began to harden now.

I started to soap him up. He had looked dusty, ashy, but when wet the wonderful dark chocolate color of his skin was brought out. He had flawless skin. He had beautiful large eyes, long curling lashes, a nose neither too broad nor too long, and wonderful little ears like precious sea shells. Close, kinky hair covered his head and beneath his belly, but there was not a single hair on the rest of his body. Flawless.

I soaped him up, then had him soap me. Our balls and cracks got a lot of suds. And we rubbed our slippery bodies together, up and down, side to side. Our hands explored everything. Then I kissed him. I knew it was wrong, but I did it anyway. I kissed his eyelids, those charming little ears, the tip of his nose. I kissed his throat and sucked his nipples. The taste of the soap didn't slow me down. I sank down, drawing my tongue down his smooth wet chest, down his belly, into his navel. I nibbled at the crisp pubic hair.

Finally I put his cock in my mouth. It was very warm, and now fully hard. It was magnificent, his cock.

After I sucked on it for several minutes, delighting in the sheer beauty and size of it, he lifted me up and turned me around. He soaped up my ass again. He seemed to instinctively know what was demanded of my slave. I could feel his fingers between my buns, exploring my crotch. They found what they were searching for and slipped in. When they withdrew, something much larger, much hotter, pushed into me.

"Oh no! I bellowed. But he kept on. I let out a whoop. I didn't know whether I was hurt, surprised, delighted or all three. Now I had taken fingers up my ass, candles, bananas, and the broom handle, but never something like that. Wow, I had never felt anything so good in my life. Before or since. The first time, they say, is always the best.

I was jerking on my prick and he was pushing back and forth into me, deeper and deeper. The pace quickened. He began to pant and moan. I felt the juices begin to move inside me. I little cry burst out of him and he bit, gently, the back of my neck, just I squirted out a big load into the bath water.

We fell back into the tub, into the cooling water, and into each other's arms.

Now, after all these years, when I think of him, I picture his nude body in my mind, and he was just so beautiful I want to cry. I lost track of the number of times I had his incredible cock up my ass, but it was at least once a day for nearly two years. I have never been fucked as well. But, of course, it was all over when the Yankees came. They kicked in the front door, pushed into Zoe's kitchen, and knocked her down onto the floor. My slave tried to throw a punch in her defense and they shot him. Shot him, right there in the kitchen. That was sure freeing the slaves!

LOOSE LOADS
Corbin Chezner

Proceedings had just begun when Dora, the department dispatcher, summoned Clint, the Sheriff, from the County Commissioners' meeting. As Clint stepped into the courthouse hallway, Dora whispered breathlessly, "Peggy Brownlee called from the lake. Some drunk has been exposing himself in the park. She's demanding an officer pronto."

Clint grimaced. "Can't one of the deputies handle it? Don't tell me they're all down with the goddamn blue flu."

"Relax, Clint. It's nothing like that. They're out on call."

"All three of them? I got no time for damn games."

Dora sighed. "All hell broke loose just after you left. Shaun's at Cobb Ranch checking out a cattle theft. Dave's in Hulbert trying to break up a fight in a bar. Don's at Sam's Diner on Highway 51. Some jerk thought he could eat without paying."

Damn. First, Dave, his top deputy, had announced that morning he would resign to take a job with the Hominy Police Department. Now, just when Clint was on the verge of making some headway on the department' s money problems, it looked like he'd have to chuck the whole thing again. With all the deputies busy, he'd have to drive 25 miles one way to investigate Peggy Brownlee's complaint. By the time he got back to the county seat town of Osage, the meeting would be adjourned. He couldn't count on the commissioners to discuss the matter themselves. With elections several months away, a budget hike was the last thing the politicians wanted to consider. Clint had hoped to convince them of the department's desperate straits, but now it looked like his plans were thwarted. It wasn't the first time this had happened.

Clint followed Dora down the hallway to the Sheriff's office. Stepping inside, he retrieved a leather holster and pistol from a drawer

129

in his desk. Hurriedly strapping the holster around his narrow hips, he plucked a clipboard off his desk and proceeded toward the exit, stopping long enough to fetch his cowboy hat off the coat rack. He fixed his intense brown eyes on the dispatcher. "Tell the commissioners I was called out, will you?"

Dora glowered at him. "What about the presentation?"

"It'll have to wait."

"Again? Why don't you ignore that old bag?" Dora fumed. "This is the third time the bitch has called this month. You know darn well it won't amount to nothin'."

It was no surprise that Dora, who always spoke her mind, was especially agitated today. The entire department was counting on the young Sheriff to convince the commissioners to increase the department' s budget. None of them, after all, not even Clint himself, had had a raise in more than two years. Even worse, last year, Toyota had built a new assembly plant, increasing the county's population by a couple thousand. Clint needed at least two more deputies to patrol new housing developments that had been built, but he lacked the funds to hire the additional personnel. As a result of the impasse with the commissioners, the department was about to lose one deputy, and if the budget crunch lasted much longer, others would soon follow. Who could blame them?

"State law don't equivocate," Clint finally managed. "It says when a complaint is made, we got to check it out. You've been around long enough to know that, Dora."

"Maybe so, but state law don't state we have to work for damn slave wages, neither."

"I know you need a raise," Clint conceded. "We all do."

"Send me to the lake, then. I can handle that old witch. That way, you can still make the meeting."

Clint was tempted, but he knew better. Although undoubtedly Dora could handle the problem, she wasn't officially deputized. If the sassy dispatcher answered the call and someone challenged her authority, the entire department could face a lawsuit. That was the last thing any of them needed.

On the way to the lake, Clint felt the world closing in on him. Just outside Osage town limits, he noticed his heart thumping against his chest. Now, as he neared Polecat Creek, a sharp pain surfaced at the back of his neck. The handsome young lawman was wound tight too tight, at the moment, to handle Peggy Brownlee's complaint in the professional manner that had become his trademark.

He had a means of solving that dilemma, but did he dare now? Years ago, when plagued by the stress of college exams, Clint discovered the therapeutic value of a quick, discreet jack-off. It calmed him, after all, and cleared his mind. Clint peered below the steering wheel at the bulging mound at his crotch. Suddenly, his cock pulsed as he imagined his long, torpedo-shaped tool stretched outside the trouser leg of his khaki uniform. His heart thumped again, more noticeably this time. Clint knew damn well (others had confirmed it after all) that he had one hell of a good-looking piece of meat. He had a cock the public expected of a cop a cock that, if he were so inclined, could make him a damn fine living in porn films. But, alas, because Clint was in law enforcement, a video career was out of the question.

Despite the report from Walnut Park, a small resort at Lake Keystone, the call of Clint's insistent cock now seemed the more urgent. He reminded himself of the benefits of what he was about to do. Just beyond the crest of a hill on a lonely stretch of County Road 112, the Sheriff slowed the patrol car and turned off the highway into a grove of cedar trees. Clint was familiar with the cluster of trees, which was dense enough to obscure a car from highway traffic. Because of the budget crunch, he and his deputies used the hideaway as a speed trap to secure additional funds for the county treasury. Pulling the car to a stop, Clint turned off the engine and closed his eyes for a moment, pressing his throbbing skull against the cool vinyl headrest.

Rolling down the window, he took in a deep breath. The pleasant scent of cedar and wild honeysuckle wafted to him and he smiled to himself. Buoyed by the clean country air, he felt desire pulse through his hefty, man-size balls as he imagined himself stretched naked across the hood of the patrol car, his legs rolled over his face, his own cock thrust deep into his hungry mouth.

At age 33, Clint could suck his own dick well, the head of it, anyhow a feat he knew damn well few men his age could accomplish. Although his physique was already lean and mean, Clint figured with the loss of a few more pounds he could take even more of his cock in his mouth. Yet, to his own surprise, he was reluctant to gratify himself regularly, fearing he might become a recluse. He enjoyed solitude at times, but not as a regular diet. When he was so inclined, rare though it might be, he handled social occasions amazingly well.

Opening his eyes, finally, the lawman unzipped the crotch of his khaki uniform and reached for his cock. Because his fleshy, throbbing tool was already rock hard, Clint had some difficulty retrieving it from his briefs, but finally he manhandled it into the open air, where it belonged. Clint's heart pounded again and his balls tingled as he surveyed his beautiful, tumescent cock. The network of cumbrous veins that fed his bloated prick reminded him of pumped forearms on a bodybuilder

When Greg Brumfield awoke and spotted a patrol car less than 100 feet from his sleeping bag, his heart plummeted. In hitchhiking through some 20 states the last year, he'd learned that law enforcement takes a dim view of transients, particularly in areas where "red-neck Bible beaters" predominate. When he sacked out for the night in this field behind a grove of trees just off the highway, he had thought he'd be safe from the prying eyes of the law. But it wasn't to be, and now he accepted the probability that his home for the immediate future would be some Oklahoma county jail. In the next few moments, however, it slowly dawned on the young transient that this cop was preoccupied by something inside the patrol car. Perhaps he was writing a report. But why had he stopped behind the grove of trees?

An overpowering curiosity compelled the young transient to investigate. Gingerly, he extracted himself from the sleeping bag and crawled closer to the patrol car, careful not to snap any twigs along the way. Just beyond the passenger side rear door, he rose to knees and peered inside the patrol car. What? It couldn't be. He shook his head in disbelief But it was true. He'd caught the cop red-handed jacking off in his patrol car!

He, Greg, was observing it first-hand. It would be a story to tell his grandkids someday, except that he doubted he'd ever have any since he didn't give a flip about pussy. Dick, on the other hand, he couldn't get enough of. He was an outdoor plumbing guy.

He caught only the briefest glimpse of the tip of the cop's cock as he jacked, but it had to be a monster tool, Greg thought, the kind of tool a cop ought to have. He got so hot watching the cop, he pulled his own tool out of his pants and started jacking off.

Mesmerized by the beauty of his own cock, Clint stroked the robust pole, slowly at first, then faster, again and again, harder and harder. Succumbing, at last, to an irresistible wave of pleasure, Clint closed his eyes and allowed a surge of gratification to sweep over him; finally, his big tool exploded, wildly splattering its sizzling load against the floorboard of the patrol car.

An instant later, Greg braced himself and silently showered the underbrush surrounding him with his own jism.

As Clint shook the remaining musty-smelling cum off the end of his dick, Dora, the department dispatcher, suddenly broke in on the radio, startling the black-haired lawman. "Headquarters to 122, 122 this is headquarters. Are you there?"

Reaching toward the dashboard, Clint, now calmed by his just-completed orgasm, plucked the speaker off its clip.

"This is 122. Over."

"We got an 1132 on Highway 51, 3 miles north of Hominy," she reported breathlessly.

In the Sheriff's department lingo, "1132" indicated a non-fatal, multiple-vehicle highway accident, generally a head-on or sideswipe. "Anybody hurt?"

"Negative. An 18-wheeler jackknifed after careening to avoid a panel truck."

"Better call an ambulance, just in case."

"10-4."

"Wrecker?"

"On its way."

Peggy Brownlee would have to wait for deputy Shaun, who was closest to the lake, to investigate the alleged exhibitionist. Clint turned the patrol car around and doubled back 10 miles to the accident. By the time he arrived at the scene, the wrecker was already there. He didn't recognize the two accident victims, who stood on the side of the highway watching forlornly as Jerry Davis, the wrecker driver, hooked on to the wrecked 18-wheeler. Parking the car a safe distance from the accident, Clint posted portable warning signs on both sides of the highway to notify approaching motorists of the accident. Afterward, he stopped to talk to Jerry, a familiar face at highway accidents in the county.

"Who you figure was at fault?" Clint asked, hoping the beefy-armed redhead could fill him in before he talked to the victims. After years of working together, Clint had gained a healthy respect for the wrecker driver's instincts. Invariably, they were on target.

"Depends on who you talk to," the redhead answered, yanking hard on one of the cables to secure it.

"What do you think?"

Jerry looked up at him. "From the way that 18-wheeler is sprawled across the highway, I'd wager he was exceeding the speed limit."

"My thoughts, too. What about that damn panel truck? Any problems there?" Emblazoned with "Snap-On Tools" on its exterior, the panel truck was parked beside the highway, about 100 feet from the wrecked 18-wheeler.

"Hard to tell. Don't doubt he should have looked before pulling out, even if the truck was speeding." He glanced at the Sheriff again. "Both of the dudes got an attitude, I can tell you that."

Clint bristled. The jack-off had helped matters, but, nevertheless, he was in no mood for lip today. From Dora, it was to be expected. Otherwise, it was something he could do without.

Before Clint and Jerry could finish the conversation, scuffling broke out from the direction of the two strangers, and when Clint looked up they stood facing each other, their fists and faces drawn tight by anger.

"You son-of-a-bitch, you better learn to look before you pull out on the goddamn highway," one of them shouted.

"Wouldn't have done no good no matter how many times I looked," the other man shot back. "You had the mother-fuckin' pedal to the metal in that damn rig. This two-lane road ain't built for a truck to go that damn fast "

"Hold it, men," Clint broke in as he raced toward the strangers. "You got differences to settle, you tell it to the law."

Before Clint could get to them, the men tore into each other.

"I said hold it," Clint repeated, squeezing between the two men. "This is the law here!"

Red-faced and grimacing, the adversaries reluctantly broke apart then, but Clint stayed between them. "I need to see your drivers' licenses both of you," Clint ordered.

Clint interviewed both drivers and called in their vitals while Jerry pulled the cab and then the trailer of the 18-wheeler off the highway. The standard procedure in such cases was to haul the cab back to town and send another tow truck back for the trailer.

Both men checked out okay but Clint chewed them out anyway. Once he'd reamed their asses good, Clint sent the panel truck driver on his way and offered Dan Gibbons, the 18-wheeler driver, a ride back to town until he could decide what he would do. In a rare moment of compassion, Clint decided not to cite either driver, although he sure as fuck could have.

On the way back to town, the trucker's ire seemed to subside, his mood elevated no doubt at having escaped a citation. "Appreciate the break," he finally admitted, absently stroking his thick blonde beard. The trucker's green eyes, damn near the color of jade, met the Sheriff's then. "To tell you the truth, it wouldn't be my first, and I can't afford to lose my license. It's my meal ticket."

Clint hated to admit it to himself, but he knew damn well why he'd let the trucker off the hook. Every time he looked at Dan Gibbons, his cock swelled. The trucker was his type, damnit, although the dark blond hair that brushed against the top of the trucker's shoulders was a tad longer than what he was used to on another man.

Actually, it was the stranger's manly physique rather than his hair that attracted Clint. When he moved, the trucker's broad shoulders and thick, muscular arms strained against the green T-shirt he wore. Gazing at the trucker from behind during the license check, Clint had discovered with a start that the stranger's buns were melon-shaped an extraordinary rear for a man who, he'd learned, was five years his senior. Too good to be true. Clint had learned long ago, to his chagrin, that men of such caliber were rarely available, save for fleeting quickies, which satisfied his powerful urges only momentarily. If not a lover, Clint needed a regular sex partner, at least. It took Clint two nasty divorces to realize, once and for all, that women were not his cup of tea.

"It's a damn tough life, being on the road so much," Clint finally managed, bringing his thoughts back to the present. Perhaps if he opened up himself, the stranger might reciprocate.

"Yeah?" The stranger was stroking his beard again. "Guess you guys put on a lot of miles yourself, patrolling the way you do."

"Not just that," Clint said, adjusting the knob on his radio to make sure it was still turned on. "I was a long hauler myself, once. Before I joined the department."

"No shit? A trucker?"

Clint nodded, and in the moment the men locked gazes, Clint sensed a mutual attraction. Or was it just wishful thinking on his part? One couldn't be too careful, especially in his position. "I guess you know the lodging's limited in Osage," Clint went on "We got only two motels, on opposite ends of town. Couldn't guarantee either would meet your standards, though."

"I'm sure they're fine enough." The trucker squirmed in his seat, as if the subject of lodging had made him uncomfortable. "But to tell you the truth, it'd be just as well with me if you take me on in to the lockup."

"You want me to take you to jail?" He gazed intently at the trucker, his brow furrowed. "I'd think twice about that, if I were you."

"I got no choice, man." He explained that his estranged wife, who'd recently left him, had maxed out his credit cards and damn well took about everything else he had of value.

"Join the club."

"Your old lady cleaned you out, too?"

Without asking Gibbons' permission, Clint turned off the highway onto the winding gravel road that led to his mobile home. "Damn near," Clint admitted dourly. "Just me and my dogs out here now, and that's the way I like it. Ten acres surrounded by nothin' but brush. If I'm inclined, I can walk around butt naked."

Picturing Clint naked sent blood surging into Dan's cock, locking in his hard-on like a charley horse.

Hungrily eyeing the growing mound in the trucker's pants, Clint met the stranger's gaze again. "I'll take some of that," he said, nodding toward Gibbons' crotch.

After less than one beer each the men found themselves naked and facing each other in bed. Surveying the lawman's broad upper torso and the carpet of black hair that fanned across his muscular chest, Gibbons sighed with pleasure. "Damn, if I knew the law looked like this, I'd be in trouble more often."

Clint grinned, returning the other man's admiring glance. "You found the place where you can loosen that damn load of yours anytime, Buddy."

That night they both loosened their loads more times than either could remember, more ways than either could forget.

Although he hadn't set the alarm, Clint awoke at the usual time the next morning at six.

Still buoyed by the previous evening's swirl of pleasure, the lawman drifted in and out of sleep, content that Gibbons' swollen dick was lodged in his butt and that it was Sunday, his day off.

Determined to impress the other man, Dan held Clint's hot butt captive with his friction-charged cock. For four hours, Dan's pole remained planted in the lawman's butt; there it would remain, he vowed to himself, until Clint begged him to remove it. Each time his dick threatened to grow soft, the trucker would resume pumping, just long enough to revive his hard-on.

The lawman, swirling high from being fucked for hours, gripped the edge of the bed, determined to keep things as they were until Dan decided he'd had enough butt.

Around noon the men dressed and drove to Sam's Diner on Highway 51, ten miles from Osage. Enveloped in a sex flush, the men sat at a corner table and ate ravenously, oblivious to the other customers.

But another customer zeroed in on the men's charged sexuality. Two tables away, Kyle Stemmon leaned toward Jason Edwards, his buddy and co-worker from the Osage Rock Quarry. "Those two dudes are fuckin'," he said, nodding toward the Sheriff and his trucker friend.

"Who you talkin' about?"

"Over there." He nodded toward the Sheriff again.

Edwards gasped. "That's the damn Sheriff!"

"I'm tellin' you."

"You're full of shit, Stemmons."

That afternoon, Clint and Dan found themselves in bed again. This time, Clint stayed awake while Dan dozed. To prove to Gibbons that he was versatile, Clint kept his throbbing, man-size cock planted firmly in the trucker's willing butthole.

At times, Clint almost dozed off himself, but each time he willed himself awake. This was not the time to disappoint, after all. Instead, he fucked the trucker's taut butt tirelessly, his eyes feasting on the beautiful, bronzed symmetry of the other man's muscular back and the mane of light brown hair that brushed against his broad shoulders.

The moment Clint reached up to run his fingers through the trucker's hair, he suddenly awoke and groaned with pleasure.

Pulsing a fresh supply of blood into his electrified cock, Clint probed Dan's stiff nipple, and the fine blonde hair that surrounded it, between his fingers. "You had enough?" he asked, pinching the hard nipple.

Gasping, the trucker managed, "No, man. Don't stop."

Clint pumped Dan's searing butt a moment longer, then hesitated. He grasped the trucker's narrow waist. "You sure?"

Whimpering, Dan finally managed. "Please...."

The next night, both men's butts were sore, so they concentrated on coming other ways.

Later, to replenish the protein they'd lost, the men returned to Sam's and each ordered a Kansas City steak.

Surveying the dining room through the order window, Greg Brumfield, the hitchhiker who'd recently hired on at Sam's as a fry cook, elbowed Michael Sears, his coworker. "That's him," Greg said, nodding toward the lawman.

"Oh, him," Michael said. "He's the reason you decided to stay here?"

"Don't you think he's good lookin'?"

"Who wouldn't?" Michael agreed. "He won't do it more than once, though."

"You sure?"

Michael nodded knowingly.

"Well, we'll see," Greg said determinedly.

Because Dan was an independent, there was no relief truck for him to use while his was being repaired. To Clint's delight, the trucker agreed to stay at the trailer until his rig was repaired. It took ten days. In the meantime, after a night of drinking longnecks at the Bottoms Up Club a few miles from Sam's Diner, Kyle Stemmons finally got into Jason Edward's pants by convincing him, once and for all, that sex between men was rampant in the county.

To Be Continued...

DONKEY DONG
Jason Carpenter

Jukebox music, amplified enough to produce deafness in cats at fifty feet, vibrated the dance floor with the bass beat of some recent Prince release, and the neon pulse of a dozen beer signs cast odd shadows in the dim room.

I sipped a weak scotch and scouted the pitiful assortment of men available. None appealed to me on a purely physical level, though a couple might suffice for a quick fuck.

The My-T-Tight lounge was deathly slow this Friday evening. Maybe thirty revelers occupied the bar or the small tables spaced around the dance floor. Three couples danced, pot-bellies bouncing to the harsh, staccato beat.

Maybe I was too old for this shit sitting in a decrepit club, listening to music I didn't like, surrounded by mindless, boring men. Christ, it would be nice to meet someone who could carry on a conversation about something besides drugs, unlimited sex partners and coming out of the old closet. And who didn't say, "you know?" after every sentence.

I'm at my peak at thirty-two and my standards are high. I work out to keep my gut and ass from drooping, have a full head of sandy-colored hair and, if I do say so myself, a pair of pale blue eyes to rival Mel Gibson's. I'm a successful designer of men's and women's clothing for a small, but elegant, shop in Dallas, drive a late model BMW and own a charming one-bedroom condo fifteen minutes from Dallas.

I demand the best in men perhaps the reason for my often lonely nights.

Then, as if God had heard my complaints, there he was. What a specimen. Through the blue cigarette haze I saw him enter and stand just inside the door. He was tall over six foot with broad shoulders, narrow hips and a crop of raven black, curly hair on his head. More hair poked from the front of the tan, leather vest he wore, with nothing underneath. Below the vest he wore the tightest blue jean shorts I'd ever seen. They were so short the cheeks of his positively luscious ass showed with each step he took. His bare legs were slim, but tight and heavily muscled.

As he passed my table he threw me a to-die-for smile, showing white, even teeth, full lips, a neatly trimmed mustache and, Lord help me, deep, pretty dimples in his chin and cheeks! My cock stood at attention beneath the table. Every head in the place was turned his way. He took a stool at the bar. His ass was a perfectly shaped inverted heart.

I made my way over quickly, taking the stool to his right; holding my empty glass aloft to catch the bartender's eye.

He approached and asked, "Another scotch?"

I nodded. "And whatever this young man is having."

The barman looked at the Adonis and raised his eyebrows questioningly.

Adonis shook his head, casting a sidelong glance from his liquid brown, Bambi-like eyes in my direction. "Old Thumper" became even more erect.

"I'm with someone ... and he has a bad temper," Adonis whispered.

Just then, a dark, hard-looking man took the seat on the left of Adonis. He grabbed the boy's shoulder, turning him roughly.

"Can't you fuckin' walk in'ta a joint without tryin' to pick up some geek?" the man asked Adonis, punching him hard in the chest.

"He wasn't trying to pick me up," I said, staring into the man's small, black eyes. "I was trying to pick him up. And if you touch him again I'm going to have to hurt you," I finished, taking a sip of my drink.

Adonis winced; he was shaking visibly.

The man got up and came to my stool. I revolved to face him.

"Get off your pansy ass and let's get it on, you little prick," he growled.

I set my drink down on the bar and looked the man over.

"Before I oblige you, asshole, you should know a couple of things. One, I'm an ex-Marine, kid, and highly trained in the martial arts. Two, I'd rather fuck than fight but I'd rather fight than be fucked with," I said, wiping my hands on my jeans.

"Three, I'm gonna use a hai kwan testicle lock and march you tippy-toeing to the door." I started rolling up my shirt sleeves.

"Four, I'm going to give you a keezu po punch at the base of your thick skull which can damage your spine. Five, I'll then turn you around and pop you with a chi itsu elbow strike to your nose, mashing it into your face." I rolled up my other sleeve. "Then six, a wah dong ahhh round kick to your rib cage will break some ribs and, if I do it just right, will rupture your heart," I concluded, standing, rolling my shoulders and bouncing lightly on the balls of my feet, my eyes fastened on his.

His hands clenched into fists. His eyes burned with anger, and his whole body shook with the effort it took for him to take a step back. Then another. Then another. Until he finally turned on his heel and walked rapidly toward the exit.

Adonis grasped my biceps. "Thanks, man. I couldn't get rid of him. The dude is crazy! Violent! And I'm not a fighter, like you," he said admiringly.

"Fighter, shit. I don't know martial arts from Marshal Dillon. And the only uniform I've ever worn was in the Boy Scouts when I was twelve," I laughed, stroking the inside of his warm, bare thigh.

He made a large "O" with his mouth. "Remind me never to play poker with you!"

"At least not the kind you play with cards," I said, slyly, extending my right hand. "I'm Wade. Wade Brents."

He shook my hand. "Cary Jenkins," he responded. "Good to meet you, Wade."

He seemed intelligent enough but, even had he been brain-dead, I couldn't have passed up a shot at him. "How long have you known him," I asked, motioning toward the door where Cary's "friend" had just exited.

Cary ran his long fingers through his curly hair. "Only a week. I met him in Las Vegas. I was dancing in one of the casino reviews but it closed down. Tony had hit on me the night before and again after the final show. I didn't find him attractive, but he said he could get me a dancing gig in Dallas.

"I didn't have many options, so here I am. We've been here four days and he hasn't introduced me to anyone in the entertainment business, like he promised. I'm glad I didn't make love with him, 'cause he is an asshole."

"Huh. Well, I don't know many people in the arts, but I'll see if I can help. By the way ... you're gorgeous, and I've got a place you can stay and a major boner. Will you come home with me, Cary?"

He touched my crotch, letting his fingers trail ever-so-lightly down the length of my rigid hard-on. I shivered.

"Hmmm. We need to see if we can make that nasty swelling go down," he teased, leaning to kiss me tentatively. His mustache tickled pleasantly.

"Let's go," I urged, tossing a ten spot on the bar.

A light rain was falling as we stepped outside, doing little to alleviate the July heat.

"You have a car here?"

"Nope. Everything I own is at the motel where I was staying with Tony," Cary breathed pensively.

I unlocked the passenger door of my BMW and held it open for him, then walked around and let myself in the driver's side. Once inside I cranked up the air-conditioning and put some Phil Collins on the CD player. The rain made a pleasant patter on the roof and windows.

I had driven about five miles when Cary laid down and put his head in my lap, facing me. He leisurely unzipped my fly, reached in, and released my bone-hard cockmeat. With agonizing slowness he circled the tip of my dick with his lips and tongue, dipping his head, taking my love-muscle deep into his throat. Up and down. Up and down, over and over, until I couldn't stand it any longer.

"Oh, Cary!" I warned, my back arching and my balls tightening in orgasm.

At the last second, he pulled away and covered my erection with a handkerchief he pulled from his pocket. He caught my steamy eruption of dick-juice in the linen, continuing to masturbate me, my own hot cum producing a slippery tunnel in the handkerchief. I plunged into it until I was drained.

Cary wiped me dry, kissed the head of my dwindling pole, tucked it into my pants with a pat and zipped me up. Then he scooted next to me in the seat, cuddling and kissing my neck the whole way home.

Once there, we noticed the rain had ended, leaving a freshness in the evening air. I led Cary up the single flight of stairs and ushered him into my home.

"Nice," he said approvingly, taking in the living room with the mauve carpeting, powder-blue sofa, love seat and recliner.

Lamps and paintings all incorporated shades of mauve, blue and cream.

"Make yourself at home while I catch a quick shower," I said, leaving him alone.

When I returned, showered, shaved and wearing a thick bath towel around my hips, Cary was looking out the window. It covered nearly the whole southern wall and offered a great view of the millions of lights necessary to illuminate Six Flags Over Texas.

I walked up behind Cary and put my arms around his firm, bare waist. He snuggled against me as I brushed his neck with my lips, then explored his ear with my tongue. He turned to me.

We locked in a tongue-thrusting kiss that seemed endless as we rubbed against each other. I felt his penis rise beneath his shorts and fisted him through the denim. He grew even harder and larger. He whimpered a kitten-like sound in my ear and I eased myself to the thick carpet, drawing him down with me.

My towel fell off, revealing my nakedness.

Tenderly, I removed Cary's vest and tugged his shorts down as he arched his buttocks off the floor. He lay there naked, a beautifully crafted man. His cock pointed toward his chin, the tip of it reaching up his flat stomach, past his navel. His pulsing dick was as thick as my wrist and I'm not a small man!

Regardless, I filled my mouth with him, gasping at the size and rigidity of his member, knowing I wanted him inside me, and eager to experience his thick, blue-veined probe.

I sucked and licked him until I felt he was close to ejaculation, amazed at his remarkable tool, his blood-engorged

man-candy. I lifted my head long enough to reach out for the circular ottoman I kept in front of the recliner. I turned it on its side, like a wide, soft donut, and draped my stomach over it, my knees spread to either side, offering my ass as sacrifice to Cary's throbbing god.

He moved up behind me, on his knees, and gently rubbed his cock against my anus, his first drops of pre-cum lubricating me.

I rolled forward over the ottoman slightly, then back to meet him. Cary stuffed that magnificent trophy inch by glorious inch up my ass-hole, stretching it to its limits. He palmed my buttocks apart, pushing deeper, until I held all of him in me. I gasped, marveling at the burning, but heavenly, sensation in and around my distended ass-ring.

He probed faster, ever deeper, rocking me now, back and forth over the ottoman. His arms snaked beneath me, his hands cupping my shoulders at the collarbones and tugging me back against him, driving more deeply up my butt-hole. My prostate, prodded and pressed, contracted within me, and I shot an involuntary stream of cum onto the ottoman just as Cary grunted and spewed his pent-up juices up my ass, bathing my guts with his hot, squirting cum.

My eyes blurred. Little black dots swam before me and I nearly passed out. The pungent, sweet-sour scent of fresh dick-juice filled my nostrils.

Cary eased his monster out of me, his cock-veins, as thick as pencils, still pumping. My anus sucked air when he pulled out. It felt like I had been fucked with a baseball bat. My god, it was simply fantastic!

"Good?" Cary breathed, pulling me to him, joining his lips to mine in a deep kiss while he fisted my cum-slick rod in his big hand.

"The best," I told him. "That's the most meat I've ever had up me. You're hung like a fuckin' donkey."

He stood and took a bow. "Where's the bathroom, Wade?"

I pointed toward the hall. "To the right. First door. Let me clean up here and I'll join you okay?"

He nodded and walked toward the hall. I cleaned my blast of cum off the ottoman with a paper towel from the kitchen and joined

Cary in the shower. We talked while the warm water cascaded over our bodies, taking turns soaping and scrubbing each other, kissing and fondling in a leisurely, gettin'-acquainted way, sated for the moment.

We slept nestled together, his naked front to my naked ass.

He held my semi-erect pole throughout the night.

I dreamed of big brown eyes and dimples.

I awoke to see Cary standing by the bed wearing a pair of my bikini briefs. The crotch was stretched to bursting by his incredible mound of meat and balls. He smiled, did a few dance steps while removing the briefs, and joined me on the bed. He went straight for my cock, sucking me to hardness, fingering my very tender asshole then slowly trailing his tongue from the crown of my cock, down the sensitive underside to my nuts.

With one gobble, he filled his mouth with my ball-sac, rolling my cods from side to side with his tongue. I humped air, my throbbing dick begging for some warm orifice to surround it.

"Want some?" Cary asked innocently, letting my balls pop out of his mouth.

"Shit, yes. I want to fuck you ... right now."

Cary turned around and knelt before me on elbows and knees, his all-seeing brown eye beckoning me to new delights. His perfect ass-cheeks, firm and white, tantalized me and his huge sac of balls and bobbing dick hung heavily between his hairy thighs. Looking over his shoulder at me he wiggled his butt teasingly.

I put my palms on his round ass and tongued his crack, wetting him, pushing my tongue deep up his ass, tasting his delicious insides. His musky scent almost made me blow my load right then, but I held back.

The swollen, purple crown of my cock eased into his ass and my cock was immediately clasped in his hot, deep cavern. He clenched muscles those hard, lovely dancer's muscles in his ass and my fuck-stick was at once pulled, squeezed and milked into a raging, violent orgasm.

I pumped and thrust, slapping my groin against his ass in a rhythmic beat, fucking into him until my cum was depleted and I had bathed his insides with my dick-honey. I rolled out of him, breathing shakily as I lay exhausted on my back.

He attacked me! Tickling my ribs, the soles of my feet ...everywhere he touched me was a sensitive mass of skin. I squirmed all over the bed, squealing with combined pain and pleasure.

"I've been waiting all night for that," Cary breathed. "Just thinking about having you in me, you fucking me. God, you're so good-looking and hot!

He hugged me, then slapped my ass. "Now, clean up while I finish breakfast."

"You cooked?"

"Yep. Love to cook. Nothing fancy, just old-fashioned crap like Mom used to make," he said, pulling on his briefs and padding barefoot toward the kitchen. His tightly muscled buttocks and thighs clenched and unclenched as he walked.

After cleaning up, I, too, dressed in bikini briefs and went to the kitchen, following delicious smells. Breakfast consisted of scrambled eggs, bacon, hash-brown potatoes, toast and strong coffee.

I ate everything Cary served me. The hell with my cholesterol and triglycerides! When I cooked everything tasted the same like shit. I was delighted with Cary's meal and with Cary, of course.

Having fallen victim to Cary's playful mood earlier, I decided to strike back. He was at the sink, his back turned to me. I took two slices of bread from the loaf on the table and wriggled out of my briefs. I crept up behind Cary.

"Hey, little boy, how about a Manwich?" I asked in a raspy voice.

Startled, he jumped and swung around. I had my cock sandwiched between the slices of bread, the tip sticking out at Cary like an albino frankfurter. He laughed, made an unsuccessful grab for my meat and chased me into the living room.

Well, one thing led to another and, in moments, we were side-by-side on the sofa 69-ing like there was no tomorrow.

There almost wasn't.

My large picture window imploded with a crash and shatter of glass, followed by the harsh, rapid pop-pop-pop-pop of automatic weapons fire. Lamps shattered around us. Picture frames exploded from the walls.

Fragments of cloth and cotton stuffing spewed from the top of the sofa.

"Shit! Someone's shooting at us, Cary!" I screamed, rolling off the sofa, dragging Cary to the carpet with me. "Stay down," I ordered, half-crawling to the telephone, oblivious to the fragments of glass on the floor that cut my knees and feet.

And still the bullets continued to spray the room, destroying everything they hit, punching holes in the walls and ricocheting off my brick fireplace to zing around the room like crazed hornets.

I dialed 9-1-1 and spilled out my address and the fact that we were being shot at. Then I heard the squeal of tires on the hot pavement below as a car roared away at high speed. Cary, ignoring me, had crawled to the window. He was looking out.

"It's Tony!" he said, aghast.

"What's his license number, Cary? Quick!" I urged.

He read it off to me, along with the make, model and color of the vehicle. I repeated the information to the 9-1-1 operator and hung up.

Cary and I hastily dressed in shorts and T-shirts and waited for the ambulance. Blood was everywhere. We both had numerous lacerations on our hands, knees and feet from the shards of glass. Unbelievably, we hadn't been hit by the two or three dozen bullets that had shredded the room.

Later, after our wounds had been cleaned and bandaged at the hospital, the police arrived to take our statements.

Seems the police had spotted Tony's car within minutes of his attack on us, and had given chase. Tony, not being overly bright, had fired on the officers. Not a good idea especially in Texas.

His car and body had been riddled with return fire, killing him, on the shoulder of Interstate 30, headed toward Fort Worth.

We also learned a few days later that Tony had been wanted for the attempted murder of a fifteen-year-old California boy who had declined his advances.

Nice guy, Tony.

But all that was over a year ago.

I'm still designing for the elite of Dallas society and Cary has been dancing regularly in shows at the Dallas Music Hall and Casa Manana Theater in Fort Worth. He's branched out into acting, too, and is really quite good.

But then, I'm prejudiced.

We have been together since the day we met and our love

grows daily. I still get a hard-on just thinking about him during the day. And, as I sit here writing this, in my remodeled living room, I call out, "Cary? Want a Manwich?"

His handsome, smiling face peeks at me from the kitchen, those glorious dimples making my cock fill with roiling blood in anticipation and ... oh, yeah, here he comes again...!

BUS STOP
Peter Eros

He was lying on his back on the bus seat, mirrored glasses shielding his eyes, his shirt open, flapping in the muggy breeze, exposing his tantalizingly suntanned and buff torso, steel nipple rings glinting. A slit in the crotch of his jeans revealed he was neither a brief nor boxer man. He really had balls and made sure you knew it. It was lust at first sight. I'd just come from the gym, disappointed that none of my regular fuck-buddies had turned up. A constant seeker after pleasure in excess, I was hot for some action. I pulled over and lowered the passenger window.

"Hi, buddy. There aren't any buses on Sunday. Can I give you a lift somewhere?"

The handsome face turned to regard me as he removed the reflecting glasses. Long-lashes shaded huge black pupils, as an unruly lock of black hair fell across his forehead. The full lips curved into a roguish smile.

"Ah ... I guess wherever you'd like to take me."

He rose and sauntered across to the door with a loose-hipped swivel, adjusting the huge dangler swelling the right inside leg of his threadbare jeans.

As I would learn later, he naturally hung left but dressed right to emphasize his principal assets, especially his thick, ten-inch prick.

He leaned in the window, tensing his midsection so that his ripped abdominal muscles popped out like they were cast in bronze. He was an inch or two shorter than me, probably five ten or eleven, but very broad in the shoulders. He was about my age, but without question a more physical guy, with a formidable upper body and forearms positively gorged with muscle. Even his stance had a potential spring to it.

151

He looked me over and smirked as he took in my blond good looks and lithe, pumped body, barely contained by skimpy muscle tank and tight gym shorts. My cock was straining the cloth.

"Yo! Man! It looks like I found me Sunday lunch! Names Ethan."

"Pete. Hop in."

He slid into the seat beside me and grasped and kneaded my bulge as he ate my mouth. My own exploring hand ripped the pliant crotch buttons apart and massaged his swollen prick. As we came up for air he urged, "You'd better get us out of here, man, or we're gonna cause a public scandal. Yo! Take me away baby! Ah'm a merchant seaman on leave, ripened by six months at sea and bored as heck by my vacation with Momma. I really want to chow down on your meat."

My apartment is only five minutes from the gym. By the time we stumbled into my bedroom, kicking our pants off as we went, we were both stripped down to our rippling muscles and ripe for action. Ethan's uncut cock simply amazed me: so long and wrist-thick, with a spiral tattoo disguising the prominent natural pattern of pumping veins on the shaft. A cock ring encircled his scrotum and a smaller ring enhanced his glans as the velvety prepuce slid back, the first Prince Albert I'd seen up close and personal.

I began jerking my own prick, making it rock hard, as Ethan lay back on my bed and I knelt to take the massive cock in my mouth. I closed my lips around it and sucked on the ring with my tongue as Ethan thrust rhythmically and deeply into my overstretched throat. I gagged and pulled back a little, lapping across the thick head and tonguing the receding folds of skin. I could taste the precum flow, which made me pump my own cock harder. Ethan began a rocking movement, meeting my suctioning mouth with every thrust, his hot sausage pushing deeper into my throat as my muscles relaxed and accepted.

"Damn, take that dick in Pete!"

Ethan grabbed the back of my head as I tried to swallow the whole thing, but I couldn't take the thick meat beyond half-way. I gagged again.

"Take it slow, Pete. Don't choke yourself. You got some poppers?"

I nodded to the nightstand and he grabbed and uncapped the tiny bottle and made me take a good hit before swiping it under his own quivering nostrils. He pulled me onto the bed with him and we assumed the 69 position. His mouth suctioned me with consummate skill, easily deep throating my eight inches as my own throat relaxed, lubricated by viscous precum, and my nose inhaled his pubic bush, hungrily sniffing the swelling odors of brine and potential sexual release. As our mutual throat probing mounted to shattering discharge of our stored-up desires and the aggressive chemical palpitated our pounding hearts my body felt like a struck gong, throbbing with pulsing tremors. We ravenously swallowed the creamy explosions of potent love juice, feeding our aching hunger, exulting in the seamy taste and odor of male justification.

Gorged and satisfied, for the moment, we lay in each other's arms, my head nestled against his massive neck, nibbling at the pulsing muscle that framed his jugular. He cradled my head there and murmured his pleasure. "I hope you aunt no vampire, Pete. But you sure are sump'n. Mm'mm!" He took my hands in his and admired them. "Lovely slim hands, babe. I'll find a use for them," and he winked. "Wanna share a joint?" He pulled his shirt over and removed the toke from his pocket.

I smiled and nodded.

As the pungent fumes suffused our lungs and relaxed our limbs we explored each other's horny manliness and massaged with lube-slicked fingers each other's resiliently upstanding fuck muscle. We passed the joint back and forth, with occasional kisses, exchanging the heady smoke, till Ethan pinched out the roach and swallowed it. Mildly chemically disordered, I was surprised when he raised his legs and urged me, "Lick my ass, man. Stick your tongue in there. Shove it in there, man!"

Always one to oblige I sucked and slurped and probed the most prominently ridged purple pucker I'd ever seen, till he howled,

"Oh yeah! Gimme your big thing. Shove it in there man! Fuckin' plow me man! Fuck this ass hard! Hard as you fuckin' can, man!"

He rolled his knees back to snuggle his ears and, to my amazement, sucked his own dick into his mouth, laying his ass open for an empowering ride at the business end of my rampant dick. His asshole was like a large rosebud, open and quivering in anticipation. I slid in smoothly and repeatedly thrust to the hilt as he gurgled and slurped his appreciation. In no time at all he was gasping and swallowing his own load, functioning as efficiently as a self-cleaning oven.

As his head fell back onto the pillow his purged dick flopped from his smirking mouth and his legs rearranged and nestled on my lower back pulling me into him. My thrusting accelerated and my mouth sought his, licking and swallowing the pungent residue of his delicious jiz from probing tongue and suctioning lips. His anal muscles went into overdrive siphoning my prong as I serviced him with aggressive pumpage. He reached up and proffered the poppers, holding one of my nostrils shut at a time as I sniffed up the other. As the vapor took possession of my reflexes and hot flushes engulfed my fluttering body Ethan's colon grabbed me with even greater insistence sucking out my very essence. He grabbed my nipples and twisted them as I shot my load, gasping and screaming in ecstatic release until his mouth smothered my joyous whimpers.

As I slid exhausted but blissful from his energetic embrace Ethan got up to explore. I caught a glimpse of his massive lats and muscular butt and heard him piss as I lay recovering my breath and my composure, euphoric tremors still rippling my body, eyes closed. He went to the kitchen and returned with two glasses of juice and a can of Crisco from the fridge.

"Yo, man, you got the supplies I need. You've given me some great natural lubrication, but a little of this will help. I want your fist up my ass, man."

My awe of him must have been obvious.

"Oh, maybe you haven't done it before? Well, man, believe me it's easy, and I need it bad. Please, man!"

"My god, I'm sorry, you're right, I haven't! I might hurt you, Ethan, not knowing what to do and all."

"Oh fuck, no problem. I'll guide you, man."

He took my right hand and kissed it, looking at me so soulfully I laughed. He grinned and ruffled my hair.

"Okay, show me."

Already lying back on the bed he was liberally lubing his amazingly prominent ass-ring. No longer a bud it had blossomed into a full-blown rose. Following the fucking his body seemed to have extruded part of itself. It was an eruption of flesh. I'd never seen anything quite like it. His anal lips were massive and sCarlet, the evidence of regular and continuous pleasurable invasion.

"Crisco your hand and wrist all over, Pete, especially on the back. Then hold your fingers in close together, like a spear."

Once I was greased he grasped my hand and folded it the way he wanted it.

"Now just ease it in gradual like. Once you get right in past the sphincter you can form a fist."

My hand slid in with ease at first and Ethan sighed his pleasure. Sure, I'd greased guys' puckers before and even my own, but this was different. My initial distaste was soon replaced by a new form of sensual stimulation. The velvety inner muscles seemed to massage my hand and wrist and Ethan's obvious bliss was a real turn-on too. Ethan's legs were on my shoulders. They tugged at me indicating his readiness for more. Ethan's breathing was very steady and focused, but he gasped as the thick part of my hand passed the inner sphincter and some inner suction took over and drew it in well past my wrist. Ethan took another deep breath and his hole opened up and swallowed my arm almost to the elbow. He leaned his head towards me and I kissed his lips. His tongue prized my lips apart and I sucked on it to let him know I was okay with this.

"Oh fuck, yeees! That's fantastic, man. Just ball your fist now and you can start fucking me for real. Pull your hand back and then thrust back in, just like you do with your cock. Oh yeah! Oh man!"

Following his instructions, I began fisting him harder and faster. He pulled his legs back farther, giving me a better angle. I pulled my hand even further out and his hole remained relaxed enough to let me piston right back in. I kept it up for almost half an hour, until my arm started to ache. Then I slowed down and let Ethan calm a bit. He seemed almost delirious. But recognizing my need he repositioned without releasing my arm. He managed to stand facing me while I sat on the edge of the bed with my elbow rested on my knee. This way he controlled how much arm was in his butt. He hugged my head as he pumped himself up and down on my extended arm. Then he fell back on top of me, my arm still embedded, his fully extended dick rubbing on my chest. I fisted while he rubbed himself against me.

I could feel his pressure building till, with a huge roar, he shot wad after wad of cum, his whole body spasming in ecstasy, his hole sucking hard on my arm. As he began to wind down I gently slid my arm out and held him to me. He sucked up the cum he'd splattered around my neck and kissed me passionately, transferring some of the savory juice to me. We drifted to sleep in each other's embrace.

I woke a couple of hours later with his energetic tongue probing my ass-ring. I stretched languidly and sighed in blissful acceptance of his attentions, though I was vaguely apprehensive about my ability to accommodate his huge prong, and I guess he was to. As he liberally greased my ass ring with Crisco, probing gently with his fingers till three had comfortably slipped in, he gazed at me with real concern and said, "I think you'd better straddle me, babe. I might be too big for you otherwise."

I did as I was told and grasped the root of his probe and positioned the embellished knob between my butt cheeks. The Prince Albert was cold against my pucker as Ethan took a tight hold on my hips. As my pucker surrendered, Ethan's swollen cockhead slid inexorably up my quivering chute, stretching my asshole to the limit. As my inner muscles relaxed then clenched again around the huge intruder Ethan sighed, "Oh babe! You're fuckin' tight!"

"Oh fuck! You feel wonderful in there. Oh yeah! I really want to ride you!"

My cock flexed and dripped, bouncing with thrilling sensation even though I wasn't touching it as I slid up and down, my colon sucking greedily on the mighty prick, and Ethan began pumping his hips to meet my down stroke. I fucked myself rapidly, smacking my ass against Ethan's loins. His cock flexed within me and he gasped and grunted as his cum exploded into my deepest recesses sending me over the brink. As Ethan pulled me down onto him and engulfed my mouth with his own, spunk jetted from my gaping piss-hole, and orgasmic throbbings pulsed through my entire body.

Then I rolled to the side of him and embraced his massive chest, sucking on the still swollen nubs of his large, dark brown nipple, tugging at the steel rings with lips and teeth, as he lay contentedly and fondled my hair.

Finally he pushed me off and rose up on his elbows, melting me with the glance from those glowing coal-black eyes."I want to try and fist you, if you're willing to try, Pete. I promise I'll be gentle and I'll stop whenever you ask me to. But I think you owe it to yourself to experience everything you can in this life. I sure as hell have and I haven't regretted one single experience." He caressed the hair back from my forehead then took hold of my chin. "How about it? My hand sure as hell ain't that much of a stretch. You can see, my hands are smaller than yours."

Dubious, but anxious to please, and strangely excited by something I'd have considered completely perverse until my experience with Ethan, I nodded my acquiescence. Without another word he pushed my legs back to my shoulders and began slathering my asshole with Crisco, pushing it in with his fingers till three digits had pressed through the inner sphincter. Then all four digits were massaging deeply inside. Then he slid the hand out and his thumb joined the spear-head of flesh and bone, sliding in smoothly till the heel of his hand, then the wrist bones, struck the sphincter. I felt like I would split apart. But Ethan soothed me and reassured me as he urged me to take another hit of poppers.

"I'll just keep my hand here till you adjust, babe. Don't get anxious; you can take it. Once you get my fist past that first hurdle your butt hole will be much less stressed than it is right now. The pain doesn't keep building. It will ease quickly, replaced by pleasurable sensations that are really intense."

I cried out in agony as my butt ring gave way, allowing the tightly furled knuckles to slide in. Ethan shushed me and stroked my thighs with his free hand, letting the other just nestle within me unmoving for about thirty seconds, then he gently reversed the process, sliding it back out of me very carefully. To my surprise it wasn't anywhere near as bad as putting it in.

After a brief pause he began the process again, insisting that I take a triple hit of poppers. My ass still hurt like hell, but the hand slid in much quicker and once the hurdle had been passed, and the chemically induced palpitations engulfed me, he just kept pressing steadily in while telling me to push out as though I were trying to shit. When he told me to relax his fist shot up my passage and through the second sphincter despite excruciating pressure at that point. Our mutual sighs of relief sealed my realization that he was in me right up to the narrowest part of his wrist. Then it slowly slid to the middle of his muscular forearm. I felt the fingers fold and bunch deep within me.

"Hmmm, you feel so warm and perfect around my hand."

He moved his mouth up to mine, keeping his hand inside me. I kissed his lips and then he slid his tongue into my mouth where I could suck on it as he started to pump on my hole. He pulled his hand back to the widest part of the palm, then slid it back in, each time going a little deeper. He started fisting me. I pulled my legs back farther to give him a better shot and he pulled his hand even farther out, and my hole stayed relaxed for him to go back in. As he explored my inner muscle rings, I learned to push down so they would open up and wrap around his arm, rapidly building ecstatic spasms wracking my body as pressure built up inside me. My whole body was sucking on his arm. I couldn't suppress an earth-shattering scream as my cock started to shoot wad after wad of cum. It just kept coming as if I had been storing up this almighty orgasm all my life. As I peaked, Ethan slowly slid his hand out. I lay in a sea of sweat and cum, quivering with unbelievable satisfaction at my accomplishment. We collapsed together, exhausted, scummy and greasy.

We hardly ate or left the bed in the next three days. I called in ill at work, and Ethan taught me all he knew about every conceivable sexual position and technique. I'm still wearing his cockring, which he presented me when he left. There were tears on both sides. He writes now and then, and about once in two years arrives unannounced on my doorstep. But I can teach him a thing or two now. I threw in my respectable job and now manage a sex shop. I've got nipples rings and a Prince Albert, and tribal tattoos that emphasize my now massively developed musculature. I've been Mister Leather in this town three years in a row, have fucked and been fucked, fisted and been fisted in numerous videos for several companies.

And, oh yeah, I've become a specialist at initiating fisting novices, with a full-blown butthole of my own that is the envy of fisting aficionados across the country. I've become a missionary for uninhibited self-expression and sexual gratification.

BULL OF THE WOODS
Thomas C. Humphrey

"That thing'll split me open! It'll hurt!"

Bobby Dean Medlin swept over me with all the force and surprise of that "no name" storm that caught the west coast of Florida off-guard a few years back. At eighteen, I'd pretty well managed to figure out that I was at least partly queer, but in my little cattle-ranching town north of Tampa that was something you hardly even thought about. You sure as hell didn't act on it. Besides, all us guys had grown up together since before kindergarten, and some kind of incest taboo must have kicked in early, so that by the time I was thirteen and the hormones got to stirring, even the thought of sex with any of my buddies would have been like wanting to kiss your sister.

Bobby Dean was different, though. He moved to town in late October of our senior year, so the taboo didn't apply to him and he became fair game for regular jerk-off fantasies. He was from a little place in southeast Georgia that, he said, made ten million of the world's worst fruit cakes and held the biggest annual Rattlesnake Roundup in the country. Football season was about over by the time he got to town, not that Bobby Dean would have played, anyway. Tall and rangy, he was more suited to basketball or cross country. But he was immediately accepted in our gang even if he didn't play football, because he was Jacob Osborne's cousin, and Jacob was the most popular guy on the team.

Bobby Dean wasn't anywhere near good-looking, even by the furthest stretch. His wiry reddish hair was always disheveled, and big jug ears framed his boyish, freckled face. He had broad, bony shoulders, a long, thin torso, narrow hips, almost nonexistent ass cheeks, and long, sinewy legs. But to hell with what he looked like. I didn't even know what "type" appealed to me. I was just a sex-starved kid who wanted to make contact with another male, without even knowing the specifics of what I wanted that contact to lead to.

I found out in the bed of Bobby Dean's pickup out in our cow pasture one Saturday night in mid-November.

The night before, we had closed out the regular football season with a big win over our main rival and were all hyped up for the first playoff game the following Friday, on what we hoped was the road to the State Championship.

The County Fair had been running all week, but none of us had gone. Coach had laid down the law that we were not to let anything distract us from "The Game." But after we won Friday night, we decided Saturday was the night to take in the fair and get drunk and raise a little hell. Everybody agreed not to bring a date, even the guys with steady girlfriends. My dumb older brother had wheedled our pickup out of Dad to go wild boar hunting, so I arranged to hitch a ride with Bobby Dean. Even though he'd never given me the slightest hint that he was anything but super straight, in a way, I felt like I did have a date for the Fair.

Everybody arrived duded out in our tightest Wranglers with the white worn circle in the rear pocket made by our Skoal and Copenhagen cans, our fanciest western shirts, and boots and cowboy hats. Even Bobby Dean was wearing jeans tight enough to stretch across his ass and make his buns look pretty tempting. And he had on his trademark belt that he wore everywhere, with a buckle half as big as a license plate embossed with a fire-breathing bull pawing the ground.

Of course, even though nobody had a date, we were surrounded by a gaggle of girls wherever we went, one of the rewards of being a jock, I suppose, if you were straight. But actually we needed them that night to smuggle in our Jim Beam and Johnny Walker and wine coolers for the couple of wusses on the team. Except for letting them hold our booze, though, we ignored them, or even had a good time putting them down.

One group of hangers-on we had nicknamed Wrangler Bunnies for the way they panted over tight-butted boys. They were mostly the overweight dogs who could only dream of hooking up with a jock, although a few of them would put out for guys who didn't care if they were screwing a knothole. To make sure I fit in, I'd even humped a couple of them, on nights when I was so drunk I could hardly get it up.

That night, Lorelle, an unattractive big blonde, was wearing a tight T-shirt that said right across her humongous boobs, "Wrangler Butts Drive Me Nuts!" She kept teasing and playing around with Bobby Dean, who hadn't dated since he moved to town. It got so noticeable that I was afraid he would be horny enough to desert me and drag her off somewhere to screw.

He put that fear to rest when Lorelle snuggled up to him, buried her cheek in his chest, and reached around to caress his ass, trying to insinuate her hands down inside his jeans. He roughly shoved her hands away and stepped back.

"Quit groping, bitch. I ain't got room but for one asshole in these jeans," he said.

All the guys snickered, and Lorelle slunk away with the other Bunnies to lick her wounds. I felt somehow pleased that Bobby Dean had turned down an almost sure piece of ass.

We ate our fill of caramel apples, rode all the dinky rides, tried to prove our manhood by throwing lopsided balls at a pyramid of weighted milk bottles, and conned our way into the sideshow where hootchy-kootchy dancers rubbed their twats in our faces while we stood against the low stage and ogled and leered.

As the booze went to work, Bobby Dean got more and more touchy-feely, punching me on the arm, slapping my back, and draping his arm across my shoulders as we strolled down the midway. On the pitiful little roller coaster, I got all excited when he leaned into me on a turn and pressed his thigh tight against mine long after the car was on a straightaway. I had a struggle to hide my boner when we dismounted.

When we were feeling just good enough, some of us entered the amateur rodeo competition, though Coach would have skinned us for risking a broken leg or something just before the playoffs. I signed up for bull-riding. When the gate opened, my bull came out of the chute like a lightning bolt. He kicked with all four feet off the ground and came down on stiff front legs. I sailed over his head and landed in front of him. A hoof caught my right hip as I scrambled to get out of his way. I limped over to the corral fence and climbed out to the jeers of my friends.

"Hey, Scott, world record: 1.2 seconds!" Dots said, guffawing.

"Yeah, Scott, you were on the ground so fast I thought the bull came out the gate riding you!" Spence added.

"You'd make a hot-lookin' heifer. That bull had been panting after you if you'd stuck around on your knees," Jacob piped in.

Only Bobby Dean moved to help me over the fence. "You okay, Scottie?" he asked, concern in his voice. "That was a pretty nasty spill."

"Nothing hurt but my pride," I said, rubbing my hip, which felt no worse than it often did after a hard tackle. A warm glow built in the pit of my stomach as I realized he'd called me Scottie, a name I'd dared anyone to use for years, thinking it was too sissy. But on Bobby Dean's lips, it sounded intimate and absolutely perfect.

Along about midnight, despite what they'd said, most of the guys began pairing off with the girls and leaving for some private fun. I resigned myself to going home to spend the night with my favorite partner: my hand!

On the way home, though, Bobby Dean and I decided to park out by the pond below my house and finish off what was left of our Jim Beam. It was a warm night for mid-November, and we sat on the tailgate of his old pickup shooting the breeze while we swigged out of the bottle and shared a can of warm soda as chaser.

"You don't date, huh, Scott?" Bobby Dean asked.

"Nah, at least not like some of the guys," I said, feeling a little embarrassed under his questioning.

"I'd figure, good-looking guy like you, on the football team and all, the chicks'd be sticking it in your face, inviting you to sniff," he persisted.

He shifted until his leg brushed against mine. Instead of backing off, he pressed even closer and leaned in until his upper arm was tight against my shoulder. My breathing was so shallow and ragged that I practically was gasping for air. I took another swig of booze, both excited and afraid of where we might be heading.

"I don't particularly like the smell of fish," I tried to joke through the distraction of this unexpected intimacy. "But what about you? Lorelle was doing everything but taking your dick out right on the midway tonight."

"That pig?" he snorted. "I ain't never been that hard up."

He was quiet for a minute and then shifted the conversation. "You know, something I can't figure is the nicknames y'all use. Like, why is Rich called Dots?"

"Easy. He had acne real bad and somebody wondered what picture you'd get if you played Connect the Dots on his face. So, he's Dots."

"Why do you call Anson 'Nat' when his name's Anson?"

"That's g-n-a-t, like the little punkie fly," I said with a laugh. "And that's an interesting story. One time we had a Top Dog contest and discovered Anson's got the tiniest dick anybody's ever seen. Somebody said he was Needle Dick the Bug Fucker, and somebody else said he couldn't even pack a gnat's ass. So, he became Gnat. It doesn't bother him, though. If anybody teases him about it now, he just smiles and says he's getting more than the rest of us, because most chicks would rather be tickled to death than stabbed to death. And he does have girls falling all over him."

"What's this Top Dog stuff?"

"It's just a game we played sometimes when we were younger. We'd be boozed up, and somebody would brag about his dick size. Somebody else would challenge him, and we'd all whip 'em out, get boned up, and compare sizes. The one with the biggest dick was Top Dog."

"And who's the winner?"

"In our crowd, it's Jesse Martin. That's why he's called Beef ... you know, like the old commercial, 'Where's the beef?' But I understand Donnell Carey's got the biggest one in the whole school. You know Donnell, the little dork who plays trumpet in the band. They say his dangles almost to his knee even when he's taking a cold shower."

"And where do you rate?"

"Oh, about second runner-up. But don't you guys have Top Dog back in Georgia?"

"Yeah, except we call it Bull of the Woods."

"And where do you rate?"

A smile lit up Bobby Dean's whole face as he flashed his belt buckle at me. "That's what my bull buckle's for – the undisputed champion. The guys bought it for me as a trophy."

163

"No shit! You're Bull of the Woods, huh?"

"Yeah," he grinned. "But let's see how second runner-up Top Dog compares." He reached over to unzip my jeans.

I almost passed out when he made the touch that I thought would happen only in my dreams, but I recovered enough to say, "Only if I get to see Bull of the Woods." I reached for his crotch and ran into a prominent hard-on that seemed determined to rip right through his jeans.

We had a few awkward moments as we grappled to unbuckle and unzip and tug down, but finally our jeans and briefs were around our ankles. With trembling hands, I reached over and grabbed what felt like a pine sapling stripped of its bark. All I could do for a minute was gawk at it.

"Good God Almighty! I didn't know humans grew them so big! Is this thing for real?" I finally gulped out.

"It's real," Bobby Dean chuckled. "But you ain't exactly average yourself, fellow." He slowly stroked my cock, sending tremors and aftershocks all through my body. Since it was my first experience, I didn't know somebody else's hand could feel so good.

We didn't do much talking after that. I just sat there in something of a fog from the booze and let Bobby Dean take the lead, hoping he knew more about that kind of stuff than I did. Except for my old friend, my hand, my total experience was wrapped up in a night of disappointment when I slipped away from the gang on my seventeenth birthday and drove over to Gainesville hoping some university student would give me a fantastic gay sex education as a birthday present. Just my luck, a sort of fat older graduate student took me to his apartment where we sipped Cokes and watched a porn flick until I got a raging hard-on and he got cold feet because I was such obvious jailbait. I got an eye-opening secondhand education on what guys do together from practically memorizing the video, but the only firsthand experience was when I parked my pickup on the side of the road on the way home and jacked off so many times my dick was sore for days.

From the start, I knew Bobby Dean wasn't so green. While I just wrapped my hand around his pole and stared with fascination at how much it didn't cover, Bobby Dean went to work on my stiff rod, sliding his hand up and down the shaft and rubbing the head with thumb and forefinger while jiggling and tugging at my balls with the other hand. I sucked in my breath in big gulps and exhaled loudly at the sheer thrill of his teasing touch.

He caught me completely off guard when he leaned over and took my dick in his mouth. I came up off the truck bed and threw my head back and howled at the little sliver of a moon overhead. Then I came back to earth and grabbed for him and held on for dear life, trying to make sure I would never be separated from the delicious feelings he was stirring up.

After laving my whole shaft with spit and sucking on the crown with enough force to pull a golf ball through a garden hose, he finally broke my grip and sat up.

"You gonna be a good buddy and return the favor?" he asked.

I bought a little time by toying with the huge prong in my hand while I carried on a quick debate with myself. Seeing guys suck cock on a porn flick wasn't quite the same as actually taking a cock in my own mouth. What would that warm hunk of flesh feel like? Would it smell or taste bad? Worst of all, by doing it I would be forever branding myself as a cocksucker. There would be no more "I'm not completely gay" thinking. It was now all or nothing!

"To hell with it! It's what I am and what I want!" I decided. I bent over, opened as wide as I could, and eased down on that massive club until it bumped my tonsils and I had to back off to keep from gagging. Not knowing what the hell I was doing, I tried to duplicate some of the moves on the video, copied what Bobby Dean had done with my dick, and just let instinct take over. I must have done pretty good. He didn't have to caution, "Watch your teeth," but once. The rest of the time, he was groaning and sighing and pulling at my hair, until he snatched his pole out of my mouth to keep from blowing his load before he was ready.

After that, we took turns going down on each other. I relaxed with it all and set out to fully explore Bobby Dean's mammoth cock with both hands and mouth. Only for a brief moment did I shiver with dread at the thought of being found out by the other guys. Bobby Dean and I both would probably get the shit kicked out of us and have to leave town if we got caught like this. But I was so hyped over the whole night's experience that even this thought did not weaken my lust.

Bobby Dean slid off the tailgate and crouched between my dangling legs. He tugged off my boots and slipped my pants over my feet and tossed them in the grass. He rose up and sucked my cock a little before he sprawled on top of me and unfastened my shirt. His big tool throbbed on my belly as he leaned down to nibble and kiss my nipples. His hands roved all up and down my flanks and onto my neck and over my cheeks. His fingers were like magnets pulling at the iron filings of my nerve endings wherever he touched. My whole body became a mass of almost unbearable sensation and I quivered beneath him as he slowly ground his prick into my belly.

His hungry mouth worked back down my body until he again took my cock in his mouth. As he sucked me, he eased a long, knobby finger between my cheeks and searched for my pucker. When he eased inside, I instinctively tightened up and flinched away. He took his mouth off my dick.

"Relax," he whispered. "Relax and push out. You'll like it." He took my cock back in his mouth.

He circled his finger against my inner walls as I tried to relax. Then I felt more pressure and some pain as he eased a second thick finger alongside the first. He sped up the action on my dick as he spread his fingers and reamed my ass, stretching and opening me up.

Before I really knew what he was doing, he tugged me forward until my tailbone was right on the edge of the tailgate. As he spat several times and slicked up his big timber, I recalled a picture I'd seen of a big-dicked statue that primitive people worshipped as a phallic icon. I knew that I would fall to my knees in awe before this one any time I got the chance.

He stepped closer and bent my legs back and threw them over his shoulders. The foreskin was pulled back all the way on his shaft, exposing his full, angry red cockhead. A thick strand of pre-cum trailed rope-like from his piss slit. His cock looked like a bull's just before he mounts a young heifer.

Maybe it was the booze, or maybe I'm just dumb, but it wasn't until he leaned forward and pushed his heavy throbber between my cheeks that I realized he intended to mount me. I suddenly panicked once I knew what he was about to do. I tried to claw my way back into the truck.

"Hell no! You ain't doing that to me. Not with that monster!" I protested.

He grabbed my hips with his big, strong hands and kept me from escaping.

"C'mon, Scottie," he pleaded. "I want to. I'll go easy, I promise. You can take it. Please."

"That thing'll split me open! It'll hurt!" I whined.

"Maybe a little at first," he admitted. "But then you'll like it. Come on, relax."

It was hard to relax, knowing what was about to be shoved up in me, but I tried. When his huge knob conquered my sphincter, it felt like Bobby Dean had crammed his fist up my ass. I let out a yell that I was afraid my folks could hear up at the house a half mile away. I tried to squirm away from the biting pain, but Bobby Dean held me fast and gradually pushed that thing on in until his dangling balls bumped against my cheeks.

Gradually, over the searing pain at the surface, I became aware of his cock sliding deep inside me and then withdrawing for a second before pushing forward again. The pain was almost unbearable, but every time I was close to crying and begging him to stop, he touched some spot in there that caused my dick to jump and throb and made me forget the pain.

But before long, I was wiggling my ass and lifting off the truck bed, trying as hard as I could to guide his hard cock to whatever it was that set me off like that.

His strokes became longer and harder; he rammed that thing in me full length with every thrust. I reached back and grabbed his flat asscheeks in both hands and pulled forward, trying to drive him even deeper. I really got turned on by his powerful flexing ass muscles on every lunge. My cock set up an urgent throbbing; I was close to coming without even touching myself.

Bobby Dean's strokes became short and spasmodic, and he started breathing in tortured gasps. His pistoning tube ballooned inside me, and after one hard lunge, he froze and I felt his thumping shaft spew wad after wad of hot spunk into me.

After a bit, he pulled out and lifted my legs off his shoulders. He crawled up the length of my body until his lips locked on mine. I grimaced with distaste at the idea of being kissed by a boy and then gave myself over to emotion and opened my mouth to accept his probing tongue. I twined my fingers in his hair and pulled his face even tighter against mine.

"That was great!" he said when we finally broke our kiss. "You don't know how much I've wanted to do this with you, Scottie. And I just knew you wanted it, too. You had to want it."

"I did want it," I said. "But I got more than I expected. I'll be walking bowlegged for a week!"

"Let's see if we can't straighten one of your legs out," he said.

He moved down and took my dick in his mouth. It grew to full size right away.

Bobby Dean must have tried out everything he knew about sucking cock on my bulging tube. In nothing flat, he had me humping clear into the air and beating the truck bed with clenched fists. Much quicker than I wanted, a wave of intense pleasure swept up my shaft and overflowed into Bobby Dean's mouth. I must have fired a dozen blasts before I settled back against the metal floor. When I began to soften in his mouth, he climbed back up my body and kissed me, the taste of my come still in his mouth.

He sat up. "Let's have a drink," he said.

After we had drained the Jim Beam, after had my first experience butt-fucking another boy and gloried in the warm wetness of his ass clutching my swollen dick, sometime before dawn I lay under Bobby Dean again. As his mammoth cock burrowed into me, I remembered how, at the fair. a lifetime ago now, the guys had kidded me about the bull riding me. Now, I wrapped my arms even tighter around Bobby Dean's back and thought how right it was to be ridden, not by just any bull, but by my own special Bull of the Woods.

Sexy porn star and stripper Sean Storm

shows off for the editor's camera. Sean loves having cocks fill his hungry hole the bigger the better.

Charming escort/model/dancer Christopher Fleur De Lis, one of the objects of Sean's insatiable lust for big dick in the following story, regularly advertises his services in Frontiers magazine. Above, a recent photo, courtesy of Black Inches magazine, available from STARbooks Press.

A STORM HITS THE BIG EASY: A Sex Diary

Sean Storm

"...I just sat straight down on Christopher's huge, very hard, black cock."

February 24:

My first night in New Orleans, and a stripper I met named Paul walked with me to a bar called Rawhide. Paul said he had had a really bad night on the catwalk and had decided not to pay the fee to get inside. I, on the other hand, had heard jean-bulging stories about Rawhide ever since I had made the decision to fly down to attend Mardi Gras. And after a long flight on AirTran, I was ready for a little "Southern Hospitality."

Once inside, a beefy daddy-type bartender served me a rum & Coke. We flirted briefly; however, my cock wasn't really interested in his stories. I thanked him for the freebie drink and headed for the bathroom. But I didn't make it very far. Within seconds my fly had been unzipped, and a pair of wet, warm lips immediately greeted the head of my cock.

Cue the music, please ... chick-a chick-a ... bow bow ... and welcome to Mardi Gras! I had only heard about the festival from college friends and from television news reports. However, nothing could prepare me for the debauchery that was to cum. And it all began with Jonah, a dance coordinator for the Mississippi River Bottom (MRB) in the French Quarter, who had invited me to be the headline featured stripper at MRB. With a word like BOTTOM in its name, how could I refuse?

Apparently Jonah and his love-toy, Josh, couldn't refuse either. I was staying with them in Metairie, which is a twenty- dollar cab ride from the Quarter. I didn't come at Rawhide, but once I got to Metairie, Jonah and Josh each took turns sucking and fingering me to my first orgasm in "Nawlins." It was awesome!

I hadn't even unpacked yet, and my first load was drying on their bed sheets!

February 25:

My second day in New Orleans, and I was making my first appearance before the cameras with award-winning videographer VidKid Timo to film footage for his next Pueris Collection release, "The Storm Surge." Alec, the model I was to shoot with, was late, so it allowed Timo and me to bond. And by the time Alec arrived I was ready to shoot my load I mean, ready to shoot my scene!

Soon Alec and I were naked, pawing at each other's aroused bodies as Timo videotaped. I was the first to manhandle Alec's cum-filled cock. He then returned the favor by pushing me back onto the bed and swallowing down to my nuts. Timo then asked Alec, "Do you have a problem eating out Sean's ass?"

Alec answered by lifting my legs up in the air, and then sticking his tongue deep into my hairy hole. He took my cheeks and spread them apart, opening my hole wide. He then spit into it, lubing it up for his fingers.

After Timo filmed Alec's four-finger fuck of my butt, he then had Alec return to sucking me. Now, normally I have much difficulty reaching a climax through oral sex, but Alec had the right touch. He gripped the shaft of my stiff eight and then swallowed it all. He used lots of spit, and hand motion as he worked his mouth up and down it. The head of my cock felt great against the back of his throat.

Without touching myself at all, I could feel the cum inside of me rush to erupt. I could see in Alec's face that he was a swallower, and at first I was afraid we were going to miss the money shot. But, at the right moment, Alec pulled it out in time for Timo to capture each glob as it exploded out of my dick and onto Alec's chin.

Filming ended around three in the afternoon. Alec needed to head home, but said he would come back in a couple of hours (with some white socks for me to use while stripping). He ended up delivering more than just those white socks. At about seven he showed up with his friend T.J. Timo and I were on the bed watching a sketch comedy series on MTV. Alec immediately joined me in the bed. He started touching my leg, which got me stiff all over again. Minutes later he pulled my cock out in front of Timo and T.J. and started blowing me. Only this time he didn't leave any evidence behind.

Showtime at the MRB was eleven. I was in the dressing room a half hour beforehand, and was trying to wake my cock up. The door opened and another stripper named Don walked in. He smiled as I stroked my dick.

"Need some help?" he asked.

Don was one of the more attractive strippers at the club, and I wasn't about to turn down another blowjob, though with two orgasms already that day, the hottie had his work cut out for him.

Fortunately, he too was a pro at oral sex, and had my throbber up in no time. He then pointed to the camera above us.

"It's all a live feed on the Internet," he told me, grinning wide.

Being watched having sex is my ultimate turn-on, so I just shrugged and smiled back.

Showtime: I was announced onto the stage. I rushed out wearing my red baseball jersey and striped pants. As a prop I had a red bat that I swung around near my crotch area. Off came my batting gloves first, followed by my rubber-cleated shoes. The DJ was playing Pet Shop Boys' "New York City Boy," a favorite of mine. I then stripped completely down to my jockstrap, at which point it became stunt time. I grabbed the base of the stage pole and swung my legs up in the air. Wearing just the jockstrap, I spread my legs apart and flashed my still-hairy hole to the crowd. One man in particular seemed to be getting off to my stage performance. He tipped me some George Washingtons, and then whispered in my ear, "How much for a private dance?"

Ka-ching!

After my set we walked to the back patio, where there were five empty picnic tables waiting for us. I stripped back down to my jock and started stroking my cock. He stuffed payment in my sock (well, my borrowed sock) and then slipped his fingers into my strap and pulled out my dick. He flicked the head of it with his tongue, getting a taste of my pre-cum. Then he opened wide and swallowed it all.

After a few minutes of cock-sucking, he then unzipped his own pants. "I'll throw in an extra thirty if you suck me back."

I thought, What the hell? and then opened my mouth and took it deep in my throat. I was getting cold, and knew I needed to get back inside, so I thought, What can I do to get this guy off?

I turned around and spread my bare cheeks wide apart. I figured showing my open hole would be just the stimulator to send him to heaven. And it worked; he stroked faster and harder until he shot his jizz all over the back of my legs. Mission accomplished and just in time for my second set on the stage.

February 26:

I woke up feeling great and was ready to shoot my first solo scene for Timo. It was a pretty simple set-up: I got naked, got hard, got lubed, then threw my legs over my head and shot a hot creamy load into my mouth. Timo and I then walked to a Mardi Gras parade in his neighborhood. It was in a residential area, so no tit-flashing or dick-flashing permitted.

I then took a cab to the MRB for my Saturday performance. Off-stage, a married couple approached me. The wife asked me what my sexual orientation was. Like a smart stripper, I answered, "I'm bi."

Ka-ching! Ka-ching!

I took them to the patio for their private dance, carefully avoiding where the guy from the night before had shot his load. We found a table in the corner, and I stripped down to my socks. The husband was the first to give head. I was having trouble keeping it up ... the air was chilly and rain had started to spit down. When the wife started to blow me I went totally soft. Still, it was rather surreal to watch a woman trying to suck me off, which was the first time in my life a woman had gone down on me. She was pretty, but neither she nor her hubby could get my dick back up.

Then I watched as he reached over to his wife's breasts and pulled one of them out of her dress. Just one glimpse of her huge brown, wrinkled nipple was enough for me to pull my pants back up. I decided to leave my sperm in the bank and call it a night.

Still, I was sublimely happy. I whispered under my breath, "Oh forgive me, Father, for I have sinned: I've had my dick sucked by nine people and have shot my load four times!"

February 27:

Sunday it should have been the day of rest, but it sure as hell didn't end up that way. It was a slow day at the MRB, except for in the beer garden. A bartender named Kyle was serving drinks, and he looked just as bored I did. He took me to the side and told me I could get up on the back stage and go totally nude if I wanted to. I smiled, thanked him, then hopped up on stage and tossed off all my clothes. A group of five men suddenly seemed interested in the activity. They approached me and started sticking Abe Lincolns into my socks. One guy in the group had a camcorder, which instantly brought my cock to attention. The other four circled around me and then touched, stroked, and groped my rock-hard bone. One guy then licked his finger and inserted it into my asshole. I spread my legs apart and began to fuck his finger. With camera rolling, I moaned and shot a huge load all the way up to my nipples and chin. Kyle smiled from behind the bar, then shouted, "Let's see the footage!"

Immediately after the cum scene I started feeling chilled. My skin was hot, yet I was shivering. The same group of guys asked me if I would give them a private show in the back patio area. Since I wasn't feeling good I knew I would have to decline the offer.

Ka-ching! Ka-ching! Ka-ching!

But of course I didn't. I led them all to the back, dropped the towel that I was wearing, and started to stroke again for the camera. I let two of the five perform oral on me. As this was going on, other customers started to filter into the back and watch the action. Ever the exhibitionist, I hopped onto a table, turned around, and spread my ass open wide for the cameraman. Two more in the group then took turns sticking their tongues up my hot hole. When I felt the orgasm build, I turned around for the camera and shot load number two.

But that second orgasm was also my breaking point. By now I had a major headache and fever. Don, the stripper who fluffed me before Friday's show, lived just two blocks from the MRB, and he invited me back to his place to get better.

Most of my clothes were at the MRB anyway because I was tired of paying for cab rides from Metairie to the French Quarter (in three days I had spend over $150 in cab fares). So I took Don up on his offer and stayed at his pad until Monday night. (We are both big bottom boys anyway, so sick or not sick, sex didn't even become a major issue).

February 28:

On Monday night, I was moving again, this time to Drake's, who is the bar manager at the MRB. He lived just five miles from the bar, and cab rides were knocked down to about 5 bucks a trip. My fever was still beating the hell out of me, and I was only interested in sleeping once I got to Drake's. Also staying there was Drake's slave, Ron.

Drake ordered his slave to sleep in the loft with me and make sure all my needs were taken care of he wanted me in top shape for the coming weekend's stage shows. I took some medication and then climbed the stairs to the loft, followed by Ron. In the middle of the night, I was awakened when I felt Ron sucking on my cock. Even though I still felt like crap, I ejaculated into his mouth anyway, then fell back into a blissful sleep.

February 29:

It was Leap Day and physically I was still feeling drained (as was my cock), but my fever and headache were now gone. Drake had left to go to the airport to send his slave back to Dallas, which left me homo alone-o.

The sun was out, and I decided to catch some rays. I walked out onto the patio and noticed it was closed in by a fence the perfect set-up for the all-over tan. I took all my clothes off and lay down. I took out my suntan lotion and rubbed it all over me. When I rubbed the lotion onto my ass cheeks I felt myself getting a stiffie. I reacted by taking the oil and massaging it all over my cock. I then kept massaging myself until cum splashed all over my chest. Naturally I was sleepy after coming, so I rolled over onto my stomach and caught some zzzzzz's in the sun.

When Drake got back, he took one look at my naked bubble butt in the sun and began to munch on it. He ended up jacking himself off with his tongue deep up my hole.

March 1:

Wednesday night found me back at Timo's doing another jack-off scene. In this one I shoved a big dildo up my hole. After getting the money shot, we then met up with his boyfriend and did something so entirely normal it was scary: we went to the theater and watched "Boys Don't Cry."

After all the sex, it was the perfect thing I needed to do.

March 2:

By now I was feeling trapped at Drake's. Cabs were getting harder to call, and when they did show, it was usually an hour later. I was sitting alone at Drake's knowing full well that the streets in the French Quarter were now teeming with people looking to party. It was time to move again. Luckily, fellow escort/dancer/porn star Christopher Fleur De Lis had arrived.

I met Christopher that night at the MRB. He too was going to dance that weekend, and together we went to Drake's, got my clothes and then moved our stuff into a condo that the MRB provided us in the French Quarter. By the time we were moved in, it was getting close to show time. We showered together to save time, which actually ended up making us late. Once in the shower, our cocks got hard, then Christopher ate my ass out on the bed while I was trying to put my underwear on. His huge black cock would have felt great between my cheeks, but there just wasn't enough time to "fit it" into our schedule (pun intended).

During our stage performances, Christopher picked up a client and scored some extra bucks on the side. I too had some offers, but instead opted to bring home a totally fucking hot circuit boy named Joe. We got to the condo and started making out on the couch. His muscles were tight, and so was the bulge in his jeans. I reached down and freed his cock from his pants it was nine solid inches in length and six inches around. He then pulled my pants down and began to lick at my now-shaved ass. But my ass was tired of getting rimmed; it needed to be fucked and hard! Joe lay down on his back and I straddled his big dick. I lowered my ass down to the tip of his cock, teasing his meat with my hole. I reached around and slid his cock along my asscrack. Just when I could tell he was losing patience, I lowered my butt down and allowed his hard shaft to slide deep up into my hole. He rode me for a few minutes before bringing us both to creamy climaxes. It was one fabulous fuck. And I deserved it. Hell, after a week in the Big Easy it was about time my boy hole had gotten well plowed.

March 3 and 4:

Friday and Saturday were lucrative strip nights. The Mardi Gras crowd was huge, and people were filing in and out of the club all night. Most stayed when they saw the strippers. After Friday's show, I joined up with the owner of the bar Oz and his friend John. The three of us hit Bourbon Street and got totally drunk amidst the party crowd.

Bourbon Street was chaos...gay boys were running around everywhere, screaming and flashing...it was Heaven! The three of us then went back to John's house, where I let them rim and suck me to a very satisfying climax.

On Saturday, I met up with Timo and porn star Chris Harding at the MRB to film our foreplay scene. I liked Harding from the moment he smiled, which made our fuck scene at his house all the more hotter and realistic.

Since my hole had already been loosened up by the circuit party boy, Harding easily slid in and out of me. After fucking me in different angles, Harding shot an impressive load onto his chest as I pinched on his nipples.

It would have been great to see Harding again while I was in New Orleans, but with less than a week to go on my visit, that seemed unlikely. I thanked him for a great time, and Timo and I then hit the road again.

March 5:

I danced but I also managed to fit a private party into my schedule. The party took place on Bourbon Street, and I was allowed to strip down to my underwear and throw beads down to the crowd below. I then walked into the living room, and, when cued by the music, stripped my Calvin's off and shook my bon bon for the 30 guys in attendance, 10 of whom took turns sucking my cock. In the end I busted my nut for everyone in attendance.

After the party, I met up with Chris back at the condo. I knew he wanted my boy-butt bad, but the timing just didn't seem to be working out. Two of his clients had invited us over for dinner at their guest house. One of the clients sucked me off for dessert.

March 6:

The madness continued in the French Quarter as if all Hell was about to break lose. I needed a break from the scene, so I decided to relax at The Country Club, a clothing-optional haven for gays and lesbians. It was crowded when I arrived; both men and women lounging around a pool in their Speedos (and less). The tits I could have done without, but seeing some of the guys more than made up for the girls being there.

I positioned myself on a chaise so that I could observe a gym god with a perfect bubble butt and a slightly hairy crack (I mean, I go totally, hmmm, crazy over butts).

I soon felt my dick getting hard, so I rolled over onto my stomach and just stared at this guy's butt. My cock hardened to full strength as the buff stud in front of me got up from his chaise, displaying his perfectly gorgeous hole in the process.

He ignored me so I ended up having to retreat to the men's room to beat off one of my few solo masturbatory moments during my visit to the Big Easy.

March 7:

Fat Tuesday; it was total chaos in the French Quarter. Dicks were being flashed for beads everywhere on Bourbon Street.

After my final MRB performance that night, I hooked back up with John (from my three-way a few nights back) and had him suck me off again before heading to the Corner Pocket to strip some more.

March 8:

I did my last solo J.O. scene for Timo and then we hung out most of the day. When I returned to the condo I found that Christopher was flying back to San Diego the next morning. It was now or never.

"I want that ass before I go," he said, eyeing me seductively.

Looking at him at that moment, I knew that everything had built up to this. I wanted his big cock up my butt just as much as he wanted it in me.

"Okay," I said.

I lubed up my butt, straddled him like I did the circuit boy, and then sat straight down on his huge, very hard cock. Christopher let me take my time getting used to his mammoth size. Until Christopher, my ex-boyfriend had the biggest cock I had ever had in me. I was in heaven. Once I was all the way down to the base of it, Christopher began to thrust.

After a few minutes of expert fucking, he looked down to watch his cock sliding in and out of my butt. He said, "We need to film a scene together."

"Yeah," I gasped. I reached behind me and spread my cheeks even farther apart.

I jacked off as Christopher thrust that huge cock into me. I imagined Chi Chi La Rue zooming in on my butt with her camera. "Okay, Sean. Show Chi Chi what you got!" I imagined her saying. "Let's see that throbbing cock explode onto Christopher's chest!" Just then I moaned loud and shot my load onto Christopher's silky ebony skin.

A porn star to the end, Christopher pulled out, removed the condom, and added more cum to his chest. "Awesome!" I cried. And he nodded in complete agreement.

Then we collapsed into each others' arms and took a power nap.

March 9:

After saying good-bye to Christopher, I went back to Timo's. I hung out with him all day, then met up with his pal, porn star Jim Buck, and Chris Harding for dinner at an Italian restaurant in the French Quarter.

Later, I hugged Timo goodbye, then went back to Chris's house and fell asleep in his arms a lovely way to end my trip.

On the plane home, I reflected on the excitement of my first trip to the Big Easy. In two short weeks, I had been fucked three times, shot off seventeen orgasms, and had my cock sucked by over forty different people! Only in New Orleans, only at Mardi Gras and just wait'll next year!

THOSE BIG BOYS OF CROSS COUNTRY (Or, MY DREAM PENIS)
Thom Nickels

"...Fred's crotch was always bulging, even when he didn't have a boner."

We were up by the football fence, sitting on the ground doing leg exercises in anticipation of the Chester County cross country meet. Coach Meterman was yelling, "All the way down! Pull those muscles! C'mon, Zach!" Zach was the star runner. He was my height and very much on the muscular side and he had the athletic stamina of two people.

Zach was always able to run out in front of the pack and keep a steady lead. During practice, he and Ned led the exercises because they were the best. Ned was small and dark haired and an excellent sprinter, while Zach was taller, with dirty blond hair and a body that made me think of a coat of armor. Ned was a quiet type. Mostly he talked with gestures and smiles or snickers, when there was something funny going on. Ned was as hairy as a gorilla whereas Zach had smooth sun-tanned legs. In the showers after practice, it was Zach who soaped down the most, rubbing the bubbles all over his chest while cracking jokes as he turned around and around under the spray of water.

Ned was running in place. He just stood up and made the move on his own. He looked very serious when he did this, and if you didn't know him you might be fooled by this look of his. I was always amazed at how easily this thin veneer of seriousness could be cracked. He was so nice!

Gradually we all stood up and ran in place while Coach Meterman watched us and shouted, "Come on!"

Some of the guys were joking and we were feeling really good, jogging in place. Even Coach Meterman seemed to have his eyes on the horizon and seemed a little less intense on running us ragged.

We still wondered what he was planning for us today. Yesterday our practice had been short; too easy. Just a mile or so up the road by the school for the retarded and then down into the school's fields and dirt roads, where the running was choppy. Today would be different though. I had heard from Donnelly that practice was going to be hard. He said this to me when I passed him in the halls between classes. I said, "Oh no!" and clutched my sneakers and pictured the two of us running alone in the middle of the pack. Donnelly was a runner very much like myself: not too good, spot not too bad. But good enough always to be considered valuable.

Coach Meterman gathered us around him. I put my eyes to the ground. Donnelly came up beside me so that our shoulders touched. His breath came out in smoke, and it was the first smoke-breath I'd seen that fall.

"You guys take the expressway run!" There was a moan from the group. I looked at the coach and decided I didn't like him. Why do the others always do what he says? We looked at one another. Zach was making believe he was falling down and clutching R.D.'s sneakers. R.D. was an okay runner. He and I were exactly even on the quality scale, except that R.D. was always spraining an ankle. He had weak bones.

Two weeks before school opened, R.D. told us that while hitchhiking to practice, the man who had picked him up said that he wanted to suck his dick. Everybody laughed or almost everybody. I think that was because we knew R.D., and the picture of him getting his dick sucked in a parked car seemed really funny. Although R.D. was muscular and he had a great head of hair, he was of a different class than the rest of us. He was what was known as a "hood" in that he wore his pants jacked up over his navel and combed his hair ducktail style. This sort of set him apart. Everything about R.D. seemed like such a joke if only because of his constant wise-cracking. He also had a little dick; in the showers it looked very small.

"I want everyone to finish the run. No walking. If I see anyone walking I'm going to penalize them," Coach Meterman warned. Meterman had binoculars and you never knew when he was spying on you. But the expressway run was out of his viewing range. He couldn't spy on us even if he wanted to, unless he followed us in his car, which is what last year's coach did. Meterman was not a car-coach. He trusted us--that is, until the day when we decided to walk because practice was getting too rough.

Zach was the ringleader. We'd been running for what seemed like an eternity, our legs funnels of hard cement and our breaths coming in short gasps. "Protest! Protest!" Zach yelled. He got us all to walk boldly down the road past the retarded school, where Meterman was sure to see us. When we heard the whistle blow, and a "Hey!" echo across the field as if it had been produced by real outrage, some of us giggled. Donnelly started to jog ahead but he was shouted back. Meterman was so mad he drove up to meet us in his car, something he never did, and he gave us a thrashing on the spot.

The expressway run was so called because you ran over a bridge that went over an eight-lane highway. It was uphill all the way, the road twisting and turning like as Zach would say "a real bitch!" He must have known what a real bitch was like because he had a girlfriend who always walked the halls with him. She was tall and thin and sometimes came to the meets, and once or twice she even got her cheerleading squad to come to the meets and cheer for us. Sometimes after a meet, especially if we won, Zach would walk arm-in-arm with her around the playing field or wherever we happened to be. Usually they would go off together, looking very serious, and then Zach would come back to us and slowly become his former self.

I liked Zach better when he was always his former self.

In the summer we'd get together for random practice runs. Only the dedicated runners came to these practices. Some of us even practiced on our own before these get-togethers. I ran through a cemetery. This cemetery had many straight and winding roads and was perfect for cross country toning up. Teenagers learning to drive occasionally made their way through this cemetery without tombstones, and cars parked next to grave sites and people standing beside graves was common too. But not that common.

Often the place was empty, and you could run and then sit under an apple tree and read the flat gravestones. which were embedded face-up in the ground as mounted plaques. I generally looked for teenagers: kids my own age who had died. I'd imagine them lying in their coffins, decayed or not decayed, depending on when they were buried. I'd already grown out of cutting flower boughs from blossom trees and walking them back to my bedroom, where I placed them before a statue of the Virgin Mary. I did this when I was a small kid, maybe twelve, and it was the only reason I ever went to the cemetery, except perhaps when I was walking with friends or when I had a lot to think about. In the cemetery there was a monument with the Lord's Prayer inscribed on it and there were steps leading up to the inscription and the effect was like a stage or a sacrificial altar. Once in a while a few of us hung out on the steps and imagined we were in an old Roman movie, dressed in gladiator skirts and shields.

This cemetery was where Dick took me when we didn't have any place to go. It was my first outdoor place, and it was summer when I was initiated for the first time. Dick parked his green Chevrolet in an out-of-the-way spot and together we got in the back seat and put a towel over our waists. Since Dick was the lifeguard at our country club pool, we came directly from swimming. My bathing suit was wet and it smelled of chlorine, and I noticed that my dick was crouched up and indented with zigzag lines from my jock strap when Dick pulled my suit off. I was one nervous guy while his was big and ready for anything right from the start. When I took off his suit I couldn't help but feel inferior.

I remember taking his dick between my hands and rolling my hands back and forth real fast like I was kneading pie dough. When a tractor came up behind us I got scared and froze, and Dick brought the towel up close to our navels as we sat there, shoulder to shoulder, until the gravediggers passed. I know they saw our bare backs through the back window and I can only wonder what they thought. But they didn't say anything. I started rolling my hands again and Dick made a noise and then there was sperm all over.

We saw each other a couple summers after that. Sometimes I'd get to the pool early and Dick would be attending to his pool duties when he'd indicate that he wanted me to follow him into the locker room. My heart would be racing as I'd enter the locker room and go in the back where the toilet stalls were. Dick would usually be in the last open stall, standing against the partition, a hard-on visible in his tight bikini bathing suit. The danger of being caught made the encounter all the more exciting. Usually I'd feel Dick up as he reached in for my boner. There would be momentary fumbling but not for long. I knew what Dick wanted.

The first time we met in the open stalls he pushed my head down over his cock. I couldn't believe what was happening because people were always rushing in and out of the locker room. I had a horror of being seen by a friend of the family's. Dick knew this as well, and that's why he wanted me to suck fast. I accomplished this easily, though I was always amazed at how quickly Dick could come. He had a truly monumental cock: Long, thick, with a fat head, perfect for sucking, and the slit was fairly large. In fact, while sucking him I'd often stop and ponder the slit as little bubbly semen segments oozed out. Dick would be on his toes, his arms stretched out to the sides, his hands grappling the ends of the partition. His body would be shaking.

The first time he came in that position I was shocked: shocked at the rush of semen flooding my mouth; shocked at his letting it happen when the act of sucking and swallowing was still new to me. I choked when he came, and after I swallowed him I thought that something terrible was going to happen to me.

Though I loved his taste and I hungered for more, I was afraid of the consequences: would I become the first male to get pregnant? I was just fourteen; I didn't know any better. For days after sucking Dick I'd lock myself in the family bathroom and rub my hands over my abdomen and worry that a protrusion was brewing in there. I'd never swallowed semen before, and I'd certainly never heard of a male swallowing the frothy mix. Was I first the first on the planet to do so? These fleeting fears gave way to the facts of science and biology: whatever effects swallowed semen had, it did not lead to pregnancy in males. The fact is, when it came time to suck Dick's dick again I was always game, always the willing Yes Boy.

"Meet me by my car in twenty minutes," Dick would say, a hard-on showing in his bathing suit, his eyes scanning the area for people who might be eavesdropping. I'd get in the car with him; it didn't matter where we went as long as it was someplace private. It was usually the graveyard, sometimes it was to the woods near the country club's driving range where boys and girls went to have sex on weekend nights.

In this isolated spot where one could find used condoms among the shrubbery, Dick would spread a blanket on a grassy knoll or between trees and bushes, then off would come our bathing suits.

We would lie on top of one another. Dick would suck me first and try everything possible to make me cum.. To no avail; I was always too nervous, and had to take matters in my own hand. I felt bad that I could not feed his hunger. I thought that something was wrong with me: why couldn't I spurt like Dick? Why couldn't I put my arms behind my head, thrust my hips up and down and then moan when I popped? What was wrong with me? Once Dick was so disgusted he called me the Jerk Off King.

"Why is it that you never come? What's wrong with you anyway?" he demanded.

I imagined myself jinxed in the world of sex.. "I'm trying, I am," I'd say, red in the face. But I could not come like him. It would be several years before I could relax enough to let that part of me rip. Every time we had sex, Dick had no choice but to push my head down over his cock and let loose. Well beyond the point of choking, I'd comply in a dutiful fashion. "That's it," he'd say, his back arching. I'd quicken my own pace and try to ascertain when he'd pop. I wanted a simultaneous explosion, two dicks coming at once. I loved it when I squirted all over his lifeguard's legs.

"Here," he'd say, holding my head over his cock. In a minute or two it would all be over, and when I stood up to wipe myself off I'd be covered with insect bites..

One day after a particularly huge orgasm in the woods, Dick put on his bathing suit, and walked away from me without saying goodbye. It was the first time anyone had just walked away from me after sex. I couldn't figure out what was wrong: had I offended him? Was he angry that I couldn't come? Or was what we did so horrible he had reached a point where he could not even bring himself to say good-bye?

Time healed this emotional slight, and soon we were meeting in the pool locker rooms and doing it in the showers when the pool was closed.

I'd suck him until the fall and then from September till June I was on my own, which meant that I had no sex at all.

# # #

Running cross country, I would run past this spot and think of Dick. Once I approximated where we parked and closed my eyes for a moment and pictured us together.

The thing that really held me to the cemetery was Mary Wiggins. Mary was an old woman who cooked for our family when my mother was seriously ill. She was famous for her snow ice cream whenever it snowed. When no one was looking I'd go to her grave and kneel down and cross myself and sometimes stick my finger into the earth next to her name plaque. Of course I kept an eye open for worms. Then sometimes I'd put a new dime or a penny into the dirt over her, or maybe a small crucifix or rosary. I was brazen enough one day to burn a candle. It was a nice spot, right under a cherry blossom tree that looked out over the hills. I knew that part of the reason Mary Wiggins became a Catholic was because I showed her an engraved letter from the pope. The letter was to me, and it smelled of incense and candle wax, and when I showed it to her she was washing dishes and she said, "Oh my!" and studied it awhile.

For a long time after that I thought that maybe I was some kind of saint, even though I did things with Dick.

I'd pretty much forgotten about Mary Wiggins when I started running in the cemetery. Some years had passed since her death, and so I tried to think of nothing. When running alone it was easy to get bored, and so sometimes I walked over to the European section of the cemetery, where there were huge tombstones with cameo pictures of the deceased in the stone. Many were dark-haired women with circles under their eyes, or stern-looking men with mustaches or little children in white bonnets. Hardly anyone came here; it was almost like traveling to a foreign country.

The team ran through the cemetery only once. I ran out front all the way, while the others, even Zach and Ned, tired out. We ran past the Lord's Prayer monument and the huge organ tower that once generated so much controversy in my neighborhood. On Sunday afternoons and all day Saturday the organ played religious music. They were mostly Protestant hymns that could be heard miles away. One neighbor, a proud atheist, complained bitterly about the hymns and threatened to sue the county. As children, we were shocked to discover an atheist in our small, quiet neighborhood. We'd also gotten used to the hymns and especially the sound of bells which came from some hidden mechanism inside the tower. Sometimes we'd stand under the tower just to see where and how the music was being played.

The team ran by the tower without so much as a second glance, though I half wanted to take Zach or Donnelly aside and show them the European cemetery. I knew they'd get a kick out of the white bonnets. I also couldn't help but think of sex whenever I was in the cemetery and the thought of taking Zach or Donnelly off behind a bush crossed my mind more than once.

One afternoon after cross country practice, Donnelly and I were alone in the boy's room pissing. We were joking around and even started making faces at one another when we combed our hair in front of the mirror. Then, before I knew it, Donnelly turned off the boy's rooms lights and said "I'm gonna get you!" as he proceeded to walk towards me in the dark like a monster. Was I supposed to run? I stayed where I was, though I did inch towards him a couple feet and hold my hands out. I had an erection, and I expected Donnelly to grab me softly down below.

That's where I wanted to grab him. Donnelly was as cute as a sandy-haired Irish lad could be with his lean build and huge dick, which I'd seen many times in the showers. Besides myself, he was the most generously hung on the team. I wanted him to grab me but he didn't. Something froze us both in our tracks.

We laughed nervously, aware for some seconds that something extraordinary was happening, but then for some reason both of us headed out the door with the bathroom lights still out. I suppose the fact that the lights were still out when we left was significant. It meant that what was happening between us was on-going and that something would take shape in the future.

I do know that Donnelly was always giving me looks and throwing me little hints" with his smiles and facial grimaces. This usually occurred in the shower, whether we were showering together or whether Donnelly was showering alone and I was passing through the locker room to go to my locker.

When I was passing through, I'd often stop and say something to him, anything to find an excuse to look over the shower wall and watch him turn his body around under the shower spray.

Donnelly also had this way of soaping his body and getting his dick to go a little beyond soft so that it gave a slight indication of just how big it got when totally hard. Sometimes when we talked at long range I'd see his arms rotate in such a way that I knew he was soaping his dick: the way he'd look at me and grimace while doing this sent very definite signals about what he was thinking about.

Donnelly had a funny way of running. He kind of wobbled while holding his arms way up around his shoulders, his hands in a fist-like clench. His head would rock from side to side.

I stole his jockstrap twice. After the first theft, I wondered whether he would be able to get a new one in time for the next meet. I'd been wanting to steal his jockstrap for ages but wasn't able to do anything until Coach Meterman had the team share the open lockers with the football team. The open lockers were just hanging stalls with the name of the athlete in each division. Since there were extra slots, our team was able to share the room with the football team. It was also easy to see where Donnelly hung his clothes since the cross country team was small compared to the hordes of guys on the football team. I always noted where Donnelly hung his clothes, and so one day before practice, when the room was empty, I went to Donnelly's slot and took his jockstrap.

Donnelly's jockstrap was particularly clean smelling, though it did have a bit of his body odor that I knew so well. I sniffed the jockstrap once before placing it in a paper bag, which I then hid among my schoolbooks.

At home, locked in the family bathroom, I put his jockstrap over my face with the crotch cup placed directly over my nose. It was as if I had Donnelly in the room, what with the smell of his dick hitting me hard and the added pleasure of a few pubic hairs getting stuck to my tongue.

Once I had successfully swiped Donnelly's jockstrap, I was on a roll. During gym class, I began staking out other guys and paying attention to where they hung their clothes. When we used the football locker for quick changes, I had my choice of the cutest boys. I'd remember where a cute boy had piled his clothes, and then when the herd left and I was alone, I'd go over and snatch a pair of underwear or another jockstrap. I was especially happy when I'd find underwear with semen stains on them or lots of curled pubic hairs in various places.

I never wanted Zach's underwear. While Zach had a good build and was cute in a brutish sort of way, he missed the mark somehow; he just didn't excite me. I could never put my finger on it. Zach, though, surprised me one afternoon when the two of us were running together through a cornfield, the rest of the boys having gone their separate way. We'd been running for a long time, and we were both drenched in sweat when Zach suggested that we lie down in the tall grass beside the corn and relax a little.

When he said, "Let's lie down in the grass," everything inside me bolted upright and I hoped that the force that motivated Dick to take control of me had moved over Zach in a similar fashion. Zach stretched out beside me and put both arms behind his head. I was too nervous to lie down flat, so I hunched forward on a small rock. This way I could admire his tanned, muscular legs and keep an eye on his crotch should any erection develop. Zach kept his eyes closed and kept saying how wonderful the rest felt as I continued to lurch forward in the direction of his crotch but not going too far. I was waiting for Zach to take my hand or do something bold but he just took in the early evening sun and kept saying how peaceful it was.

It was not peaceful, for I couldn't help but feel that Zach, like Donnelly before him, was waiting for me to make the first move. And so I continued to sit and look at Zach and wait for an erection that never came, or if it did come I didn't see it because Zach was not big and it's conceivable that he could be hard without anything showing. Just as quickly as he suggested we lie down, Zach jumped up and continued the run. For months afterward I often wondered if I had blown my one and only chance to make it with the captain of the cross country team.

Somebody on the team kept talking about the mirror in the locker room. This was the mirror all the boys stood in front of whenever they combed their hair.

Our teammate, Ralph, was saying how he looked terrific in some mirrors and so ugly in others that he'd mutter to himself, "You ugly bastard!" Ralph's comment was what I'd been thinking all along. The mirror in the gym made most of us look good. Pimples didn't show up like they did in the mirror on the first floor by the school library. In that mirror, pimples came out looking blue, red; even casual blackheads showed up while in the gym mirror they never showed.

I had two pimple patches on either side of my face. They were up high, around my cheekbones, and there was always a cluster there. I thought that maybe the reason for this was because this part of the face was closest to the bone. I'd get one side healed, then a patch would come up on the other side. When this happened I'd walk real fast past the library mirror and avoid looking at myself because I knew if I did I was going to get depressed.

It's funny how the boys who have the fewest pimples are the ones who most complain about them as if they were victims of a plague. Ralph had only a few blackheads on his chin, and his complexion was good. His real problem was baby fat. He was too heavy to be a cross country runner, and I would never have thought of ever stealing his underwear!

There was a mirror by the art classrooms that was in the path of the afternoon sun. Looking into this mirror was like putting a microscope up to yourself. The crinkles and the acne stood out like plaster of Paris mold created by Mrs. Holland of the Ceramics Department. (Mrs. Holland was "way out" and wore long hoop earrings and was so her girl students kept saying "really different.") I would look into the Art mirror and then walk straight into the little boy's room, which was tucked away around the corner. (I say 'little' because even when classes were changing, hardly anybody went in there; it was also a good place to hide out when you wanted to cut class or jerk off.) The lighting was so dim in that tiny boy's room, everyone looked good standing in front of the mirror. I'd always examine my pimples close-up there after racing in from the Art mirror and tell myself, "See! there's nothing to worry about. The Art class mirror exaggerates!"

Then I'd go outside again and pass the Art mirror and sort of sneer at it, though I'd be glancing at the side of my face with less pimples. This made me feel better. Nevertheless, passing a fellow student after getting a face full of your own plaster of Paris in the Art mirror was a real chore. The entire Art corridor was illuminated by the sun and logical thinking had it that if the Art mirror had you looking awful then the Art corridor did also, and so you were ugly when you walked it.

Our team kept doing the expressway practice run and during these sessions I was always somewhere in the middle. Running is strange, because sometimes I excelled and sometimes my performance was poor. I could never figure this out. There were days when I ran astride Zach and Ned; it felt good knowing that Donnelly and R.D. and the others were far behind as we three jumped over logs together or made a single formation like a team of horses. It was really something, especially when Zach would say, "Okay, we really got 'em now!", meaning the other boys like my friend Lewis, who'd just joined the team and who was getting better every day and who I knew would be as good as me one day.

I've seen many extraordinary improvements in runners. An extra wind is like a gift from God and it comes unexpectedly. You'd be running along and all of a sudden some boy who was never any good will pass you. I never understood how this happened, though I could always tell just by the way a boy moved when he passed you that he was feeling good about it. "Hmmm, he thinks he's got it made," is a thought I frequently thought, watching boys pass. Yet sometimes I didn't care. Sometimes a long distance run was so exhausting you felt you couldn't breathe and, somewhere inside you, you gave up because you just couldn't go on. That's when you thought of faking something to explain your performance, like a stomach ache or a sprained joint.

A sprained joint never happened to me. I don't know why. My feet should be a lot like the next guy's the next guy is always twisting his ankle or getting a sprain but I never even had bad ankles. Other guys wore ACE bandages over their ankles or were always rubbing red hot over their legs in the locker room. Perhaps they had weak bones. I envied them, that's for sure, because Meterman always played nursemaid when a boy complained of any sort of sprain. "Watch that ankle Eddie, take care. If you find it hurting too much, take a breather and walk the rest of the course." Take a breather? Meterman seemed to know that there was no sprained ankle in me, just ordinary tiredness, which didn't count.

On the away-meets, Zach and Ned and Donnelly and I would try and sit near one another in the back of the bus. I'd usually have a sandwich bag with cheese sandwiches on a special bread that contained no sugar (because of my pimples), and some apples. We'd put these snack bags on the racks above our heads. On the bus Meterman would always sit beside us for a while and tell us what we had to do.

"I want you boys to get in there. Put some red hot on those legs. Take deep breaths!" Whenever Meterman went on like this one of the runners would roll up his sweat pants and rub on red hot. Red hot smelled like something out of a gas station and it didn't take long for the smell to be everywhere. It tingled the skin with a slow warmth and sometimes you felt a burning sensation. Sometimes when I applied red hot I felt too prepared or something, and the knowledge that I had it on seemed to weigh me down so I was convinced I didn't run as fast. My best running was always when I thought least of the meet or of elaborate preparations but when my mind dwelled on sitting next to Donnelly on the bus on the way home, our legs pressed together like a tight clamp.

Lewis joined us the second year I was on the team. He was a quiet guy and mostly fun but he was obsessed with talking about girls and making fucking motions with his hands. He'd usually make a hole with two fingers and then slide the rest of his fingers in and out of it. This was usually enough to get the rest of the boys to talk about girls, something that hadn't happened before Lewis joined the team. Before Lewis joined, we were happy laughing and joking amongst ourselves, and we certainly didn't need girls as a topic to get us going.

Whatever Lewis did or didn't do had little effect on Donnelly, who'd sit next to me whenever he could and spread his legs far apart. I don't know whether this was from being tired or what, but I do know that they stayed in the same position almost glued to mine as we sat there, locked to one another.

#

I had my best times with my brother. He was younger than me but he was in the same high school just the same. He was a freshman when I was a senior, and as I watched him walk the halls I'd think how good he looked in his white tennis sweater. I also noticed that my brother was getting in with one of the cliques, though I couldn't tell whether it was a major or minor clique because I was out of that age group and didn't have a hook on the freshman class.

But I want to talk about my brother's hairbrush.

My brother's hairbrush was very much like mine in color, size and weight except that it was smaller, like a toy brush. Now, my brother had better hair than I, much better I mean it swirled and twisted this way and that and it was thick. I was jealous. I didn't want to admit it, of course, not even while looking at myself in the bathroom mirror. You see, my hair was curly and I had an irregular hairline that looked as though it might recede at any moment. And I was quietly panicking. So I would get my brother's hairbrush, bring it to a shelf in the basement where my father kept oil, gasoline and various engine fluids, and squeeze the oil that was used to lubricate screws and bolts, into his brush.

The purpose was to have the oil contaminate his hair in some way so that he might lose his hair before or while I lost mine. Since his hairline was straight and low on his forehead, and since some of our relatives called him a handsome brute, many thought that he was cuter than I. Since I couldn't do anything about the stuff he used on his face I mean, I couldn't contaminate his after shave I kept oiling his hairbrush. At first my brother didn't know what was happening. He would bring the brush to our mother and show her the oil in between the bristles and say, "Look at this?"

"What is it, dear?"

"Who is doing this?"

Mother was perplexed too. I mean, what could she do? Everybody was scratching their heads. For a long time my brother would just wash the brush out with soap and water and forget about it, thinking maybe that an accident had happened. I'd feel a little guilty about this but my remorse always dissipated when I saw that my brother continued to look pretty good. Occasionally I'd convince myself that the oil in the brush was making a tiny bald spot on the top of his head, but not always. When he looked better than usual his hair as lush as Ricky Nelson's I'd squeeze on more oil, and then sometimes mix oils so that the brush looked as though it had been dipped into a car engine.

"It's you who's doing this, isn't it?" he said to me one day, wet, oily brush in hand. I thought he was going to punch me, and maybe he did. I forget. I do know that we had it out and that he waved the brush around a lot. Then he poured motor oil into my brush and told me to smell it.

"Life is hard," I told him, "I'm having difficulties in school." That was my only excuse. But I'll say one thing for my brother: he understood. He walked away so that I felt pretty cheap like a second-rate thief.

The fact is, I was spending too much time alone. Whenever I wasn't running cross country, I was sitting in the library reading books and magazines like The Nation, The New Republic, and Time. I was evolving into something. I felt it, and it frightened me. The librarians all noticed me, of course, coming into the library before home room and reading before the class bell, sitting alone, talking to no one.

I did like the librarians, though. One was short and acted sort of dumb: she was a female absent-minded professor. The really nice librarian was the one who probably should have been a teacher. They said she had a son in private school somewhere. She wasn't pretty; she had a big nose and she had me bring her The New York Times to the library every morning. I liked that job. I would go to a classroom where they delivered the papers, take a copy off the desk and then walk it back to her. A very pretty World Cultures teacher was in charge of unwrapping The Times and keeping track of how many went out. I never had her for anything but they always said she was smart and a real nut for newspapers.

The librarian would thank me for the newspaper when I put it on her counter when, really, I should have been thanking her. I didn't know what else to do before home room.

Once in a while I'd walk the corridors by myself but it got monotonous to keep going it alone. I would keep bumping into the same kids and they'd always be with friends and it got to be embarrassing. Only fat, or black girls roamed the halls by themselves cracking their gum to keep from getting lonely. Whores with teased hair and runs in their stockings roamed the halls alone too, when they weren't with their hoodlum boyfriends.

All in all, Valley High was really strange. When I was a freshman I had lots of friends. We did silly things together. We had parties. We sat and joked in a glass-enclosed partition before home room. This was when I was seeing a lot of a boy named Fred, who was from North Carolina and he lived in a trailer park not far from my family's home, which was next to a cornfield. Fred was tall and muscular, and he seemed to take to me right away. We did everything together, even sit together every morning on the school bus.

Fred got on the wrestling team, and sometimes before home room, he'd weigh himself in the gym locker room. I watched him take off his clothes and stand nude on the weighing scale. Fred had the kind of body that populated my dreams. Muscles, big cock, small "bunched up"' ass.

One day I gave Fred a story I wrote about two boys getting it on in a hayloft. The boys were supposed to be us. In the story I had one boy, a cute, blond farm boy, falling through a hole between the bales of hay. The other boy (dark-haired, of course, for contrast), his best buddy, dove in to rescue him. When the second boy pulled the first boy out of the hole, they relaxed together in the hay. Then the blond noticed his buddy had, in the excitement, popped a boner. The blond started massaging his friend's boner, but only as a joke. What began as a joke turned into a big barn blow-job scene, with the blond boy sucking off the dark-haired boy as nearby cows mooed and as pigeons fluttered from rafter to rafter. It was one of my favorite fantasies and I made it come true on paper.

In a later draft, I completed the fantasy:

...Jake Swanenberg, the farm boy, fresh in from the outer cornfields, wiped his brow and looked at his friend, Frank, who was sunburned from being outside all day. Jake knew what was on Frank's mind when he asked, "Is your mind up in the clouds or are you sick?" He said this as he threw bales of hay off the flatbed truck.

"It's nothin'," Frank answered, trying not to let his feelings show. Jake had been working with his shirt off and pitching the bales in rapid motion.

Frank could barely take his eyes off his friend's muscles, especially the way the lad's jeans kept riding low on his hips.

For his part, Jake knew what was up. He'd caught his friend's eyes looking before. He caught his eyes looking hard. Sometimes it made him horny to think what might happen if Frank would only speak up and tell him what he wanted. Why was he so afraid? "You know we're buddies, and buddies do everything and say everything. They keep no secrets, so speak!" he'd joke to Frank.

In the cornfield, the feeling from Frank was even hotter than the sun. And Jake was thinking how the small spray of freckles looked on Frank's shoulders and what it would feel like to take his dick out and have Frank lick it, or have Frank lie down so he could lie on top of him. That would be a lot like lying on top of Frank's sister, which is what Jake always wanted to do.

"The hayloft is where it's cool. Up top where its dark and cool, though first we got to climb up the stacks. Want to go?"

Frank said yes, a hot chill shooting through his body. Something was different about Jake's voice but he didn't know what. In the loft with Jake, high up in the dark, away from people and girls. That was some kind of dream.

They headed for the big barn down the road a ways, Jake walking fast as perspiration wet his back. Inside the barn Jake felt the tingling hot force collect in his cock, one week's worth of build-up, an unusual savings since he was always fucking this girl or that. Jake scrambled up the first bales of hay arranged like steps that went up into the immense loft, reaching and climbing until the steps became smaller and narrower, Frank following almost as fast. Higher up, off in a corner, was the darkest area. From that perch people on the barn floor looked small. The area was six bales of hay laid across but to get to it you had to hurdle a hole that shot straight down to the barn floor. It was an area Jake's father said was off-limits. Too dangerous. "If something slips down, like a little boy, they'd all but be swallowed up like Jonah in the belly of the whale dead, dead, dead!" was his father's refrain. Jake's father couldn't help talking like that. He was a Mennonite.

Jake hurdled across the hole, his wide wrestler's legs straddling like the athlete he was. Frank copied the stride almost to a tee but caught on to a loose bale of hay as his legs slipped into the hole. Jake spun around and caught his arm in plenty of time, even though Frank was well on his way to pulling himself up. His passion for Jake provided him with accelerated energy.

"Almost lost ya," Jake said, a strange blush visible on his cheeks. (Almost like he was talking to my sister, Frank thought.) Jake's hand rested on Frank's shoulder in Red Cross fashion even though Jake was stretched out on his side, his beautiful navel taut and the lump in his jeans now an erect, straight arrow that seemed to want to push through. (That big cock that had been inside so many girls, Frank thought.)

"I feel good now," Frank found himself saying.

"Cool. Just lie back and rest," Jake said. He was burning up. What was happening? In the dark, Frank's auburn hair reminded him of the sister. She was the lush one, the virgin. Even his freckles, his white skin, his smell. Frank was stretched out before him, eyes closed, pale face of an angel, waiting, too shy to do anything. "Take this," Jake said, letting a small gob of spit fall from his mouth and land on Frank's right nipple. A foamy web then linked his lips to the upright little mount. Jake breathed in then let his tongue go down and touch the pink tip. He made a circle like he did on girl's tits, then brought his full lips over it in a kiss that clamped tight. Frank had the faraway look of someone who was comatose or too shocked to register any emotion just yet.

Frank, through closed eyes, heard Jake unbuckle his belt, unzip, then do the same to him. He lifted his body so that Jake could

195

slide his jeans over his legs. Jake put both jeans in a pile to the side and then climbed on his friend. Frank felt the great wrestling cock settle down between his legs, the rocket tip pressing in and out of his balls as it also took a nosedive near his ass. He'd never felt anything so big, so utterly splendid.

"Let me hear you go 'Uuuuahhh...ooooooh,' real soft, real soft. Say it, say it, Frankie, 'Ooooooooh, ahhhhhhhh,' real soft," Jake was saying.

Frank was afraid to open his eyes but when he did he saw a different look on Jake's face. He reached down and grabbed Jake's cock, slid his fingers over the tip and then down the long shaft. Jake brought his cock out from between Frank's legs and let it flip-flop on his buddy's belly. Then he directed it up towards Frank's chest, dangled it in the air in a show of shows, then let it sway from side to side over Frank's belly. The motion left a web of sticky trails.

"Take it in your mouth, go 'Oooohh, ahhhh,' say it soft." Jake was now on all fours poised above the boy's mouth. Neither boy wanted to move too fast but Jake couldn't help himself.

When he released himself into his friend's soft mouth, the chains from the sister broke and he knew now that life was gifted with more options than the narrow one that claimed to be all there is.

Fred didn't say anything when he handed back the original draft of my story, but I was sure I saw him blush. I wanted to crawl underneath the table we were sitting at to see if he had a hard-on, but of course I didn't dare. I was waiting for a reaction of some sort, but I noticed nothing. In my own way I was planting a seed, telling him what I wanted to do to him one day when he was bored and when he couldn't find a date among the many girls who made themselves available to him.

The glass booth where our little group sat was the scene of many outbursts. One day for no reason at all just to be funny, I guess I threw my sister's pocketbook in the air so that all the contents fell out and everybody in the booth screamed. All the "in people" walking around the booth looked in on us like we were a bunch of monkeys. This was about the time that our group began to disperse.

Was I dumb? I didn't know, yet down deep I knew that I knew things that most kids didn't. I could write stories, for one thing. I wrote mysteries in English class, got good marks, and was asked to read aloud during class. People applauded, voted me top writer, and teachers hung my compositions on bulletin boards. What a thrill. In English, I beat them all even the son of a famous writer that freshman year when everything in that public school was so big, so new. My English teacher, Mr. Flank, was a dandy of a man who knew how to dress and quoted Oscar Wilde. He was the best-dressed teacher in the school. And he always had on talcum powder that made you want to sniff and sniff. You loved it when he walked up and down the aisles past your desk. His shoes, made of the finest leather, would always creak when he walked, and I was really impressed.

One day we came to school and Mr. Flank was not there. Students and teachers said that he'd been arrested on a morals charge. He'd been buying booze and letting the sexy A-list boys in the Boys' Leaders Club, all top athletes, drive his sports car so long as he could photograph them nude and give them blow jobs. Mr. Flank had become the talk of the town. I wouldn't see Mr. Flank again until after high school graduation, when I spotted him selling men's underwear in a large department store not a very good place to spout Oscar Wilde jokes.

My retreats into the school library had special significance when Fred was there. Usually I'd sit at the same table with him, only across from him so that I could stretch out my legs next to his and slowly rub my legs against his. Since Fred always sat slouched in a chair with his legs stretched out in front of him, this wasn't too hard to do. For the longest time Fred didn't seem to notice what I was doing; or if he did, he kept quiet about it.

Sometimes I felt he noticed it but was just enjoying himself by getting into the sensation of having his legs massaged by my leg under the table. Of course, I knew that Fred had thick tufts of black hair on his legs and that his legs were really strong because he was on the wrestling team.

Sometimes I would feel the warmth of his legs and then I really got excited and closed in on him with both legs and pressed in and out. This action on my part seemed to go on for the longest time without Fred saying anything about it. And while I was doing this I would always look around the library and see other boys in under-the-table leg locks. Or maybe it was an ankle-lock or a knee-union; whatever it was it involved touching.

But one day Fred said to me, ''Hey, man, what are you doing under there?'' He wasn't mad, just curious, but I had to stop. "Nothing," I said. "I always do that to people I sit across from." I nearly meant it, but the funny thing is Fred didn't move his legs out from under mine. He kept them there, as if testing me. So it was hard for me to stop.

At the beginning of my sophomore year was when Fred started to really fuck. I would get on the school bus and go to where he was sitting and he would tell me about it. How he waited till the end of the bus line with this new girl, and how he unzipped her dress there in the back seat, and how he fucked her just as the sun was going down. Fred always shook his head when he talked this way; much like a horse shivers in the cold or makes a noise of some kind. Then he would describe for me what she looked like. I listened and once in a while looked at his crotch to see if it was getting big. I also liked to push my leg against his leg when we rode on the bus, as I did with Donnelly. But Fred's crotch was always bulging, even when he didn't have a boner.

Fred asked, "You ever had a girl?"

I stammered some feeble excuses, but he knew the score. Generous fellow that he was, he said he would fix me up. Sure enough, he told me that if I asked Dee-Dee to the party that was to follow a football game she just might let me take her. Dee-Dee was a cheerleader, a rosy-cheeked, pretty student with, as Fred said, good boobs. I just happened to mention to him one day that I liked Dee-Dee. Only in a "friendly" sort of way or as a person with a good personality. But since it was the first football game of the season, and Fred had a date, and my sister had a date, and all these dates were being arranged, Fred felt I was in dire need.

"There she goes! Ask her now!" he shouted to me one morning as Dee-Dee passed the outside of our booth. I felt my face turn red, and before I could feel anything else, Fred pushed me out the booth door and raced up to Dee-Dee himself. "He really does have something to say to you!" he said. Dee-Dee smiled. She really was a nice person. She just blinked and stood there, half looking at me and, well, I felt forced to walk over to her. As soon as Fred took off, I asked her to the football game. When she said yes I said I would phone her and tell her when my father and I would pick her up. When I told Fred Dee-Dee said yes he said "Ya!" and gave me a hard slap on the back.

This was way before I was always alone in school and before I flunked Algebra and Spanish and wound up in General Math I as a junior, in a class full of freshmen and sophomores. When I was in this class I would think back to the day I asked Dee-Dee to the game and something in my stomach would roll up into a ball and I would say to myself, How could I? Because since that football game Dee-Dee had climbed to higher scholastic heights, heading committees and giving talks and cheers while throwing her pom-poms around at athletic events. I barely even glanced at Dee-Dee when I was a senior, though once in a while she would throw me a "Hi," though I thought it was because she felt sorry for me, walking around the school corridors all alone loaded down with library books and acne.

Fred and I continued to be good friends; I'd go up to his trailer and visit and the two of us would sit and watch TV and I'd listen as he'd tell me about his parents or a new girl he fucked. He would make vodka and orange juice and we'd get high. Fred, through all of this, had a thing for my sister. She was in the same grade as I and the three of us often rode the school bus together. Fred would always kid my sister about her frizzy hair just to get her goat. "Here she comes, Miss America," he'd sing, knowing darn well she didn't look her best. He really just wanted to fuck her. My sister knew this too and this is why she never went out with him because he always got fresh and started to let his hands roam as that penis of his grew to monstrous length as it "begged" to be let out so it could do its sex duty.

In junior year, Fred and I went to the gym so that Fred could weigh himself for an upcoming wrestling match. This was when our friendship was on the downhill slide. It was morning, and I remember the sun shining through the gym windows as I sat on a gym bench beside the lockers.

Fred undressed in front of me, taking everything off, and soon his huge, nearly erect penis was just a few inches from my face. I could scarcely believe my eyes. It was the first time I had seen it standing straight up, so long and thick. Fred was talking to someone on the other side of the lockers and stood naked and hard like that for some minutes before slipping on his underwear. I kept looking at his cock and then looking away. I didn't know what to do. What was he trying to tell me? I imagined it in action in back of all those buses, in the lakes of New England where he said he fucked girls in the water. I also imagined him in his trailer where he probably fucked on his mother's sofa.

Everywhere! His penis shooting sperm into countless vaginas! Here it was! I had only to reach out and take it, gobble it up, stretch it, flip it from side to side, blow on it.

That penis of his appeared in my dreams long after he left the locker room. It stood, detached from him, like a plant walking, going to school, spurting cum, looming high on the horizon like the Washington Monument.

The penis came in many forms. It came as a great blimp in the skies over the cemetery, balls hanging way down so that they touched the tops of the trees. It came to me as something detached from Fred, something packed inside a pair of trousers. In these dreams Fred's hand would unzip his zipper and put it in front of my face. No words, no warning, no preliminaries: out would come the great cock, the long slit open at the top as if it knew it was the release-valve of copious flows.

Then I would suck ... suck and kiss and then stop-motion so I could gaze at it a moment, in complete worship, then suck again, always knowing when it got close. I could hear Fred's whimpers, feeling the penis move on its own, so hot, little bits of cream slipping out until I could only think "More! More!"

It would come to me at odd moments, in the middle of dreams about my parents or school or Auntie Dorothy. Fred in shorts or jeans or dress pants, just the crotch intruding with the hand coming around and unzipping. The full, rocket-like penis in my face like I was nursing on it in some cock cradle, suck, suck, suck, until, of course, Fred came, and I was awash in a river of foam. His smell, his essence, overwhelmed me. Sometimes the penis came again and again until, choked with cream chalk, I awoke gasping for air like an asthmatic. A "cock asthmatic" wanting more and more....

This was my dream penis that I saw get longer and longer and actually poke through the rim of his Bermuda shorts the day of the hayride. He had his arm around my sisters, consoling her about something, his legs spread far apart so that the outline of his dick was immense so immense, so obscene that it was embarrassing. Everyone around him saw that it was alive and solid, and, of course, so was mine!

SCHOOLBOY DREAMS – AN INTIMATE MEMOIR by WILLIAM COZAD

"You're the spitting image of a boy I always wanted to fuck in
high school but never had the nerve to approach...."

Brett Easton Ellis in the novel "Glamorama"

1 Mark, from English Class

In senior English class, Miss Greene gave us dictation, words
in a sentence that we had to learn to spell because we were tested on the
list at the end of the week. I don't know where she got those words.
chuckie, the class clown, did an imitation of Miss Greene that had us
boys howling before she came into the classroom. He joked that Miss
Greene played Dictaphone, she took the phone and dicked the phone up
her ass. When Miss Greene came into the room the noise hushed at
once. She was an old woman with beady black eyes behind the wire-
framed glasses she wore. She had thinning gray hair and a pot belly.
She lived in an attic room in the house on the corner across from
Herbert Hoover High. The high school was in Iowa and our claim to
fame was that the state had produced a U.S. president. Of course that
pride was overshadowed by Harry Von Zell's (the announcer on the
"Burns and Allen" show) boo-boo while introducing the president as
Hubert Heever. Hebert Hover. Hobart Haver. Tongue-tied, he never got
the name right. That true story was legendary even after the former
president croaked in '64, and still rival schools razzed us about it.

Miss Greene was a taskmaster. Her red-inked marks on our
themes, which she required every week, made you wonder if you spoke
the same language she did. Chuckie joked that she learned the language
directly from the Anglo-Saxons themselves.

But I digress. While I liked English and literature because of Miss Greene, I was often distracted from her dictation. I'd stare out the window and look at the grounds below the second story and at the traffic on Hillside Street.

Miss Greene's list of words to learn to spell often included trees like Joshua, cypress and eucalyptus. Chuckie joked that eucalyptus was the Jewish tree, which was funny after he explained it, about the rabbi's revenge.

While I listened to Miss Green's whiny voice and rasping cough, my eyes roamed over to my classmate Mark who was assigned to a front row seat since the seats were assigned in alphabetical order. I sat a couple rows behind him on the end near the windows.

Miss Greene seemed to have memory lapses sometimes. Once when a girl asked her a question the teacher said "What school? Where?" That got a big laugh, which she didn't understand. At times like this my classmate Mark would turn around and smile at me. He lived across the street from me. We used to walk to school together in junior high until Mark got a bike. Then he'd pass me on the street and wave.

There was something about Mark that triggered feelings and urges in me that I didn't understand. When I'd first noticed him in the locker room after gym class in high school I was shocked by the size of his dick. It was huge, fat and uncut. Different, because most of us boys were circumcised. In class I liked to look at Mark's rump in the ass-hugging jeans he wore. Mark was medium height with jet black hair and brown eyes. In high school Mark and I were still friendly but hung out with different crowds. He had a paper route and I got a job at Gold's department store, working after school and on Friday nights and Saturdays.

I used to think about Mark when I jacked off after school before I went to work, and at work when I thought about him I often got random boners. I wanted to touch his muscular body. I wanted to touch his dick and jack it like I jacked mine. I shot dozens of loads while thinking about him.

My first sex experience happened with Mark. I invited him to come over to my house and drink a Coke when I saw him on his bike. Even though we didn't hang out together he agreed. Both of my folks worked. I had a half hour before I had to be at my after school job.

In the kitchen I got Mark and me a Coke, and we went upstairs to my room. He sat down in the chair. I sat on my bed.

"Getting any?" he asked.

I didn't understand what he meant at first. When I realized it was sex.

"Naw, I don't fool around."

"Doesn't Connie put out?"

"No, we're just friends."

"Karen lets me touch her tits. She jacks me off sometimes." Looking at Mark rubbing his crotch gave me a boner.

"God, you got me horny," I said.

Brazenly I jumped off the bed and groped Mark. I'd goosed and given wedgies in the locker room after gym class but never with Mark. This was different somehow.

"Hey man, whatcha doing?"

"You got a big dick."

Mark grinned.

"Whip it out. Let me see it hard."

"Why should I?"

"'Cause we're horny and can beat off. Ain't nothing wrong with two buddies jacking off together. Not like it's queer or anything."

"I don't know. I did it once with my pal Joe and it changed our friendship."

"C'mon, Mark, let's get off."

Kneeling, I unzipped his fly and freed his boner. I literally dragged him by the dick over to my bed.

His dick was hot and throbbing. I jacked it, fascinated by the throbbing, the cowl of foreskin and his big balls.

While he lay down on my bed I played with his dick. It was just a tad bigger than mine. The piss hole breathed.

"Oh shit, I'm gonna shoot!" he shouted.

Splash! Big gobs of creamy cocks not hit his belly.

Seeing that, I shot my load in my shorts. I didn't even take out my dick.

Mark smeared the cum onto his belly. He zipped up his fly. "Gotta go, man," he said.

Mark left in a hurry.

Looking at my watch, I had to rush or be late for work. I made it to the store in the nick of time. I was all flushed and sweaty. I smelled kind of rank with a load of cum in my shorts.

No one seemed to notice but me. I did my job and went home to supper.

My relationship with Mark changed after that incident. He avoided me. He didn't look back and grin at me in English class like before. I guess he was embarrassed or scared by the homo experience.

Later, he started going steady with Karen. He stopped speaking to me altogether. I was confused but eventually accepted it.

2 Mike, the Mechanic

With my class schedule I had study hall during fourth period before the lunch hour.

The teacher monitor was Mr. Hart. He was also a history

teacher. He'd worked at a radio station in Des Moines. He'd done the sign-off newscast at midnight. He left the station when it was sold and settled for a teaching gig in our town. There was an overflow of students in the study hall at that hour so some of us were assigned to a nearby classroom that was empty during that period.

Of course you were supposed to study during study hall, but without the teacher in the overflow room little studying got done. There was mostly chatter among the students from all grade levels. In study hall I met Mike. He was a junior. Short, with cropped brown hair and big blue eyes. He sat next to me and started to talk to me. Since I was a lordly senior and he was a lowly junior, I guess it gave him status to suck up to a senior. There was something about Mike that attracted me. It wasn't his brains but his looks. He had chiseled features and sensuous ruby lips. He had a deep voice which sounded sexy.

Mike was into cars, which he rattled on about. I listened, not because I was interested. I listened because I liked Mike's looks. He had a muscular build and a big basket. I kept wondering what his dick looked like. Looking at him and listening to him made my balls tingle.

One time I went to my last period gym class and Mike was standing on the bench in the locker room in his briefs. He was in the gym class the period ahead of mine. He had a gorgeous, smooth body. He spoke and smiled while he tugged on his clothes. I got a half hard-on while I changed into my gym trunks.

I never let on to Mike how attractive I found him. I was sure he was totally straight. I thought that I was the only budding queer in my high school. After the rebuff from Mark after the hand job incident which I was sure he'd blab about but didn't to my knowledge, I decided to cool it. I could lust after Mike and he would never know.

I idolized him. I went home after gym class that day and flopped down on my bed. My dick raged in my jeans. I reached down inside my shorts and fondled my dick. I shot off pronto while I punched up the image of Mike in his briefs.

For a long time afterwards I had to stifle the urge to somehow bust into his locker and steal his shorts while he was in gym class. How I'd love to sniff them. How I'd love to lick them. Just thinking about those white cotton briefs which held his jewels made my cock get hard as a rock. There were piss and cum stains on them and the taint from his butthole.

I never got those briefs but I got a lot of jack-off mileage out of seeing him standing on that bench in his drawers.

Mike worked after school and on weekends at the Chevron gas station which his father owned.

On Sundays, I got my dad's blue Chevy to tool around town in. I stopped at the Chevron station on Fifth and Maple where Mike worked by himself on Sundays. He wore blue coveralls and tinkered with an old junker Ford that he was restoring.

He was real friendly with a big smile on his face. I got a couple bucks worth of gas and had him check the oil dipstick. That's when I got a big boner. When he bent over the fender. I could see the slit in his coveralls and his bare skin and those white shorts underneath. I almost creamed my pants on the spot.

Alas, nothing ever happe.ned between us. But I had this wet dream of Mike that haunted me for many moons. In the dream I went into the station at closing time. He shut off the pumps and closed the overhead door at the station.

I went into the toilet to take a piss. I was surprised when Mike came in and joined me at the urinal.

He reeled out his dick which was fat and cut. He took a leak. I stared at his dick. He shook off the piss drops.

"Shake it more than three times and you're playin' with yourself," I teased.

He shook it several times and it got hard. It was huge, jutting out from his coveralls. He stroked it.

I had a pretty big boner myself from watching him. I stroked my dick.

"Whoever shoots first is the winner," he said. "Five bucks, okay?"

"Hey, you're on!"

I was so horny I thought I'd bust a nut. I fisted my meat like crazy but he beat me to the punch. He shot huge globs of cum all over the white porcelain urinal.

I handed over the fiver.

"Gotta stash the cash. See you later."

When Mike left the toilet I did something real nasty. I

leaned over the filthy yellow-stained urinal and licked up all his cum drops. They tasted real sweet.

In study hall I talked to Mike but he wasn't real friendly like before. I wondered what was wrong.

When he left the study hall to go to the toilet, by accident I bumped his desk and knocked off his loose-leaf notebook. picking it up, I looked at it.

I was shocked at what I saw. He had itemized things about me. I read the list: 1) This senior guy acts like a queer: he gawks at my crotch. 2.) I hate fags. They're the scum of the earth. 3) Queers are evil and should be burned like witches. That's what all my buddies say. 4) If a queer ever hit on me, I'd bust him in the mouth. So this senior guy who sits by me in study hall better be careful. 5) Maybe I could blackmail this queer. Make him give me money not to tell about him. That's what one of my buddies did to this old man and the sucker paid.

I didn't finish reading the list. There were three or four more items. But I was worried that Mike would be back real quick. He was. But he didn't catch me.

Despite his macho good looks I decided that he was bad news. So I asked the study hall teacher to let me stay in the big room because it was too noisy and I couldn't get any studying done in the overflow room.

I guess Mike realized that I'd seen his nasty notes because he looked the other way when I saw him in the hallways. That was fine with me.

For awhile I thought I was going crazy. I was getting paranoid that other people knew my secret, but no one ever said anything about it to me.

3 The Blond Boy

I became obsessed with a blond underclassman. I saw him on campus. He was tall, with wavy hair and shiny brown eyes. He was only a sophomore, but I thought he was a living doll.

I sniffed around and eventually learned that his name was wayne and that he was the kid brother of a girl in my class, Betty. I'd have plotted to ask Betty for a date in order to get close to her brother. But I heard through the grapevine that she was going steady with a guy who'd graduated last year. She was blonde, with the same dark eyes as her kid brother.

It didn't seem possible that I'd ever get a shot at Wayne. Lordly seniors just didn't fraternize with sophs. Every time I saw Wayne in the hallways at school between classes I ogled him. I stored up lots of bits and pieces like his pouty lips and big hands that I later used in fantasies during my nightly jack-off sessions.

There was a god after all because, lo and behold, one Saturday I was working in the men's department at the store alone when the regular clerk was on his lunch break. In strolled my fantasy boy in the flesh. I felt my heart lurch in my chest. Sucking in my breath, I approached him. Can I help you?"

"Yeah, I need some jeans."

I led him over to the area where the jeans were.

"Do you know what size?" I asked.

"I'm not sure. My mom usually buys them for me."

"Let me check." This was just too much! I was trembling as I got the tape measure out and wrapped it around his waist.

"Thirty," I said.

When I measured his inseam, I was even more nervous. I dropped the tape, quickly picked it up again. I ran the tape from his crotch to his shoes.

"Thirty-one length," I said.

I located the size on the stacks.

"Maybe you should try 'em on just to make sure."

"Yeah, I guess," he said, not too pleasant about it.

Wayne went into the small corner dressing room. I felt my dick stir in my pants. I'd measured plenty of guys for their pants size but never thought about it like I did now. My hand had even brushed against his dick.

There were no other customers in the men's department at that time and I paced around nearby the dressing room. Just the idea that Wayne was in his shorts, changing his pants made my dick ooze. I was afraid I'd show a wet spot and checked my crotch, but I looked in the mirror and my dark blue slacks didn't show anything.

Suddenly Wayne opened the door. He stepped outside of the dressing room and looked into the mirror on the door.

"They feel okay. Whaddaya think?"

I checked the waist from the back, cinching the jeans with my fingers. I looked at his basket and the inseam.

"They're your size," I said.

"I'll take 'em."

He went back into the dressing room to change into his other pants, but he left the door open. He didn't seem to notice or care that I stood there watching him take off the new jeans. He stood in his briefs and shirt. He had a big bulge. I wanted to touch his basket and butt, but I didn't dare. He might slug me. He might tell and get me fired. I just couldn't risk it. His legs were dusted with blond peach fuzz. I stared at him as he put on his other pants.

Watching him, I almost shot off in my pants. My dick was slanted sideways but I don't think he noticed.

I went to the counter, bagged his jeans and rang up the sale.

I walked him to the front door.

"Good game last night, the Tigers kicked butt," he said.

"I didn't see it. I had to work. But I heard we won."

He gave me a quick replay of the game, the overtime field goal that put the tigers over the top.

Wayne had a husky, sexy voice. When I looked into the dark pools of his eyes I thought I saw fire. He was a real hot looking kid.

"See you around," he said.

He gave me a big smile.

"Thanks for your business...."

I realized that my dick now tented my slacks. He had to have noticed that while I was bagging up his jeans. I felt sweaty.

I got the notion to go sniff the dressing room for a whiff of Wayne, but the room was stuffy.

Soon as the clerk returned, I took my lunch break. I hightailed it home, about six blocks from the store.

My folks were out shopping or something. I went to my room. My dick was hard as a rock and leaking like a sieve as I dropped my pants and lay across my bed. I grabbed my dick and leisurely stroked it.

I raved on out loud while I pounded my dick. "Oh wayne, you're such a beauty. I want you so bad. I can taste it. If you only knew."

In my fantasy, I followed Wayne into the dressing room after he modeled his jeans. He looked as sexy as Marky Mark with his jeans down on the bus shelter posters I saw in Minneapolis while on vacation last summer. Only Wayne was the real thing.

In the dressing room, Wayne dropped his jeans and I tugged down his shorts like the dog with the kid in the Coppertone billboard ad on the highway outside of town. I kissed his butt. He looked over his shoulder at me with those big black eyes.

"Suck my ass, you queer."

I spread his butt cheeks. I licked his funky crack with the blond fuzz.

"Tongue my shithole. I like that."

209

I tongue-fucked him. I stroked my dick faster. I wanted to shove it up Wayne's hole.

He turned around suddenly and slapped me in the face with his monster cock which was rosy red. I licked it.

In a quick maneuver, he spun me around and "de-pantsed" me. "I'm gonna fuck you in your queer ass!"

"No, don't, Wayne. Your dick's too big."

What was I saying? Was it even possible to fuck a guy like a girl?

He shoved his dick up my ass. I thought I'd die.

Now I beat my meat furiously as he screwed my butt.

Just when he shot his wad up my ass, I opened my eyes and watched my dick spurt pearly cum drops all over my belly.

"Oh Wayne, I gotta have you. I gotta suck your big dick. I gotta feel it up my butt."

I licked my own sweet cum off my fingers. I rubbed my cum into my skin.

Hurriedly I fixed a ham and cheese sandwich, wolfed it down and hiked back to my job at Gold's.

In reality I never had Wayne. But a guy can dream, can't he? And dream I did. And jack-off I did. Over Wayne. Over and over and over. And every time I saw him at school I greeted him and smiled. He liked the attention, just because I was a senior. I ate him alive but only in my dreams.

4 Andy, the New Guy

A boy named Andy transferred to Hoover High in Weston for his senior year. The word was that his family moved from Nebraska to Iowa when his father was promoted as a regional manager at Midwest Oil Company.

I didn't pay much attention to him, except to note that I noticed he wore tan, neatly tailored chinos and Ralph Lauren shirts. He was known as a nerd. He wore wire-framed glasses and was real smart. I know because I was in biology class with him and he knew the names of all the human bones when the teacher pulled down a skeleton drawing. I thought that was weird. Mr. Cooper, the biology teacher, was also the athletic director, and he spent more time in class talking about sports than biology. But I liked him because he'd been a college jock and was real good-looking some even said movie-star handsome, with his wavy black hair and big brown eyes.

Andy sat next to me in class because of the alphabetical seating chart the teacher used. Since he was in the nerd classification, part of the labels assigned like jocks and stoners, no one paid much attention to him. He started talking to me a lot, since the teacher was often late and was often called out of class because of his athletic director duties.

When Andy took off his specs to rub his eyes, I noticed that he was really a good-looking guy. He had brown hair, brown eyes, smooth features with sensuous lips and chicklet teeth. He was medium height and kind of skinny.

I scoped out his crotch but couldn't detect much of a basket in the tan chino pants he wore out of the blue Andy invited me to stay overnight at his house. I wasn't used to doing that. I had friends at school but no bosom buddies. His folks were going to a big party at the Country Club and we'd be alone since he was an only child like me.

When I asked permission from my folks, Mom thought it was a good idea to befriend the new guy and Dad liked me associating with the son of a man of substance in our town.

That Friday night I went home after school with Andy. He lived at the edge of town in a real expensive brick ranch style house with a manicured lawn and evergreen trees.

Inside the house was plush with thick blue carpet. Nice furniture with original oil paintings hanging on the walls. I was impressed since I was from a working-class family where my folks fought constantly over money.

Andy's room was furnished with a ship captain's bed and matching desk, chair and dresser. Custom-made red drapes with a nautical design at the windows. He had a large tank of tropical fish which he was proud of.

He got us frosty bottles of coke from the fridge. He played rock music cassettes on his state of the art stereo system, which he blasted loudly since his folks were gone. He even had his own color TV in his room. I envied his life of luxury, compared to mine.

When it got late we decided to hit the hay. Since he had a single bed I figured maybe he'd tell me to sleep in the guest room. The drapes were open and the light of the harvest moon, which I heard them call it on the weather report the other night, bathed the room in shimmering silver.

Andy slept in his shorts. So did I. He climbed into bed and I crawled in beside him.

"Sweet dreams," he said.

I thought I'd drift off to sleep but I had a boner, just like I always did when I went to bed at home.

A few moments later Andy's hot, bare leg brushed against mine. That made my cock throb. I thought it was just accidental.

Later, I felt his hand touch my thigh. At first I thought I was dreaming. Not only touch my thigh, but his hand crept over to my crotch and grabbed it. Maybe it was accidental, but I preferred not to think so. Well, I thought, two could play that game. I brazenly reached over and grabbed Andy's crotch. His dick was hard like mine.

He ran his hot hand down inside my shorts and wrapped his fingers around my dick. He stroked it slowly. I did the same thing. I ran my hand inside his Calvin Klein briefs and grabbed his dick. I could tell by the feel that it wasn't as big as mine, but it was real stiff. slowly I tugged on his dick. I could feel the slimy goo seep out of his pee hole.

The cat was out of the bag. We were jacking each other and then he flung back the blue comforter. Not a word was spoken. Both of us were horny teenage boys who needed to get our rocks off before we could get to sleep.

He peeled down his briefs and kicked them off. I did the same thing. We beat each other's meat in earnest.

I stopped him because I didn't want to squirt right off. I wanted to prolong the sensation. He squeezed my balls. I fondled his.

In the silvery moonlight it was obvious that my dick was much bigger. It seemed to fascinate Andy, who leaned down and looked at my dick while he fisted it. I continued to jack his dick. Both of us picked up the pace. It was now like a circle jerk competition to see who could shoot first.

"Oh, I'm gonna fuckin' shoot!" he hissed.

"Me too!"

It was a photo finish as both of us got our nut at the same time. Gobs and gobs of pearly teenaged cum drops decorated our smooth chests and bellies.

Without saying another word Andy retrieved our briefs off the floor. He wiped his cum on his shorts. I did the same. Then we put them back on.

I went out like a light, the way I always did once I got my rocks off at night.

I had a horny dream that night. A dream of Andy. He had his dad's new white Oldsmobile. He gave me a lift home after school, but he took a detour out into the country. He parked the car. Both of us got out.

Suddenly Andy was all over me. He ripped open my fly. He licked my dick until I was ready to squirt.

He bent over the front fender and dropped his tan chinos, exposing his smooth, round butt. He spread an ass cheek.

"Stick it up my butt," he begged.

I had no idea he was gay. He was just like me.

I eased my drooling pecker into his vise-tight butthole. Damn! I came off just as my dick eased into his warm, moist shithole.

I was startled awake. There was Andy jacking my dick like crazy.

"Shoot it! I wanna see it shoot!"

He was jacking his dick at the same time. I squinted at the light that streaked in from the window.

"It's coming!" I moaned. Splat! I shot a puddle of cum all over my belly.

So did Andy. He aimed his cocks not onto my belly. Then he rubbed it into my skin, mixed with my spunk.

Both of us got dressed.

His folks were home, and they were real nice people. His mom fixed us a big breakfast with eggs, pancakes and sausages. Then I went home.

I thought Andy and I would become best friends now that we explored our sexuality and exchanged hand jobs. He did stay friendly with me, unlike Mark after I'd jacked him off, but he seemed to keep his distance. He started dating a brainy girl named Carolyn. I was kind of confused, but figured that he was really straight but was just lonely in a new town and a typical horny teenager who got his kicks wherever he could. Kind of like the joke they told in the locker room about the guy who opened a whorehouse but ran it by hand until he got some girls.

5 The Jock

In Modern Problems class, which was required of all seniors, I began to fantasize about another one of my classmates. His name was Carl, and he was the captain of the football team. He was the son of the coach, the spitting image of his dad. He had a shock of sandy blond hair and big baby blue eyes.

With the approaching last game there was a lot of pressure on Carl, the quarterback. Because the team was having a bad season and rumors were flying about dumping Coach Conway. But a big upset win might change things with the school board.

Fat chance, I thought, that Hoover High could upset Winters, considering the opponents were undefeated this season.

In my fantasy, while Mr. Fitch the teach was rambling on and writing dates of historical events on the blackboard, I glanced over at Carl who sat at the end of the row. There was something about him. Animal magnetism maybe. He was a talented player and was being checked out by college scouts. It wasn't his fault that the other players had butterfingers and couldn't hold onto the ball after he passed it to them. I felt sorry that he had to be with those losers on the team. He was like a rose in a manure pile. Other students said the same thing. So Carl was still a big man on campus.

During my last period gym class, I took my sweet time showering and dressing. Sometimes I got a sneak peek at some of the football jocks when they suited up for practice after school. Once I was blessed and got to see Carl wearing just his jockstrap. His beefy body was dusted with golden fleece.

After seeing Carl in his jockstrap, he became the star of my jack-off fantasies. The pouch of his jockstrap was really packed. He was hung big, I could tell. But I wondered just how big and whether his dick was clipped or not.

Looking over at Carl in class, I noticed how macho he looked. He was probably thinking about football plays while the teach droned on and while I thought about Carl in his athletic supporter.

The day of the big game rolled around. There was a big pep rally and lots of pressure on the team to pull the upset.

I even took off work that Friday night to see the game. The manager of the store didn't like it but reluctantly agreed after I told him that they'd treat me like a traitor at school if I didn't go to support the tigers.

The last game of the season was a disaster. Especially when the tight end fumbled the ball just before halftime when our team was deep in their territory. A touchdown would have tied the same at halftime.

The second half was worse if that was possible. The crowd started to leave before the game was over. Winters flat out skunked Hoover.

After the game I hung around the parking lot, trying to get a glimpse of Carl. I saw several of the other players leave. My dad had even let me have the car that night. I wanted to console Carl somehow.

After they turned off the stadium lights, I knew it was time to go.

Just when I started to leave I spotted Carl. He was all alone. I pulled up beside him.

"Tough luck," I told him. "But it wasn't your fault. Can I give you a lift?"

Miracle of miracles, Carl climbed into my car.

"My dad's history. I let him down. I let the whole school down.

"Hey man, that ain't true. Besides, it's just a game."

"Tell that to my dad. He says that winning isn't everything, it's the only thing. I'm a loser."

"Aw man, don't beat yourself up. That's bullshit talk. The team might be losers but you're not."

"What do you know? You're not even on the team."

"But I'm a fan, a big fan of yours, Carl."

"I still feel like shit."

"You need to relax, cut yourself some slack."

"I know one thing: I hate to go home tonight."

"You don't have to."

"Even my girl didn't wait for me."

"I waited for you, Carl."

"Why?"

I made a right turn onto Seventh Street.

"Where the hell you going?" he asked.

"It's a nice night for a ride."

"I'd better get my ass home and face the music."

Brazenly I reached over and groped Carl.

"What the fuck you doing?"

"I can take care of that big thing for you."

"You're fuckin' crazy, acting like a queer."

"It won't take long, Carl."

I ignored his protests and headed out Ashley Road. I parked along a deserted country road. I shut off the engine and cut the lights.

My hand never left his crotch. His cock was rock-hard.

"What if someone comes?" he asked.

"No one's comin', except maybe you."

I don't know where I got the nerve but I leaned over ripped open the metal buttons of his fly. In the moonlight I could see that he was wearing his jockstrap I started licking it. I felt his dick stiffen even more.

"Oh yeah. Take it out."

I tasted his funky jockstrap, the piss and cum stains on it. With my teeth, I pulled it down. He lifted up on the seat.

His dick was huge, at least eight inches of cut meat, and beer-can thick. Gripping his shaft, I swabbed the mushroom crown. "Suck it. Suck my fucking dick."

I spit on it, stroked it. It gleamed. It was magnificent an absolutely magnificent penis.

"God, you're good," he said as I applied more spit to it. "I've been trying to get my girl to do it but she thinks that's dirty. She don't put out. All I can do is play with her boobs and dry fuck her. But she jacked me off a couple times."

While I listened to his rambling confession I kissed his dick, the first one I ever did.

"Put it in your mouth."

216

I wrapped my lips around the jock's crown and jacked the shaft while I bobbed my head up and down.

He roughly shoved my hand away.

"Oh, yeah, suck it."

He clasped my head and thrust his dick down my throat. He battered my tonsils. I thought he'd choke me to death.

"Oh shit. Aw fuck, I'm gonna come!"

Somehow I managed to keep my mouth on his dick when it squirted and gushed wads cum down my throat. I savored the taste of him. I pulled off it and continue to stroke it.

"Hey, I gotta get home, buddy," he said.

My dick raged in my pants. I squeezed my crotch, and my dick creamed my jeans.

I flipped on the car radio and drove Carl home.

"See you later," I said, but he didn't answer me.

I drove home savoring my conquest of Hoover High's star jock. It never happened again, but he still spoke to me whenever our paths crossed.

6 A Quick Stop at the Bus Station

School let out early one day because of a teachers' meeting. So I wandered around downtown before going to my job at the department store.

I was going to stop at Van's, the drug store, and get a soda at the fountain. But I made a detour to the bus station at Fifth and Elm in order to take a quick piss.

The lobby of the bus station was deserted, except for a guy in an Army uniform. When I looked at him he stared back. He wasn't much older than me. He had a muscular build. Black hair fringed his garrison hat and he had bright brown eyes.

I hurried into the john. At the urinal, I whipped out my dick and let go with a splash of frothy golden piss. Then I went over to the sink on the opposite wall and washed my hands.

Suddenly the door creaked open and the soldier in uniform came in. He glanced at me, then went over to the pisser.

In the mirror over the sink, I watched his back. Knowing that he had his dick out aroused me. Just like in a wet dream, he turned sideways and flashed me his dick. It was big, hard and uncut. Looking at me, he lewdly stroked his dick.

In a trance-like state, I ambled over to him. I touched his throbbing, drooling dick and he moaned softly.

He groped me and unzipped my fly, freeing my stiff dick. He wrapped his hot hand around my dick and jacked it.

I was nervous, aware of where I was. Anybody could come in and catch us. The danger excited me all the more.

The horny soldier shoved me down on my knees.

"Suck it, boy. Suck my soldier cock."

Faced with his throbbing boner, I grabbed it and licked it. I opened my mouth and engulfed it down my throat. I took only a few slides on it and it was like a crowbar.

"Sonuvabitch, I'm gonna fuckin' blow!"

He crammed his big dick down my throat and it exploded. Rivulets of sweet, creamy cum flooded my mouth and I drank every drop, nursing on his big meat until it softened. When his dick fell out of my mouth the crown was covered by the cowl of foreskin.

"Stand up, cocksucker," he barked.

For a moment I thought maybe he'd hit me in the mouth to show his disgust and teach me a lesson for being queer. I shivered all over when I stood up. My legs were wobbly.

The soldier shocked me when he kneeled down and grabbed my dick, which had gone limp out of fear. He yanked on it hard and it stiffened at once.

Opening his mouth, he gobbled up my dick. I couldn't believe it. The feeling was overwhelming. He had no idea that he was giving me my first blowjob. It was the most delicious feeling I ever had. I'd waited all my life for this moment, even though it

turned out to be a stolen moment of lust in the bus station john. He sucked my dick hungrily, which let me know that he'd sucked dicks before, this macho looking young soldier. I wondered where he learned his technique. Maybe from other horny soldiers.

Looking down at him groveling at my feet gave me an awesome sense of power as he serviced me.

"Yeah, eat my big dick, cocksucking soldier. Take it all the way down your fucking throat."

In a fit of fury with my dick hard as a rock, I stuffed it down his throat and it erupted, pushing wads of my hot schoolboy cum into the queer soldier's mouth. Damned if he didn't swallow every drop of my load. He siphoned my balls, then stood up.

My dick stayed hard after I got my gun, the way if often did. In hot solo jack-off sessions I could shoot five loads with the right fantasy material, images of boys' dicks in the locker room at school, replays of my sexual encounters, the notches on my gun;, the dick trophies I'd collected so far.

Standing up, the soldier proudly flashed me his big, soft dick. I clutched his meat but he shoved my hand away.

Then he did the sexiest thing I could imagine. He placed his dick in tandem to mine and sheathed his fleshy foreskin over my rosy crown and masturbated our dicks together until his dick got hard. After docking our dicks he held them together, bone against bone, and jacked them at the same time.

It didn't take long before I felt the familiar buzz in my balls. Both of us popped our nuts at the same time and the mixture of our cum coated our dicks.

The soldier stuck his cum-coated fingers into my mouth and I sucked on them, tasting the sweet and salty flavor of our loads.

He stuffed his softening dick back into his uniform trousers and I got my clothes arranged.

Looking into each other's eyes, I knew this was something that both of us would remember and jack-off over for a long time. The silence was broken by the crackle of the loud speaker and the announcement that the bus for Des Moines, Omaha and points west was now departing.

The soldier hugged me. I hugged him back, noting that the name tag on his uniform blouse said Torres. Which meant he was a Latino, as I suspected.

"Gotta go, amigo," he said.

He dashed out of the john for his bus. I splashed cold water on my face, relieved that no one had caught us fooling around.

Going to my job at the store, I had a big smile on my face and a song in my heart.

7 Copsucker

Weston was a small central Iowa town located near Des Moines, the capital. It had formerly been called Valley Junction because it had been a switching station for the Rock Island railroad. An overflow of people from the capital city moved westward, settling into the area which eventually grew into fairly large "bedroom" community.

Iowa was noted for its rich farm land. It was Bible Belt country and conservative. Although the landscape was changing. Banks had foreclosed on farms. But there was a thriving business community in nearby Des Moines, with banks and insurance companies and the Solar Aircraft plant.

One thing that I loved about the Midwest was the change of seasons: Cool autumn winds and the changing color of the leaves to red and gold before the advent of winter with snow, ice and freezing temperatures.

Sunday was my favorite day of the week when I was a senior in high school. I didn't have to go to school. I didn't have to go to work at the store. When I'd turned sixteen, my folks no longer made me go to church. That was a blessing. And my folks no longer attended the Methodist church on a regular basis.

I could sleep in late. Although I usually. got up early. I'd wash the family blue Chevy in the garage and wipe it dry of water streaks.

My folks let me take the car for a spin on Sunday afternoons after I got my driver's license. Away from school, I was kind of a loner. I drove to Des Moines, where I circled the loop at 7th and Locust. Although there wasn't much traffic on Sunday. Sometimes I parked by the river downtown, where the old-timers hung out near the public library. I looked at the water and thought about the future. I knew I'd leave after I finished high school. I planned to go to the University of Iowa.

Heading back to Weston, I approached the highway. I was surprised when I heard a siren. Looking in the rearview mirror, I saw the whirling cherry red light of a police car. I pulled over to the curb.

I'd never been stopped by the cops before. I wondered what was wrong because I was careful to obey the traffic rules, especially when my dad threatened to ground me if I got any tickets.

In the side view mirror, I noticed the cop got out of his prowl car. He was a big fat cop. He came over to the car.

"Somethin' wrong, officer?" I asked.

"Yeah, I noticed you made a Hollywood stop at the sign back there. A rolling stop. you're supposed to come to a complete stop even if there is no cross traffic."

"I thought I did."

"Got a driver's license?" he barked.

"Yes, sir."

I pulled out my wallet and opened it.

"Take the license out of the holder."

I did, noticing that the big cop's crotch was at eye level. So was the gun in the holster on his right hip.

"Okay, William. Get out of the car."

I obeyed.

"Turn around, put your hands on the hood."

I couldn't believe this was happening. Just like in the movies.

"Is this your car?"

"It's my dad's."

"You got his permission to drive it?"

"Of course."

"Well, it matches the description of a car that was used in a gas station robbery."

"I'm no criminal."

"Spread your legs. Carrying any weapons?"

"No, sir."

Suddenly I was scared. This was a mistake. Maybe I'd go to jail. My dad would really be pissed off.

The fat cop frisked me. Reaching around, he felt my front pockets and my dick, which stiffened at his touch.

"Put your hands behind your back."

"What?"

"Just do it."

Before I knew what happened I felt the cold metal bracelets clamp around my wrists.

"Are you going to arrest me?"

"Depends. This is for my safety, cuffing you stay right where you are."

I froze while the big cop went over to his car. I heard the crackle of the police radio as he spoke into the mike. He came back.

"The car's not stolen, I swear."

"Well, there's the matter of your traffic violation, the stop sign."

"It won't happen again I promise."

"A ticket might teach you a lesson."

"No, please don't. Can't you let me go with just a warning? I've never got a ticket before. My dad will ground me. The rules are the rules."

"Looking into his steely blue eyes, I knew he wouldn't just let me too."

"Please let me go this time," I begged. "Why should I?"

"Do anything you want."

"Hell, this is an unusual situation, you've got a clean record. If you were a babe, I could take out the ticket in trade. you can with me."

"Say what? You one of them queer boys? One of them fairies? Made a Hollywood stop and everything, hee-hee. Do you like dicks?"

"Uh, no sir. I mean, I'd do whatever it takes not to get a ticket."

The idea appealed to me of sucking the cop's cock. He was around my dad's age and tough dangerous, maybe, carrying a gun and all. Hell, I'd like to suck his dick, sure, but maybe he'd bust me for being a queer when he was finished.

The big cop grabbed his crotch. "I sure as hell could use some action. Okay, boy?"

I just stared blankly at him.

He shook his head in disgust. "You listen up. Drive over behind that warehouse and park. I'll be right behind you. No funny stuff or I'll throw your ass in jail."

He took off the cuffs.

I rubbed my wrists. Getting into the car, I was ashamed to admit I had a boner. I drove over behind the closed warehouse and parked.

The fat cop came over to the passenger side and climbed in.

"Okay, boy, do your stuff."

I groped the cop. I unzipped the fly and freed his dick. It was fat, cut and stubby. He had balls like a bull.

"Suck it and get it hard."

I wrapped my lips around his dick and sucked it.

"Oh yeah, baby, you take your time suckin' Daddy's dick."

I jacked the shaft while I sucked the knob. I was amazed at how big his cock got. When it was fully erect, it had to have been at least eight inches and thick as my wrist.

"Eat that cop dick. Go for it. Yeah, keep sucking. Doin' good, boy. You're doin' real good for such a young 'un."

He thrust upwards and shoved my hand away. I bobbed my head up and down on his dick. He clamped my head and battered my tonsils. I had trouble breathing.

"Oh, yeah, this is what I need to haul my ashes. I need a cute queer boy to fuckin' get me off. Oh fuck, I'm gonna shoot!"

His dick exploded like a bomb and gushed wads of hot cum down my throat, whitewashing my tonsils. He flooded my throat with salty cop cum. I couldn't believe it I had creamed my jeans. He stuffed his dick back inside his pants and zipped up. He wiped the sweat off his brow. "You okay, boy?"

I nodded.

"You just keep your trap shut about this. Comprende?"

I nodded.

"What?"

"Yes, sir."

"Okay, now get your ass outta here."

He got out of the car. I switched on the ignition and peeled rubber just to show off.

Driving back to Weston, I couldn't believe my luck. I'd actually sucked off a real man, a fucking cop.

That incident proved to me that there were lots of men around who might appreciate me. Like they say: bloom where you're planted.

8 Bart the Barber

During my senior year of high school, I became obsessed with my looks. I spent a lot of time in front of the mirror on the inside door to my closet. I had a hard, natural body, not pumped up like a jock.

I spent all my extra money on clothes, since I got them at a discount at the store. They were just average sports clothes made for working class people. But I mixed and matched combinations and colors. Like Billy Crystal posing as Fernando Lamas said, it's better to look good than to feel good. And I wanted to be noticed by other guys, not by girls. In a poll for the school paper, I was even voted the best-dressed boy on campus.

All the time I spent in front of the mirror, usually before going to bed at night, inevitably led to my getting turned on, even if by my own reflection. I mean, the sight of my jewels sent horny messages to my brain. I liked to watch my dick get hard. I liked to stroke it while I admired my chest, butt and legs. Splat! I shot my load onto the mirror and watched the pearly cum drops drip down it.

Not only did I spend a lot of time modeling and planning my wardrobe but I spent a lot of time bathing, shampooing my locks and styling my hair. My brunet locks looked best dry and shiny, not the greasy-kid style of some guys at school, which, inevitably, led me to the Downtown Barber Shop near the store where I worked. I was constantly fussing over my looks. Old Kenny was the barber. He did a decent job but I swear he nipped while he waited around for customers because he had boozy breath.

I got my hair cut every couple weeks, more often than necessary, after work. If you got inside his door before the 8 o'clock closing time, which I managed to do by a few minutes, he stayed and sneared your locks. This time when I got to the barber shop in the nick of time, so to speak, I was surprised to see a different barber. He was young, short, blond and blue-eyed and not much older than me. He looked vaguely familiar. Wait a minute, he looked like Kenny if he'd found the fountain of youth. He was trimming an older man's hair.

"Can you cut my hair?" I asked.

He smiled. "Have a seat. You're my last customer of the day."

I flipped through a dog-eared issue of Time magazine but I glanced at the young barber cutting the old man's hair with scissors and comb in hand.

The old man looked into the rectangular mirror and was satisfied with his trim. He paid and left.

I climbed into the barber chair. "Where's Kenny?" I asked.

"He's taking some time off...."

To continue his drinking career, I thought, but didn't say it. Aren't you his son?"

"Yeah, I'm Bart. I remember seeing you at school. You've grown up."

"So have you."

"Yeah, I just got out of the Navy. Did three years on a kiddie cruise. I was a barber aboard ship."

He combed my hair.

"How'd you like it cut? It would look better as a buzz cut."

"Huh?"

"Short. Military style."

"Yeah, I guess. You think so? Okay, do it."

I watched in the mirror across the room as the young barber deftly clipped my hair off. He danced around the chair and his crotch pressed against my hand. I could feel his jewels and I got a boner.

When he took off the bib to shake it he obviously noticed my tented slacks. I was kind of sweaty. He didn't say anything.

He smeared on some shaving foam and trimmed around the edges with a straight razor.

"I look different, huh?"

"Better, I'd say...."

He strapped the vibrator on his hand and massaged my shoulders, like his father often did. That had nothing to do with cutting your hair but it felt nice.

I was shocked when he placed his vibrating hand on my crotch. I squirmed.

"Looks like you need more than a haircut...."

"Whaddaya mean?"

"You know what I mean...."

Before I could respond, he went over and closed the Venetian blinds on the large window and turned the sign on the door to CLOSED.

Bart stood beside the chair and whipped out his dick. It wasn't real big, but it was cut and hard.

"Go on, lick it."

Leaning over, I grabbed his stiff red dick and swabbed my tongue over the bulbous crown. I was amazed when it started to squirt right away. Cum drops hit me in the face and in my freshly-cut hair.

"Jesus, I was so horny. I couldn't hold back. Suck on it some more."

I nursed his cock, tasting his salty load. I wiped the cum off my face.

"How'd you know 'bout me anyway?" I asked.

"Shit, I was a sailor. I can spot a queer or wannabe a mile away."

He groped me. He unzipped my fly and freed my boner.

"Hey, you got a big one, kid."

"Will you suck it?"

"Hell, little ones are for sucking. Big ones like yours are for fuckin'. I bet a b0oy like you'd like some sea pussy."

I wasn't exactly sure what he was talking about until he yanked me out of the chair by my dick. He placed the chair in a horizontal position. He dropped his pants and shorts and lay down on the chair on his belly with his butt exposed. Reaching back, he spread an asscheek.

"Come and get it, baby."

If I wasn't sure what to do my dick was. I straddled the chair and slapped my boner against his smooth butt cheeks.

"Stick it up my ass," he said.

I couldn't believe my luck. I was about to get my first piece of ass!

"Use some spit," he said. "Get it nice and wet."

I drooled spit into his crack. My dick was leaking like a sieve. I punched it into his hole, which was hot and juicy.

"Fuck me. Fuck me in my ass."

I probed his hole, enjoying the delicious sensation, feeling every nook and cranny.

"Bet you were fucked a lot aboard ship, huh?"

"Oh, yeah, I was a slut. I couldn't get enough d.ick. Even the chiefs fucked me. I gave haircuts and blowjobs like Santa passin' out Christmas candy."

"I've never fucked anyone before."

"Well, you enjoy it. You got a big dick, kid. Fuck me harder!"

I crammed my dick all the way up his hole and he humped back. I tried to make it last and prolong the sensation, but my nuts were ready to bust. I buried my dick up the barber's butt and flushed them in his hole. He clenched his butt muscles around my cock and siphoned my balls. He bucked me off.

Leaping off the horizontal barber's chair, he grabbed my dick which was still hard, and he licked it clean, eating all the cum and assjuices off it.

He hoisted his pants and I stuffed my dick back into my pants.

I tried to pay Bart for the haircut but he refused.

"It's on the house."

A couple of weeks later, I went back for another free haircut and another hot fuck session with Bart, but his dad was there. Bart, he said, had gone back to sea.

9 A Little Christmas Cheer

'Tis the season to be jolly, like it or not. There was tawdry gold garland strung around the street posts downtown. Christmas trees showed in the picture windows of houses. A light blanket of snow covered the ground.

The new mall in Des Moines stayed open on the Sunday before Christmas to accommodate the late shoppers like me. I had no idea what to get Mom and Dad. So I went browsing in the stores. Christmas carols sounded over the speaker system.

In the Jolly Giant store near the toy department I spotted Santa in his red suit sporting a fake white beard. It was Big Al from my class at school. I'd heard that he got the job because of his size and cheerful disposition and because his father was one of the store managers.

So there was Fat Albert, as he was known in grade school and later as Big Al when he played fullback on the football team, with a little boy sitting on his lap, telling him what he wanted for Christmas. Amused by the sight, I stood and watched. Big Al noticed me and waved. I watched while he held a little girl on his knee and asked her what she'd like and she rambled off a list of things.

Big Al stood up when he was finished. There was no one else waiting in line to talk to him.

"Time for Santa's break," he said.

He ambled over to me.

"Wanna tell Santa what you want?" he smiled.

"A blowjob," I whispered.

He laughed. "I'd like one of those for Christmas myself. Hey, I'm dying for a smoke. You got any cigarettes?"

"Yeah."

"Follow Santa."

I walked with Big Al to a storeroom in the back, where there was a small toilet. I followed him in and he locked the door. He pulled off his fake beard.

"This is where you gotta sneak. Smoking isn't allowed in the store."

I gave Big Al Marlboro, put one in my mouth, and lit them.

"Excuse me but I gotta take a leak," he said.

He unfastened the red Santa suit and took out his dick at the urinal. I watched him. I was surprised at how fat his cut dick was. He splashed pee into the porcelain bowl. When he was finished he shook his cock. He looked over at me, and, seeing me staring at it, he lewdly stroked his dick.

"Yeah, Old Santa's horny," he said. "I'm used to sleeping in late on Sundays and playing with my Yule log. But I woke up late and didn't have time today."

"What about your girlfriend, doesn't she take care of you?"

"Hell, there ain't no whore once football season is over. I ain't been laid since then!"

I wondered who Big Al was referring to. Maybe he'd banged one of the cheerleaders. There was a rumor around school that Martha, the sluttish-looking cheerleader, had taken on the whole team once but I suspected that was just bullshit.

"You wanna jack off together? I'm horny myself."

I pulled out my dick and started in.

We stood there, gazing at each other's cocks for a few moments.

"We gotta be quick," Santa said.

"Well, maybe I could be Santa's helper," I teased.

Brazenly, I reached over and grabbed Big Al's stubby prick, which was like a steel pipe.

"Always wondered about you, guy."

"Oh?"

"Yeah, you're too pretty to be totally straight."

"Oh?" The way he said emphasized totally made my chuckle. Was anyone totally straight?

"Yeah, I'm so goddamn horny. Any port in the storm will do." That was a green light as far as I was concerned. Kneeling on the wooden floor, I grabbed the store Santa's fat pecker.

"Are you really gonna suck Santa's candy cane?"

I licked it up one side and down the other, tasting his sweet pre-cum. Slowly, I took the big head and some of the shaft in my mouth.

Santa moaned. While Big Al stayed in character as Santa he dropped his cigarette in the urinal. I left mine on the sink against the wall.

Big Al clutched my head. He rammed his cock in and out of my mouth. It was weird, looking up at him in the red suit. He had a twinkle in his cobalt blue eyes.

"Oh fuck, yeah. This is what I need. Oh yeah, you've done this before. I didn't know you were the school cocksucker. Ain't life full of surprises?"

I would have answered him but my mouth was full of dick.

"Oh, yeah, kid, keep sucking my dick. Man, you suck better than that bitch Martha. She was a lousy cocksucker but she had a hot box. Now she's fucking the basketball players, I reckon. She don't give me the time of day no more after the football season's over."

I let go of Big Al's bloated meat. I jacked it while I. lapped at his hairy balls. I stuffed them both into my mouth.

"Oh shit, look at you...."

I put his cock back into my mouth just in time. Suddenly, waves of cum blasted down my throat. I squeezed his balls until I got the last drops.

"Oh man," he sighed as he pulled his cock away. "Time for Santa to get back to the little bastards. You made my day, kid."

After Big Al got his Santa suit re-arranged he left the toilet.

He never finished his cigarette. I stayed in the tiny john with the sex scent in the air. I locked the door. I whipped out my dick and beat it until came, then took a whiz through my boner. I relit my smoke, took a drag, then split.

I waved at Santa as I passed him. He had a little boy on his knee, a future cocksucker maybe. He waved back.

Outside in the car I laughed like a hyena. Suddenly it struck me as hilarious that I'd actually sucked Santa's dick. I'd probably not get anything for Christmas since I'd been so naughty. But Big Al's hot load was a nice gift in itself.

10 The Basketball Player

Like most kids, one of my chores at home was to take out the garbage. Garbage cans lined the alley behind our house.

It was a lazy Sunday morning. I'd slept in late and just eaten a bowl of cereal. The thin blanket of snow that had made the holiday season magical was gone. But the winter weather was still cold. For some reason my folks had decided to go to church. So I was alone in the house.

Crushing the sack of garbage into the can, I looked up and saw Steve, my neighbor. He was a long drink of water. Over six feet tall and slim. He obviously had the same chore as me, the garbage detail. I liked Steve but we weren't buddies since he hung out with the jocks on campus and got a ride to school with one who had a car. I used to walk to junior high with him sometimes. He was brunet with sparkling blue eyes.

"How's it going?" he asked.

"Okay. what's up?"

"Oh, just another borin' day. I was going to shoot baskets. wanna play with me?"

He had a hoop on a post in his back yard but had never invited me over to play before. Play with him indeed. Yeah, I'd like to play with his dick. As I remembered from the junior high locker room he had a big one and it was uncut. I wondered how big it was now.

"Sure," I agreed. I liked basketball but Steve was way out of my league, considering he was the star center on the school team.

Steve got his basketball and came out of the house.

"One-on-one. Okay?"

It was a joke; he could beat me on his worst day.

"What you wanna play for?" he asked.

"I might as well give you the money now."

"I'm not talkin' about money. How about the loser's gotta do whatever the winner wants?"

It was still a losing proposition for me, but I was intrigued by what Steve wanted from me.

He let me make a couple shots, then he showed me his stuff and skunked me.

"So what do you want, Steve"

"I noticed your folks left earlier when I was shooting baskets. How about going into your house?"

"Sure."

Steve hadn't been inside my house since junior high days.

Inside the house, I took him to my room upstairs. We chatted about our college plans before I got down to business. I asked him what I had to do.

"How about a blowjob?"

"Say what?"

"I heard that you like dicks."

"Who told you that?" I blushed crimson.

"Just talk. They say that about all the smart guys in school. You know that."

"No, I didn't know that." I figured somebody had been squealing.

"You mean you don't like to suck dick?"

Steve rubbed his crotch and I saw his big dick tent his jeans.

"I wouldn't know if I'd like it or not."

"I'll bet you'd love this one...."

He sat down on my bed, unzipped his fly. Out came an enormous cock.

"My god," I gasped. It was at least nine inches, with the rosy head out of the hood.

"Like that?" he asked, stroking it.

Kneeling between his splayed legs, I grabbed hold of his pulsing prick. I wrapped my lips around Steve's monster meat. I bobbed my head up and down on it.

My own dick raged in my pants and my butthole twitched.

"My god, that's great, man. Really great...."

I let go of Steve's dick.

"What's the matter?"

Suddenly I got the big idea that Steve was my ideal: a hunk, a macho stud. I'd been thinking a lot about being corn holed. Ever since I banged Bart the barber's box, I had been wondering what it felt like. I'd fingered my hole all the time lately when I beat my meat at night.

Standing up, I stripped naked. Steve stared at me. He seemed to like my smooth, taut body.

I lay down on the bed beside him on my belly. I glanced over my shoulder.

"What the hell's goin' on?" he asked, stroking his wet cock.

"How'd you like to fuck some boy butt?

"Are you crazy?"

"No, I've always wondered what it would be like," I said, reaching over and taking control of his tool. "I'd love to see if I could take this one. You wanna try?"

"Oh yeah, man. I just can't fuckin' believe it."

"I got some Vaseline there on the nightstand. Grease me up."

"You've never had anybody try it?"

"Not yet."

"Hot damn! I've only dry-fucked a girl. I never got to stick one."

By the looks of his throbbing boner, he was willing and able. He practically tore off his clothes. His body was smooth and slender. He straddled my legs.

Steve spread my butt cheeks and greased his prong.

"Put a little grease in me," I begged.

He did as I told him and then, anxiously, he nudged his crimson crown into my pucker. I held on to the pillows as I offered my butt up to him. When he got the head in, I squirmed.

"Stay still."

"Oh shit, it's so fuckin' big. Don't think I can take it."

Steve stayed still with his thick head embedded in my hole. I relaxed. I wanted it real bad. I backed up on his big meat, inch by inch, until I felt his pubes scratch against my asscheeks.

"Okay," I cried. I buried my face in the pillow.

He probed my hole slowly at first, then he picked up the pace and really let me have it. He was soon huffing and puffing. He dripped sweat onto my body as he rammed my hole for all he was worth.

The idea of being fucked especially by a jock like Steve took me over the top. Without even touching my dick, I shot my load onto the green bedspread. My hole was on fire and it spasmed around Steve's cock.

Steve came after I did, then collapsed on top of me and kissed my neck. He stayed still until his big dick softened and fell out.

I scooted around and grabbed his boner. I spit-shined it, cleaning all the gunk off it.

Steve hopped up and got dressed.

Just then I heard my folks' car in the driveway. Steve sneaked out the back door so I didn't have to offer any explanation, not that it would have been a big deal, considering he was my neighbor and a classmate.

I was all flushed and managed to clean up before Sunday dinner.

I went to all the basketball games I could, even watched him practicing with his buddies in the driveway. I was hoping for some more one-on-one, but it just didn't happen.

11 The Stockboy

Both of my parents worked. Dad was a service repairman for Whiting Appliance Company. Mom was a waitress at Mo's Diner. Sometimes Mom called me at Gold's and asked me to pick up some bread, milk or whatever she needed for dinner. She got a ride home with another waitress from the diner near the Interstate and didn't have time to shop on weekdays.

After the store where I worked closed at six, I'd stop at Sam's Market and get whatever items she needed.

That's where I ran into "Sam Junior," the owner's son, one day. I'd seen him at school. He was a year ahead of me and graduated last year. Now he stocked shelves, bagged groceries and made deliveries in a van. He was short with brown hair and brown eyes. He had a thin mustache which made him look older than nineteen. The other thing I noticed about him was the tufts of hair that stuck out from the open white shirt he wore.

Gold's wasn't busy after the holiday season. I marked the new merchandise that came in and helped tidy up the stock in the men's department where I worked as a clerk on Saturdays. Chet was the assistant manager, an older man in his fifties. The manager Max was the owner's son-in-law and he was out a lot with salesmen, being wined and dined while he ordered merchandise for the spring season.

Since business was slow, I asked Chet if I could leave early since there was nothing to do and I had to stop at the store to get some bread and eggs at the market. He said it was okay since Max was out, and I wouldn't get docked for the time off. Of course I always looked the other way and took over sometimes for Chet when he'd drunk too many beers on his lunch breaks last summer and was kind of woozy.

At Sam's Market I got the items Mom wanted. As usual, I looked around for Sam Junior, just to feast my eyes on him for a bit, but didn't see him. That is, until I left the store.

I was walking down Maple Street heading home when he pulled up to the curb in the delivery van with the Sam's Market logo on the side.

"Hi, Billy. Get in. I'll give you a ride," he said.

I climbed into the passenger side of the van. There were some boxes of groceries in the back that he was delivering.

"Man, I wish I was still in school like you."

"Huh? I can't wait to graduate."

"Shit, all I ever do is work work work."

"Don't you meet some lonely housewives when you deliver groceries?" I teased.

"I wish. All I meet is old ladies who want to give me cookies and milk instead of tips, like I was a little boy."

I laughed because Sam was so serious. But he did look like a little boy, even younger looking than me!

"Don't you have a girlfriend?"

"Nope. Not right now. Just Mrs. Hand and her five daughters," he laughed.

Turning onto Fourth Street, where I lived, I didn't want the ride to be over. Something about Sam Junior made me horny. I think it was the chest hair that stuck out of the top of his white shirt. It was so incongruous; he looked like a kid, but there was all that hair.

"I'll bet you could use a good blowjob."

"Do you know some babe who sucks dick?"

"No, but I learning fast, let me tell you."

"Learning fast?"

"Yeah, I never thought I'd like it like I do."

"Really? You're a cocksucker?"

"I told you, I'm learning...."

"You need some practice? Is that what you are trying to tell me?"

"Yeah, I guess."

He glanced over at me. He took my hand and placed it back on his crotch. I rubbed the bulge and felt his dick get hard.

He stopped the van near the small field where the kids played baseball in the summer. It was deserted in winter.

"You got a big dick, Sam," I said, kneading the bulge.

I put my head on his lap. He stroked my hair.

"Go ahead. Take it out. I'll keep watch, in case somebody comes. You can practice on me."

I unzipped Sam's jeans and freed his dick. It was clipped, only around six inches long, but it was fat as a beer can, with a big mushroom glans. I stroked the shaft while I stretched my lips around the reddish-purplish crown. I started sucking.

"Oh shit yeah. That feels real good. Ain't had my joint copped since prom night."

He shoved my hand away. He clasped my head and pumped his dick down my throat.

"Oh, Billy, suck it. You're a quick learner."

I gobbled up Sam's hefty meat all the way down to his wiry brown pubes. coming up for air, I took my mouth off his dick.

"Why'd you stop?

"Gotta breathe, you know."

That wasn't the reason. I didn't want to stop sucking his dick; the last thing I wanted was for him to change his mind and make me stop. But I wanted to see his hairy chest. He didn't stop me when I unbuttoned his white shirt. Just as I expected, it was the hairiest chest I'd ever seen one of the sexiest sights I ever saw. I rubbed my face against his chest and licked the hair until it glistened with spit. His nipples were small. I tweaked and alternately sucked them until they got hard.

"Whatcha doing?"

I covered his hairy chest with kisses.

He grabbed my head and plugged his boner back in my mouth. He guided the sucking rhythm with his strong hands.

"Now," he cried.

Wads of his cum shot down my throat. I nearly choked on his load. The overflow flooded my mouth and dripped out of the corners.

I nursed his cock which was obviously tender after he got off because he winced. But I kept my lips sealed around his thick meat until I drained his nuts. Letting go, I licked my chops.

Impulsively, I just did it. I unzipped my fly and whipped out my throbbing prick. Stunned, Sam just stared at my dick while I reared up in the van and jerked off until I exploded, my free hand never leaving his hairy chest.

"Billy, that was a terrific blowjob," Sam said, buttoning up his shirt.

I stuffed my prick back in my pants.

He revved the engine and sped down Fourth Street like he was fleeing a crime scene. I pointed out my house, the white one with the green shutters.

"Thanks for the ride, Sam."

"Anytime, Billy."

12 The Horny Trucker

A week later, I went to another basketball game. The Hoover Tigers were having a winning season, mostly feeding the ball to Steve at center, who'd spin around and hook the ball into the hoop. I never got tired of watching him and his flashy moves. I remembered the feel of his nuts on my buns when he got my cherry butt.

After the game, I hiked out to Mo's Diner near the Interstate. Mom brought me a slice of their delicious hot apple cinnamon pie and a cup of coffee. I chatted with her when she wasn't busy.

Seated across the counter was a guy around twenty-five. He wore a red baseball cap with Peterbilt written on it in white letters. I wondered what that meant. He wore a red plaid flannel jacket. He had a stocky build and emerald green eyes like a cat's. peterbuilt indeed. All I could think about was his peter and I wondered what it looked like and how big it was. He caught me eyeballing him while he wolfed down a burger and fries. Embarrassed, I glanced away.

Finishing my pie and coffee, I said goodbye to Mom and went outside. I fired up a Marlboro. She knew I smoked but didn't approve of it.

In the parking lot, I noticed a huge Peterbilt truck parked at the back, gleaming with chrome. I sauntered over to have a look at it. I figured it must belong to the guy in the diner with the cap with the same logo on it.

When I turned around there he was, the guy from the diner.

"This your truck?" I asked.

"It belongs to the bank, but I drive it. I'm an independent. "Cross-country?" I asked.

"Yup. Wanna see it inside?"

"Yeah. It's a beauty." And so was he, incidentally.

"Well c'mon, get in the cab."

I climbed into the cab beside him.

"Hey, this is neat. CB radio and everything. Riding up high. Bet you see a lot of stuff on the road."

"On I-80 I looked down and saw a man feeling up a babe. She had her skirt hiked up. Made me horny."

I wondered why he told me this. Maybe he was interested in some action. But he looked real macho. I'd better cool it.

"What are you hauling?" I asked.

"Container cargo off a ship. Electronic stuff from Japan, going to the Big Apple."

"Have a big load, huh?"

He rubbed his crotch.

"Got that right, kid. You wanna see, uh ... the sleeper?"

"Sure."

"Go ahead, crawl in the back."

Curious, I crawled back into the sleeper. The trucker sat looking at me for a few moments. I looked back at him and smiled. "This is neat."

He smiled. He crawled in behind me. He rubbed his crotch again.

"You like dick, don'tcha?" he said.

"How'd you know?"

"Seen you eyeballing me back in the diner, but I thought you were too young...."

"Oh, I just look young. I've been around."

"Oh?"

"Yeah," I said as I reached over and groped him.

He leaned back, as if he was comfortable with me now. He didn't object as I unzipped his fly and freed his dick. It was soft, fat and cut.

I stroked it.

"Suck on it, kid. Get it hard for me."

I gripped the shaft and wrapped my lips around the crown and sucked on it. His dick ballooned into a massive eight inches, it was nearly as big as Steve's.

I licked his reddish gristle up and down and darted my tongue into the wide slit and tasted his salty goo.

I took out his big balls in their wrinkled sac and lapped at them. I tried to stuff both of them into my mouth but they were too big, 80 I sucked on them separately.

"Yeah, lick them suckers. Got the cum boiling in them. That's the ticket. Get back on my dick. I'm about ready to blow my wad."

I wrapped my lips around the trucker's cock and deep-throated it down the shaft to his balls, which I tugged on.

"Doing good, kid. Oh yeah...."

I gobbled up the veiny shaft and his dick belched cum into my mouth. I kept my mouth on his dick until it deflated. I savored his cum which tasted like buttermilk.

It was fun to service the trucker. For a moment I wondered if Mom saw me get into the truck. Maybe someone else did and told her. I thought I'd better get the hell out of there. But the trucker grabbed my crotch. I didn't expect it. My dick throbbed.

"Feels big, kid. Take it out and let me see."

I flashed the trucker my hard cock which was about the same size as his. crawling over beside him, I waved my dick in his face.

"Like schoolboy dick, don'tcha?"

"Hey, that's a piece of man meat...."

I lewdly stroked my dick in his face. I painted the trucker's pouty lips with my goo. I slapped my dick against his face. His beard stubble felt like sandpaper and made my balls rumble. Suddenly I felt powerful, high on "prick power". The trucker opened his mouth and I speared my dick down his throat.

He grabbed the base of my dick but I shoved his hand away.

I held his head, knocking his baseball cap askew, but I didn't stop. I dick-fed him. He swallowed the length of my meat, showing me that he was no stranger to dick.

I pumped my dick lustily down his throat. I tried to hold back but it was impossible.

"Oh my god...."

I crammed my dick all the way down his throat and whitewashed his tonsils. The overflow of my load trickled out of his mouth and down his chin.

I yanked my dick out of his mouth and wiped it off on his cheek. The feel of his beard stubble against my tender meat made me shiver all over.

"Man, that hit the spot," he said. "But I gotta get on the road. Wanna make it to Chicago before I shut down."

Impulsively I planted a big sloppy kiss right on the trucker's luscious lips. That surprised him but he hugged me and kissed me back.

I stuffed my dick back into my pants and zipped up. So did the trucker.

"So, maybe I'll see you again when I come back this way the next run."

"Hope so. I'll keep an eye out for you."

I got out of the truck and looked around but no one noticed me. I watched the trucker start his rig and wheel out of the parking lot. He tooted his horn and flashed his lights.

I forgot to ask him his name. But I knew I'd see him again, if only in my wet dreams. For a long time afterwards I got a big hard-on whenever I saw a Peterbilt truck.

13 The Pizza Boy

One night a couple of weeks later, I was home alone. My folks had gone to a shindig at the lodge they belonged to.

Usually I'd fix myself a Dagwood sandwich and gorge myself on it, wash it down with a couple Cokes. I usually got my homework done in study hall or in boring classes when the teachers rambled on. That cleared the time for my part-time job, which my folks were convinced would teach me about responsibility and respect for money that I earned. And I could channel surf on the TV, which was often as much a drag as homework.

Tonight I was in a horny mood. I could take a long bath, suds up and pull my pud. But I liked to wait until I hit the hay. Then I'd beat my meat and drift off to sleep. Sometimes I had wet dreams and woke up in the night with sticky shorts. Sometimes I woke up in the morning with a boner that wouldn't go down until I whipped off a load.

My dick was begging for attention. It stirred in my pants. I had a mental jack-off file of my various encounters, to which I added mental snapshots of boys' bulging crotches I'd seen at school or dicks I'd scoped out in the locker room after gym class.

I was both hungry and horny. A quickie jack-off session and then I could chow down. What would I eat and who would I fantasize about?

Suddenly it dawned on me that I could kill two birds with one stone. I thought about Alex, a classmate I'd seen in the showers. He had a big dick.

As I was fantasizing about him, I remembered that he worked in the evenings as the delivery boy for Joe's Pizza.

Suddenly, I was in the mood for a big pizza smothered with sausage and cheese. Actually, I was in the mood for Alex if only in my dreams. At least I'd get to ogle him in the flesh before I jacked off.

I called Joe's and ordered a large sausage pizza. They delivered within half an hour. It was a long wait. I flipped on the TV. Sometimes I caught sight of an actor who made my balls buzz. But not tonight. I had Alex's big cock on the brain.

Eventually I heard the car pull into the driveway and saw the lights flash into the windows. The doorbell rang.

Opening the door, I saw Alex in the flesh. He was medium height, muscular, with a shock of chestnut hair and big brown eyes, bedroom eyes.

"Got your pizza, buddy."

"Hey, come in."

He came into the house and followed me into the kitchen at the back. He placed the pizza down OD the table.

"You want a slice?" I asked.

"No, thanks. I eat so much pizza that I'll probably turn into one."

"How about a Coke?" I offered.

"Hey, sounds like a winner. I'm done for the night now."

"Really?"

"Yeah, real slow tonight." He sat down at the kitchen table.

"No ladies wanting to give you a tip?"

"Haha! Never happened to me, buddy."

I got two cold bottles of cola out of the fridge. He gulped it down. I sipped mine.

Alex lewdly grabbed his crotch. I could tell by the twinkle in his eye that he was a natural-born prick teaser.

"Just the thought of it turns me on, though," he said, then he finished his cola.

"Go ahead, take it out. I'll give you a tip you'll never forget."

"You're crazy."

"Yeah, crazy for cock."

"Serious?"

"As a heart attack."

"Well, I'll be damned...."

Damned if Alex didn't unzip his fly and flop out his fat, cut prick. I was impressed, like I'd been in the showers at school. Alex tugged on his cock and it became stiff. It was a beautiful, sculpted dick with leafy veins and a rosy mushroom head. With my eyes feasting on his dick, I pulled out mine and stroked it slowly. I was hotter than a firecracker from looking at Alex's dick and I got even hotter when I went over to him and touched it. It throbbed wildly. He stared at me. His brown eyes were smoldering.

I kneeled down at his crotch. He slapped me in the face with his big dick, which was drooling lube. He stuck his finger into my mouth and I sucked on it. He replaced his finger with his big dick.

I put Alex's dick in my mouth, and he held my head. Leaning back, he plugged my throat. He moaned. He groaned. He buried his dick down my throat and battered my tonsils. I held onto his denim-clad thighs while he slammed his big dick in and out of my mouth until he came. It took only a couple of minutes.

I swallowed his cum, then nursed his cock until it softened. At the same time, I fisted my dick with my hand until it splattered cum onto the linoleum.

Alex's limp dick fell out of my mouth. He took a deep breath and stuffed his dick back into his jeans. He pushed me back and stood up. Zipped his jeans, he said, "Pizza's on me, buddy."

"No," I said, handing him a ten.

"Hell, no," he said.

I watched through the living room window while he drove off. My dick hardened again.

Returning to the kitchen, I scooped up a gob of my cum off the floor and smeared it over my dick. Reliving the face-fucking I had just endured, I shot another load.

I cleaned up the mess. Then I wolfed down the pizza which tasted all the better because my mouth was coated with the cheese from Alex's big dick.

14 The Dark Runner

On a wintry Sunday afternoon I was tooling around town in the family Chevy. I took a ride out to the country and looked at the barren trees. The car interior was cold and I flipped on the heater. A light snow began to fall. My late afternoon it would be dark. How dark I could never have imagined.

I was about to head back home when I noticed a figure in gray sweat pants and a blue parka jacket running along the side of the road. As I approached him, I noticed that it was Antoine, one of my classmates. He was a muscular black guy.

He smiled and waved at me. I pulled over in front of him. He came up to the driver's side window and I rolled it down.

"Hey, what's happenin', man?" I asked.

"Just out jogging. Gotta keep in shape, you know."

"Gonna freeze your balls off."

The flurry of snowflakes covered him.

"C'mon, I'll give you a ride back to town.

"I didn't expect it to snow," he said.

Antoine got into the passenger side of the car. He rubbed his hands together.

I drove along in silence, watching the snowflakes fall onto the car. I glanced over at the black runner.

"Gonna win the state mile this spring or bust a gut trying," he said with a grin.

"Jesus it's colder than hell out here. They'd have found you frozen stiff."

"Only one thing on me that's stiff." He rubbed the big crotch bulge in his sweat pants.

I wasn't sure if the gesture was a joke or an invitation. Lately I began to realize from my experiences that most guys straight, gay or whatever were as horny as me.

Antoine was a hot black dude. He wasn't so much handsome as he was macho. He had the most sensuous lips and a deep voice like that black singer Barry White. I'd heard locker room talk that black guys had the biggest dicks. I wondered how big Antoine's dick was. Suddenly I just blurted out what I was thinking about.

"Ya know, I was reading this book by Norman Mailer in which he said that white men are intimidated by black men's sexual prowess or something like that."

"I guess it's true. Us brothers are blessed with big dicks."

"I dunno. I think I got a big one."

"How big?" he asked.

"Bigger than most guys I've seen. Show me yours, I'll show you mine."

I almost drove off the road when Antoine slid down his sweat pants. He was wearing a jockstrap. He slid the pouch aside and showed me a fat black dick that was at least six inches soft, with an ebony shaft and pink crown.

"Yeah, but it's just big soft. What about hard, any bigger?" "If I didn't know better I'd think you was some kind of 'mo. All this talk about dick and wanting to see mine."

I figured that Antoine was game. Maybe he'd let me play with that juicy meat. I pulled off of the road onto a field. Risky, because if it snowed heavy I might get stuck. But my brains were in my dick which was oozing in my pants from me seeing Antoine's cock.

Unzipping my fly, I freed my by now semi-hard dick. I stroked it.

Antoine tugged on his dick and it was getting harder and harder.

"Well, you got a big one for a white boy. But you ain't seen nothing yet."

My gasped. Antoine's dick, now fully erect, was a whopper, the biggest one I'd ever seen. It had to be ten inches!

Unable to stop myself, I reached over and grabbed his throbbing dick.

"It's fucking awesome," I said.

I fondled my own dick with my left hand while I jacked that big black dick with my right hand. He had hefty, heaving balls and kinky black pubes. clear goo drooled out of his wide piss slit.

"You're a fucking 'mo. Oh wow, I don't believe it. Don't look like no sissy boy neither. But hey, that's cool. Bet you suck dicks, don'tcha?"

"Ain't no big deal," I said.

"Bet you never sucked a black dick before. Ain't many at school. Shit, I'd of heard about it if you had. SO you're a 'mo. Damn, if that don't take the cake."

He was wide to me so I saw no reason to deny myself the pleasure of sucking on that big black meat.

Bending over, I clasped the base of his dick. Up close, it was like an ebony pillar. The shaft was black as midnight and veiny. The pink knob turned purplish and dripped sap.

"Kiss it," he hissed.

I obeyed. Not only that, I lapped the sap off the spongy crown. I dug my tongue into his piss hole.

"Oh, yeah, put those honky lips around my black dick. yeah, suck on it."

I worked on the knob with my mouth while I stroked the shaft.

"I like a blowjob as well as the next guy. But I'm really a stick man."

"Huh?"

"I like to fuck. I fuck anything, so can you dig it?"

The thought of taking that big boner up my hole was scary.

"It's too big, Antoine."

"Shit man, you're afraid of my dick. Maybe you're just prejudiced."

"No way. Racism is stupid. But I got a little hole. You got a monster dick."

"Well, they say, 'Once you've had a black man....'"

"Well...." I took a deep breath. I decided to take up the challenge. My butthole itched for that big black dick.

"Let's get into the back seat where there's more room," I said.

I crawled over the front seat and so did Antoine. I slid down my pants and shorts and lay on the back seat.

Looking over my shoulder, I watched Antoine examine my ass. He licked my funky crack. I couldn't believe it.

"Gotta get it all ready for my big dick, just like you do with a pussy."

Soon he mounted me. I couldn't watch. The size of his dick was too intimidating. I cradled my head in my arms.

He rubbed his fiery, drooling prick into my crack and popped the crown into my asshole.

"Oh no, it'll kill me!"

"Relax your butt. Just let my dick slid right in."

He shoved several inches up my hole.

My ass ring stretched to the limit. Hungry for it, I backed up on it. "Aw fuck!" I yelled.

He probed my hole slowly. Finally, the pain subsided.

I now found that Antoine was an experienced pussy-prodder. He began slowly, then he bore into my hole lustily.

I moaned and shoved back.

His big nuts slapped against my butt cheeks.

"Oh yeah," he said, pulling it all the way out, them slamming it back in. "I like to watch my dick go in and out of your lily white butt."

"Keep fuckin' me, Antoine. Please!" I was delirious.

He was huffing and puffing and dripping sweat onto me while he hunched over me. He had incredible staying power.

"Finish, Antoine! I can't take much more. It's ripping my ass apart."

He pistoned my hole mercilessly. Just when I thought I'd pass out or die his cock got hard as a rock. He crammed every inch of his fat prick up my hole and blasted bolts of scalding black man cum deep into my assguts. He held onto me until his dick softened and plopped out.

At first I thought I was bleeding from the butt, but it was just the overflow of his load trickling out of my abused hole.

The car windows were fogged from our breath. We pulled up our pants and crawled back into the front seat. I turned on the defroster. The field was covered with snow.

I managed to get back on the road and drive Antoine to his house on the other side of the railroad tracks. He might be a poor boy but he had meat for the cock hungry.

Antoine and I became better friends after the incident in the country. I think I walked bowlegged for a long time . afterwards because of the track star.

15 The Chubby Plumber

An overhead water pipe was leaking in the basement of the house. Dad tried to fix it but wasn't able to because the pipe was all rusted. He bandaged it with waterproof tape and called a plumber who promised to show up first thing in the morning. My folks left for work before I left for school, so I hung around to wait for the plumber, who showed up bright and early. He was thirty something, short and chubby, with thinning blond hair and bright blue eyes.

He stood on a chair, examined the rusted pipe and grunted.

"I think I have a piece of pipe in my truck that I can use to replace the broken one with."

I watched while he measured the pipe. He shut the water valve off in the garage.

I followed him out to his battered pickup in the driveway. He had a mounted vise. He took a pipe, measured it and cut it off with a hacksaw.

I liked his jolly disposition. He had a big belly and his blue twill pants slid down on his butt, showing the crack of his ass. Seeing that made my cock stir in my pants.

He got a utility ladder and a plastic bucket with some tools and stuff in it.

Back in the basement, I watched him work. He danced around, removing the rusted pipe and replacing it. He put some clamps and sealing goo OD it.

"You're still in school, huh?"

"Yeah."

"Whatcha gonna study?"

"I dunno."

"Get a good education, that's the key. So you don't end up a working stiff like me."

"I heard that plumbers make big bucks.

"Haha! Not in this town. But it's a livin'...."

He looked like he ate well.

"Always been a plumber?"

"Yup. Since I was out of the Marines. My uncle owns the business. "

He checked his handiwork and I gawked at him. He caught me and smiled.

I trailed him out to the garage. He turned the water back OD and checked the pipe. Not a drip.

"You're pretty good," I said. "what did you do in the Marines?"

"I was an MP, picked up drunken jarheads and swabbies OD the beach. Ah, those were the days. I was all muscle in those days." He patted his belly.

"More to love, they say."

"What would you know about that?"

"Ha! You a chubby chaser?"

"No, you're not what I would call chubby." He'd let himself go to pot after being so muscular.

"I'm chubby, chubby all over," he said, groping himself.

I stared at where he was rubbing himself.

"Sonuvabitch. I can't believe you're a cocksucker."

"Been known to. I'm sorta in training."

"Ha!"

I nodded. He straddled the utility ladder. I kneeled down on the floor. He unzipped his fly and hauled out his stubby, clipped dick.

"Suck on it, baby."

I circled my lips around his soft dick and it stiffened immediately. It was a nice fat seven inches, hard.

While I showed him my oral expertise, I freed my own stiff prick. He took a look.

"Jesus, you're hung big...."

"I don't get any complaints," I said.

He startled me when he pushed me away and reached down and grabbed my dick.

"Are you in training for fucking too?"

"I dunno...." I kept stroking his cock.

"How would you like to fuck me with that big cock?"

"Really?"

I was shocked when the chubby plumber dropped his pants and shorts and mooned me while hugging the utility ladder.

"You man enough to fuck my fat ass?"

"You bet."

My dick throbbed at the prospect.

"Spit in my crack and go for it...."

I drooled spit into the crack of his ass. I spread his cheeks. He watched over his shoulder while I rubbed my dick in his steamy crack. My dick was like a pipe when I rammed it into the plumber's pucker. He clamped his hole around my dick.

"Screw me, kid. Last time I got fucked was by this petty officer. He went with me on shore patrol. He'd suck the drunks while he fucked me. Then we'd cut 'em loose and not throw them in the brig." He went on babbling about different cocks he'd sucked while being fucked by the petty officer. Occasionally, a guy was sober enough to fuck him after the petty officer finished.

I was amused by the plumber's rambling confession but my concentration was on fucking.

"Oh yeah, you got a real man's dick. Oh, it's so big. Keep fuckin' me!" he screamed as I came. My dick softened and slipped out.

The chubby plumber got up on wobbly legs and flashed me his hard dick.

I wrapped my lips around it and chowed down. I chewed on his gristly dick and he didn't complain.

"Suck faster, faster! Shooting my wad in your mouth, boy."

After he came, and I swallowed his heavy load, he had to pry his dick out of my mouth. The plumber hoisted his britches and I zipped up.

"Hey, time is money, like my uncle always is reminding me. Gotta shag ass."

The plumber took a crisp Andrew Jackson out of his wallet and tucked it into my pants pocket.

"Buy yourself somethin'. I wouldn't charge your folks for the service but I couldn't explain that to my uncle."

"Thanks, I understand."

The chubby plumber took his utility ladder and plastic bucket and waddled out to his truck. I watched him drive off, and waved.

I had to get a late pass at school but Mom had written a note of explanation just in case.

In school I thought about reaming the plumber's butt and draining his pipe. He paid me and made a whore out of me.

16 The Obscene Caller

I was puttering around in my room at home, thinking about going to bed and pulling my pud. I heard the phone ring downstairs.

Mom yelled up the stairs that the call was for me. I wondered who it could be. Probably some dork from school wanting to know about some class assignment.

I bounded down the stairs and picked up the phone.

"Hello," I said.

"Bet you're getting ready for bed. So am I, but I got this problem. I got a big hard-on." The voice was husky.

"This some kind of joke? Who is this?"

"I can't go to sleep until I jack-off."

I thought about hanging up. But I was curious about who it was. I peeked around the corner into the living room where Mom and Dad were watching the news on TV.

"Just do it, pervert," I whispered.

"I thought maybe you'd like to join me. "You're crazy."

"Did you hear the one about the obscene caller who got arrested? The police allowed him a phone call and he called the woman back."

"Very funny. Story of your life. So who is this, really?"

"Hey, I saw you looking at me when I was naked in the locker room at school."

That could be almost anybody. I didn't recognize the voice. He probably had a hankie over the receiver to disguise his voice. So it had to be someone in my last period gym class. Or it could be a track runner who was changing into his running shorts.

Suddenly I heard a slapping sound. hat's that t noise?"

"Don't you know? It's my hard dick slapping against the mouthpiece."

Just the idea that it was some guy from school with a boner made my dick stiffen.

"Does that sound get you hard? Wanna beat off with me?"

"My folks are in the other room."

"So are mine but I'm in the kitchen whipping up something, you might say."

"I gotta go...."

"No, don't hang up! I know you've got a boner. I know all about you, you fucker."

"Who told you?" I asked. "What did they tell you?"

"It's a secret. I heard that you give head."

"Do you believe everything you hear, asswipe?"

"In your case, yeah, I sure do. C'mon, don't waste time. Go ahead, take your dick out."

The power of suggestion was too much. I just did it, even though my folks might catch me. I could hear his heavy breathing. "Whatcha doing?" I asked.

"I'm strokin' it. Do it to yours. Bet you'd like to know what my dick looks like."

"Okay. How big is it?"

"Real big. A true eight inches and thick. Got a big knob. There's stuff drooling out of my piss hole right now!"

I slowly tugged on my dick and felt the pre-goo ooze out and down my shaft.

"Jack it off," I hissed.

"Aw fuck! I got a hair trigger. I'm gonna blast. Here it comes! All over the floor!"

Imagining a big, squirting cock, I was about to get off but I stopped jacking. I wanted to save it for later.

The guy on the other end of the line was breathing hard. "Maybe next time I'll let you suck it off. Wanna do that, don'tcha?"

"Okay, I'll play along. Where? When?"

"Tell you what, I'll meet you after school tomorrow. In the boys' room on the second floor. Be there. Gotta clean up this fucking mess before the news is over."

I hung up the phone. I stuffed my dick into my pants, said goodnight to my folks and went upstairs with a hard-on that wouldn't quit. I didn't even bother to brush my teeth. I stripped naked and got between the sheets. Slipping my hand down between my legs, I jacked my prick while I fantasized about guys in the locker room at school. I thought about some of my classmates'. dicks and about the dicks I'd scoped out on some of the track team members. In no time I felt the cum boiling in my balls. Lifting up the sheet, I squirted hot cum drops all over my belly. I smeared it into my skin and dozed off to sleep.

I was awakened by the disc jockey's chatter on my alarm clock radio. I rubbed the sleep out of my eyes and sat up in bed. I could feel the cum caked on my belly.

All day at school I thought about the dirty phone call. But I didn't think the caller would show up in the john after school and reveal his identity. It was just a prank. He was horny and got off on teasing me.

After school, I hightailed it up to the boys' room on the second floor. It was empty. I went into the stall and sat on the crapper. I looked at my watch. Nobody was going to show. I couldn't wait long. Even if I didn't stop at home, I had to be at my job at the store in less than an hour.

What the hell. I felt my dick stiffen. I could have a quick beat off session right here and then split. It was kind of kicky and risky but I liked the thought of jacking off at school. Something new. I wrapped my fingers around my dick.

Suddenly the door squeaked open. Better be careful. It could be someone just coming in to whiz. I looked through the crack in the stall door.

Some guy was at the pisser against the wall. I didn't recognize him from behind. I didn't hear any piss hit the water.

The guy turned around and flashed his dick. It was hard. Looking up, I realized it was Tony. He was on the track team. He was the obscene caller!

He was tall, brunet, with brown eyes. His shirt was open at the neck and I could see the tufts of brown hair on his chest.

With a grin on his face, he strolled over to the stall where I was. I opened the door.

He didn't say a word. He just rubbed his dick against my lips and shoved it between them.

I grabbed his denim-clad butt cheeks and bobbed my head up and down on his big dick. It really was big.

"Suck it, cocksucker. Suck my dick."

He pumped his big meat down my throat, splitting my tonsils. He had big fuzzy balls which slapped against my chin.

"Oh yeah. Been wantin' one of your blowjobs for a long time. Couldn't get my girlfriend to do it. When I heard about you I knew I'd score sooner or later."

I coated his cock with spit. I deep-throated it down to his nuts, which I squeezed.

"Gonna fucking blow! cumming in your fucking mouth!"

He burrowed his shooting prick down my throat and whitewashed my tonsils. I drank every drop of his nutty tasting cum.

With a big shit-eating grin on his face, he stuffed his big dick back into his jeans. He split without saying a word.

My dick was throbbing wildly. I just aimed it in the commode and squeezed it, draining my balls.

I had to rush to get to work. But I made it on time. No one seemed to notice that I was all sweaty and had the smell of cum on my breath.

17 Lust on Spring Break

Spring is the time when a young man's thoughts turn to love. In my case it was lust.

During spring break from school I worked at the store. Bored and horny, I got my dad's permission to borrow the car one night. I drove to Des Moines. I circled the downtown loop at Seventh and Locust. I drove out to the shopping mall on the west side.

I stopped at Castle Lanes, the bowling alley. They had a sign on the marquee outside that was supposed to be funny. It said "Take the kids off the street and put them in the alley."

Inside the bowling alley there was a bowling league, teams with their logos on their shirts. Mostly older people.

I wandered over into the pool room. That's where I spotted two young guys around my age who were shooting a game, so I hung out and watched them.

The blond one had a pretty face, the black-haired guy was real macho looking. The blond was real cocky. He beat the other guy at the game. He looked over at me.

"Wanna shoot a rack?" he asked.

"You're too good for me!"

"C'mon. Try me."

I looked at the dark-haired guy who smiled.

"Sure. Why not."

I wasn't much of a pool player. I used to shoot pool in a place near the railroad tracks in my town. When Dad got wind that I hung out there, he put a stop to that. He said he didn't want me hanging around pool hall bums, that was a bad influence. So I stopped going there.

"I'm Mel. My buddy's Jake. We go to Roosevelt High, seniors. Never seen you around before."

"I go to Hoover in Weston."

"Oh yeah? Whaddaya wanna play for?"

"Five bucks okay?"

"Ha, I bet you're a hustler," he said.

"Nope. Ain't played in a long time."

"I don't need your stinking money. What about the loser's gotta do what the winner wants?"

"Humph. You're on," I said.

I had no idea what he had in mind. Probably some prank like mooning someone. I sure knew what I'd like to do if I won. I'd like to suck the blond's dick. Hell, I'd even do his buddy.

Well, I didn't win. Mel was the hustler; my game was rusty. He let me make a couple shots. Then he ran the rack.

"Well, you win, Mel. What do I gotta do?"

"Well, what do you think, Jake?" the blond asked his buddy.

The black-haired kid shrugged his shoulders. It was clear that Mel was the dominant one.

"Let's go to my place and drink a brewski. I'll figure somethin' out. My folks are away," Mel said.

Outside in the parking lot, Mel told me to follow them in his car. He had a late model Ford Mustang with racing stripes on it.

255

This looked interesting. Maybe they'd get drunk. Maybe I could suck Mel's dick.

I had to speed along Grand Avenue to keep up with them. I was a little afraid I might get a ticket.

When Mel drove south of Grand, I was surprised. He pulled into the driveway of a really expensive home. Looked like his folks were loaded.

I parked in the driveway behind them. And I went into the house with them. It was posh to say the least, with thick white carpeting and fancy furniture.

I followed them into the den, whatever. It had the biggest TV screen and stereo system I'd ever seen. It even had a wet bar. Mel got us all beers.

"Nice pad," I muttered.

"Yeah, well, my old man's a stockbroker. Makes money the old-fashioned way he steals it." Jake guffawed. I laughed along with him. We all sipped the beer.

"You gotta strip naked, kid," Mel said.

"Say what?"

"You lost."

"I know. You want me to streak or something?"

"Get undressed first."

Hell, I was game. I did it, slowly, as if I was stripping to please him.

"Now what?" I asked.

Mel seemed to like my little strip. He rubbed his crotch. He ambled over to the chair where I sat and shoved his crotch in my face. "Take out my prick."

"You're joking?"

"Do it, dude."

If Mel thought he was going to humiliate me he was dead wrong. Little did he know that I'd gladly suck his dick.

I groped him and he moaned. I unzipped his fly. His dick got stiff right away. It wasn't real big, only about six inches, but it was real stiff.

He grabbed his dick and slapped me in the face.

"Lick it. Lick my big dick."

I rolled my tongue over his circumcised crown. Looking out of the corner of my eye, I saw Jake watching us.

Mel was obviously showing off for his buddy. He shoved his dick between my lips. Holding my head, he pumped his dick down my throat.

"Oh Jesus, that feels good. I knew you'd sucked dicks before. I knew it when I first laid eyes on you! Oh fuck, I'm gonna come."

I captured the wave of cum and swallowed it.

"Now you gotta do my buddy Jake."

"Hey, that's okay," Jake said.

"Do it, punk. You lost. Blow Jake."

When I reached over and groped Jake, his dick was stiff from watching me suck Mel. When I took out his dick I was surprised. It must have been doubled up. It was a whopper, at least seven thick inches of nicely cut meat.

Kneeling down between his legs, I serviced him with gusto. I really liked his dick. His cock throbbed in my mouth. It got super hard, and scooting to the edge of his chair, he clasped my head and mouth-fucked me. I was delirious with joy.

"Oh, man, look at that!" Mel shouted.

Looking over at him, I watched him stroke his dick while I was being face-fucked by his buddy.

"Gonna shoot...!" Jake hollered.

His cock exploded and fell out of my mouth. It splattered gobs of cum all over my face. I licked my lips and tasted his syrupy cum.

I reached for my clothes.

Mel kicked them away.

"Not done with you, buddy."

"Let 'im go, Mel," Jake said.

"Hey, he lost. He's from Hoover, you know."

For a moment I thought maybe he would kick my ass. I looked into his glassy blue eyes and saw a fierceness there that scared me. The next thing I knew he had me positioned down on all fours. Looking over my shoulder, I watched him drop his pants and shorts. His dick jutted out from his blond pubes.

He mounted me. I felt him drip spit into my crack. He rubbed his hot, hard dick between my butt cheeks. He nudged it inside.

"Oh, no. It hurts," I cried.

It hurt because it was small and skinny.

He ignored my protests and started to bang my butt. He sawed his dick in and out.

"Suck on Jake while I fuck you."

I looked up at Jake. He dropped his pants and shorts. He held his dick out. I gobbled it up. While Mel screwed my butt I sucked on Jake's dick.

Mel was a fast cummer, thank goodness his dick felt like a knife in my guts.

"Jesus, you suck like a vacuum cleaner."

"Whaddaya expect, coming from Hoover," Mel teased, and his dick got steely-hard. "Fucking shooting up your ass, kid!"

Mel sprayed his hot cum into my ass and yanked his prick out.

"C'mon, Jake, you take his ass...."

Jake looked at me and I smiled. He knew that I wanted his dick up my hiney.

Jake got behind me and popped his boner into my filthy asshole. I backed up on it.

Mel stroked his semi-hard cock as he watched his buddy fuck me.

"Oh, yeah, fuck that queer's ass, Jake. Give it to him good!"

Jake reamed my ass and I loved every thrust. I clenched my butt muscles and humped back.

"Oh, yeah, fuck me harder!" I begged. I said it without thinking, I was so taken with Jake.

"Yeah, he's queer. Didn't I tell you? He fuckin' loves it," Mel cried. I couldn't have agreed with him more.

Jake pistoned my hole. His big balls slapped against my asscheeks. Just when his dick got hard as concrete, I shot my load on the floor, without even touching my dick. My asshole spasmed around the dick buried in it and the black-haired boy shot a big load of molten cum deep into my guts. He pulled his prick out.

"He takes it like a little slut," Mel said, working his dick with a blurry hand. He sprayed his cum all over my back. I felt it drip down my sides.

"Clean your fucking scum off the floor, you fuckin' pig."

Mel shoved my face into the cum puddle and I lapped up my own jism.

I donned my clothes while Mel and Jake hoisted their britches.

"Now get the fuck outta here, you pussy Hoover punk," Mel growled.

I glanced at Jake and he winked at me.

And I left the luxury home of the rich boy and his hung macho sidekick. It was my first three-way and I knew I'd never forget it. I just prayed I would have Jake again.

18 The Preacher's Son

On Easter Sunday I went to the Methodist church with my folks. I hadn't been there for so long I was afraid the roof would fall in. But I went mostly to please my mom, who seemed concerned about my soul. If she knew what I'd been up to she'd die. If my dad knew he'd kill me in cold blood. He'd once told me to stay away from homosexuals.

I drifted in and out of pastor Hightower's sermon. Every Easter Sunday that I could remember he preached about the resurrection, pointing out various members, who I suspected were big contributors to the church, as various disciples in various places, and saying that none of the disciples had denied that Jesus was the son of God and resurrected, despite some dying horrible deaths. The gist of his sermon, I discerned, was that without belief in the resurrection of Jesus that Christianity was meaningless.

Glancing across the aisle at Tommy, the preacher's son, I caught his eye. His hands were folded across his crotch. He was a senior in school like me. He was tall with flaming red hair and green eyes.

I wondered about him, how he acted so goody-goody. At the same time he seemed to have a lusty look in his eye, the way he looked at me. I wondered if he even masturbated because his father had once ranted on about the sin of Oman, spilling his seed on the ground, how sex was to be only in marriage. The preacher must have done it at least once because Tommy was proof, and he was the spitting image of his father. pastor Hightower had harangued that homosexuality was a sin that you'd burn in hell for. It was after that message, when I was aware of my own desires, that I decided to stop going to church when I was sixteen and my folks no longer made me go.

After the Easter Sunday sermon and the hymn sung by the choir, the pastor dismissed the congregation.

Leaving the service, Tommy stopped and shook my hand.

"Nice to see you in church again," he said, with a broad smile on his cute face. "I'd like to talk to you, if you've got a moment."

"Sure," I said.

I told my folks to go ahead, that I'd walk home.

Well, I wasn't sure exactly what Tommy was up to but I was damn curious. Maybe he wanted to save my soul and put my scalp on his belt.

I followed the preacher's kid down into the basement of the church, which was deserted. He led me into a large closet with a lot of cleaning supplies and equipment. He switched on the overhead light. He looked around furtively and closed the door. What's up?" I asked.

"This!"

He took my hand and placed it on his crotch. His dick was in an upright position and hard.

"If I'm wrong about you, I'll kill myself. You want this, don't you?"

I squeezed his dick and he sighed.

He hugged me and kissed me on the lips. He stuck his tongue down my throat. He groped me and my dick was already stiff.

"They say you're queer if you get a hard-on when another guy kisses you."

That sounded funny but Tommy seemed serious. He shoved me down on my knees. I rubbed my face against the crotch of his suit pants. I unzipped the fly and freed his boner. His dick was a big fat seven inches of clipped meat. He had bull nuts and a flaming red bush.

Holding his veiny dick, I licked it up and down, doing a butterfly flick on it. Clear cum oozed out of the wide piss slit. "Suck on it, man."

I wrapped my lips around his prick and gobbled it up. Gripping the throbbing shaft, I bobbed my head up and down on the spongy crown. He shoved my hand off his shaft.

"Take it all the way down your throat. Yeah, that's it...."

He messed up my hair as he rubbed my head. He rocked on his heels and fed his big meat down my throat. He was as surprised as me that I didn't choke on his big dick. He battered my tonsils.

"Holy shit, I'm gonna lose it...!"

I deep-throated his big dick down to the red pubes and captured every drop of his cum that tasted like buttermilk.

He helped me up to my feet. He unbuckled the belt to my slacks and they fell down around my ankles. He peeled down my briefs and my dick saluted him. He grabbed hold of it with his hot hand and milked it.

"Blow me, Tommy."

"No, I got a better idea," he said.

He spun me around and bent me over. He slapped his dick which was still hard against my butt cheeks.

"Whatcha doing, Tommy?"

"I think I'm gonna fuck you."

"I don't do that," I teased.

"Sure you do. You're queer. Queers take it up the ass."

"Your dick's too big. It'll hurt too much," I pleaded.

"I'll go easy. You'll like it," he said.

"Have you ever done it before?"

"Hell no. I love Jesus. But I'm a man now and I know my weaknesses."

That was pretty worldly talk for a preacher's kid. But my butthole was twitching at the prospect of being boffed by Tommy after having been royally fucked by Jake.

"Spit in my crack."

He dripped warm saliva into my ass. His cock was drooling goo into my crevice.

"Stick it up my ass, Tommy. I really want you to do it."

He pushed his big cockhead into my pucker and I let out a scream.

"Quiet. Someone might hear us," he said.

"Tell that to my butt. Your dick feels like a fence post."

He slid his entire dick up my hole because I could feel his wiry red pubes scratching against my asscheeks.

Bent over, I grabbed my heels for support. He gripped my waist and stayed still for a moment while my ass ring stretched around his bloated prick.

"Yeah, do it, Tommy. Fuck me."

He clutched my waist while he slammed his dick in and out.

"Fuck deeper! Harder!"

He began to piston my hole, with his hefty balls slapping against my butt cheeks.

"More!" I begged.

He plundered my butthole, ramming it for all he was worth. In no time his dick was stiff as a board.

"Oh my god....!" he cried as he came.

"Oh, please, stay inside. Don't pull out."

He obeyed me; he kept his big meat buried up my hole. I balanced myself against the wall with one hand. With the other hand, I grabbed hold of my stiff prick and stroked it. He flexed his dick up my ass.

I quickly whipped off a load. My butthole clamped around his big dick while I spurted a hefty load onto the floor. I moved forward and his big dick slid out of my by now well-fucked hole.

Tommy turned me around and helped me onto my feet. He crushed his lips against mine.

Coming up for air, I squatted down carefully to avoid the cum puddle. I held his softening prick and cleaned it off with my mouth.

Tommy and I got our clothes arranged. He wiped up the cum puddle with a rag.

Slowly he opened the closet door.

"The coast is clear."

"You sound like the weather bureau," I said.

"Yeah. Just make sure no one gets wind of this."

"My lips are sealed." I blew him a kiss and left the church. I laughed to myself about Tommy shoving the fear of God into me like Elmer Gantry did to his whore.

19 A Trip to the Lake

It was tradition at Hoover High for the seniors to declare a Skip Day and go somewhere to party.

Lake Keomah was chosen to be the place. A bus was chartered and a caravan of cars would make the trip.

I'd intended to go on the bus. But when Nelson asked me if I was driving I said yes. Sure, I'd give him a ride.

I had to practically get on my knees and beg my dad to borrow the car. It was only once in a lifetime, a day I'd remember for the rest of my life. other students were counting on me. I swore there would be no drinking. There were going to be faculty chaperones. It was just going to be swimming and a picnicking. Using the car could be my graduation gift. When Mom came to my defense, Dad relented and gave his permission to let me use the car.

Nelson just asked me out of the blue because the bus spots were all taken. I'd had my eye on him lately. He was short with buzz-cut black hair and big brown eyes. He had a big basket and I figured he had a big dick.

When Skip Day rolled around I was excited. I picked up Nelson, and he was surprised that he was my only passenger.

The drive to Lake Keomah was slow, like a funeral procession. It was a bright, sunny spring day. I turned the car radio onto a rock 'n' roll station. We were rocking while we were poking along.

At Lake Keomah, the students hung out in clusters, the jocks and their girls, the nerds, the brown-nosers who hung around with the faculty chaperones, and the outsiders.

Some of the students wore swim suits. Some wore shorts. Some wore regular street clothes.

Swimming and soaking up rays from the sun was on most of the kids' minds. It was a perfect day but the water was a little chilly.

I wore my green plaid swimming trunks under my jeans and the matching green plaid short-sleeved shirt which I'd bought at the store where I worked just for this occasion.

When Nelson pulled off his white tee he showed his naturally muscular body. When he tugged off his jeans he wore a skimpy red, brief style swim suit which left little to the imagination about his jewels.

He jumped in the lake and splashed me. I jumped in and splashed him back. We swam around with several other students and then lay on our towels on the sand.

There was loud music blasting from a portable radio and lots of flesh to ogle and make comments on. Nelson seemed content to just hang out with me.

Around noon there was a big picnic lunch with hot dogs, potato salad, beans, chips and cakes.

Mostly it was lying around in the sun, although some of the jocks set up a net and played volley ball.

"Wanna take a hike and get away from the noise?" I asked.

"Sure, why not," Nelson agreed.

I had a devious plan in mind after we got away from the clusters of students. I'd noticed that a few other couples had strayed away, with probably similar ideas in mind.

On the other side of the lake, we found an isolated spot among the trees and shrubs.

I made no secret of eyeballing Nelson. He was a hunk in his own right, a compact model. There was sparse black hair on his chest between his pecs. His legs were covered with spidery hair. His ass was a perfect bubble butt.

Sitting in a clearing, we lit up cigarettes. I was sure that some of the other straying students were smoking funny cigarettes or had smuggled beer in their coolers and were making out.

"So what are you going to do after graduation, Nelson?"

"I dunno. Got no money for college. Maybe bum around the country awhile. Then maybe join the military. My dad was a Marine. He said they build men."

"By that bulge in your swim suit, you already look like a man."

"Ha! You mean my big dick? My brother's got a big one. SO does my dad. Runs in the family, I guess."

He cupped his crotch. I coughed on the cigarette smoke and snuffed the butt.

Brazenly, I reached over and groped Nelson. His dick stiffened slightly.

"What you doin'?" he smiled.

"I'd really like to see it...."

He smiled. "You just want to see it?" He had thick lips and perfect, pearly white teeth. He snubbed out his cigarette.

"Well...."

"I've seen the way you look at me. I thought you might know somethin' about makin' a man feel good. That's why I asked to ride in your car."

Leaning over, I lay my head against his damp red swim suit. I sniffed its musky scent. I licked it.

"Oh, yeah, you know all about makin' a man feel good, dontcha?" He leaned back and stretched. I peeled down his swim suit and his semi-hard cock was at a forty-five degree angle. It was fat and uncut.

I grabbed hold of it and slid back the overhang and looked at his bullet-shaped crown. His dick became engorged.

"Oh yeah, you know all about it. Yeah, lick it. That's it."

I swabbed his rosy crown which turned purple. I pinched his foreskin over the crown while I licked his shaft. I tongued his hefty nuts in their chicken-skin sac.

"Oh, yeah. Suck my balls. That feels so fuckin' good."

I stuffed both of his hangers into my mouth and sloshed them around before spitting them out.

He grabbed his dick with one hand and my head with the other. He poked his fat prick between my lips.

"Suck it. Suck my big dick."

I gobbled up his pecker until his bristly pubes tickled my nose.

I shed my shirt and tugged down my trunks and freed my boner. I kicked off my trunks. Nelson kicked off his. Both of us were bare-assed naked.

Looking up at him, I saw that he was staring at my hard dick. I fisted it in the same rhythm that I ministered to his.

He thrust his dick down my throat.

"Suck it good and I'll come in your mouth. Is that what you like?"

I nodded. I tugged on his wet balls while I bobbed my head up and down on his prick.

"Aw fuck, I'm gonna blow!"

His cock dribbled, then spurted waves of hot, sweet cum down my throat. I sealed my lips around his prick and captured every delicious drop. I kept his big dick in my mouth until it softened and fell out. The crown retracted into the foreskin.

My own dick was hard as a rock. My balls were heaving in their sac. I let go of it.

In a quick move, I rolled Nelson over onto his belly. He glanced over his shoulder at me.

"Whatcha gonna do?"

"I wanna taste that beautiful butt of yours."

"Huh?"

I showed him what I had in mind when I spread his muscular butt cheeks. His crack was sparsely-lined with black hairs. I dove in and lapped at it.

He squirmed around underneath me.

Mounting Nelson, I slapped my hard dick against his muscular butt cheeks.

"What are you doin'?"

"Nothin'. Just relax."

I slapped his butt with my hand.

"Oh, god...."

Scared or embarrassed, I don't know which, but Nelson cradled his face in his arms.

Mounting my horny classmate, I punched my prick head into his ass ring and lay still while it stretched around my cock.

"Aw fuck, I don't think I can take it."

"Relax, you'll like it."

He lay still and whimpered, but after a few moments, he backed up on my dick.

"Oh, please. Go slow and easy."

My stiff prick was deaf to his pleas. Once I knew that he could take it and wanted it I began to sluice my dick in and out of his steamy ass.

He moaned plaintively which encouraged me all the more. I picked up the pace. I couldn't believe how I took to this. I rammed his asshole, with my balls banging against his asscheeks.

Mel thought I was a slut! Hell, Nelson was a real slut. I pounded his ass like there was no tomorrow, riding the crest of the wave of orgasm. Before I wanted it to happen, he clutched my cock with his butt muscles and drained my balls of their juice.

Surprising me, he bucked me off. I rolled over onto my belly, panting.

Rearing up, Nelson flashed me his boner.

"Look what I got for you, pal."

"I don't get fucked," I lied.

"Who cares? Fuck with me, I'm gonna fuck you back."

Nelson manhandled me. He was much stronger than I thought. I fought him as best I could. For a moment I thought maybe he'd flip out and hit me. His brown eyes were glazed. I relaxed, finally. I didn't want him to get the idea I was an easy lay.

He spread my butt cheeks and spit into my crack.

He horned his big dick right up me.

As he thrust in and out, I moaned and groaned, showing my appreciation. "Oh Nelson, you're a real stud," I said.

I clutched his cock with my ass muscles.

He slammed his big dick in and out, relentlessly.

"Oh Nelson, it's so hard. It's gonna shoot. I can feel it. Oh fuck! Sonuvabitch! Hot cum shooting up my ass!"

He flooded my hole with his cum. When he pulled out the overload trickled down my thighs.

"That's it," he said, happy that he'd given me what I'd given him. He slapped my ass as he lifted off me.

Nelson and I got our swim suits back on. We hiked back to the other side of the lake and joined our classmates. No one seemed to notice or care about our absence.

At dusk with the sun setting in the west, we drove back to Weston in our caravan. Nelson acted as if nothing unusual had transpired. When we reached his house, he gave me a high-five and ran from the car.

20 Prom Night: The More the Merrier

I invited Connie to go to the senior prom. She was a raven-haired girl with blue eyes who worked with me on the school paper. I liked her a lot. She was smart and had a great sense of humor. But there were no romantic sparks between us.

Her best friend, Jean, was being escorted by Scott, a jock who played on both the football and basketball teams. Scott lived with his divorced mother and didn't have a car. When Connie asked me if we could double date with them I said sure, the more the merrier. The idea of being around Scott had a special appeal to me. He was a tall blond with baby blues and was friendly.

On prom night I had my dad's Chevy all shined up for the occasion. I wore my good blue suit that I hadn't worn since Easter Sunday at church.

I picked up Connie at her house. Her folks were real nice people. I don't know if they saw me as possible husband material, but I sensed that Connie was wise to my roving eye for my male classmates, although we never discussed it. She looked pretty in her light blue satin formal.

The next stop was to pick up Scott. He looked marvelous, with his blond locks slicked back. He wore a white dinner jacket with a pink carnation in the lapel buttonhole, black slacks and a black bow tie.

With Scott in the back seat, we proceeded to Jean's house. She was a statuesque brunet with hazel eyes. She looked nice with her hair in a French twist. She wore a pink taffeta evening gown. The four of us drove to the Starlight Ballroom on the outskirts of Des Moines. A live band was playing. The school faculty chaperones were there. The dancing was already underway.

I danced with Connie; Scott danced with Jean. We got some punch, which someone had spiked with vodka, and sat at a small table. Everyone was high and happy. The girls gossiped and commented about the other girls' dresses and dates. Scott and I just grinned and bared it.

The party was fun. I enjoyed it and danced the night away. I even danced with Jean and with Miss Ellis, the old maid speech teacher, who went on and on in class about how she attended Grinnell College with Gary Cooper before he went to Hollywood and became a star. Behind her back, the kids joked that she was on the stage, the one that went through Dodge City. She had to be way past retirement age. But she was a nice little old lady who could tear up a rug and enjoy herself.

When the evening wore down and the kids danced close to slow music there was a sense of sadness that our carefree high school days were over and that we'd soon go our separate ways. There had been a lot of talk among guys in the locker room at school that prom night was a time when a lot of girls would go all the way. The crowd started to thin down.

Connie and I, along with Scott and Jean, drove to an A&W root beer joint for a burger and fries. Then we drove out to the edge of Weston and parked in an area that was known as a lovers' lane.

I gave Connie a peck on the cheek and squeezed her. Glancing in the rearview mirror, I could see that Scott and Jean were going at it pretty good. She was moaning, which made me think he was feeling her up. Eventually they came up for air.

"It's after midnight," Connie said. "Both Jean and me gotta get up early, since we both teach Sunday school."

Scott groaned. But I was secretly relieved that the party was about over. I was kind of bored by all the pretense that I was the all-American stud. I was perfectly content to leave that act to Scott and the guys like him.

We dropped Connie and Jean off together since they lived in the same block. I walked Connie to her door and gave her a smooch. Scott escorted Jean to her door.

I waited in the car for Scott to drive him home. He took his sweet time. I was even thinking about splitting since he went inside the house with Jean to smooch and maybe even get a little, but I doubted that since her folks were home and all the lights were on.

At last Scott came back to the car. He got into the passenger seat. I started the engine and drove away.

"Big-time bummer," he said.

"How's that?"

"Jean's holding out for a ring. Oh man, I had my hand up under her dress, inside her panties. I can still smell her pussy on my fingers. All she ever let me do before was play with her tits while I beat off."

"Well, she's a religious girl like Connie."

"You didn't even try to score with Connie."

"I knew better. Besides, who needs women?"

"Oh, shit, I do. I still got a half hard-on most of the time. Right now my pants are all sticky."

"What you need is a blowjob."

"Got that right."

"But most girls don't understand that."

"Right. Hell, I'd settle for anything from her to get some relief but she wouldn't even jack me off at the movies."

I edged the car onto the street where Scott lived. I parked in front of his house.

"Next week at school all the guys will be bragging about how they scored with their dates. Me, all I can brag about is how I went home and jacked off."

"All lies. Guys that get it don't always kiss and tell."

"Oh?"

"You know what I'm saying. The ones who are gettin' it don't talk. Believe me."

"Well, you didn't even try, from what I saw."

"Maybe I didn't want to."

He looked into my eyes. "What do you want to do?"

I turned away, stared out the window.

"Hey, my mom's not home. She's got a date. Wanna come in and drink a coke or something?"

"Sure, Scotty. I'd like that. I'd like that a lot."

I followed Scott into his small house. I sat on the sofa while he got a couple cokes out of the fridge in the kitchen. Both of us sipped the cokes.

He sat down next to me. He took off his bow tie and the white dinner jacket. I unloosened my tie.

Reaching over, I groped Scott.

He sort of jumped up, startled.

"What the fuck you doin'?"

"Just checking to see if you were telling the truth about how horny you are."

"You don't have to feel it to see how horny I am."

No, I certainly didn't. His trousers tented tantalizingly before my hungry eyes.

"Oh man, I'm so hot I'm gonna beat off the minute you go."

"Hey, you can do it now. Ain't no big deal. Maybe I can help you out."

"I don't think so...."

I groped him again, and he let my hand stay on it. Taking that as a green light, I smiled and unzipped his fly. I pulled out his dick.

He had a big dick like I expected. It was uncut, fat, seven inches long.

Kneeling between his legs, I rolled my tongue over his spongy, cheesy crown.

"Oh shit, I don't believe this. Man, I'd never have guessed you was a cocksucker."

"Want me to stop?"

"Hell no. Go ahead, man."

I gobbled up his throbbing dick and he moaned.

I tugged on his plump balls and bobbed my head up and down on his shaft. Apparently I wasn't going fast enough because he scooted

271

to the edge of the couch. He clasped my head and rammed his dick down my throat. He wasn't kidding about being horny. Gobs and gobs of hot cum the consistency of cottage cheese spurted down my throat. I swallowed every drop.

His dick stayed hard when I let go of it. He stroked it.

"I still got cum in my nuts," he said.

I was glad the drapes were closed and no one could see in, even though it was in the wee hours. I stripped off my clothes.

"Whatcha doing?"

"Since you're such a horny big stud, I thought maybe you'd like some man-pussy."

Lying on my belly on the rug, I reached back and spread an asscheeks.

"Jesus, you can take it up the ass?"

"Only because it's you, Scott. I've always dug you. Now you can dig me."

He grinned and dropped his black slacks and boxers. He straddled my legs.

"Yeah, stick it up my ass, Scott. I want you all the way up my ass."

I managed to get a gob of spit in my crack before he stuck me. I was glad that his dick was oozing. He nudged in the head.

"Oh, man," he moaned as he stuck it in. "I can't believe this."

Despite the initial pain, I backed up on his dick.

"Screw me, Scott. Screw my ass."

He pumped my hole.

"I don't believe it. A boy-pussy. I can't believe it."

He was sweaty and breathing heavily. I cradled my head in my arms and enjoyed his mighty thrusts.

"Oh, Scott. It's so fucking hard. It's gonna shoot again. Do it, man."

With his balls banging against my butt cheeks, he plowed my ass. He crammed every inch of his hard dick up my hole and

grunted. He came, and, at the same time, I jerked off, my cum splattering the carpet.

The jock stud collapsed on top of me until his dick softened and slid out.

Turning around, I noticed that his cockhead was in the hood. He pulled up his boxers and slacks.

"I'd better go before your mom gets home," I said.

I left Scott with a smile on his face and a tell-tale cum stain on his carpet. I told Scott I hoped to see him again.

21 A Study in Weirdness: Graduation Day

Commencement ceremonies were held in the high school gym which was converted into an auditorium for the occasion. The students looked weird in their caps and gowns.

The commencement address was boring, a long-winded speech by Mr. Wells, the school board president, who rambled on about his own success story. He owned a dry cleaners for chrissakes. The principal passed out our diplomas as our names were announced. Baldy Clay, as he was called behind his back, shook our paws and congratulated us.

There were several parties to celebrate by various groups and clubs on campus. I opted for the reception at Doc Hall's digs. He was a strange duck, to say the least. He came to Hoover High for the spring term when Miss Greene, the English teach, got sick with tuberculosis.

Doc was weird, very different from any teacher I'd ever had before. A short, skinny man with thinning red hair which he obviously dyed, he had rheumy blue eyes and had to be at least sixty years old. He spoke in a clipped British accent. He rambled on about himself, how he'd traveled the world, and dropped the names of writers he'd known in Paris like the black writer James Baldwin and Kay Boyle. He knew a lot about literature and could quote a lot of Shakespeare and passages from many books. He wrote copious notes on the themes he assigned us.

I drove to Doc's apartment on Maple Street. He rented the upstairs rooms in an old widow's house. His flat was clean and cheery with travel posters on the walls and stacks of books.

At Doc's invitation, I had joined the yearbook staff. He was the faculty sponsor. With his help we students put together a chronicle of our high school days. He carefully edited our various accounts and the finished project was quite stunning in appearance.

Most of the kids who showed up at Doc's party by invitation were on the yearbook staff. Doc served us punch and cheese with crackers. The small group of us sat around as Doc regaled us with fascinating stories of his world travels and adventures. Doc said he had taught English to natives in Africa. He'd studied at Oxford, where he'd earned a doctorate. He'd done post graduate work in Rome and Paris. He encouraged us all to follow our dreams because we could do anything we set our minds to, that the future was ours He was much more inspiring than the commencement speaker.

After the other students left I sort of hung around. I helped clean up the paper cups and empty the ashtrays into the garbage can in the kitchen. Doc was a chain-smoker himself.

"You know, you're my prize student," he told me. "If I had a son, I'd want him to be exactly like you. You're young, bright and so handsome."

"Yeah, right." I knew it was bullshit, but I was pleased and basked in the glow of his compliment.

"If I didn't know better, I'd think you were putting the moves on me," I teased.

"Oh please. I'm an old man," he said, pouring some vodka into what remained of the punch. "Not over the hill, ha-ha, but my time is past and yours has come." He sipped his spiked drink and offered me some. I took it, saluted him, and downed the now-heady brew.

Sensing his attraction to me but knowing that he'd not make a move on me, I decided to be seductive. I put my cup down and said, "Yeah, coming is what I had in mind all right." I tore off my shirt.

He finished his punch, his eyes fixated on my torso.

"Do you think I've got a nice body?" I asked.

"Ah yes. The bricks are all in the right place.

"Wanna see more?"

"Well, I always say that if you've got it, flaunt it."

I dropped my pants and flashed Doc my dick.

"Oh baby, it's so big."

"You think so?" I said, stroking it.

"Oh, yes. One of the biggest I've seen."

"Feel it, Doc. I know you wanna."

"I've suppressed my desires for students all these years...."

"I'm no longer a student, Doc."

He took another shot of the spiked punch. He shook his head in dismay. "I don't know...."

"C'mon, touch it." My cock was hardening.

Finally he reached over and grabbed it. He manipulated it, examined it. "I must say it is a beauty. You've got it all, the brains, looks and hung like a horse."

"Why don't you make it feel real good...."

"I don't know. I'd like to, but...."

"Oh, go on. I've been this route before. Lots of times."

Kneeling, Doc held my dick and admired it. Then he kissed it while he played with my balls. Finally, he took it into his mouth. He took a few slides on my dick, then let go of it.

"What's wrong?"

"I can't believe I'm doing this to a student."

"I graduated, remember?"

"Oh, yeah, what a difference a day makes."

"Got that right. Go ahead. It's all yours."

So there in the kitchen he blew me. About half-way through it he pulled out his little wiener and got off, his cum dropping on the tile floor. While he came, he nuzzled my crotch and was gasping so hard I thought he might be having a heart attack.

When I was close, I held his head steady and shot deep down his throat. He didn't gag.

When I was finished, I pulled out and sighed.

He said, "I came so quickly ... I don't believe it. Goes to show you that just because there's snow on the roof don't mean that the fire's out below. Oh baby, you're precious."

I stripped off my clothes and sat around in the nude while Doc admired and worshipped my young, hard body. I remember thinking that perhaps some boy would do the same for me someday when I got old. I drank more punch and listened to Doc ramble on about his world travels which he spiced up with some erotic accounts of baths by Japanese boys and fucking Arab boys under their robes.

#

After graduation, I began what I thought was going to be a long hot summer in Weston, working at Gold's store and looking for action. One day another former student of Doc's came in and gave me the news that Doc had been caught with a neighbor boy, a thirteen-year-old. There was some evidence, apparently, that he may have been fooling around with the kid from the first day he arrived in town!

I grant you the kid wasn't one of his students, so Doc had not technically lied to me, but I felt weird about it all the same.

June was hotter than usual and the heat seemed to keep the natives inside and my adventures ground to a halt. But I had all those memories of fall and winter and spring to get me off, twice or three times a day. Then came the big surprise that changed my life.

It all started when my older sister Mary dumped her husband Matt. I thought she had to be out of her mind. I had always envied her. Matt was a hunk: chiseled features, big brown eyes, black hair cut high on the sides and short on top. He was nearly six feet tall and about 170 pounds of solid muscle. His upper body was completely smooth, and tanned from working shirtless at his yard maintenance business in a town about thirty miles from Weston. Now Mary's main complaint, it seemed, was with his struggling lawn business. Mary was always a pretentious bitch as far as I was concerned and had often expressed dissatisfaction with Matt. She was tired of working as a receptionist to support her husband's business. So one morning she took off with her boss's son. He was a nerdy guy in thick glasses, but he was set to inherit a pile of dough. Now she was in Reno working on a quickie divorce.

Mary's departure left Matt singing the blues. Everybody in the family pitied him, and tried to be extra nice to him and make him feel better especially me, as it turned out.

I had always had a secret crush on him. Or at least I hoped it was secret. I wasn't sure, on account of I couldn't keep my eyes off him whenever we were in the same room.

It had been about two weeks since Mary flew the coop when my mom made some banana cream pies at the diner and asked me would I take one over to Matt's. She knew it was his favorite and it would cheer him up. Would I? Would I ever! I got dressed in my khaki shorts and tightest white T-shirt and drove over with the pie next to me on the seat. It took me about an hour to get there, plenty of time to fantasize about sucking Matt's cock.

Matt took a long time answering my knock, and I was afraid he might not be home. I almost felt like crying.

Finally Matt showed up at the back door, wearing a pair of faded jeans which showed off his big basket and a filthy black T-shirt.

In the kitchen, Matt stuck the pie in the fridge and took out a can of beer." "You want one?" he asked. "You old enough?"

I laughed. "Yeah, I'm old enough."

Carrying our beers, we went into the living room. The place was in a terrible mess. Matt had no reason to pick things up, obviously.

"I'll bet you wish I was Mary, huh?" That was a dumb thing to say. I guess it was one of those Freudian slips kinds of things. He looked at me kind of funny, but didn't say anything.

He sprawled out on the sofa. I eased my body into the big armchair across from him.

"Cheers, man."

"Cheers," I squeaked, still blushing like crazy.

I didn't drink beer at home. I didn't much like the taste, but I pretended to be a regular guy.

I was surprised at the way Matt chug-a-lugged the beer. He turned on the stereo loud and went for reinforcements. At this rate I figured he might get drunk and pass out. Maybe if he passed out I could even sneak a look at his dick. Maybe even touch it. Just looking at him and listening to his deep, husky voice made the blood pound in my head and in my dick.

I counted five beer cans on the floor while he was out of the room. He returned with a sixth in his hand. "You probably think I'm a loser, like Mary does."

"You're no loser."

"My old man said Mary is out of my class."

"That's bull."

"She wants expensive stuff I can't give her."

"So fuck her," I said.

"Oh I'd like to," Matt answered, looking away, as if deep in throat. "Hell, you don't know what it's like. Not used to doing without it." He rubbed his crotch. I blinked my eyes in disbelief. "God, I get so horny. What about you, sport, you got a girl?" He guzzled his beer.

"No ... uh... not lately...." I replied.

"You and me, we're in the same boat!" He laughed, finished his beer.

I gulped what was left of my beer.

Matt dropped his empty beer can on the floor and stretched. "Man, I'd kill to have a body like yours," I told him.

Matt smiled. "Yeah, that's me, all body, no brains."

I ignored that; he may have been a bit dim, but I knew he was a hard-working guy. "Yeah, I'm planning to really work out this summer," I told him. "I'm really too skinny."

"Take off your T-shirt. Let me see how you're developing."

I couldn't believe that I tore off my T-shirt in front of him but I did. I flexed my biceps.

"Come over here."

I did like he said. He looked me up and down, felt my biceps, my pecs. "You look pretty good to me." He leaned back on the sofa and chuckled. "And you look like you got a big dick."

I was shocked. I didn't say anything. I couldn't. It wasn't until I looked down that I realized that my cock was tenting my best khaki shorts. "It's not as big as yours, I bet," I said nervously.

"Maybe it is, maybe it isn't."

"Show me," I said. I was nervous. My mouth was dry. My hands felt clammy. I could do this with a perfect stranger but doing this with Matt....

I blinked as Matt whipped out his cock. He was uncut, and his cock had to be eight inches to start with and it just kept getting bigger. And thicker. It must have been a full ten inches by the time it finished swelling. Why would Mary leave this? I wondered.

"So is that what you've been wanting to see all these years?"

"Yeah. You knew?"

He nodded, looked down at his incredible cock. He stroked it. "God, I'm tired of beating it. Ain't been getting any. Sure wish I had a cunt to fuck right now. I've been missin' it so much." He went into a long ramble, describing how he fucked Mary morning, noon and night, and then she cut him off. He knew she had another man, that she was involved.

I stroked my cock through my khakis. "You still got me, Matt."

"Don't say something you're gonna regret...." Matt flipped his cock around. It was fully hard now; a silver strand of pre-cum drooled out of the pee hole. He stared up at me. "You know, you and Mary got the same pretty face. Same blond hair. Same blue eyes."

"Can I touch it?" I whispered. "You can close your eyes and pretend it's a bitch if you want. I don't care."

"Go for it, man." Matt smiled.

I did it: I touched his throbbing cock. Then I just stared at it, hypnotized.

"Yeah, I knew I was right about you, Billy. The way you looked at me all the time, I could tell you wanted it. I got nothin' against it. I've had guys makin' moves on me for years."

"I'll bet."

He spread his thighs. I kneeled on the floor. I stuck out my tongue. I was finally getting to lick his dick. After a couple minutes of adoring it, I engulfed Matt's big dick with my mouth.

"Oh yeah," he murmured.

I worked my tongue and lips on my soon-to-be-ex brother-in-law's giant cock, knowing I was giving him real pleasure. Caught up in the blowjob I was giving I grabbed my own cock and stroked it slowly, letting go when it got too close to blasting. "Oh, Billy, get me off."

By now Matt was pulling my hair and dick-feeding me, ramming his dick down my throat, battering my tonsils until he came. I couldn't help it. I gagged, pulled off. His cum foamy from my mouth. I squeezed my own cock and spurted cum on the carpet.

My cock went soft but Matt's didn't. The bullet-shaped cockhead was out of the foreskin. The long, veiny shaft glistened with cum. "That was great, Billy," he said as he lifted himself off the sofa. He pulled up his pants, and ruffed my hair. "Let's clean up," he said.

I followed him into the master bedroom suite. He stopped me as we passed the bed. He turned me around, squeezed my ass. "God,

279

you know what chicks like best is a nice ass, and you've got one helluva nice one."

"I do?"

"You know you do," he chuckled. He sat on the bed and pulled down my shorts. He started to knead my asscheeks. "Look at this thing," he said, positioning me so I could look in the mirror across the room. "Is that an ass or is that an ass?"

"I guess...."

"I know, man. You know, Mary'd never let me do it. She'd never let me stick up her ass."

"You wanted to?"

"Yeah, why not?"

He shoved a finger up me. "You got a tight, pink, cherry butthole."

Cherry?! I thought. I wasn't about to tell him.

"Want it, Billy? Want a big dick in your asshole?"

"Only your dick Matt."

Matt sighed and grabbed my butt cheeks. He licked them and bit them. Looking at his throbbing prick I was kind of scared, but I wanted to give up my butt to my sister's hunky husband.

Matt shed his clothes, and I followed suit.

He gently shoved me down on my belly on his bed. He straddled my legs.

Looking over my shoulder, I saw he had a big grin on his face while he slapped his boner against my ass.

"Never thought I'd be fucking you, Billy." He kneaded my melons and spit into my crack.

"Me neither."

The pain of entry was excruciating. Matt was so eager too eager. I sympathized with him, though, all that fucking morning, noon and night and then nothing. I bit into the pillow.

"Oh god, it's so fucking tight." My ass ring stretched around his thick prick and the pain amazingly subsided. "Yeah, you want it, huh, bro? Want this big dick to bang your butt?" All the while he was shoving it in.

"Give it to me, Matt. I want you. Only you."

He slid his dick in and out, slowly at first, then faster and faster, deeper with each stroke.

Matt kept humping my butt, with his big balls slapping against my asscheeks. He was breathing hard, and sweat was dripping off his body onto mine.

"I could fuck you all night long, you know."

"That'd be okay with me." I pushed back and squeezed his cock with my butt muscles. He was getting close. His cock got steely hard. It began to hurt again.

Now I begged him to come. His cock responded by hitting my butthole like a battering ram until it squirted, flooding me with his fiery wads.

I rolled over onto my side with Matt's cock still embedded in my butthole. I wrapped my fingers around my cock and pumped it furiously until it rained hot cum all over the bed. I felt my butthole spasm around Matt's cock.

He pulled his prick out, and his glistening rosy cockhead retracted into its hood.

"Got a hot ass, bro."

"It's yours, Matt. All yours. Whenever you need it."

Matt took me at my word and fucked me again before he sent my sore ass home for the night.

The next day, Matt offered me a job on his crew. Delirious with happiness, I quit Gold's and went to work for Matt for the summer. Because of the long drive, my folks were the ones who suggested I stay with Matt during the week. They thought I was sleeping on the couch, but in reality I was sleeping right next to Matt in his bed. He'd fuck me in the morning and again at night, and sometimes in between, if I got lucky. It was the best summer of my life.

Come fall, I left Matt and Weston for the university in Iowa City, where I planned to hunt big men on campus and service them.

I hadn't been on campus a month before my mom called me and gave me the news: Matt had gotten engaged! I knew he was seeing an old school sweetheart on the weekends when I wasn't in his bed, but I had no idea it had gotten that serious. I was depressed for several days, but finally I let Matt go, along with all my other schoolboy dreams. Reality, I vowed, would make those dreams seem mild in comparison.

About the Editor

JOHN PATRICK was a prolific, prize-winning author of fiction and non-fiction. One of his short stories, "The Well," was honored by PEN American Center as one of the best of 1987. His novels and anthologies, as well as his non-fiction works, including Legends and The Best of the Superstars series, continue to gain him new fans every day. One of his most famous short stories appears in the Badboy collection Southern Comfort and another appears in the collection The Mammoth Book of Gay Short Stories.

A divorced father of two, the author was a longtime member of the American Booksellers Association, the Publishing Triangle, the Florida Publishers' Association, American Civil Liberties Union, and the Adult Video Association. He lived in Florida, where he passed away on October 31, 2001.

Connor Maguire

#oneclickaway

www.ingramcontent.com/pod-product-compliance
Lightning Source LLC
Chambersburg PA
CBHW052015020726
47501CB00004B/1076